ELIZABETH STREET

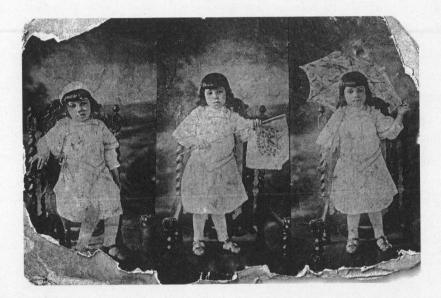

ANGELINA SIENA ON HER FOURTH BIRTHDAY, SEPTEMBER 11, 1909.

ELIZABETH STREET

A Novel Based on True Events

LAURIE FABIANO

Mariner Books
Houghton Mifflin Harcourt
Boston   New York

The characters and events portrayed in this book are fictitious.
Any similarity to real persons, living or dead, is coincidental
and not intended by the author.

First Mariner Books edition 2011

Text copyright © 2006, 2010 by Laurie Fabiano

For information about permission to reproduce selections from this book,
write to trade.permissions@hmhco.com or to Permissions, Houghton Mifflin Harcourt
Publishing Company, 3 Park Avenue, 19th Floor, New York, New York 10016.

www.hmhco.com

First published, in a slightly different form, in 2006 by Fig Books
Published in 2010 by AmazonEncore

Library of Congress Cataloging-in-Publication Data
Fabiano, Laurie.
Elizabeth Street: a novel based on true events / Laurie Fabiano. — 1st Mariner ed.
p. cm.
ISBN 978-0-547-74494-0 (pbk.)
1. Italian American families — New York (State) — New York — Fiction.
2. Immigrants — New York (State) — New York — Fiction. 3. Italians — New York (State) —
New York — Fiction. 4. Little Italy (New York, N.Y.) — Fiction. 5. New York (N.Y.) — Fiction.
6. Mafia — Fiction. 7. Mafiosi — Fiction. I. Title.
PS3606.A243E45 2011
813'.6 — dc23
2011028594

Ransom notes by Siena Della Fave
Author photo by Steve Winter

Printed in the United States of America
DOC 10 9 8 7 6 5

FOR MY FAMILY

PAST, PRESENT, AND FUTURE

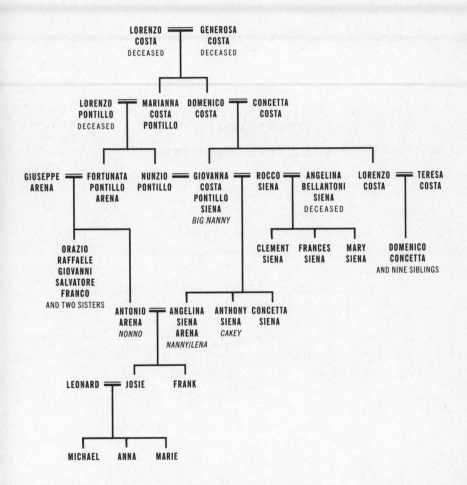

AUTHOR'S NOTE

The events described in this book are true and the dates accurate.
All the central characters are based on real people.
Giovanna Costa Pontillo Siena was my great-grandmother.
Angelina Siena Arena was my grandmother.
Most of the names of primary characters that are deceased remain the same;
the names of characters based on people who are living have been changed.
Some primary characters are composites, and some details and
minor characters have been fictionalized.

PROLOGUE

"We lived at 202 Elizabeth Street." My grandmother looked away from the video camera to my head. "How come you don't do anything about your hair? Why don't you go to the beauty parlor?"

I ignored her. It was a refrain, not a question. "Nanny, try not to move around so much. You keep coming out of the frame."

For the tenth time, I got up to adjust the camera. My grandmother was seated on the couch and wore a red polyester shirt. Her dyed blonde hair had been set so that two curls framed her face, which was overwhelmed by her gold-rimmed glasses. She was eighty years old and could remember details from more than half a century ago, but not what she had eaten for lunch.

"How many more questions?" complained Nanny halfheartedly.

As Nanny had gotten older, she had mellowed. She said hello to people she didn't know well and showed her grandchildren more affection. It had taken two decades, but at twenty-eight, I was as close to my grandmother as anyone could be. Still, she was stubborn, and if I was going to get what I wanted on tape, it would take manipulation and coaxing.

"We just got started," I said, trying to sound sweet and patient.

"I don't know why you're doing this anyway," she grumbled.

"I told you. My memory isn't as good as yours. You don't want me screwing up the facts if I try to tell these stories to my kids someday."

"Some things you shouldn't tell."

PART ONE

SCILLA, CALABRIA, ITALY
1890–1901

ONE

Giovanna Costa gripped her father's arm as he escorted her down the aisle. Nearly everyone from the tiny southern fishing village was in the church of the *pescatori,* Santa Maria di Porto Salvo. People smiled at her, some whispered. Giovanna wondered what they were whispering and guessed it was nothing she hadn't heard before. Comments like, *"Finalmente,* it's about time!" and "What took them so long?"

Nunzio glowed at the base of the altar. He was tall, taller than Giovanna even, and with the sun blazing through the windows making his deep red hair a bright gold, he resembled a lit taper. Even from this distance she could feel his warmth and see beyond his eyes. His gaze lifted her up and sent them both spinning into their own little world, which was where they existed most of the time.

The village of Scilla was their *pezzo di cielo caduto in terra*—piece of heaven fallen to earth. They lived in the Chianalea, the oldest part of town, which housed the fishermen. Cobblestone alleys led to their stone houses, perched on the water. The crystal-clear azure sea lapped at their front doors, and their boats were docked at their doorsteps. Their backdoors and terraces led onto the narrow streets and alleys that wound up the mountain.

Scilla was situated on three levels, divided into three parts. The town jutted into the sea. At its point was the ruin of a castle that had been conquered and inhabited by countless invaders and clergy since it was built in A.D. 500. On one side of the castle was the Chianalea. On the other, the half-moon-shaped Marina Grande. There the houses were set in from the sea, and the sandy beach served to dry the fishermen's nets. Above the Chianalea was San Giorgio, the newer part of the city, where the town square and city hall overlooked the splendor of the Calabrian

coast and Sicily's Aeolian Islands. And beyond San Giorgio were ter-
raced lemon groves and farms that reached to the top of the mountains.

It was here that Giovanna and Nunzio grew like the vines on the village
Indian fig trees, intertwined in such a way that it was impossible to
know where one branch started and where the other ended. Giovanna
did not know life without Nunzio. Her father and his mother were
brother and sister. Their houses were two doors apart, and they were
born two months apart. Although her earliest memories all had Nunzio
at her side, it wasn't until she was six years old that she realized that
life did not exist without him. Nunzio was hoisting baskets of smelts
onto the dock from her uncle's fishing boat. As Nunzio turned to say
hello, he slipped, sending the fish flying. Giovanna laughed. Giovanna
had a throaty, hearty laugh even at that age. Instead of getting angry,
Nunzio did it over and over again until Giovanna laughed so hard she
had to gulp for air.

When Giovanna and Nunzio weren't doing chores, they were in the
water. They would swim out to one of the many rocks that dotted Scilla's
coastline and use it as home base to explore the sea around them. The
clear water showcased a kaleidoscope of color, created by hundreds of
species of fish and coral. Over the years they had developed the ability
to hold their breath for long stretches and dive underwater to explore
the reefs and wrecks.

Early on, Giovanna's father and aunt had assured each other it was
a childhood crush. There was a road to Scilla now; the people of Scilla
were not obliged to marry cousins. With each day, though, it became
more apparent that Giovanna and Nunzio were a matter of destiny, not
circumstance. If someone commented, Giovanna's father and aunt sto-
ically repeated what their father said on the subject of marriages within
the family: "It makes the blood stronger."

When Giovanna reached puberty at fourteen, they were no longer
allowed to spend hours alone together. Because they were cousins and
neighbors, they saw each other many times a day, but their unchaper-
oned adventures came to an end.

As Giovanna made her way down the aisle, she glimpsed the faces witnessing her journey to the altar. Each face held a story about her life with Nunzio. There was Paolo Caruso, who had saved her leg. Early one spring, she and Nunzio had climbed the narrow steps out of the Chianalea, raced through the plateau of San Giorgio, and picked their way through the lemon groves and then headed to the farms to trade fish for goat cheese and milk. Giovanna fell over a stone wall, cutting her long, thin leg to the bone. Paolo was the first to hear Nunzio's cries and carried Giovanna home on his back. Nunzio trotted alongside, bravely singing Giovanna's favorite songs while holding his shirt around her leg to stop the bleeding.

Giovanna smiled at her older cousin Pasquale. Many times, this still formidable man had served as their protector. As children on the beach, Giovanna and Nunzio would search among the water-polished stones and fragments of terra-cotta for the ancient Greek and Roman coins that frequently washed ashore, particularly after a storm. They would use these thousand-year-old coins, with bits and pieces of heroic images still visible, for a pitching game played in the narrow alleys of the Chianalea. Once, older boys had cheated them out of their prize coins during a game. All burly Pasquale had done was knock on the culprits' doors, and the treasure was quickly returned to its rightful owners.

Zia Antoinette's cracked face brightened when Giovanna passed. Zia Antoinette had been the first of many to catch Nunzio and Giovanna kissing. She'd whacked Nunzio so hard with her broom that Nunzio would later joke that kissing Giovanna made his head spin and *culo* hurt.

Giovanna passed the row holding Nunzio's sister, Fortunata, her pregnant belly, and six children. The older boys, Orazio and Raffaele, were already fishermen. They stood tall next to their lean, muscular father, Giuseppe Arena. Fortunata's youngest boy, Antonio, waved to Giovanna from the pew.

Giovanna was also conscious of who was missing. In her mind she placed her brother, Lorenzo, who lived in America, and Nunzio's father, who had succumbed to cholera a decade ago, at the end of the aisle with her mother, Concetta, and Nunzio's mother, Zia Marianna.

Tears streamed down Concetta's and Marianna's faces and over their delicate features. Giovanna always thought the sisters-in-law looked like matching porcelain dolls: one with dark chestnut hair like her own, the other with red hair like Nunzio's. They were close, and even now they did not separate to sit on opposite sides of the aisle, as was customary for in-laws, but stood together holding hands.

Nunzio and Giovanna had grown up listening to their mothers talk and gossip while they wove linens and embroidered late into the night. They marveled at how quickly their mothers turned the simple string into strong and beautiful cloths. When Giovanna and Nunzio were twelve, they heard Concetta and Marianna planning to sew together two tablecloths they had made to create one large enough to cover the Christmas dinner table. On the night before their mothers were to stitch the two cloths together, Giovanna and Nunzio each took the string from their mothers' sewing baskets, and out of sight in the moonlight reflected by the sea, they pulled the string slowly through their mouths. When Concetta and Marianna knotted the stitches that wove the two halves together, they did not know they were accomplices in Nunzio and Giovanna's first act of commitment. And only the week before the wedding, Concetta still did not know why Giovanna was so insistent that the stained and tattered Christmas tablecloth be part of her trousseau.

Nunzio took Giovanna's hand after she had kissed her father and he'd shuffled into the pew beside his wife and sister. The couple's eyes locked. Nunzio said he saw the sea in Giovanna's eyes. He often told her that when he was out fishing he imagined himself sailing on her gaze, and that like the sea, the color of her eyes changed before a storm. Nunzio could tell from the color of the water what the day's catch would be, and he could tell from the color of Giovanna's eyes whether she was tranquil or had dark undertows. For her part, Giovanna felt that Nunzio's eyes were windows. When life held her captive, she could escape through those windows. She could see farther and more clearly through Nunzio's eyes.

Unlocking their gaze, they turned toward the priest and faced the altar of Santa Maria di Porto Salvo. The church was humble on the outside, simple stone and stucco. But inside, the frescoes that covered every wall turned the village church into a cathedral of dramatic proportions for the fishermen. Scilla's history surrounded the parishioners and was interrupted only by windows onto its subject; and if the light was right, the view outside became one with the paintings. The tale of the creation of the frescoes had become part of village lore. It was a story built on stories:

One hundred years ago, an itinerant painter wandered into Scilla looking for work. The church had just been built, and the whitewashed walls mocked the parishioners with their poverty. The fishermen invited the painter to a town meeting in the church, where young and old regaled the painter with tales of Scilla. As they spoke, he sketched their faces and gestures in charcoal on paper they normally used to wrap the fish.

The oldest person in the village, Nunzio's great-great-grandfather Giacomo, told the oldest tale. "Scilla," he began with great flourish, "was the town Scyllae from Greek myth." He made it known to the painter that they were all good Christians, but that didn't mean there wasn't something to the legend—otherwise, there was no explanation for why the waters between Scilla and Sicily were so treacherous.

The painter apologized. "Signore, I am an illiterate man who only knows the stories of the Bible."

Giacomo smiled. He had hoped the artist did not know of Scylla. He relished the opportunity to recount the chilling legend and to watch his friends' and family's faces as they reacted to different parts of the story.

Giacomo eased back into his chair and moved a candle closer to his face. When he described in detail the beautiful nymph Scylla, who was loved by the god Glaucus, he studied the men's expressions. Giacomo knew they would miss the next part about Glaucus asking Circe for a love potion because their minds had not yet finished caressing Scylla's lithe and silken body. When he told of Circe's jealous rage, as she herself was in love with Glaucus, Giacomo saw the disapproval of the women. They sucked in their cheeks and shook their heads at such selfish emotion. The children's eyes widened when he told of how Circe had turned Scylla into a hideous creature with twelve feet and six heads. "Scylla was cursed to remain on a solitary rock and devour sailors as they attempted to navigate the Straits of Messina," Giacomo recounted dramatically. The children hugged their legs and drew them into their chests.

"Ever since," Giacomo directed his closing comments to the painter, "should a sailor survive Scylla's wrath, he would soon encounter the deadly whirlpool

Cariddi, which lay in wait across the strait on the Sicilian side. This is why we say, 'Tra una pietra ed un posto duro'—'Between a rock and a hard place.'" Giacomo *punctuated the ending by lifting his wine glass to Scylla and Cariddi. The artist captured the gesture perfectly, immortalizing Nunzio's great-great-grandfather Giacomo as Saint Paul.*

Another villager had been waiting for her moment. She had listened attentively to her father's stories of ancient Scyllae, and when he died at sea she had become the unofficial town historian. Rocking her sleeping child in her lap, she began with great drama: "The blood of one hundred nations courses through our veins." She pointed into the night as if the painter could see the view beyond her hand. "There," she announced, "Sicilia. You can practically touch it. Every king and warrior believed they had to control Scyllae to control Sicilia. Scyllae was conquered so many times that the villagers lost track of who ruled the town—and were often reminded by the tip of a sword."

After many more stories, most of which were true, the oldest fisherman, Agostino Bellantoni, cleared his throat to gain the floor. His feet shuffled beneath him, and he hung his head humbly. "Signore Artista"—his voice was at first tentative but gained conviction as he continued—"we enjoy these old stories. But Scilla is what it has always been, a village of simple fishermen and goat herders. This may not be exciting to an artist, but Scilla is for us the sea, Scilla is the cliffs, the trees of lemons, and now, our church."

The most beautiful painting was behind the altar. Giovanna had studied it a thousand times, but today she felt herself standing in the boat with the disciples hauling in nets full of fish. The disciples looked at her with the familiar faces of the Costa, Pontillo, and Arena families of Scilla. Saint Paul, holding high a crucifix, gave her a warm smile from underneath his intense expression. Gazing from the boat, she saw Scilla's mythical cliffs, and beyond the cliffs was heaven.

Giovanna was a devout Catholic. Nunzio occasionally accompanied her to church, but she knew Nunzio treated his faith merely like an important tradition. She had decided his scientific mind wouldn't allow him devotion, but she forgave him because she loved the way his mind worked. She marveled at how he would use numbers to solve problems and how he could look at a building, a boat, or anything in three dimensions and know intuitively how it was built.

Nunzio was fixing fishing boats by the time he was eight. When he was twelve he was improving on them. From May through August, the fishermen of Scilla caught the best *pescespada*—swordfish—in the entire world. They had built a special boat and developed a unique system for spearing the elusive giants. A pole jutted fifteen feet into the air from the center of the boat. A man acting as lookout balanced at the top of this pole, his feet perched on two small blocks. Beneath him, four standing men rowed the boat, and a sixth man stood at the prow, spear and rope at the ready to launch into the speeding pescespada.

When Vittorio Macri's boat was not moving quickly enough, it was Nunzio who figured out that the boat's balance was off because of a misplaced center pole. And when he was only a teenager, Nunzio worked with the forger to create a better spearhead, which locked into the fish when the rope was pulled back.

Nunzio enjoyed his elevated position in the village. He was proud that his father's friends came to him for assistance; it only made him love Scilla more. It was decided that Nunzio had a gift and should become an engineer. It meant leaving and going north to study. Felipe, the sometime village schoolmaster, warned him that he would be treated badly. He said they would call Nunzio a peasant and laugh at his clothes and dialect. But the prospect of losing status, of being mocked, all paled next to the thought of leaving Giovanna. In the end, Giovanna made the decision easy. She said that she would not marry him unless he went to school and came back an engineer.

It took Nunzio more than five years to finish his studies. Being from the Mezzogiorno, he was forced to work for less pay than his fellow students in his apprenticeship, and the professors often held Nunzio's work to a higher standard, forcing him to repeat lessons. While these injustices kept him away from Scilla longer than planned, Nunzio reminded himself that it was a miracle he was studying at all. He would not spend his life, as every man of his family had before him, taking fish from the sea. Giovanna cursed their decision; life was intolerable without him. But her chest swelled with pride when someone asked if she had heard from "Maestro" Nunzio, a title reserved for respected professionals.

To make the time pass while Nunzio was away, Giovanna worked day and night. In the early mornings she cleaned her family's narrow three-story house, starting from the top floor, with its terrace that over-looked both sea and village, and moving on to the second floor, which opened to the alley behind the house, and ending with the bottom floor, which faced the sea and the family's fishing boat. After cleaning, she would go to her parents' fish store to ready it for the day's catch. She would return to the store in the afternoon after the midday meal to sell fish to the people of the Marina Grande and San Giorgio. When this routine left her with too much time in the evenings, she started trailing Signora Scalici, the town's midwife.

Giovanna had long been the person to whom villagers in the Chianalea brought sick animals. When Giovanna held a hurt animal, it would calm down, and if she couldn't help the animal, she would hold it until it died to ease the creature's passing. She was equally as nurturing with plants. On the family's terrace, a garden flourished in pots, and this became Giovanna's laboratory. She devised poultices for drawing out infections and healing wounds using a variety of herbs.

So when people saw Giovanna with the midwife, they acted like they had known all along that one day Giovanna would deliver the babies of the village. While it was a natural progression, some of the women were not happy at first. They thought Giovanna had airs. They disap-proved of how she took charge in the fish store and had no problem scolding men about the quality or price of their fish. And the women were puzzled and suspicious of her decision to allow Nunzio to go north without marrying her.

As each year went by, more and more of Giovanna's time was spent helping Signora Scalici deliver Scilla's next generation. After their initial mistrust, the mothers liked having Giovanna around. Signora Scalici was kind, but all business. Giovanna could help take the minds of birth-ing mothers elsewhere when the pain was unbearable and focus them when the time was right.

Early in her training, she had helped deliver her childhood friend Francesca Marasculo's third baby. It had been a fast delivery. The women had cleaned up and left. Giovanna was to forever remain haunted by the screams of Francesca's husband echoing off the stone houses as he ran through the Chianalea calling for help. He had woken up in a pool of Francesca's blood, as she lay hemorrhaging and unconscious beside him. By the time the midwives reached her, Francesca was dead, her two young children clinging to her limp hands.

Francesca's death became a scar that knit itself on Giovanna's soul. From that time forward, after birthing a baby, Giovanna spent the night with the mother, cooking, cleaning, and keeping a watchful eye. For that, too, she had earned the respect and trust of the women of the village.

The wedding guests had returned to their pews following communion. The church was silent. Nunzio and Giovanna knelt before the altar. The priest nodded, and Nunzio squeezed Giovanna's hand as they got up. Giovanna's mind stopped wandering. The joyful weight of the moment nearly made her fall.

"Do you, Nunzio Pontillo, take Giovanna Costa to be your wife?" Nunzio was at sea as he looked into Giovanna's blue eyes and said yes from their depths.

"Do you, Giovanna Costa, take Nunzio Pontillo to be your husband?" Giovanna felt complete when she said, "Yes." Life was as it should be and how it was meant to be.

Sì. Finalmente.

TWO

Nunzio and Giovanna were born not long after the unification of Italy. As a child, Nunzio would climb on his uncle's donkey, with a stick for a bayonet, and pretend he was Italian revolution general Giuseppe Garibaldi, riding into town to exile the foreign rulers. Giovanna would cheer and wave a red cloth. When their elders said the word "*Risorgimento!*" Giovanna and Nunzio could hear the defiance, hope, and passion in every syllable. Now, years later, it was different. It was as if the adults were saying an ex-lover's name. There was still an attraction in their voices, but you could hear the betrayal.

One of the changes since unification was that sometimes Giovanna and Nunzio went to school. School was the rented room of a teacher sent from the north. The *professore* never lasted long, but when there was a professore in town, Giovanna's and Nunzio's parents insisted that they go. The town was supposed to build a school with money from the north, but the school was never built, and the money disappeared. Despite fleeing teachers and nonexistent classrooms, somehow Giovanna and Nunzio learned to read and write, and this alone distinguished them from most of the other children. But the majority of their education came from proverbs, legends, and conversation they overheard in the town square—the *chiazza*.

The chiazza was Scilla's heartbeat. It was on the third level in Scilla and overlooked the castle, the neighborhood of the Chianalea, and the beach. Its western end jutted out over the sea. Adjacent to the square were rows of pino marino trees and flowering bushes; in June the air was scented with honeysuckle. In good weather, which was nearly every day, people would gather there in the evenings, and on Sundays.

Children were scooted away to play so that the adults could have a glass of wine and gossip. Giovanna and Nunzio had a spot under a bougainvillea bush where they could listen undetected while they shelled and sucked on pistachios.

They loved when the talk turned from the village to the news of the world. Town gossip was boring. Generally it was a topic the men all agreed upon, and it made for uneventful conversation. "The fish are running good," and they would all nod and grumble in agreement, "Sì, the fish are running good." But when the subject was the politics of Italy, that was an entirely different matter. Arguments and curses flew fast and furious, fists were raised in dramatic thrusts, and unlikely alliances were both made and broken.

When Giovanna and Nunzio heard that a northern newspaper had made its way into town, it didn't matter how many chores they had, they would make sure they were under the bougainvillea bush with an extra stash of pistachios and a flask of wine. On these nights, Vittorio, one of the few *contadini* in the village who could read, would scrub his hands and muscular forearms with lemons to rid them of the fish smell and put on his best shirt. He would stride to the chiazza and sit in the prime spot that had been reserved for him. Within minutes, scores of men would gather around Vittorio with the women on the perimeter pretending to be absorbed in their sewing.

Vittorio would read aloud from what was usually a Roman newspaper, although sometimes a paper made it all the way from Milano. Their local newspaper was published in Reggio and written in their dialect, but it didn't have the same incendiary content of the northern papers. The northern papers were written in Italian, which was only vaguely similar to the dialect spoken in Scilla. Also, the paper was invariably three months old, and along the way pages had been torn out to blow a nose or to wrap the day's catch. So Vittorio would struggle to read what was left of the words that most closely resembled his own language.

"And then, the pig says"—Vittorio was prone to commentary—"our Italia must be protected by an Italian army. Our good men from l'alta Italia are serving, and so must the lazy dogs of the south whose families whine that they can't leave their farms."

"That stupid son of a whore!" Luigi DiFranco, a goat herder, shouted, jumping on his chair. It wobbled on the uneven cobblestones beneath. "If my son goes in their goddamn army, who will take care of the goats and make the cheese to pay their taxes!!??"

Every man shouted at once.

"Who will fix the nets?"

"Dogs! They are pigs! *Sporcaccioni!*"

"How come they tax my mule but not their rich friends' cows? I'm not stupid!"

"Will their sons plow my land?"

The men were so loud that Vittorio's brother lit a firecracker to stun them into silence.

Cesare, one of the oldest men in the village, was the first to speak. "Who is this Italia and why does she need an army? Is she a Roman queen?"

After a moment there was laughter, but Vittorio was getting impatient; he wanted to continue reading. "Cesare, do you know nothing? Italia is the country we live in. The north, the south, Sicilia, we are all this country of Italia."

"Cesare's right!" The firecracker had done little to change Luigi's mood. "Who is this Italia? I'm *Calabrese*. I can't afford to be an Italian. They taxed my goat, they taxed my mule, and now they want to take my son. Italian my ass!"

"It's the price we pay for a united Italy. Do you want to be conquered every time the winds blow?" Vittorio felt he had to defend unification.

"No, but I want to eat!" shouted Luigi.

"I hear the northerners aren't running to join their army," another man shouted. "A ship captain in Naples told me the northerners are leaving in droves for South America."

It was like another firework had exploded. Voices overlapped. Hands and arms were not enough for gesticulation. They jumped up and down and acted out emotions. Someone fell off a wobbly chair. From afar, the group looked like it was engaged in a bizarre ritual dance.

"Leave their homes? When do they come back?"

"If there are no northerners in the north, let's move!"

"Have you ever seen a *Piemontese* row a boat?"

The men talked until Luigi's one-eyed demented rooster crowed midnight, and Giovanna and Nunzio stayed under the bougainvillea bush until their mothers pulled them out by their ears. Giovanna couldn't remember if that was the first time she heard talk of people going to other lands, but from that moment on it was a constant topic.

It was unthinkable to leave your home. It was a concept, like Italy, that was too difficult to fathom. Didn't her papa teach them that while the rulers always changed, the Calabresi remained? If no war or event in Italy's history had forced them from their home, how could unification?

Lorenzo, Giovanna's older brother, played with the little bit of food on his plate. The air was thick at the dining table. Concetta knew her son well. She knew he was trying to say something, and she was doing her best to stop him from saying it. Every time he started to speak or even sigh, she picked up a plate or shifted in her chair to break his concentration. Domenico peered at his son expectantly from under his eyebrows, afraid to meet his gaze.

In the past three years, Giovanna had watched her proud brother move from anger to frustration to defeat. There was a slump in his once-square shoulders, and his lean body now just looked skinny. Giovanna felt that she and her brother had aged. It wasn't simply because he was a man of twenty-two and she a woman of twenty, but because life had become more and more difficult with each year.

When they had buried the last of the dead from the cholera epidemic, including Nunzio's father, they thought that the worst times were over. But cholera turned out to be an overture to a tragic opera where events spiraled out of control and the audience was left trying to keep track of the villains.

The other villains were not as dramatic or forthright as cholera; they were more insidious and masked. Since the government started taxing goats, the mountain peasants had to reduce their herds. Soon there wasn't enough milk and cheese to trade, and they had to reduce the herds further. For a while they ate a lot of goat meat. Now there was no milk, no cheese, and no goats. Then they taxed the mules, so farmers had to plow the lands themselves. One year the crops would be eaten by parasites, and the next they would die of drought. When there wasn't enough food from the farms and people were forced to grow what they could in their yards, they taxed the gardens. Only the *padroni,* the large landowners, who were mainly foreigners or northerners, had farms and animals anymore. The goat herders and the farmers were reduced to serfdom on the manors of the padroni.

When the people rebelled with sticks, the northern police mowed them down with guns. The only option for many men was to become a brigand. First the sons and then sometimes the fathers left for the mountains to make their living robbing rich landowners and travelers who traversed the region's few roads. In the dead of night, the men would scramble down cliff paths to leave money or food with their families, never staying more than minutes. When they stopped coming in the dead of night, their families knew that the police had killed them.

Lorenzo planned on marrying Pasqualina, Vittorio's daughter, but he was waiting for things to get better. Pasqualina got tired of waiting. When Luigi DiFranco's son, who was living in America, wrote Pasqualina's family with a proposal of marriage and the money for passage, she accepted. After Pasqualina left, Lorenzo considered *brigantaggio,* but he knew that he would not be a good brigand. He came from a family with property; the best brigands were of pure peasant stock. It was their way to rise up in the world, to gain respect, and to reap the justice that the law failed to give them. And it was their fate for their severed heads to be displayed as an example for other justice seekers.

Lorenzo wanted his turn at life—to become a man like his father, with a house and a business. The Mezzogiorno had turned him into a contadino without power or a future.

"I'm going to America." There. He said it.

Concetta sucked in air and began to clear the dishes as if a word had not been spoken.

Lorenzo looked at his father. "I'll send money. I can't help you here."

His father walked out the door in silence and sat on the dock. Lorenzo rose to hug his mother, who sobbed at his touch. She didn't want her son to see her this way, so she waved him out of the house. He heard Giovanna comforting his mother as he walked to his father and sat down beside him. Domenico didn't look up and continued staring into the water that reflected his weather-beaten but still handsome face. In a soft voice and with tears etching his skin, Domenico said,

"Dami centu lire
E mi ni vaiu a l'America
Maladitu l'America
E chi la spiminata"

Give me a hundred lire
And I'm off to America
Goddamn America
And the man who thought it up

Domenico pulled at the ropes holding the trunk to test their tightness. Lorenzo checked his pocket many times for the address of Luigi DiFranco. It had been arranged that he would first go to Luigi's home until he found his own place to sleep in New York. The piece of paper seemed so fragile. What if he lost it? He had already memorized the address, Mulberry Street, 141, but he did not trust his memory. He copied it again and put it in his shoe. The immigrants who returned described a city of black smoke and soot. He had waking nightmares of wandering around trying to see obscured numbers and not being able to ask directions.

Domenico put his hand on Lorenzo's shoulder and said, *"Andiamo."* Concetta and Giovanna were inside the house. Having said their goodbyes, Concetta did not want to see her son walk off. She was in her rocking chair, the one where she had nursed Lorenzo, winding her rosary through her knotted fingers. Giovanna sat beside her, resting her hand on her mother's leg. When Concetta heard the mule's hooves scrape on the cobblestones, she rocked faster and faster until Giovanna had to grab the arms of the chair to keep it from falling over. As the frantic rocking stopped, her mother let escape a wail from deep inside her chest that Giovanna knew was echoing off the cliffs of Scilla.

THREE

Maria Perrino groaned. Her mother absentmindedly patted her head and continued her diatribe. "L'America's worse than a cheap whore, a *mala femmina*, who lures away our men."

Giovanna and Signora Scalici tuned her out as they prepared the room for the birth. Giovanna had heard Maria's mother give this speech before. Maria's father was one of the first to go to America. Initially, he had sent the family a letter with money each month; now it was once a year at best. After Lorenzo emigrated, the Costas' fish store had become one of the primary places for women who had already lost their husbands and sons to America to come and commiserate with one another. In their minds, the Statue of Liberty was not lifting her lamp, but her skirts. She was l'America's Scylla, a beauty beckoning from a rock in the water. And she was going to devour them.

Not getting a reaction, Maria's mother asked Giovanna a question. "Have you heard from Maestro Nunzio in Rome?"

Giovanna nodded. "Last week," she said, and continued scrubbing her hands while Signora Scalici tended to the young woman. Giovanna no longer apprenticed; she delivered the firstborns and Signora Scalici delivered the children of women she had already helped birth. Today was different. Signora Scalici had asked her to come knowing it was going to be a difficult delivery.

"And what of Lorenzo? Has he married that girl he met in New York?" The mother interrogated Giovanna while she dried her hands.

"Next month they'll marry."

"Lorenzo Costa marrying a girl from Puglia." The woman clucked her tongue. "L'America is diluting Calabrese blood."

Giovanna wished the Signora would shut up and pay more attention to her laboring daughter.

"The head's to heaven," whispered Signora Scalici to Giovanna. "I've tried to turn the baby for weeks. We'll have to deliver it breech."

The mother fluttered around the room commanding her daughter, "You need to push more. Be strong."

"Signora," directed Signora Scalici, "we need more belladonna. Can you get it?"

"Sì, sì, of course." Maria's mother swept out on her mission, heading to the *farmacia*. The request for belladonna would be the pharmacist's cue to keep the meddling mother occupied and out of the way for as long as possible.

The young woman calmed when her mother left. "Maria," Signora Scalici spoke directly in her ear, "we must do this together. Lean on Giovanna and follow her directions."

Giovanna braced her body against Maria's back and held her beneath the arms. At the next contraction, Giovanna instructed, "A long push, make it long and slow." Maria's sweat-drenched hair was matted, and the veins in her neck and face looked as though they might break through her skin.

After a long hour of pushing, the baby's culo emerged as Signora Scalici looped the cord around her finger to protect it from tangling. With Giovanna applying pressure to Maria's lower pelvis, Signora Scalici reached in and unfolded the baby's legs, drawing them out.

"Ah, as I thought, Maria, you have a girl." Turning to Giovanna, she said, "We must quickly birth the head."

Maria was exhausted. "Can't we let her rest through the next contraction?" muttered Giovanna. Giovanna was still young and occasionally her empathy got the best of her.

"Clear the nose and mouth when you see them," instructed Signora Scalici, ignoring Giovanna's question. "*Forza*, Maria. We will soon see your child's head." Signora Scalici draped the baby's body over her forearm and reached into Maria, putting her fingers into the baby's mouth. The fingers of her other hand cradled the back of the baby's neck.

"Push, Maria," gently coaxed Giovanna. Maria no longer looked human; it was as if all the blood had drained from her face, into her eyes. The strain of pushing had broken all the blood vessels.

Signora Scalici lifted the lower half of the baby's body upward. Maria pushed, the midwife pulled, and the nose and eyes emerged. Giovanna quickly wiped them.

"This is it, Maria, but a slow push this time." Giovanna realized the cruelty of her words. This baby was only centimeters from being born, and the mother had to take it slow. But Maria listened, and in one slow, long push, the rest of her little girl's head emerged.

"*Brava*, Maria!" exhorted Signora Scalici. Maria fell back on the pillows, panting and moaning.

Giovanna cleared the baby's passages and laid her on her mother's chest. All three women felt such relief that laughter accompanied their tears.

"Maria, they say that with a girl born backwards, the birth is the easiest part. She will be strong and stubborn. Look at Giovanna! When I delivered her, I was first introduced to her *culo*!"

They were soon quiet. Giovanna looked at Maria cradling her daughter. The baby was black and blue, Maria was covered in blood, and yet they looked beautiful. A peace descended in the room as the baby suckled for the first time. Giovanna's thoughts turned to Nunzio. With his return imminent, she could not attend a birth without thinking of their children. Her faith in the future was strengthened as she imagined cradling Nunzio's child. They would finally be inextricably bound and live forever in their generations.

Through scores of births, Giovanna would imagine birthing her own children, so when nearly a year had passed since marrying Nunzio and she had not become pregnant, Giovanna's disappointment became all-consuming.

Nunzio and Giovanna sat on the edge of the cliff above the village and looked out at the moon-drenched sea. It was a night so clear and bright that it was timeless. This moment, too, was timeless. They were married adults in their late twenties, but two decades before, they had often sat in the exact same spot talking of their future while they devoured fresh cheese and bread that they had traded fish for. There was no longer cheese and bread, but they still dreamt.

While Nunzio wove fantastic plans that included wealth and status, Giovanna prayed that her self-diagnosis was wrong. She hadn't menstruated in three months; she believed that this wasn't because she was pregnant but because she was starving.

"You know, Giovanna, one day we will sit here and I will call you Doctor," declared Nunzio.

This comment was so outrageous that it interrupted Giovanna's thoughts, and she laughed.

"No, Giovanna, I mean it. When things change, I will work in the north for a few years while you go to school. We will come back to Scilla as a doctor and an engineer with our five little children."

She almost laughed again, but she saw that Nunzio's eyes had hardened, which meant he was serious, so she kept quiet. She loved planning the future with Nunzio, but this dream was impossible. She would be happy if their plans simply included no separations, food, and children.

"Giovanna, you will make the most wonderful doctor. When I was in school, I read about women who had done many things, and I even met a woman doctor. That's when I thought my Giovanna could be a *dottore*. Why not?"

It was impossible for Giovanna to say anything, so she simply gazed at the sky. Were life not currently a contest for survival, it would have been unthinkable to hear a husband encouraging his wife to become a doctor. But in times of turmoil, tradition became a detail.

After their wedding, Nunzio was forced to travel to find work. He spent time in Reggio helping to build ships and went as far as Naples to oversee the construction of a dock. At first Nunzio and Giovanna considered moving to a city with more work, but it soon became clear that there wasn't any city in the south with enough work to keep Nunzio employed more than a few days a month. In the north there were public works projects, but after five years in Rome he knew that, engineer or not, in the north he was still considered a southern peasant.

Within a few months there wasn't even work in other cities. Nunzio would fish, but there was little to trade for the fish, and no one had the money to buy it in the store. To make matters worse, the sea's bounty had diminished, and often they would return with barely a basket of fish to sell. Occasionally, the *glantuomini*—the gentry—walked into the fish store. Their felt hats set them apart from the villagers wearing worn wool caps. Giovanna cringed when they entered. Even though there would soon be coins in the coffers, she hated the manner in which she had to greet them, *"Vosia, sa benadica"*—"bless me, your honor." She refused to kiss their hands as the others did. The gentry were in full control of the local government and the police. They made the laws, enforced the laws, and exempted themselves from them. Giovanna often heard the men in town end a story with, *"Chi ha denaro ed amicizia va nel culo della giustizia"*—"he who has money and friends fucks justice in the ass."

Giovanna and Nunzio's families survived on fish and the food and sundries that were given to Giovanna in exchange for delivering babies. But it was the money sent by Lorenzo from l'America that allowed them to keep their house and pay the taxes.

Giovanna knew they were better off than most. A year ago, she started to notice curious dents in the walls of houses she visited. The mystery was solved when she entered a home to check on a mother who had delivered a few days before and saw her scraping plaster from the wall and adding it to the little bit of flour on the table.

To keep them nourished, mothers breast-fed their children long after they would normally have been weaned. Giovanna watched as hungry people unconsciously stared at the breasts of nursing mothers, who would tug at their shawls to cover their chests as they walked quickly past.

"Giovanna, are you listening to me?" Nunzio took her chin in his hands and turned her face toward his own.

"Sì, sì, *scusa*, Nunzio, but before anything else, I want to have our children."

Nunzio turned, dejected. "I know," he whispered. This blow of reality changed his mood. They sat in silence for a long time. They could hear the water lapping up against the boats, could see the sea sparkle and smell the lemons in the air. They were being forced from the piece of heaven that their families had inhabited for generations.

"Giovanna, Scilla will always be our home and our children will marry here. I promise you this. Before we go to the north for your studies, I must get money to feed us and make things good again."

Giovanna shivered. She knew where this conversation was going. The stars started to blur. The village where they traded food was totally empty. Immigration had started at the mountaintop and trickled down to the water. The fishermen were the last to go. Sometimes, Giovanna felt Scilla was hemorrhaging and would envision the town as her doomed friend, Francesca Marasculo. The blood had drained from the top to the bottom, and only a few were left behind clinging onto the dying village.

"It's the twentieth century now, Giovanna. Things will change. They are changing all over the world; it is just coming more slowly to Scilla."

Giovanna didn't utter a sound.

"And engineers, the world needs engineers. I'll come back to Scilla and build us a port." Nunzio was using his big public voice.

At the words "come back," a wail escaped from Giovanna. She pulled her knees to her chest and began to rock.

"Giovanna, I am sorry." Tears streamed down Nunzio's face. He tried to compose himself and reached into his pocket. "Look at this." He pulled out a tattered piece of paper. It was an advertisement in English. "Lorenzo sent it."

Giovanna's eyes flashed anger at the betrayal. She knew Lorenzo thought he was helping, but how could he have done this?

Nunzio held the paper before her. He had learned some English in school, and he read it slowly to Giovanna.

CROTON RESERVOIR DAILY WAGE:
Common laborer, white $1.30–$1.50
Common laborer, colored $1.25–$1.40
Common laborer, Italian $1.15–$1.25

"Giovanna, more than a dollar a day! That's a wealth of lire! Lorenzo said he would help me. I'll be back in no time with all the money we need."

"Lorenzo also said he would be back."

"Lorenzo's wife is in l'America. Mine is here." Nunzio kissed her.

They cried together for so long they were saturated in each other's sorrow. When they could cry no longer, they tangled their long legs together and made love, adding sweat to their tears.

Giovanna prayed that Nunzio would leave her with a child. In the month before Nunzio left, Giovanna ate more than her share and uncharacteristically took all that was offered, hoping to make herself healthy enough to conceive. She focused all her energies on this project, which was a diversion from the constant pain and foreboding she was living with.

The preparations for Nunzio's departure were similar to those for Lorenzo, except she was now the one packing the trunk instead of her mother. Giovanna made it a mechanical task. She gathered, sorted, and wrapped items as if she were leading a demonstration on how to pack for the New World. She especially wanted to be sure he had dried fruits and nuts. For years they had heard stories about the horrible passage to l'America. The immigrants considered it the penance they had to pay for leaving their villages. But penance or not, Giovanna was determined that Nunzio would not eat vermin-infested food.

The only time her emotions revealed themselves was when she was baking *mustasole,* the hard cookies that would keep for a year or more. She shaped three of the cookies: a swordfish for Scilla, one that resembled a pretzel but was really a *G* and an *N* intertwined, and a crucifix. Wrapping the special cookies separately in fabric torn from her wedding dress, she buried them in the bottom of the trunk.

With every item that Giovanna packed, Nunzio assured her this was a brief chapter in their lives. He would soon return to Scilla with the money they needed to move north and have Giovanna start her studies. Giovanna never laughed at his plan again, but she felt like she was playing along with a child's fantasy. All she wished for was that Nunzio would return to her and the child she hoped she was carrying. She wondered why Nunzio's dream had to be bigger than her own and reminded herself that was how it had always been. He was the idealist and she the pragmatist. Yet, like everything in their lives, there were contradictions. He was the idealist with little faith, and she was the pragmatist who believed in miracles. Nunzio dreamt and Giovanna prayed.

Giovanna insisted on going with Nunzio and her father to Naples. On the night before they were to leave, they both had trouble sleeping. Nunzio awoke at one point to find Giovanna carefully unraveling the Christmas tablecloth and winding the yarn into a ball. He did not question her and instead helped her undo the stitches. When the last of the string was wound on the ball, he simply took her hand and led her back to bed. They found it difficult to speak to each other and spent what little time they had in an entangled embrace.

It took them a day to walk to Reggio. They avoided the roads, knowing they might be stopped and forced to pay a tax, or jumped by brigands who would assume that if they were traveling on a road they were wealthy. Instead, they took to the hills, and when they did encounter brigands in the mountains, they were given a hot meal and advice for safely navigating the streets of Naples. Sitting by the fire, a man with many slashes on his face, some scarred and others fresh, warned, "If the ship is not ready, go back into the mountains. The port is filled with thieves and hucksters."

From Reggio they took a boat to Naples. Emotionally and physically drained, they slept for most of the trip. Giovanna had never been to Naples, or to any city so large, and she was at once repulsed and awed. The smells and voices assaulted her, and the buildings made her jaw gape. With the brigands' words ringing in their ears, they avoided the peddlers selling "Americani clothes," the "dentists" who offered to extract troublesome teeth before the voyage, the "monks" who sold blessings for safe passage, and the cures for trachoma, the dreaded eye disease that would prevent an immigrant access to l'America.

Giovanna was relieved that the Spartan Prince was leaving the next day. She couldn't imagine being able to act so strong for much longer. Nunzio bought a ticket for steerage and was examined by the ship's doctor. The shipping companies did not want to run the risk of transporting back a rejected immigrant at their expense. After Nunzio passed the physical, they coached him. The shipping agent asked in Neapolitan dialect, "Do you have a job in America?"

"Yes," answered Nunzio, thinking of Lorenzo's promise to find him a job.

"No, the answer is no," reprimanded the agent. "If you say yes, you will be rejected. A yes means that you are contracted labor, and that's illegal."

"No, I have no job," Nunzio repeated.

They slept in a *pensione* near the port and woke to the sounds of a ship's departure—the vendors' cries, the clopping of heavy hooves hauling luggage, and men shouting orders. Nearing the ship, they also heard the wails and sobs of the many women who had come to bid their husbands and sons good-bye. Peddlers circled in and out of embracing families in a last-ditch effort to sell their wares. They knew their prey was vulnerable, and a distraught mother might pull out her last coin for a blessing or extra food.

Domenico cut the awkward silence between Giovanna and Nunzio with the first of many reminders to kiss Lorenzo's children and to tell his son to write more often. Domenico seemed desperate to lessen their pain by ignoring it and pretending all was well.

"Carry your luggage? I'll bring it right on the ship." A young boy pestered them.

Nunzio ignored the child and knelt on the dock. He reached his cupped hand into the water and poured it on the back of his neck, letting it spill into his shirt. The Italian waters made their way down his back and started to evaporate. When he stood, Domenico reached up to fix Nunzio's collar and took him by the shoulders, turning his son-in-law's face toward his own. "Our blood is your blood. No country can separate you from your family." At the gangplank, Domenico told him, "Go, go, I expect you to be a big man in America. Don't forget you are a maestro."

Giovanna reached in her bag and handed Nunzio the ball of yarn from the tablecloth. All she said to him was, "I'll be here."

Nunzio gripped her so hard that she forever had a scar where his nail had dug into her neck. She called the scar "Nunzio's good-bye." Domenico separated them. Nunzio walked up the gangplank and went to the ship's rail above where Giovanna stood. He held one end of the string and threw the ball down to her.

The noise around them became deafening; people shouted, horns blew, and donkeys brayed in a whirl of motion. In the midst of this chaos, Giovanna and Nunzio stood perfectly still, staring into each other's eyes, each holding tight to the string. Another horn blew shriller than the rest. Smoke billowed around them as lines were untied and the ship's motor roared. Giovanna and Nunzio did not move, only the string began to unwind when the *Spartan Prince* slowly pulled out of port. The string stretched between them, becoming longer and longer as the ship became smaller. When the ball was at last unwound, the string left Giovanna's and Nunzio's hands at the same moment and drifted into the sea.

Cedar Grove, New Jersey, 1963

Everyone remembers that day. I just remember it a little differently. I was in the first grade, seated alphabetically, staring at the bulletin board. The second grade teacher walked into the room and whispered into my teacher's ear. My teacher, who was old and very upright, slumped back onto her desk and covered her gaping mouth. It took a few minutes, but in a shaky voice, she told us to put our heads on our desks because the president had been shot. From our lowered viewpoint, we could catch glimpses of Mrs. Robinson pacing and whimpering. The principal's voice came over the loudspeaker. It didn't boom like usual. "Children, President Kennedy was shot and he has died. School is dismissed so that you can all go home and mourn with your families." We didn't quite get it. Mrs. Robinson had to tell us to leave.

My best friend, Thea, and I ran home to tell our mothers. As we ran into the circle at the dead end, there was a big black car, a funeral parlor car, in our driveway. I remember asking Thea if she thought they brought the dead president to my house. My mother was sitting with a strange man. I ignored him to announce the president's death to my mother. Instead, she told me that my great-grandmother had died. She said my Big Nanny died at the same moment as the president. I spent the remainder of the day trying to figure out if my great-grandmother's death and the president's death were connected.

My mother and grandmother took me to the wake. I overheard them say, "It will be fine; she barely knew her." They didn't realize how well I remembered brushing my Big Nanny's long gray hair, how holding her enormous silky hands always made me feel safe, and how I had memorized her face as she said words to me in Italian that I didn't understand.

I studied my great-grandmother, her coffin, and the red roses that spelled

M-O-T-H-E-R from the kneeler in front of the casket. She looked like a fairy princess with a rosary knotted in her fist. Her dress sparkled. It was blue, the same color as her eyes, the blue that they painted heaven in church. I absent-mindedly played with the sequins on her gown and wondered about heaven. Did you eat in heaven? If so, would Big Nanny make the president gravy and meatballs? My musings were interrupted when my grandmother swatted my shoulder. "Get away from here now."

As always, my grandfather came to my rescue and drew me onto his lap.

"She didn't have to hit me, Nonno."

"She's upset, Anna. Everybody love your Big Nanny, but most of all your nanny."

I watched Nanny take something from her vinyl purse. She unwrapped a small religious medal, kissed it, and placed it under the pillow that held Big Nanny's head. For the first time ever, I saw my grandmother cry.

A month later I sat at my alphabetically arranged school desk. Mrs. Robinson handed out the new *Weekly Reader*. The president's picture was on the cover and the headline was HERO. I taped the card from the funeral parlor to my *Weekly Reader*. At the top of the card was the Blessed Virgin Mary with outstretched arms. Underneath Mary's robes of heavenly blue was printed, GIOVANNA COSTA SIENA 1873–1963.

PART TWO

NEW YORK, NEW YORK
1901–1902

FOUR

Nunzio stood at the prow of the ferry with the throng of new immigrants released from Ellis Island. The ferry rocked as it approached the dock in Battery Park, where Nunzio could see a huge crowd of people waiting. Moments earlier, he'd overheard one of the ferry operators say, "You can always tell when we're releasing eye-talians. There's five of them at the gate for every one off the boat."

The boat bumped up against the dock, and both crowds roared. The searching for familiar faces began even before the first person disembarked. The passengers gripped bags and lifted children, nervously inventorying their families and luggage as they jostled forward through the ferry gate as one. Within seconds, people were being hoisted into the air, embraced, and patted on the back. There was uncontrolled weeping and laughing. When all had disembarked, the crowd became a knot of humanity—relatives weaving in and out in search of loved ones, or padrones looking for fresh recruits for the mines and farms. At Ellis Island, Nunzio had been handed a pamphlet warning him of the swindlers that would greet them at the Battery and how much to expect to pay in rent or for a carriage ride. Watching the solicitors swarm the crowd, he wondered what would happen to those who couldn't read or who hadn't heard.

With most of the crowd dispersed, Nunzio continued squinting into the sun, looking for Lorenzo. He was trying hard not to be distracted by the tall buildings in the distance. Finally, one hundred yards away he saw a man running, carrying a child with one arm and holding the hand of a small woman with the other. Another child held onto the mother's skirt and struggled to keep up. He couldn't see his face, but he hadn't forgotten that Lorenzo ran like a goat.

Lorenzo reached him, breathless, and caught him in an embrace. "The walk was longer than I remembered. I'm sorry, brother." He kissed Nunzio's cheeks. Nunzio had not yet heard Lorenzo call him brother. Lorenzo had always called him cousin, but after Nunzio and Giovanna married, Lorenzo's letters began to refer to him as "*mio fratello*." Seeing Lorenzo made Nunzio miss Giovanna even more. He hadn't counted on Lorenzo being a constant reminder of his wife. Lorenzo too had smooth, clear skin and was tall and straight, but his face didn't hold the conviction of Giovanna's—it was more relaxed.

Lorenzo stepped back. "Teresa, this is my brother, Nunzio Pontillo. Nunzio, this is my wife, Teresa, and my children, Domenico and Concetta."

Nunzio bent to kiss Teresa and lifted Concetta from the ground as she wiggled back to her mother. He took off Domenico's cap and tousled his hair.

"Thick hair like your father's. Are you as strong as your father?" Nunzio asked.

Domenico put up his fists and pummeled Nunzio's legs. "Ah, stronger! How old are you, big boy?"

"Seven." Domenico punctuated his age by making a muscle.

Laughing, they gathered the bags and turned to begin their trek to Elizabeth Street.

"It's not as far as Naples," teased Lorenzo, who was holding one end of the trunk with Nunzio holding the other. Lorenzo was grateful that Nunzio didn't question him when he saw other arrivals get into horse-drawn carts with their families. And when Nunzio stared at the elevated track, Lorenzo knew that it wasn't because he wanted to take the train but because he didn't know what it was. Nunzio's head was locked in the up position as they walked underneath the El. The track trembled and there was an enormous roar. Nunzio dropped the trunk, grabbed the children, and rushed from beneath the elevated track. Teresa and Lorenzo ran after Nunzio to assure him they were safe, but before they uttered a word, a train thundered on the track above, explaining everything. Nunzio stood in amazement with the children still clutched to his sides.

"The cars, none fell off! A railroad in the sky! This America of yours, does it always build what you dream?" Nunzio exclaimed.

Lorenzo dragged the trunk to where his brother-in-law stood and greeted Nunzio's childlike enthusiasm with a parental answer: "Nunzio, I promise we will take a ride soon." Lorenzo felt guilty again, especially because their route to Little Italy followed the El. He wished they had the extra money for train fare, but they had moved into a three-room apartment in preparation for Nunzio's arrival and for the third child that young Teresa was carrying.

Nunzio didn't know whether to look down or up, and if Lorenzo hadn't been attached to the other side of the trunk, leading him out of the way of carriages, he would have been run over. Nunzio stomped his foot on the pavement and looked down.

"It's a sidewalk," said Lorenzo. "They are on some streets."

"Where does it lead?" asked Nunzio.

"Wherever you want," answered Lorenzo, smiling.

Nunzio thought his head was going to burst trying to absorb it all. When Lorenzo asked about Giovanna, Nunzio realized that for the first time in his three-week voyage, he wasn't thinking about her. He was too caught up in the sights, heights, and sounds of this strange city.

More people passed speaking a foreign tongue.

"Does no one speak English in America, Lorenzo?"

Lorenzo laughed. "Even when we all speak English, our accents are so different we don't know if we are speaking the same language. Language is not so important in this country. If you want to understand one another, you do."

"This way. We'll walk up Broadway," directed Lorenzo.

Concetta and Domenico kept stealing glances at Nunzio, who only occasionally caught them because his head was spinning. A cherry tree was in bloom next to a church with a tall spire that Nunzio was scrutinizing.

"It's not a Catholic church," Lorenzo said. "It's an American church, Trinity, and people think it is very old."

A streetcar pulled by horses thundered toward them. Not bony horses like the ones in Calabria, but enormous ones that dwarfed the pedestrians. The streetcar carried more people than Nunzio could count men and women pressed so close together that Nunzio imagined Father Clemente would be outraged. When the car passed, Nunzio had a full view of an even more amazing sight; it was a building taller than he imagined possible.

Lorenzo looked back at Nunzio and smiled. "I knew you would have your head in the clouds."

"What is it? What is it called, Lorenzo?"

"And I knew you would ask me about the buildings, so I found out their names. This one is called Park Row. They finished it last year, and they say it is the tallest. But this seems to me a big competition these Americans have. If they don't stop, they'll scratch the sun."

Teresa smiled at her husband and directed her pride at her children. "See how much your papa knows?" Lorenzo had told her all about Nunzio, how he was a maestro, and how he had gone to school in the north. She was nervous to meet him, embarrassed that she couldn't read and write. But she was feeling less uncomfortable already; Nunzio had a nice smile, and she liked how he treated the children. Teresa was only fifteen when she married Lorenzo. She had never gone to school, but she had been in the country since she was a little girl, and this gave her the edge to maintain the balance of power in their marriage.

Nunzio stopped in front of Park Row. Lorenzo tugged. "Brother, you will see the sights when I don't have forty kilos hanging off my arm. Forza."

They walked through an area with large, wide buildings, not as tall as the others, but mammoth structures that were grouped together. Lorenzo would narrate when he saw Nunzio's eyes lock onto something. "This is the city hall and the court."

Nunzio thought about Scilla's small stone building near the chiazza where they brought the babies and where they recorded their marriages. In his mind, he saw Giovanna at his side as he signed the ledger recording their marriage before the *sindaco*. Diverted from this memory by the row of skyscrapers that loomed before him, he focused on the one that was bigger than the rest, which had a gold dome.

"Is this the Jewish church?" Nunzio had heard that many Jews lived near the Italians.

"No, a newspaper building. They all are. That one is the *New York World* building."

Nunzio sighed. "There must be a lot to write about."

Conversation about newspapers made Teresa insecure, so she pointed beyond the buildings toward the east. "Nunzio, *guarda!*"

Nunzio had caught a few glimpses of the structure, but it was distant and too unbelievable. Within range of his scrutiny, he was forced to drop the trunk and marvel at the towers and suspension wires of the Brooklyn Bridge. Lorenzo knew that he had no choice but to stop and rest, and this was as good a place as any. Teresa smiled with a child's pride that she was the first to point out the most spectacular of all the marvels to him.

Nunzio stood in awe. Had Giovanna been there, she would have been convinced that such reverence proved that Nunzio saw God in the works of man. When they eventually picked up the trunk, it was as if a prayer had ended, and they continued on in silence. Nunzio glanced back at the bridge, and only then were his eyes able to take in the river, the ferries, the barges, and the bustle of waterfront activity.

Their walk had taken them up Park Row, but now Lorenzo led them left onto Mott Street. The English letters on signs turned into Chinese characters. Nunzio knew many different people lived in New York, but he hadn't expected them to have their own cities. He imagined that China didn't look much different than life on this street; pigs and hens hung in store windows, people ate with sticks in restaurants, and baskets of clothes were piled to the ceiling in cellar laundries. Nunzio saw a shop with small bottles of every color and shape arranged neatly on shelves over barrels brimming with herbs. He knew Giovanna's eyes would burn bright if she saw such a place and he envisioned her rubbing the herbs between her fingers, smelling them, and concocting recipes for new poultices and salves.

Two Chinese men in Western dress walked toward them, but when they passed, Nunzio saw that long braids fell from their felt hats. He wondered how you decide to wear the Western suit but keep your hair in a long tail. What would change about him in this l'America? Nunzio thought of the Calabrians who returned home but thereafter were called Americani. There was no time to figure out the answers to these and other questions; he was trying too hard to navigate the strange streets. He simply had to take it all in and have faith that the curious would soon explain itself.

A Chinese peddler, balancing a large wicker basket on a long stick, walked beside them. Nunzio was sure that whatever the teetering basket held would soon fall on his head, and he tugged Lorenzo farther away. They followed the stone path that Lorenzo had called a sidewalk, but many streets, including this one, were also paved in stones, and it made the noise around them deafening. The sounds of wagon wheels, boxes being dragged, water splashing from pots—all were amplified with no dirt to absorb them. There was such a rhythm to the noise and motion of the street that Nunzio's closest comparison was Scilla's Feast of Saint Rocco. Life in this New York was a parade without an order of march.

"Lorenzo, is every day like this?" shouted Nunzio.

"It's quiet today because it is Sunday."

For the first time, Nunzio felt exhausted.

"Ah, we are on Elizabeth Street," exclaimed Lorenzo.

The Chinese characters changed to Italian words. Even from the signs, he could tell that much of the dialect was Sicilian.

This street was not paved with stones. Dust and dried manure swirled through the air with each breeze. Some pushcarts, stripped of their inventory, lined the road.

Responding to Nunzio's glances, Lorenzo said, "On weekdays, there are so many sellers it's difficult to walk. It can be a good living. This block here"—Lorenzo nodded—"is where all the fish peddlers live. Elizabeth Street is mainly Sicilians. There are more Calabrians on Mulberry Street, but we found a better apartment here." Since marrying a girl from Puglia, Lorenzo crossed lines more easily.

"Here we are. Home. Elizabeth Street, 176."

They entered a narrow, dark hall and climbed three flights. The children ran up the stairs ahead. If it weren't for the strong and familiar smells on each landing, and the laughing and arguing that characterized Sunday dinner echoing in the halls, Nunzio would have thought they had entered a cave. Lorenzo pushed open one of two doors on the third floor. They entered an apartment with not much more light than the hallway.

"We moved in last week," said Lorenzo nervously. By the expression on Nunzio's face, Lorenzo knew that Nunzio's reaction was similar to his own when he first saw the houses of l'America.

Nunzio walked between the three small rooms thinking, "How do you get outside? Is the only way out really down those narrow stairs?" Looking for an escape, he ducked his head under the fabric hanging on a string in front of the window. Raising the curtain, he leaned his body on the sill and was startled by all the people looking back at him. Hundreds of people were leaning out their windows above and beneath him, across the street, and up the block. The tenement dwellers stared at the newcomer, and Nunzio nodded awkwardly. A man smoked a cigar; a woman called to her children; but mostly, they leaned forward, watching the seething street with their elbows resting on pillows or burlap sacks. "So, this is how you go outside in l'America," thought Nunzio. He had heard descriptions of New York apartments, but like everything thus far about l'America, until you saw it, you wouldn't believe it, and even then it was hard to comprehend.

Upon arriving, Teresa immediately set about preparing a meal in the cramped kitchen. "I was only a child, but I remember the food on that ship."

Teresa had done most of the cooking before going to meet Nunzio at the Battery. Sunday dinner was always extravagant—they had meat and salad—but today she had prepared all of her specialties with Lorenzo's blessing. The children lifted the cloth to pick at the *pasticcini,* but Teresa slapped their hands and shooed them into the hall to play. Lorenzo poured Nunzio a glass of wine and explained that he had traded a few things for a soft mattress to put in the kitchen for Nunzio's bed.

"The kitchen is not so bad, Nunzio. In fact, in the winter, you may find your niece and nephew joining you," Lorenzo warned. "Later tonight, Luigi and Pasqualina DiFranco will come by to pay their respects . . ."

Lorenzo kept talking, but Nunzio wasn't listening. He was looking at Teresa's table with as much reverence as he had the Brooklyn Bridge. He couldn't remember the last time he had seen so much food. He was ravenous.

Domenico watched his uncle's eyes follow his mother's every move. He snatched a meatball and secretly handed it to Nunzio. Nunzio took a breath to protest, but then winked at Domenico and took the meatball.

Lorenzo was chatting nervously, and Nunzio surmised it was because he was avoiding asking a question. Correctly guessing the cause of Lorenzo's angst, Nunzio said, "Lorenzo, your parents are well." He continued, and Lorenzo's shoulders relaxed. "If there was more food, that would be better for everyone. But your mother still sews like no one else in the village, and if there is a fish to catch, your father will catch it."

Lorenzo's face radiated relief. "And Giovanna, is there no child?"

It was Nunzio's turn to be pensive. "I wait for a letter. I wait."

Teresa ordered everyone to the table, and her pride was evident. Her ink black hair was swept back in a bun, and although her plain face still looked young, she had the weary but confident bearing of an older Italian woman. Teresa stopped fluttering while Lorenzo said a prayer and continued serving when he finished. She refused every entreaty to sit down and instead concentrated on keeping Nunzio's plate full—something that hadn't been possible for many years.

FIVE

Lorenzo laid brick in the spring, summer, and fall, and, if he was lucky, sold sweet potatoes in the winter. During the first of his eight years in New York, Lorenzo had had such a difficult time finding work that he had even considered listening to the lies of the padroni and going off to lay track for a railroad or to work in a mine. He knew he would be cheated, but at least he would be working.

In the end, what kept him from indentured servitude was Teresa, who was wise in the ways of finding a job. Teresa made the rounds with Lorenzo to the barbershops, cafes, and markets to chat and listen to rumors of work. Before long, Lorenzo was on the laborer circuit and rarely spent more than a day or two between jobs.

Nunzio now benefited from his brother-in-law's experience. Lorenzo wrote down the addresses of three places where he could look for work. At the first location, after having trouble finding the place and waiting in line for five hours, he was told he was too late, all the jobs were filled. He cursed himself for getting lost, and the next day woke at three in the morning to ensure he would be at the next site well before six.

After again waiting for hours, he was told they already had too many Italians on the job. A small boy with a pimply face and hands much older than his years explained when he saw Nunzio's puzzled expression, "They think if there's a lot of one kind, the unions will get you." Nunzio had no idea what the kid meant.

On the third day, he hiked down to the Brooklyn Bridge long before the sun came up and walked across to where they were building a waterfront warehouse. There were already three men in line, all Italian, and each had heard a different story concerning how many men were to be hired. Lines were a new experience for the Italians, but they caught on quickly to this American phenomenon. The men had queued up in front of a misshapen small shack made out of scrap wood. It stood alone on a lot strewn with rubble, which had the beginnings of a foundation. They watched in silence as a short, fat man with ruddy skin placed a plank across two crates in front of the shack, making a table for himself. One by one, workers and foremen arrived at the site carrying trowels, buckets, and tins of food. It was hours before the fat man called them forward.

"Hey, this wop says he's an engineer!" yelled the hiring boss to the foreman. "And he speaks English."

The tall, thin foreman sauntered over. "So, you're an engineer."

"Yes, sir," answered Nunzio proudly, "I studied in Rome."

"So, I bet you built that there Col-es-see-um." The hiring boss laughed heartily at the foreman's joke.

Nunzio ignored them. "I know how to build. I work hard."

"You eye-talians haven't built anything that isn't falling down. This is America, wop-boy, and you don't 'build' here—you carry brick." He turned to the hiring boss. "Hire 'im, but keep your eye on 'im. I don't trust no English-speaking eye-talian with red hair."

Nunzio twirled his sandwich, which was harpooned on a wire, toasting it over the flame. Six laborers, all *paesani*, ringed the fire, eating their lunch. Nunzio never thought he'd think of Sicilians, Abruzzese, and Napolitans as paesani, but here in this country they were all Italian. In his most recent letter to Giovanna, he wrote of the irony that, in America, Italy was more united than in Italy.

Two-Toed Nick opened his flask of wine. "Nunzio, where you go after this joba?"

"Joba." "The job." The word was always said with such reverence that Nunzio envisioned it as a satin-coated deity. He had been on this job eight weeks, and it was coming to an end. "I don't know. But I want a big one so I lose no days and return to Scilla."

"You Calabresi, always thinking you're going home."

"Sicilians are so different?" Nunzio nodded to another man at the fire. "Saint Carmine told me he counts the days on his bedroom wall."

Two-Toed Nick looked offended. "Saint Carmine is not *Siciliano*. He's *Napolitano*. And besides," he said with a smile, "he's not right in the head."

"Don't tell that story." Carmine didn't move as he spoke and continued puffing on his cigar.

"Nunzio, didn't you ever wonder why they call him Saint Carmine? It's certainly not because he worships at a certain house on Mulberry Street."

The laughter started.

"It's not funny," protested Carmine, who got up in a dramatic huff and pretended to go back to work.

Two-Toed Nick took Carmine's exit as permission to continue.

"Like I said, Saint Carmine is Napolitano and every few years the Napolitanos have to deal with Vesuvius coughing up hot lava. One time the lava, it was coming straight for Carmine's village. Carmine went to the church, and he ripped the statue of Saint Gennaro from the altar and carried it halfway up the mountain. Then he takes Saint Gennaro, and he puts him down in the path of the lava."

Two-Toed Nick stood to reenact the story, shaking his finger and mimicking Carmine's gruff voice. "Carmine says, 'Saint Gennaro, we pray to you, we give you a big festival, we give you money. Now, you do your job—make this lava go away from our village.' Then Carmine, he stood and waited as the hot rock flowed. The lava, it headed straight for Saint Gennaro and Carmine's village. Carmine, he sees the saint is doing nothing, and he goes *pazzo*. He starts throwing rocks at the statue screaming, 'You dirty bum! You freeloader!' Carmine keeps throwing those rocks as he's running for his life down the mountain."

The men, despite having heard the story before, cried from laughing so hard. Nunzio, who kept trying to catch his breath, laughed hardest and at the same time debated whether to write Giovanna to tell her this story. He knew she would let loose the throaty laugh that he loved, but he could also imagine her crossing herself, filled with guilt for laughing when a saint was involved.

When Nunzio caught his breath and ended his silent debate, he asked, "And what of the village? *Cos'è successo?*"

"Who knows? Carmine, he kept running right onto a boat and came here!"

The men collapsed again into laughter as the foreman walked by. "Hey, you gang-o-dagos, enough lounging around. Get your sorry garlic asses back to work."

Nunzio had started on the job as a laborer. He mixed mortar and loaded wheelbarrows with piles of bricks, delivering them to the bricklayers. He hadn't done such mind-numbing, backbreaking work since he was a child.

The foreman who had hired Nunzio called him to his "office," the misshapen wood shanty. "So, hotshot, you can drive a wheelbarrow. Now we're gonna see if you can lay brick." The foreman stood up, and Nunzio almost smiled, not because he was being "promoted," but because the man so lived up to his nickname. Carmine called him *"Linguine con Pomodoro"* because he was tall and thin with red splotches all over his white skin. Linguine con Pomodoro handed him pointing and bricklaying trowels. "Borrow these today; tomorrow you bring your own."

Nunzio had spent two weeks watching the fluid movements of the bricklayers, so it didn't take him long to master the bricklayer's art. He stayed out of Linguine con Pomodoro's eyesight until he could dip his trowel and ice the brick like a seasoned artisan. He missed the freedom of movement he'd had as a laborer, but he loved climbing the scaffolding and working high off the ground. This warehouse was only six stories, but that was three stories higher than most of the buildings in Scilla.

Nunzio could also see everything that went on around and below him. He could see the inspector coming even before Linguine con Pomodoro, who always had the inspector's favorite scotch waiting. The inspector would enter Linguine con Pomodoro's "office," and after an hour or so, the two would emerge singing songs or laughing at the punch line of a joke.

Accidents on the job were to be expected. There were the petty nuisances of the trade—skin burned and chafed so badly by mortar that the only way to relieve the pain and heal the wound was to urinate on your own skin. Or the sore and bent backs that needed both hot and cold to straighten them out. But these were the daily annoyances, not the events that earned workers their nicknames.

Two-Toed Nick was simply Nick before a pile of brick crushed his foot. One-Legged Paul, who sold fruit from a Mulberry Street pushcart, was formerly Paul the Riveter. *Uno Occhi* (One-Eye) Nardone, who lived in Lorenzo's building, used to set the dynamite to build the tunnels. Now he dug them, because you didn't need good eyesight to shovel dirt in the dark. Nunzio prayed that his nickname would not change. His paesani had taken to calling him "Professore," and it was his hope that he did not become the Professore of a missing piece of anatomy.

Sundays were the only day of the week that "Joba" was not worshiped. The women went to church and cooked, and the men gambled and relaxed in the cafes. It was also the one day of the week to be an individual. The man in the apartment on the first floor played his mandolin when the Sunday meal ended until the first of the *bambini* were put to sleep. Carmine, not surprisingly, loved the theater and was a vocal member of the audience at performances in Little Italy. Lorenzo made extra money by painting idyllic landscapes in tenement foyers. Apartment seekers rarely saw the actual rooms for rent and instead met the landlord in the foyer. The effect of scenes reminiscent of the Italian countryside apparently made the potential tenants feel at home, and it allowed the savvy landlords to charge even more for the airless dark rooms that were more reminiscent of railroad cars than open villas.

So on Sundays, Teresa cooked, Lorenzo readied his paint box, and Nunzio would kneel and say a prayer of apology to Giovanna for missing church before scrubbing himself and the children clean. He would fuss over little Domenico and Concetta, making sure that their Sunday clothes were pressed properly and that their hats were on straight. The three would leave the house on their weekly adventure, brimming with excitement, and Teresa, who was large with child, would smile and shake her head.

Nunzio, his niece, and his nephew would retrace their steps back to the Battery, stopping at each skyscraper to explore the building and to ride the elevator. The first time Nunzio charmed a watchman in the Park Row building and they rode the elevator to the top, Domenico emerged from the gilded marvel with his hand cupped under his chin, holding the contents of his stomach. Undeterred, Nunzio took them on every elevator he could sweet-talk his way into until Domenico's stomach adjusted to life in the twentieth century. When the watchmen weren't watching, Concetta and Nunzio would run their hands along the marble in the lobbies to feel the cool of the stone. Nunzio would point out details in the carvings, and if there were paintings, they would memorize the colors and scenes to describe them later to Lorenzo. Sometimes while waiting for the elevator, Nunzio would show them how to measure the lobby with their strides. They did all of this in silence. The rule of thumb was "no talking" for fear they would broadcast their immigrant status more loudly than their appearance already did.

On the way home, Nunzio would buy the children sugared almonds and pistachios. They would sit on the bench overlooking the Brooklyn Bridge that they had claimed as their own and discuss the merits of all the buildings they saw. Concetta chattered about the animals she saw in the marble patterns; Domenico bragged that someday he would carve the greatest gargoyle; and Nunzio imagined Giovanna was on the bench with him and these were their children.

The trio would make their way home just in time for Teresa's feast. The children would collapse into chairs as Lorenzo rubbed the paint off his hands with turpentine. The music of the mandolin player—whose family ate one hour earlier—filled the exhausted silence. By the time Teresa piled the table with nuts, fruit, and pasticcini, they would have revived and would all be talking at once. When the meal ended, Lorenzo would smoke his pipe with his children on his knees before leaving for the cafe. "The Goat"—Nunzio wasn't the only one who noticed that Lorenzo ran like a goat—would try and persuade Nunzio to go with him, but Lorenzo knew that Nunzio would opt for his solitary walk instead.

After Sunday dinner Nunzio would walk up to Twenty-third Street and stand at the intersection of Fifth Avenue to assess what work had been completed since the previous Sunday. These men, how lucky they were! They were building the most marvelous building in the entire world. They had shaped it like a triangle, and it was going higher than Nunzio could have ever imagined before stepping foot on the Battery. But this building was different from the others. It had poetry. Its shape mimicked the crossing of Fifth Avenue and Broadway, and it played with your eye. This was a masterpiece. And the way it was being built! This building was not held up by its walls, but by the steel of its interior. Nunzio marveled that the exterior of the building was like skin; it merely served to cover the interior structure. The middle of the building was covered in its facade first. Nunzio wondered whether they did this for any engineering reasons or if it was just to prove to the world that they could. He yearned to work on such a building.

SIX

"Giovanna must be praying for me," Nunzio thought on his last day at the warehouse job. Carmine had gotten a tip that they were looking for laborers for a project in Brooklyn that could keep them employed for a year or more. Nunzio had already calculated what he could save and had determined that he could return to Giovanna at the end of the year with enough money to move north so she could study.

"It's a tank to hold the gas for the lights," said Carmine, knowing that this explanation would appeal to Nunzio—the job might not be building a skyscraper, but it was about progress. "They're hiring tomorrow morning. But it's even farther north than here; we'll be dead before we get there," pronounced Carmine dramatically.

Nunzio picked up Carmine at three in the morning from Mulberry Street for the three-hour walk to Wythe Avenue and North Twelfth Street in Williamsburg, Brooklyn.

"*Brutte Americane* waters!" cursed Carmine, as they followed the river south to the Brooklyn Bridge. "With no current, we could swim there in half the time."

Nunzio looked at the stocky, bald man from the mountains and thought, current or not, he'd sink like a stone. But Carmine's comment stoked his yearning for the turquoise waters of Scilla. They walked past another bridge being built that, if finished, would cut their walk in half. Nunzio studied the construction and could tell that this structure would not be as grand as the Brooklyn Bridge. Still, he'd love to work on it, and if that wasn't possible, he simply wished it would open quickly and lessen his commute—were he lucky enough to get this job.

They weren't dead, but they were exhausted by the time they

reached Wythe and North Twelfth. There was already a line, but not a long one. Joining the line, Nunzio shifted the weight of his canvas bag holding his chisels, level, trowels, and hammer, which he brought in case the foreman wanted them to start right away.

Carmine gave Nunzio a disapproving look. "For me, no job, no tools. They give me a job, I bring my tools," he blustered.

Nunzio suspected Carmine's bravado had more to do with laziness than conviction. Nunzio had always thought there was a lazy streak in Carmine, but of course he had never voiced such a thing. It would have been the ultimate insult to an Italian. Poor, okay, but lazy—never.

TAYLOR, WOOD & CO., BALTIMORE was printed on a sign above the building housing an office. This was good. Nothing makeshift; it meant they planned on being around a while. Nunzio looked at the barren land and imagined the tank they would build there. Carmine said he heard it was to be a giant cylinder. Nunzio thought of building curves, not angles, and was intrigued. Approaching the office, he instinctively straightened up.

The men entered one by one. An Italian translator stood next to a balding man in a suit. Nunzio had never seen a man wear a suit at a job site. The translator addressed Nunzio.

"*Come si chiama*?" asked the translator.

"Nunzio Pontillo. I speak the English, sir."

The man in the suit looked up. "What's your experience?"

Nunzio rattled off a progression of jobs, some true and others not, that took him from laborer to skilled mason. He had learned they didn't check, and he had also learned not to say he was an engineer.

The boss looked approvingly at his tool bag. "You start tomorrow as a laborer. If you work out, you'll be on this job at least six months, could be longer."

"*Grazie*. No, thank you . . ."

"Sign up over there," interrupted the translator.

Carmine was put on a "reserve line"—if no one better came along, he would be hired. Nunzio waited in the shade of one of the few trees and watched. It was July, and the sun was high at noon. He knew Carmine was on the verge of cursing them for keeping him waiting in the scorching heat, so Nunzio shot him an occasional look that said, "Behave." At two in the afternoon, when the line had dwindled, Carmine was pulled from the reserve and signed up.

They were halfway back to Little Italy before Carmine calmed down. "They take all of those jerks right away and they don't take me? *Stronzi*. They are all stronzi."

Nunzio ignored him. "Carmine, let's celebrate. When we get to Mulberry Street, we'll eat clams." Nunzio was not usually so extravagant. Buying clams on the half shell from a pushcart was standard fare for some men, but it was an unnecessary expenditure for one with big plans.

That night, lying in bed, Nunzio wrote to Giovanna in triumph. In all of Giovanna's letters to Nunzio, she found a thousand ways to tell him not to worry and not to be disappointed at how long it was taking them to achieve their goals. Nunzio saw through every line. He knew when Giovanna was trying to be strong, although he was sure that no one else could pick up on this because Giovanna's voice and body spoke with such conviction. But Nunzio could see what others could not, like the tiny flutter beneath Giovanna's left eye. When she was suppressing emotion, Nunzio saw that twitch in Giovanna's letters, but tonight, he imagined her reading his good news with a smile creeping across her face. She might even allow herself an open grin before she ran off to church to give thanks.

Unable to sleep because he was so happy, Nunzio got up and wrote Giovanna another letter, this time drawing what he imagined the tank would look like. And maybe because he was delirious or because he again wanted to imagine Giovanna's laugh, he did a second drawing of the tank. This time it was situated on Scilla's north coast and looked like a pasta pot.

They were building two tanks, one at a time. Nunzio couldn't understand why they weren't being built at the same time, and although he asked as politely as possible, he got a stinging rebuke from the foreman and a raised eyebrow from the supervisor. The first task was to dig a circular hole 10 feet deep and 192 feet in diameter. When the ground was excavated, they were to lay the concrete floor on which the tank would rest. The month of July was spent mixing and laying concrete in three-foot-square sections to cover the floor area.

Nunzio was lead man in a crew that included Carmine, "Pretty Boy," "Meatball," and "Nospeakada." He liked to imagine that he was in charge because he was the most skilled, the engineer, but he knew it was only because he spoke English. Nunzio had a hunch that Nospeakada spoke English, but whenever he was asked a question not in Italian, his quick reply was "Nospeakada eenglish." Pretty Boy was both pretty and young. He was lean with thick eyelashes and delicate features, but Nunzio could count on him to work the hardest. Meatball, an older man, had indulged in one meatball too many, which earned him his nickname and a stomach he struggled to bend over. Carmine was only useful when he knew the supervisor or foremen were watching, which left most of the work to Nunzio, Pretty Boy, and Nospeakada.

The supervisor, Mr. Mulligan, no longer wore a suit to work, but he was always impeccably clean and often on the telephone in the office. He communicated with the men through his foremen, who made a big show of shouting orders after Mr. Mulligan had quietly given them instructions. To get his information, Nunzio stole glances through Mr. Mulligan's windows at the plans for the tanks tacked on his wall.

Before they had finished laying the concrete floor, large pieces of wrought iron, five by twelve feet and three-eighths of an inch thick, were delivered to the site. Nunzio's spirits lifted when he saw the iron, and he urged the men on to finish the floor. He could imagine the largest gas tank in the world taking shape.

With the concrete set, it was time to build the tank. Supervisor Mulligan had a short meeting with the foremen, who broke from the circle, shouting to their lead men. The first step was to build the bottom of the tank. Over the next few days, they erected scaffolding on the concrete floor. When that was completed, the men hauled the sheets of iron into place, which would then be riveted together. Nunzio peered at the drawings through the windows, looking for clues as to why large numbers of jacks and timbers were showing up on the job. Unable to figure it out, he approached one of the foremen during a lunch break.

"Mister, why all the jacks? What are we going to do with them?"

"What's it to you, wop?"

Mr. Mulligan heard the exchange, gave his foreman a look of disapproval, and answered Nunzio.

"That's how we're going to get her down, son."

Nunzio was so fascinated he forgot he was just a laborer talking to the supervisor. "But how are we going to use the jacks without making holes?"

"We will make holes, but we'll seal them when it's lowered." The supervisor walked on, and the foreman angrily waved Nunzio away.

"Your job's not to ask questions, you hear?"

Nunzio couldn't follow the supervisor's logic—they were riveting the plates of iron on scaffolding to ensure tight seals, but then they would compromise the metal by piercing its surface. After thinking it through, he came to no conclusions but dismissed his doubts. This was America. They knew how to build with metal, and Nunzio didn't know metal like he knew wood, stone, and brick. He would watch and learn.

There was creaking as Nunzio climbed into his cot in Lorenzo's kitchen, but it was his body, not the bed. Settling on top of the sheet, he cursed his complaining joints and tired muscles. All was quiet in the apartment, except for the muffled sounds of Teresa's new baby suckling at her breast. Nunzio had waited until everyone had gone to bed to read Giovanna's letter, wanting to savor it without interruption. He unfolded the paper and marveled at her steady, fluid hand, thinking that if she didn't become a doctor she could work in the office of the sindaco recording the births, deaths, and marriages. He excitedly refocused on her words, lingering on "*Caro* Nunzio" for a moment. Nunzio's eyes skipped through the sentences with Giovanna's voice echoing in his mind. The letter opened with reassuring words about the health of their parents, as it always did, and went on to chronicle the news of the village.

"Ah, she got my letter!" he thought delightedly, reading further.

I am so proud that my Nunzio is shaping this America.

I think of you on this job and know that all the men must look up to you. I imagine that there is a chorus of 'Ask Nunzio' all day long. I have my own question: what does the name of this job, Brooklyn Union Gas Company, mean?

Oh, but how I wish you did not have to travel so far to get there! Nunzio, you must send less money and pay to take a cart, at least for the trip home. I can't

bear to think of you working so hard all day and having to walk home. I would do
anything to take those steps for you.

   At least I know that Lorenzo is giving you plenty of wine with dinner. I have
not showed your drawing to anyone for fear they would say that America has
made Nunzio soft in the head.

   I did laugh, very hard, and then, of course, I tried to imagine how much pasta
we could cook in such a pot.

Nunzio smiled, pleased with himself. After commenting on Nunzio's
letter, Giovanna usually would end with assurances that time was passing quickly, even though it didn't feel that way, and they would soon be
together in Scilla. But this letter did not follow its usual course. Nunzio
could see the speed in Giovanna's writing, and he reacted by sitting up
on his elbows.

   Nunzio, today I delivered a little girl. It was a difficult birth, and the baby's
lungs are infected. I don't think she will live. I was frustrated during the deliv-
ery, because if I knew more I could have helped that child. I have always relied
on my instincts, which have served me well, but today, as other days, I faced my
ignorance. Until this moment, I thought that if I were to study further, it would
be because Nunzio wanted me to. Now I share your dream, improbable as it may
seem. Thank you, my dear Nunzio, for knowing what is in my heart even before
I do. Sometimes I feel like you inhabit my soul.

"Brava, Giovanna, brava," whispered Nunzio, running his hands
across the page, caressing Giovanna in its surface. He wondered how he
could feel such a connection with a woman an ocean away. Carmine had
tried to bring him to the house of the *puttane*, and he had allowed himself to go through the door. A dark-haired woman approached him, but
even with her breath on his face, he felt physically closer to Giovanna.
He turned and left Carmine to his comforts; and now, he folded the
letter, laid it on his chest, and fell into a satisfied sleep.

Nunzio became lead man for three crews because so many men had
quit during the next phase of construction. The metal bottom of the

tank sat on wooden stilts thirty-two inches above the concrete floor. The metal plates were being riveted from above—and below. The first time he crawled into the dark beneath the disc, he sympathized with his countrymen who had become miners. But within days, he was jealous of the miners, for while the miners had to endure the soot, he believed that at least they labored standing in the cool beneath the earth. Nunzio and his co-workers entered hell each time they slithered under the tank bottom. The August sun baked the iron and the noise from the hot rivets being pounded into the metal from above created an ear-piercing, broiling torture chamber.

Nunzio's job was to crawl on his belly to the plate that was being riveted and position the anvil to take the blows and steady the tank bottom's weight of two hundred tons. He felt like a worm. His mind flashed back to his fantasies of building the Flatiron Building. If he weren't so miserable he would have laughed at the irony. He tried to cheer himself by imagining this project as one part of the web that was being spun throughout New York, spanning rivers, reaching into the sky, burrowing tunnels, and stretching in every direction. He tried even harder to convince himself that he was an important piece of this puzzle and not simply cheap Italian labor.

Meatball had a heart attack the first week they worked under the disc, but he survived. He was now helping to sell fruit on Mulberry Street at half his paltry laborer's wage. In the late afternoons, when Carmine and Nunzio made it back to Mulberry Street, they would head for Meatball's cart. The garage behind his fruit stand housed Meatball's friend's ice truck, and he would take Nunzio and Carmine there to sit inside its cool walls and eat the bruised fruit that he had saved for them.

Near the end of August, they finished riveting together the plates of the tank's bottom. "Ah, just in time for winter, we'll come aboveground," Carmine mocked.

They drilled holes in the plate to insert the jacks. The plan was for the scaffolding to be removed and for the jacks and screw logs to hold the bottom of the tank above the concrete floor. Nunzio noticed that Mr. Mulligan looked more worried than usual and was making many phone calls. When Nunzio couldn't contain himself any longer, he asked what the procedure was going to be for lowering the structure onto the floor. One of the foremen grabbed him by the shoulders and yelled inches from his face, "Stop asking stupid questions!"

In that instant, Nunzio realized the question wasn't stupid, and he was not the only one who didn't understand the mechanics of how this disc was to be lowered. Work slowed for a day or two, and another man in a suit showed up. Supervisor Mulligan and the man went into the construction office. Supplies were stored near the office door, so Nunzio walked over pretending to need a new drill bit.

"Mulligan, we've got six jobs to worry about. If you can't handle this one, let us know," was the first and last thing Nunzio heard before a foreman walked by and snapped, "What are you doing? You're supposed to have a runner get that."

Lowering the disc to its surface could be put off no longer. On the morning of September 2, the men arrived at work and were surprised to see an additional crew of twenty-five laborers on site. Mulligan called all the foremen and lead men together.

"Alright, we're going to lower this baby to the bottom today. I want one man to every two jacks and one to every screw log. We got extra men here to help. Take it down. Slow as you need to. And we'll need a few men underneath to oil the cups of the jacks."

Go underneath when it was being lowered? Even the company's foremen were stunned. Mulligan answered the silence. "The head engineer says that unless those jacks are oiled she's not going to come down smooth and easy." The silence continued, and eventually so did Mulligan.

"Okay, let's try it without men below the disc and see how it goes."

The men, including Nunzio and Pretty Boy, who was now also a lead man, broke from the circle relieved and went to round up the crews to work the jacks and screw logs. By ten o'clock the disc had been lowered two inches in a tedious, arduous process. The jacks and men groaned from the weight. Nunzio overheard the foremen calculating that it could be three to four days before they got the tank floor to the ground. Supervisor Mulligan nervously circled the disc when he wasn't being summoned to the phone. At noon the men were promised an extra hour's pay if they took ten minutes to eat and skipped their lunch. They were hot and exhausted, but it was too good an offer to pass up.

By two o'clock the disc had been lowered to twenty-six inches. After another phone call, Supervisor Mulligan brought the foremen and lead men together once again.

"We're going to oil the cups; it's going too slowly. I figure if eight men go underneath, that should do it. At twenty-six inches, they need to work on their backs, so the skinnier the better." Mulligan walked away, leaving them in stunned silence.

It took a few moments for the chief foreman to speak. "There's eight crews. Each lead man should pick one person from their crew to oil the cups."

The eight lead men stared at the Irish foreman, who knew them well enough to know that they would pick themselves. It was a matter of honor. They were the lead men; they were making five cents more an hour. It was their responsibility. Nunzio looked around at the other men and wordlessly asked the question. The lead men all nodded.

"We're the men," intoned Nunzio.

They gathered again at the bottom of the disc to discuss positioning. The foremen figured they needed five men in the interior and three along the perimeter. The chief foreman called off names. "Lagato, Fiero, Constantino, Romano, and Idone will work toward the center. Pontillo, Amato, and Jones will handle the perimeter."

Pretty Boy, whose real name was Mariano Idone, tried to control the shaking in his hand as he reached for his oilcan. Nunzio noticed and offered, "Pretty Boy, I positioned most of these jacks, why don't you stay around the edge and I'll go in."

Pretty Boy stared at Nunzio and quietly said, "Alright Professore, if you think so."

Nunzio slithered on his back under the disc and headed for the center. He used his heels on the concrete and his palms on the metal tank bottom to propel himself through the space. He held the oilcan in his mouth. It was dark, and the few inches that were lost with the lowering of the disc made a huge difference in the amount of air and anxiety that flowed through his body. To keep going, Nunzio was forced to use a mental trick Giovanna had taught him that she used with women in labor. His body was sandwiched between sun-scorched steel and concrete, but he visualized himself sitting with Giovanna on the cliffs of Scilla. A sea breeze cooled them, carrying the smell of lemons.

The laborers above were instructed to lower the tank an inch while the men underneath oiled the cups and checked the jack pins to ensure they were working. The strain of the jacks on the metal was amplified beneath the disc. Nunzio's head felt like it was going to explode from the noise and the heat. It was almost pitch dark under the disc, but when Nunzio saw how the pins played loosely in the cups, he knew he had found the problem. He decided to check one other jack cup before telling the foreman. Nunzio shimmied over to the next jack. He glimpsed the bottom of a boot and called out.

"Do the pins seem okay to you?"

"I can't see a thing, I'm getting out of this goddamn inferno," came Lagato's voice.

"I'll be right behind you."

Aboveground, Supervisor Mulligan noticed that the strain on the jacks and screw logs had not changed. He was furious with the engineer for backing him into this problem. It wasn't his fault it was taking so long; the engineers had come up with a lousy idea. Mulligan decided to tell them he was stopping the job until they came up with a better plan and marched off to the office to call.

Nunzio had checked a second jack cup and found the pin just as loose. "No oil is going to help this situation," he thought. "They're strained."

It was going to be a long crawl out from under the disc. His panic worsened, making it harder to get out, so he narrowed his mind's focus to the blue of Scilla's water, skies, and Giovanna's eyes. He stared at the blue and heard the rushing sound of the tide through small stones that seemed to sing "Ssh-illa." Within seconds his concentration was shattered by a strange creaking sound.

"Forza!" yelled Nunzio into the dark. Curses and the sounds of desperate scrambling came in reply. Nunzio ripped the skin on his elbows, hands, and legs as he frantically tried to move his body faster along the concrete. The next few moments, like the metal inches above him, hung in the air. Nunzio felt the disc lurch westward and heave a heavy groan. He had a split second of recognition that he was going to die, and he let his mind flash onto the blue before all two hundred tons of steel heaved, fell, and crushed his body.

The police, firemen, and the laborers identified a few areas with minor elevations and worked in teams with heavy sledges and chisels to rip up the plates. An hour after the metal jacks and timbers had snapped like toothpicks and the tank bottom had crashed to the concrete, one rescue team had ripped up enough metal to locate a body. Work stopped and there was a hush when they brought Lagato into daylight. It was his clothes that held the pulp of Lagato's body together. At the sobering sight of the first body reduced to a fleshy mass, work slowed, perhaps because it was evident that survival was impossible or the thought of finding another man was too gruesome.

Carmine, however, refused to give up his urgency. He urged his crew on. Pretty Boy, whose leg was cut open from the ankle to the knee, wouldn't allow them to take him to the hospital until they found Nunzio. He lay by the edge of the disc muttering, "Nunzio, he yelled, 'Forza.'"

The rescue crew took advantage of the void left by the removal of Lagato's broken body and wedged long sticks underneath, poking to pinpoint the location of the other men.

Several thousand people had gathered at the scene, including a number of reporters and a priest. To Carmine, the priest looked like a black crow waiting to pounce on a corpse, and he spit in his direction without interrupting the swing of his hammer on the chisel.

Work stopped briefly again when Constantino's body was removed and taken, as Lagato's had been, to the police station to be examined by the coroner. Finding Constantino made Carmine work faster, because he was now sure it was Nunzio beneath the slight elevation where they were working.

Near six o'clock, Carmine's crew removed their fourth panel and found Nunzio. His legs were visible, and although they knew he was dead, Carmine made the men lift the final metal plate as gingerly as possible. He wanted to keep his friend's body intact. With the last blood-stained metal plate removed, Nunzio's body, every bone broken and arms and legs at unnatural angles, faced the sky.

PART THREE

SCILLA, ITALY, TO NEW YORK, NEW YORK
1902

SEVEN

Giovanna woke with a start, shivering. She pulled the quilt tight around her body but soon realized nothing would make her warm. She got out of bed and paced, eventually going outside to look at the sky as if it would tell her something. There were no signs in the stars or the breeze, only the terror that coursed through her body.

Six hours later, Concetta awoke to an eerie silence. She went looking for her daughter, and when she did not find her in her bed, she ran outside to where Giovanna still stood facing the sea, drenched in morning dew.

"Giovanna, get inside!" Concetta pulled the wet quilt from Giovanna's body and tried to lead her indoors, but she would not move. Concetta's pleas drew Domenico from his bed. He begged Giovanna to tell him what was wrong. With every unanswered plea and vacant stare, Domenico and Concetta became more convinced that death had visited, and Giovanna had lost Nunzio. They gave up trying to get her inside and instead forced her to sit in a chair facing the sea at the door to the house. Concetta spooned hot tea into Giovanna's mouth and wrapped her in dry shawls while Domenico dressed to go to the telegraph office.

The telegraph operator sat behind a long oak desk. Dead flies flew again on flypaper that flapped in the breeze of a humming black metal fan. Domenico stared at the telegraph machine for a long time. It was as silent as Giovanna. The operator told Domenico to go home, commenting that Giovanna's condition was probably from something she ate. Domenico knew his daughter's silence was not caused by her diet, but he also knew that the news would come whether he watched the mysterious machine or not.

Domenico walked home and drew up a chair next to Giovanna. Word of Giovanna's condition had traveled to Nunzio's mother, Marianna, who arrived at the house distraught. She pleaded with Giovanna to speak to her. Giovanna could only answer with her eyes, but her aunt could read the loss. Concetta took a stunned Marianna inside and handed her a rosary. Together, on their knees, they began their prayers. They prayed to their patron, Saint Rocco, they prayed to Saint Anthony in case Nunzio was lost, and they prayed to the Madonna, because she was a woman and would understand.

Nunzio's sister, Fortunata, got word as she was preparing to board the boat for Messina, where she made money as a wet nurse. She ran from the dock to her home to gather her family, and they arrived together. Seeing her mother and aunt praying sent Fortunata into wails. Her daughter took the baby from her breast, and her older sons left for the chiazza in search of information. Her second youngest boy, Antonio, who was six, would not leave the women and sat at their feet, rocking to the rhythm of their prayers and the sway of the crosses at the end of their rosaries.

Domenico and Giovanna continued their vigil, seated in chairs that wobbled on the uneven cobblestones. Domenico would lean forward looking down the narrow street each time he heard footsteps or hooves approaching. The Scalici family came by with food and placed it in their laps. They then left plates inside on the table for Concetta and Marianna, who remained on their knees beseeching the saints to intervene.

In the late afternoon the sunlight made the leaves of the olive trees flash silver and the ripples in the sea glitter gold. Domenico and Giovanna were equally oblivious to the light and to the untouched food on their laps. When they heard the sound of gentle footsteps approaching, Domenico did not need to lean and look. Telegraphs were delivered by boys with gentle, purposeful footsteps. The telegraph boy came around the bend holding a paper trimmed in black. Notices of death were trimmed in black. A gang of children respectfully followed ten yards behind him, waiting to run home and tell their mothers the news. The young messenger gave the paper to Domenico, but only Giovanna could read.

"I am sorry, Giovanna," Domenico said, crying, handing her the telegraph.

Moving for the first time, she took the paper from her father, but instead of reading it, she crumpled the paper and handed it to the boy. The telegraph boy was flustered. He would be punished if the message wasn't delivered.

Domenico motioned for the boy to read it. He flattened the paper with his palm against his leg, and in a halting falsetto the boy delivered the news they already mourned. "With great sorrow stop Nunzio killed in accident stop I will bury him in New York stop Lord have mercy stop Lorenzo."

Concetta, Marianna, and Fortunata had ceased praying but remained on their knees inside the house, listening to the boy read their sorrow. Marianna collapsed into Concetta's and Fortunata's arms with thunderous wails when he read "Lord have mercy." Little Antonio, frightened by the sobbing, buried himself in his mother's skirts. Tears flowed down Domenico's cheeks. Nothing flowed from Giovanna. Nothing.

The pots on the terrace of the Costa house were barren. It was late October, and an early frost had killed the last of the vegetables and herbs, but Giovanna scraped at the potted soil, trying to find even one remaining sprout she could nurture back to life. Giovanna was on her knees when Concetta passed the door to the terrace and stopped to stare at her daughter. For Concetta, Giovanna's state of mind had become as heartbreaking as Nunzio's death.

It had been nearly two months, and Giovanna still had not spoken a word. She spent her hours staring silently at the sea, gardening, or doing chores in the house. The first time Giovanna had been called to deliver a baby after Nunzio's death, she simply shook her head and retreated inside the house. Signora Scalici traipsed the town, exhausted from the burden of being Scilla's only midwife.

Giovanna's silence was the loudest sound Concetta ever had to endure, and now, watching her once proud, strong daughter futilely digging in the dirt, Concetta snapped. She ran out the door to Giovanna and pulled her to her feet.

"Stop it! *Basta*! There is nothing there!"

Giovanna bent to resume her scraping, and Concetta pulled her up again and violently shook her shoulders.

"Do you think you're the only woman to lose a husband?" Giovanna tried to wriggle free of Concetta's grip but was rendered motionless when her mother's hand hit her face with a loud slap. "Talk to me!"

The sight of Giovanna's vacant stare in reply defeated Concetta, and she collapsed, sobbing. Only then did Giovanna's face register any emotion, and she tenderly picked up her mother, wiping her tears.

"There's unfinished business," pronounced Zia Antoinette, Concetta's eighty-year-old aunt, who was the town expert in all matters pertaining to the evil eye. Concetta had called together Zia Antoinette, Father Clemente, and Signora Scalici to discuss what to do about Giovanna. The participants in this precarious caucus sat in the chiazza far from Giovanna's eyes and ears. Never before had these three natural enemies come together and their mutual mistrust was obvious in their glances and in the way their bodies did not relax into their chairs. Father Clemente condemned Zia Antoinette's pagan beliefs and Signora Scalici's superior airs. Signora Scalici resented Zia Antoinette's inexplicable cures and Father Clemente's wealth in the face of poverty. Zia Antoinette was angered when Signora Scalici's knife did what her remedies could not and when Father Clemente acted as if he alone owned the saints.

Concetta had organized this unprecedented gathering because she reasoned that if these three souls could agree on how to help Giovanna it would be the right path, and the trio consented to the meeting because the one thing they shared was a love for Giovanna. The spectacle of seeing these icons together drew a crowd, but the crowd kept its distance out of respect and fear. The mood in the chiazza was never so self-conscious.

A cat played with the rosary hanging from Father Clemente's vestment, and everyone, including the priest, chose to ignore it. With each swing of the cat's paw, the anticipation in the chiazza rose. When the father's shiny black shoe finally sent the cat flying, the animal's screech broke the tension, and people, even those in the tribunal, started to relax. Concetta called for a child to get a basin of warm salted water for Signora Scalici's visibly swollen feet, and they resumed their discussion with less formality.

It was fairly easy for all of them to agree that Nunzio's death had caused Giovanna's state, but they were in spirited dispute about why his death had taken her speech.

Signora Scalici was frustrated with Zia Antoinette and Father Clemente's complex conclusions. "It's simple! Her heart is broken!"

"In Scilla hearts are broken every day! No, it is because of something Nunzio told her when he died," spat back Zia Antoinette.

"*Stre—*," Father Clemente stopped himself from calling Zia Antoinette a witch and offered his explanation. "No. Giovanna is worried that Nunzio is not in heaven." When even Concetta looked at him puzzled, he continued. "Nunzio didn't share Giovanna's devotion, and she fears that she will not be reunited with him in God's kingdom."

"If that's the reason, can't you say a prayer and get him in there? He's your padrone." Signora Scalici was not usually so irreverent, but her feet were killing her.

Sensing Father Clemente's disgust, Concetta jumped in. "Does it matter the reason?"

"She should say prayers at his grave," said Father Clemente, dusting off his vestments.

"Giovanna must see the place of Nunzio's last breath," proclaimed Zia Antoinette.

Signora Scalici took a foot out of the bath and rubbed it. "She needs a change of scenery."

So they agreed without agreeing, and all spoke the truth.

Maria Perrino, with her once breech child at her side, broke from the distant circle of onlookers and walked forward. She put coins on the table in front of Concetta. "For the passage of Signora *Levatrice*."

Slowly other villagers followed until there was a pile of coins on the table. When the last person had added to the ante, Concetta made the sign of the cross.

Zia Antoinette put her weight on her cane and rose from the chair. "She should go after Christmas and before the new year."

When there was no dissent, Concetta nodded and thanked her

counselors, kissing their cheeks. The crowd in the chiazza slowly dispersed until only Concetta remained. Concetta was not surprised to see Domenico emerge from behind the bougainvillea bush where he had been listening. He had told her that he could not bear to hear the three old windbags talk about Giovanna's fate, but Concetta knew it was because he was afraid that they would come to the conclusion that they both dreaded and suspected. Domenico took Concetta's arm and escorted her home. It was their turn to be silent.

EIGHT

The *Lombardia* left the Bay of Naples on the twenty-eighth of December with Giovanna and 1,301 other passengers in steerage. They would arrive in New York to a new world and a new year. But such lofty thoughts did not occupy the minds of Giovanna and her fellow passengers; instead, they concentrated on enduring the smell of vomit, urine, and excrement that hung in the stifling air and on the deafening sounds of babies' cries and the ship's boiler. If for even a moment the immigrants were able to block out the assault on their senses, they were left only with relentless boredom.

It was day three of the fourteen-day voyage. Giovanna thought that time had taken on the character of a long labor where every minute lasted an hour and was filled with anticipation. Conversation, the most common way to pass time, was not possible for Giovanna. Nunzio's death had her by the throat. She would listen to people talking and even tried to join in a few times, but her vocal cords still could not vibrate. No one questioned her silence. There was so much more to worry about.

On the bunk beneath Giovanna was a young woman with her two-year-old daughter. Giovanna had been assigned the bottom bunk but had given it to the woman for fear that in one of the ship's many keels, the child would fall to the floor. The top bunk was considered preferable anyway. You were less likely to be splashed by vomit. Nearly everyone was horribly seasick; the winter seas knocked the boat around like a toy. Giovanna's life on the water had given her an iron stomach, much to the benefit of the woman beneath her and to those on either side. The peasants from the sea towns fared better on the ship than those from the mountains, many of whom had never even seen a twig float. When the ship rocked suddenly to the extreme, steerage echoed with the terrified screams and prayers of immigrants who were certain their real destination was the bottom of the ocean.

Occasionally, the passengers would brave the icy wind aboveboard to get air. A section of the lower deck that caught the soot from the ship's smokestacks was reserved for steerage. There, crammed on the deck, the immigrants would suck in the fresh, salty air, ignoring the crew, who were using the same deck to slaughter livestock and wash chamber pots.

A small portion of the upper deck jutted out over the lower deck, and from here the first- and second-class passengers would gaze down on the immigrants. Sometimes, a well-dressed man or woman would throw bread or an orange, trying to get it into the hands of one of the waiting children. One day, Giovanna watched boys on the deck above shouting to children below who gathered in hopes of catching food. The first-class boys let something drop, and there was a scramble. When the child who retrieved the prize uncupped his hand revealing an apple core, the immigrant children angrily cursed, "Sporcaccioni!" throwing the offensive trash overboard. The boys above, getting the reaction they wanted, doubled over in laughter and ran.

Below in steerage, families were put in separate cubicles that resembled sties. Among the Italians, there were few families; it was difficult enough to scrape together the money for one fare, never mind for the whole brood. A blanket hung on a rope separated the men and the women, although it did not hang in the middle of the hold, for there were far more men than women. Among the women, there were two groups—those traveling alone with children, presumably to join their husbands already working in l'America, and young women whose faces bore all the promise and fear of their arranged marriages. As far as Giovanna could tell, she was the only woman traveling alone who was not in her teens or with children.

A number of the women were pregnant, but it took an experienced eye to tell because their stomachs were hidden under layers of clothing. Giovanna prayed that no one went into labor. She was surviving by going through the motions of life; delivering a child would confront her with the pain and beauty of living and breathing and with what she could not have.

The passengers already knew to call Giovanna for their aches and pains. On the first night, when she could no longer bear the sound of a child's rattling cough and his mother's admonishments to be silent, Giovanna rose from her bunk and walked to the buckets of saltwater that were set aside for baths. She poured water into a washbasin and headed to the ship's boiler room. The crewman was stunned into compliance at the sight of such an imposing, mute woman motioning for him to make the water hot. While the soot-faced young man heated her water, Giovanna dug in her trunk for the poultices and herbs she was carrying and put together a salve for the child's chest. Retrieving the hot water, she went and sat on the woman's bunk. Because the steaming saltwater made her intentions apparent, or because Giovanna's manner was so matter-of-fact, the woman did not protest. Giovanna rubbed an oil of eucalyptus and archangelica on the child's chest and, taking the shawl from the mother's shoulders, created a tent filled with saltwater steam for the sick child.

"Grazie, mille grazie, signora," mumbled the mother, kissing the hands of Giovanna, who then left as wordlessly as she had come.

"Signora," an arm tugged on her skirt. Giovanna got up and reached for her bag of herbs. "No, no, signora, I want to talk to you. I know you can hear; I see how you listen. Why don't you talk, signora?"

Giovanna looked down at a girl of perhaps eleven with cascading dark hair who steadfastly gazed up at her. Her first instinct was to shoo the girl away, but something in the girl's quizzical expression and forthrightness softened Giovanna. She came down from her bunk and sat on the floor with the girl.

Realizing that Giovanna wasn't going to answer her question, or any questions, the girl decided to do all the talking.

"We're going to l'America," she said proudly.

Giovanna nodded and pointed to her chest indicating, "Me too."

"You see, my father died. Now it's just my mother, my little sister, and me. My grandparents said they couldn't take care of us, and in our village there are no men left for my mother to marry—they all went to l'America. My grandparents wrote to my father's sister and asked her to take us in. They work on a big farm and pick red berries in water. I'm going to do that, too!"

Giovanna noticed that the girl had not stopped scratching her head. Retrieving a small comb from her bag, she motioned for the girl to sit with her back to her.

"Mamma may even find a husband, and I'm going to make enough money to buy new shoes for the entire family!"

Giovanna combed small sections of the girl's hair and used her nails to catch and crush lice and pick their nits off each strand.

"My aunt, she went to l'America when she was fifteen to get married. I don't want to get married. Boys are disgusting. Don't you think so?"

She stopped talking long enough to turn and look at the smile on Giovanna's face. Hours passed this way with the girl recounting her life story and her grand plans for l'America while Giovanna methodically deloused her head.

At some point Giovanna tuned the girl out, wondering what Nunzio's voyage had been like. He had written little about his time on the ship, only saying that his plan was to work hard enough so that if Giovanna were to ever visit l'America she would travel with a second-class ticket. She wondered if Nunzio had met a young boy and if they'd built boats out of nutshells. Had he slept on the top or bottom bunk? Did his ship smell as sickeningly awful as this one? She imagined that boredom drove Nunzio to join in one of the many games of *briscola* or *scopa*, even though he didn't like playing cards. It was one of their few differences—Giovanna loved card games.

The shuffling of bodies and the clanging of tin plates signaling a meal snapped both Giovanna and the girl out of their own worlds. They rose and each got her plate, which had been issued by the shipping company, and stood in line. The evening meal was no different from the previous evening's meal or the noon meal for that matter. When each passenger reached the head of the line, a crewman ladled broth with unidentified floating objects into their shallow bowls and handed them a piece of stale bread. Giovanna was grateful for her stash of salami, mustasole cookies, and wine. She rationed herself, dreading the prospect of running out and having nothing but the greasy broth.

It was too cold to take their evening meal above on deck, although a few souls did brave the night winds rather than eat in the stench of the steerage quarters. At mealtime, even the most private passengers became sometime conversationalists. Giovanna found that she noticed and heard so much more since she had ceased to speak and vowed that if her voice returned, she would remember this lesson. The primary mealtime topic was news and gossip relating to their voyage and new life in l'America.

"You must all be prepared for when we arrive at the dock in l'America," pronounced Luigi, who had been designated the authority on America.

"*If* we get into l'America," shot back a man whose dress and demeanor indicated he was from the mountains. "My brother-in-law, he got to America and it was all filled up. They made him go home."

"*Stupido*! That's impossible. They send you home, but only if you have a disease of the eyes," countered Luigi. "They lift your eyelid, and if they see the disease—bam—you are back on the boat."

Another man, having finished his meager meal, took out his mandolin and was playing softly. This prompted another announcement from "Mayor Luigi."

"Tomorrow is the night of the New Year. We must have a *festa*!"

Just then, as if to counter the suggestion, the ship rolled over a huge wave, and people and baggage went sliding and falling to one side of the boat. When the screams stopped, the prayers started. Someone yelled, "God is punishing us for leaving!" Giovanna, exhausted from the hopelessness, went to her bunk looking for solace in scripture.

The next day on deck, Giovanna studied the crew, who were working furiously. Crates of fruits and vegetables were being stacked and candelabras polished in record time. She guessed they were preparing for a party.

Nunzio once described a fabulous party that his professore hosted for the New Year in a villa in Rome. The professore had offered Nunzio a few extra lire to help, and Nunzio was thrilled to be holding the silver trays and sparkling glasses until he realized that his fellow students were also present, only they were guests. But even in his humiliation, he had remembered almost every detail and told Giovanna of inlaid marble floors on which the women's heels made wonderful clicking sounds, and of an entire orchestra all dressed finer than any southern bridegroom.

Giovanna tried to envision tonight's party and the ship's grand staircases and sparkling chandeliers that she would never see, even though they were no more than one hundred feet from where she sat. She imagined the first-class passengers moving among the splendor, the women draped in fine fabrics accented by jewels. The party continued to swirl in her thoughts, and Giovanna decided the guests would laugh with delight if the ship suddenly careened, secure in their knowledge that they were safe, as opposed to the steerage passengers, who would scream and shake with fear. The cold, wet air got to her, and Giovanna climbed down the many metal stairs that brought her back to her reality.

Shortly after the evening meal, the music in steerage began. Within an hour it became a cacophony of sound. The orchestra above deck was drowned out by the rhythms of Sicilian dances, Calabrian folk songs, and Neapolitan love songs emanating from each steerage compartment. People from one town or region tended to travel in the same compartment, so were the setting different, it would have been an impressive revue of southern Italian music.

Giovanna watched the festivities from her bunk. She was becoming accustomed to her role as an observer of life. Successful at blocking out all thoughts of what the new year and new country would bring, she was less successful in stopping the what-ifs. What would it have been like to greet Nunzio on the dock? Would 1903 have been the year they had a child? Giovanna's fingers went to her temples to stop her thoughts from causing her so much pain. Rolling onto her stomach, she squinted at the revelers, trying to concentrate on the here and now.

A crewman walked into their compartment holding a tray and shouting in bad Italian, "The captain sent this for the kids. Happy New Year." He set the tray, holding a large cake, on a trunk in the center of the compartment. The "3" of "1903" had been cut out, and a bit of the decoration had slid off, but it remained three glorious layers high and covered in pink frosting. The children squealed with delight and pressed forward, trying to get as close to this marvel as possible.

The authority on l'America, Luigi, took control and shouted for everyone to stand back. Taking a knife from his pocket, he cut the cake into squares and placed them into the upraised, cupped hands of the children clamoring around him. When all the children had been served, a small section of the cake remained. The unspoken question became who among the adults would get to enjoy this luxury. After much debate and no consensus, it was somehow decided that everyone would take a crumb, which turned the eating of the cake into something akin to communion.

Giovanna had fallen asleep during the great cake debate and was awoken with a tug.

"Signora, signora, it is the New Year!"

Giovanna squinted down at her young friend and patted her head in greeting.

"Signora, I ate the most wonderful thing. On the top and sides was a cream the color of the roses in the father's churchyard, and inside, it was soft, like bread, but sweet like biscotti. I closed my eyes when I ate it, and I could see the most beautiful things. It was sunny and clean, and my sister and I had on white dresses and hair ribbons the color of the cream. In my stomach, the *torta* filled me up and sang songs. And do you know what the best part was, signora? Luigi's son said that in l'America, they have this cake for breakfast and supper! I am going to love l'America, signora!"

Giovanna smiled, caressed the girl's face, and rolled over.

"Signora," the girl was whispering. "Signora!"

Giovanna rolled back over and looked at her.

"I saved you a taste of the cream, signora." The girl uncupped her hand, and there in the middle of her palm was a dab of pink frosting. "Here, signora," she said, flicking the frosting onto her finger and holding it up to Giovanna's mouth.

Giovanna's first instinct was to shake her head no, but when she looked at the girl's face, she compliantly licked her finger. The sweetness of the sugar and the girl's gesture burned Giovanna's throat.

"Happy New Year, signora," whispered the girl, smiling.

NINE

When the *Lombardia* approached New York City's harbor, everyone scrambled up the metal stairs and packed onto the deck, desperate to catch their first glimpse of their new home. There was a reverent hush as people watched and waited in anticipation. Slowly they saw New York seemingly rise from the sea. Prayers of thanks and animated voices rose in volume as each new detail revealed itself. Someone who had made the trip before pointed to a landmass covered in snow and shouted excitedly, "Itsa Brookalyn!" The message was passed and murmurs of, "Ah Brookalyn!" rippled through the crowd. Giovanna could make out spires on buildings and shivered at the memory of Nunzio's descriptions of the architectural detail.

The *Lombardia* sailed closer to New York, and they all got a better look at the large shape holding a torch in the water. "Is that where Columbus is buried?" shouted a man on deck, trying to be heard over the jubilant shouts. "No," thought Giovanna, remembering Maria Perrino's mother, "that's the whore." The first cries of joy turned into thunderous cheers when the Statue of Liberty came into full view and she was recognized as the American Madonna. Or, in the eyes of those left behind in Italy, the American Scylla on the rock.

"Viva l'America!" was shouted, men waved their hats, women bounced and kissed the children in their arms, prayers were murmured, and tears swallowed.

Sailing forward, Giovanna's eyes didn't leave Liberty's face. "You welcomed my Nunzio, but you didn't protect him. You devoured him like the women said," accused Giovanna, although her face bore none of the emotion that her heart felt.

She felt both excitement and paralyzing sadness at the idea of soon walking where Nunzio had walked and sleeping where Nunzio had slept. The boat turned into a dock away from the statue, but before Giovanna lost sight of Liberty's face, she asked her, "And what plans do you have for me here in l'America?"

At the pier, the steerage passengers waited while the first- and second-class passengers were cleared through onboard customs and then disembarked. From the deck, the immigrants watched the happy reunions on the dock. They were only a few feet from l'America, but still an ordeal away. The people in steerage were boarded onto a barge that had pulled alongside the *Lombardia*. Standing shoulder to shoulder, they waited in anxious anticipation for the sound of the motor and the last leg of their journey. But nothing happened. Instead, torturous time passed while they stood rocking in the wakes of passing boats. Word filtered through the immigrants that Ellis Island was crowded.

"I told you l'America was filled up!" the man in Giovanna's steerage compartment shouted to Luigi.

"*Boccalone!* We'll be there soon," reprimanded Luigi.

It wasn't soon, but six hours later the barge pulled into the dock at Ellis Island. The mood was solemn as the immigrants stepped onto land to waiting crew members who pinned a paper number to each foreigner's clothing. Giovanna looked at her "27" upside down and wondered if they had her age wrong, but then she noticed a child with "102."

They entered a large redbrick building where they were instructed to leave their baggage. Giovanna hesitated but let go of her belongings when she saw the fear that she felt mirrored on the faces of the other immigrants as they parted with all that they had.

The crowd moved up a staircase into a huge hall that was divided into aisles by iron railings. They were no longer being prodded by the ship's crew but by people in uniforms who filled one aisle at a time. Instructions shouted in many languages by exasperated and overworked immigration officials echoed throughout the great room, and nervous whispers were amplified in the cavernous hall. In an attempt to understand what was happening to them, the detainees whispered messages up and down the rows.

"There are men checking people and writing on them with blue chalk," was the first message to reach Giovanna. *Writing on them? Didn't they have paper?* In the aisle next to her, the line of communication broke down at a group of Poles sandwiched in among the Italians.

Giovanna advanced far enough down the line to glimpse an inspector in a navy blue uniform outlined in braided trim holding a piece of blue chalk in his hands. From the moment someone reached the head of the line, the man scrutinized that person. Giovanna watched him order a mother carrying an older baby to put the child down and make him walk. The mother set the boy on the floor. He stared at the shiny, black knee-high boots in front of him and screamed. His nervous mother swatted his bottom, forcing him forward.

When each immigrant reached the inspector, after walking a closely observed ten feet, the inspector thumped on the foreigner's chest, picked up their arms, lifting their sleeves to look at their skin, and then inspected their fingernails. Giovanna looked at her own fingernails. Would they not let you into l'America if you were dirty? The pungent body odors in the room convinced Giovanna that cleanliness couldn't be the reason for checking fingernails. The smells were so strong that Giovanna was taking long breaths with her face nearly imbedded in the basil plant of the man in front of her. Various plants were clutched like gold throughout the hall, and Giovanna busied herself by identifying them.

After banging on their chests, the man in blue listened to their breathing. A few of the immigrants tried to talk to the inspectors, but the inspectors ignored them or put their fingers to their lips. For a line that moved so slowly, it all happened quickly; Giovanna counted no more than six or seven seconds for each person.

The immigrant was then guided forward a few feet to another man with shiny buttons who snapped back the immigrant's eyelid and took a look. Sometimes he scrawled an *E* on their clothes. Numbered and possibly "lettered," they moved on to an area that Giovanna couldn't see from her place on line.

When Giovanna reached what she had thought was the front of the line, she realized it snaked around and she was nowhere near being examined. She was in a maze, never knowing what the next corner would bring and searching for an elusive and uncertain exit. Her head moving like a searchlight, she saw her young friend from the boat and waved. She barely recognized the girl, who was twice her size from wearing count-less layers. Instead of leaving her luggage, her mother had dressed herself and the children in all the clothes that they had brought with them. The girl, her face shiny from sweat, smiled and waved back at Giovanna.

A voice and an arm prodded Giovanna farther. From this vantage point, she could see the step after the exam, and she froze in fear. The inspectors spoke to you, and they expected you to speak back. Her hand rose to her throat; she had heard rumor of the examinations, but no one had ever told her you must speak. Here, too, they held blue chalk, and she saw an X marked onto a man's lapel.

Giovanna was flushed and sweating. She cleared her throat and tried to say, *"Buon giorno."* Hot raspy air was all that emerged from her lips. So what if she didn't get into this l'America? What difference did it make? Although she asked herself the question, she knew the answer. When her parents first suggested going to New York, after her initial shock, she realized that that was what she wanted. She needed to kneel at the place where Nunzio was buried.

With her panic rising, she prayed to Nunzio and to the Madonna to give her speech. She prayed to the whore in the harbor, and she prayed to Saint Rocco. Her pounding heart reminded her that the physical was first, and she was sure to be marked if she didn't calm down. She instructed herself as if she was coaching a laboring mother to concen-trate. Focusing on Nunzio's face, she imagined tracing the outline of his jaw with her finger, playing with the flesh of his earlobe, lingering in the warmth behind his ear, and then following his hairline down the nape of his neck. It was working; her body and breathing were returning to normal. Her finger had circled round Nunzio's head and was touching the end of his eyelashes when she was pushed toward the first inspector.

She met the eyes of the inspector while he watched her walk. Within seconds of reaching him, he had thumped and listened to her chest and checked her skin and hands. His hand went up and a uniformed woman took the pins from Giovanna's hair, releasing her long dark chestnut braids, which had been wrapped around her head. The woman's fingers moved like lightning, pulling apart the braids and checking Giovanna's head and scalp before motioning her forward. Out of their clutches,

Giovanna braided and repinned her hair, feeling as if she had been disrobed in public.

Her relief at making it through that part of the exam was nullified by the sight of the officer snapping back the eyelid of the woman in front of her with a buttonhook. Giovanna responded by forcing her mind back into focus and letting her finger go from Nunzio's lashes to his brow. So strong was Giovanna's concentration that she didn't even flinch when the cold hook brought her eyeball to eyeball with the inspector.

Guided into the next line without an *E* on her clothing, Giovanna began to notice once again what was happening around her. An older man, who was slightly stooped, was surreptitiously trying to wipe a chalked *B* from his sleeve by brushing against a pillar and quickly patting at his arm with his other hand.

The inspectors who asked questions were again in view, and Giovanna tried once more to concentrate, except she wasn't as successful and kept lapsing into prayers. She could see the paper the inspectors held and realized it was the answers to the questions asked by the ship's crew before they sailed. Her father had answered the questions for her and explained her silence as modesty. Desperately she tried to recall the queries so she could practice the words in reply. As the questions came to her, she recited the answers in her head. " 'Twenty-nine.' Please, Madonna, I beseech you. I must feel the dirt between my fingers where Nunzio's body lies. 'Twelve dollars.' Make my voice heard. 'Widow.' "

A Russian family in front of Giovanna stepped forward. The same inspector, who had just been speaking another tongue, spoke to this family in their language. "How smart these Americans are," flashed through Giovanna's mind between prayers. "Please, Madonna, I will light many candles in devotion and thanks. 'I come from Scilla, Calabria.' " Or was the answer, "Scilla, Italy"? To the last question on the form, "Who paid for your transport?" Giovanna decided to keep it simple and say, "My family paid my fare of twenty-eight dollars," and not tell of villagers contributing to the cause.

Giovanna jumped when the inspector looked at her and shouted, *"Avanti!"*

"Italian too!" she managed to marvel, walking forward. "Perhaps this is a dream, and as in a dream, I will speak."

"*Nome*?" quizzed the inspector.

Giovanna pushed the air from her stomach and moved her lips forward to form the first sound of her name. It happened so slowly that Giovanna could feel the air travel up her throat and her muscles reshape her lips. Her mind blocked out the noise in the hall, and all she heard was deafening silence before the air escaped her mouth.

"Gi-o-vanna Pontillo."

Both Giovanna's and the inspector's heads jerked back at the force of the sound. It wasn't loud; it was strong and deep as if it had been buried and gaining strength.

"Your mother's name?" With this next question, Giovanna was assured that he, too, had heard her voice. The inspector then glanced at Giovanna's letter from Lorenzo and at her hands. She wondered if her shaking hands would be reason to pull her from the line, but he only asked to see her money. Giovanna took the satin pouch that was tied to her waist and opened it to display her small fortune of twelve dollars in lira.

"You can keep moving."

Giovanna tucked the precious pouch into the folds of her dress, and when out of sight of the inspector, she grabbed at her throat and massaged her cheeks in wonder and appreciation. As she made the sign of the cross, her prayers of thanks rushed forth.

In her quiet exultation, she could hear the next person being questioned. It was a young man traveling alone who had impatiently shifted from one foot to the other for the past four hours, punctuating his movements with sighs of exasperation and curses of complaint. His behavior stood in stark contrast to the bewildered and compliant demeanor of most of the immigrants.

The inspector had finished the twenty-nine questions from the ship manifest and asked the restless man another: "Would you wash stairs from the top down or the bottom up?"

"I did not come to America to wash stairs!" he answered indignantly.

The inspector tried to hide a smile. "Move on."

Five hours after she entered the great hall, Giovanna could see what looked to be the last step—a series of desks where inspectors reviewed and stamped the papers. Behind the desks were three staircases, all

marked with different words. People were gathered in front of the staircases, many saying good-bye to one another.

After a few minutes of shuffling along in line, Giovanna approached
one of the desks. The inspector took Giovanna's papers from her hand.
He looked at them and yelled over to the next desk, "Martin, is Scilla
north or south?"

"When in doubt, it's the south."

"I don't know why we have to mark them as two races anyway.
They're all eye-talians," complained the inspector.

"It's only eye-talians these days," answered Martin.

The men frightened Giovanna. Had she come this far for there to
be a problem?

"At least this one reads and writes."

The inspector handed Giovanna a pen and indicated she should sign
on the line. He then handed Giovanna her papers and motioned for her
to go to the staircase marked NEW YORK DETAINED.

"God, she's big. But good-looking," Martin called over when Giovanna
strode past the desk. "Wonder how she got through alone."

"A brother and plenty of calluses," answered the inspector.

Giovanna walked into the swarm of people in front of the staircases.
At each staircase was yet another uniformed man, the kind who spoke
all the languages, checking their documents. Out of curiosity, Giovanna
went to the staircase marked NEW YORK OUTSIDES. The inspector
looked at her paper and said in Italian, "No, signora, a woman alone
must be picked up. You take that staircase and meet your brother."

"Where does this one go?"

"To the ferry that takes you to New York."

"And that one?" Giovanna asked, pointing to the third staircase.

"That is for people taking the railroads. A ferry takes them to the
trains in Hoboken."

Now Giovanna understood all the tears of farewell—people from the
same village were splitting up to join relatives or friends in different
parts of the country. With no one to say good-bye to, she descended
the staircase.

She entered yet another large room with benches around the perimeter. An iron fence from ceiling to floor divided the room. Giovanna

couldn't get to the gate, but she knew those on the other side were here to pick up their friends and family. Was Lorenzo really that close? Another guard told her to take a seat until her number was called. A teenage girl holding a photograph of a young man sat next to her. Giovanna wasn't normally so nosy, or so friendly, but she wanted to hear her own voice again.

"Is that who is meeting you?"

"Sì, signora. It is my uncle's nephew. We are to be married."

"Do you know him?"

"Only from this picture. But I think he's handsome, don't you, signora?"

Giovanna nodded.

"What if he doesn't like me, signora? What if he sends me back on the boat?" Not waiting for an answer, she continued nervously. "My mother told me not to worry, that he used all his money for this ticket and will have no choice, but my sister's friend, she traveled all the way to l'America and her fiancé wouldn't take her. She was sent back. She never married. She's all alone." The young woman seemed to look at Giovanna for the first time and, noticing her black dress, said, "Oh, I'm sorry, signora."

Giovanna patted the girl's leg. "He will like you."

Hours later, Giovanna was half asleep when she heard number twenty-seven called. Snapping out of her stupor, Giovanna went to the guard who had her trunk at his feet. She helped him open it and he did a cursory inspection of her meager, worn belongings. He motioned for her to go to the door of the gate and hand her papers to the guard. The gate guard announced Giovanna's name to the crowd. How could he be heard over the din? But she saw the head of someone fighting to get through. When he reached the first few rows of people clinging to the bars of the gate, she could see that it was Lorenzo. While the guard checked Lorenzo's identification against Giovanna's papers, Giovanna and Lorenzo locked eyes, saying nothing. The guard noticed the uncommon silence and questioned Giovanna. "You sure this is your brother?"

"Yes, he is my brother," answered Giovanna. That recognition was all she needed to collapse into Lorenzo's arms.

PART FOUR

NEW YORK, NEW YORK
1903–1904

TEN

Lorenzo and Giovanna walked up and down the rows of stone markers in the Queens cemetery.

"I know it's here somewhere," lamented Lorenzo.

Row upon row of stone markers lay imbedded in the ground, most with only numbers chiseled on them. Giovanna's heart tightened. How could Nunzio be buried in such an anonymous, sprawling place? Her Nunzio, with hair that could be fiery red or golden, who could touch a building and recite its history, who could make her laugh and dream, how could her Nunzio be buried in foreign soil beneath a number?

"I found it," called Lorenzo from two rows over.

Giovanna's feet rooted to where she stood. Her brother came, took her by the arm, and led her to the stone that was numbered 304.

"Giovanna, I'm sorry, but when we make more money, we will get a proper stone marker with his name—a big one. They don't put a photo on the stone in this country, but the carver could make a boat. No, it's better a building, maybe the triangle building." Lorenzo babbled over the silence until he realized he should retreat.

First, Giovanna brushed the dirt off the stone. With her finger, she traced the outline of the new grass. There was nothing else to fuss with, nothing to arrange. All of a sudden she understood the reason for vases and candles in the cemeteries in Italy. It gave you something to do, a connection, a way to take care of the dead.

Left only with her prayers, she knelt at Nunzio's head, kissing her fingers and touching them to the ground repeatedly. When that wasn't enough, she laid her palms flat to the ground while she beseeched

Nunzio to guide her and tell her how to live. The cold anonymous ground gave her no answers, and she collapsed forward on top of the grave. From afar, Lorenzo wondered if he should go to her, but not knowing how to comfort her, he turned away. Giovanna lay on top of Nunzio's grave, letting the wails and sobs that she had locked deep inside escape. Lorenzo sat behind a tree for fear that someone would question why he wasn't helping her, but he knew that this was a passage she must go through alone. He picked up a small branch, took out his penknife, and scraped at the stick.

It was one or two hours later when Lorenzo noticed that Giovanna's cries had tapered off to exhausted whimpers. He walked to where she lay on top of the grave and lifted her into a sitting position. Taking the corner of his jacket, Lorenzo wiped the mud and tears from her face, and, sitting beside her, he planted the stick, now a slender crucifix, in front of the stone. This gesture reminded Giovanna that she, too, had brought offerings.

The first time she had walked into Lorenzo's airless, dark apartment, she had looked for signs of Nunzio. Finding none, she had asked Lorenzo if he had any of Nunzio's things. Lorenzo had produced a small box and explained that the clothes and tools had been given to those in need. Giovanna had taken the box to the farthest corner of the apartment and turned her back to the others while gently lifting out each object, starting with Nunzio's cap. She had cradled his cap and then run his razor blade across her own skin, using it to cut the string holding a package of her letters. At the bottom of the box there had been two of the mustasole cookies that Giovanna had made Nunzio for his voyage. They had remained wrapped in the fabric of her wedding dress. The G and the N had been chipped but were still entwined, and the swordfish was missing part of its fin. Giovanna had remembered that she had made a third cookie, a crucifix. She had smiled, and the smile had turned into a big, throaty roar when she realized Nunzio had eaten the cross. "Ah, Nunzio," she had laughed aloud, "I will say your prayers."

The sight of this new woman laughing at their dead uncle's things had frightened Lorenzo's children. They hadn't known what to make of her and of the urgency with which she hugged them. They had loved their uncle and understood that this was his wife, and their papa's sister, but she had seemed sad and strange. Their mother, too, had seemed uneasy in her presence.

Now at the cemetery, Giovanna took the two mustasole cookies from the pocket of her skirt. She had also brought two of the ancient coins that they had played with as children and a lock of her own hair cut with Nunzio's razor. She had thought she would leave these relics at his stone, but she feared they would blow away, leaving her husband anonymous once again. Instead, she laid them on the ground and dug four small holes while Lorenzo searched for a rock to help scrape at the dirt. When the holes were dug, Giovanna buried each talisman with a prayer and a promise.

Covering the swordfish with dirt, she said a prayer to Saint Rocco and vowed to Nunzio to watch over all that he loved in Scilla. She took the coins and dropped them into the second hole. She told Nunzio that if there was justice to seek in his death, she would pursue it, and she prayed to Saint Joseph to guide her efforts. Her tears began flowing down her cheeks once again when she buried the *G* and *N* cookies wrapped in her wedding dress. Her prayer and promise became one as she vowed to Nunzio and Saint Valentine that she would never love another as she loved Nunzio.

The chestnut curl of her hair was tied with a thread, and Giovanna held it tight before putting it in the dirt. This was the hardest promise to make, and she prayed to Saint Anne, the patron saint of laboring mothers, for help. Lorenzo, seeing her silence and concentration, tipped his hat and walked away. With Lorenzo gone, Giovanna took the hair and pressed it into the ground with both hands and vowed to Nunzio Pontillo what she knew he would want the most—that she would go on living.

Life in the Costa household settled into a routine. Giovanna helped Teresa, who was in the fifth month of a difficult pregnancy, with the housework and children. Domenico and Concetta were in school, and the baby who was born before Nunzio died was now toddling around. After a month, Giovanna mentioned to Lorenzo that she would try to find work as a seamstress or take in piecework, but Lorenzo asked that she continue to help Teresa until the baby was born.

Teresa encouraged Lorenzo to let Giovanna find a job, because in truth she was not comfortable with her around. It was not because Giovanna was not helpful; in fact, Teresa thought Giovanna was too helpful. Teresa came up to Giovanna's chest, so she felt diminished even before Giovanna did anything. And when Giovanna did something, in Teresa's mind, she always did it better than Teresa did. Giovanna could lift and carry double what Teresa could, but it was how quickly and efficiently Giovanna accomplished everything that intimidated Teresa. Teresa still did the cooking—she would not relinquish her kitchen—but even when Giovanna remarked that a dish was delicious or asked how something was made, Teresa felt threatened.

Nothing bothered Teresa more, however, than seeing Giovanna help the children at the table in the evenings with their letters—and watching them teach Giovanna English. One evening when Lorenzo was out at the cafe, Giovanna asked Teresa to join them, saying, "Come, Teresa, we'll learn together." Teresa pretended to be too busy and brushed them off with a terse, "I don't have time for that."

For his part, Lorenzo was oblivious to his wife's discomfort. He was glad to have his sister with him; it eased his homesickness and allowed him more freedom, because he worried less about his wife's precarious pregnancy with Giovanna around.

But Giovanna saw that Teresa needed her privacy, and on her fourth Sunday in America, she decided to leave her alone to prepare the meal. The children watched Giovanna dress in hopes that even though Zio Nunzio was gone, they could still have a Sunday adventure; eventually, little Concetta worked up the nerve to ask Giovanna where she was going. When Giovanna answered that she was going to the cemetery, the children were only slightly disappointed. They knew the outing would at least involve a trolley ride, so they enthusiastically asked to join her, heads rotating from their mother to their aunt for approval. Giovanna waited for Teresa to answer first. Moved by this respect accorded her and by the children's longing, Teresa reluctantly said yes. The children ran for their Sunday clothes, because leaving the neighborhood meant dressing their best. Giovanna waited by the door in her black dress and head scarf while Teresa nursed her toddler in the awkward silence.

Giovanna only had the memory of her trip to the graveyard with Lorenzo to go on, but she was certain she could retrace their route. Out of their mother's gaze, the children were more comfortable talking to their aunt and rambled on about their walks with Nunzio, and they were rewarded with Giovanna's rapt attention. From high in the El heading east, the children turned in their seats and pointed out buildings to Giovanna. Giovanna was so enthralled that she missed their stop and didn't realize it until the train pulled out of the station. She nudged Domenico to ask another passenger for directions and smiled at Domenico with pride when he sat back down. He was a bright boy, lean and tall.

Following the passenger's directions, they got off at the next stop and waited for the No. 5 trolley. The area was desolate, making Giovanna anxious. When the trolley appeared, Giovanna grabbed the children's hands and whisked them onboard and into their seats with great relief. The conductor came toward them. Giovanna opened her purse that was hidden in the folds of her dress and for the first time confronted the strange American money that Lorenzo had put there. Domenico, seeing her bewilderment, pointed out the coins she needed to give to the conductor.

The horses trudged up the street, pulling the car along the tracks. The street was lined with factories and construction sites, which explained the area's desolation on a Sunday. Ahead of her, Giovanna caught sight of a strange building taking shape. The frame appeared to be round. She squinted, the trolley drew closer, and her pulse quickened. There was no mistaking the stucture. It looked like a gigantic pasta pot.

Giovanna pushed to the opposite side of the trolley to get a better look. A long stretch of the road was fenced in, and near the gate to the site she could see a sign. Sounding out the words, Giovanna nearly collapsed. BROOKLYN UNION GAS COMPANY. She had to stop herself from leaping off the trolley—and she would have had the children not been with her.

Falling back into her seat, she tried to breathe normally. She had asked Lorenzo to take her to the gas tanks, but he said that he didn't know exactly where the site was because he had picked up Nunzio's body from the coroner's office. The children pestered her for an explanation, and she told them through controlled breaths that this was where their uncle had been working when he was killed. Domenico and Concetta had been told how Zio Nunzio had died, but seeing the site prompted questions about the accident that Giovanna couldn't answer. Questions that she too began to ask.

"Basta, Giovanna! What for? Nunzio is with God. Nothing will change that!" blurted Lorenzo in exasperation.

Giovanna peppered Lorenzo with questions, trying to learn every detail she could about Nunzio's death. How did he find out about the accident? What did he do next? Who was at the coroner's office?

Lorenzo would protest, and she would pause only to repeat the question a few moments later. Defeated, he began giving her one-word answers. Lorenzo watched the determination and concentration on Giovanna's face as she recorded his answers, and he finally understood. He cursed his stupidity for not recognizing sooner how desperately Giovanna needed to do this. She sat before him writing, but in his mind he saw Giovanna in control, delivering babies, and generally being her fearless self. Giovanna couldn't allow Nunzio, or herself for that matter, to be a victim. Understanding that this exercise was fundamental to his sister's survival, Lorenzo became a more cooperative player.

It was hours before Giovanna ran out of questions, but Lorenzo's answers simply raised more questions. Her desire to keep going was strong. She knew in her heart that she had started something she would finish, whether or not it was the right thing to do.

ELEVEN

"Dio mio!" Teresa's screams rang through the apartment. Labor had started a month early. Giovanna was relieved when Teresa ordered Domenico to fetch the doctor who had delivered her other babies. She didn't feel ready for the miracle of birth. Giovanna imagined that she would simply keep the children out of the way. Smiling, she thought someone might even send her to the pharmacist for belladonna as she and Signora Scalici had done to Maria Perrino's mother. But Domenico had returned breathless and in a panic, announcing that the doctor was nowhere to be found.

Giovanna calmly sent Domenico back out, ordering him to wait on the doctor's stoop. She closed the door behind him and turned to her sister-in-law. "Teresa, this baby is not going to wait for the doctor. Do you want me to help you?"

Having birthed three babies, Teresa knew Giovanna was right and managed to nod yes before the next contraction.

Two hours later, Domenico burst through the door with a panting American doctor who had been dragged through the streets. The apartment was quiet; Teresa was feeding her newborn, and Giovanna was scrubbing sheets.

"Why do you women all have to deliver at the same time?" groused the doctor. He pulled the blanket from the baby and gave her a quick once-over.

Giovanna didn't stop washing but kept an eye on the doctor. She didn't understand what he was saying, but she followed his actions.

"She's little but looks healthy. Let's take a look at you." He motioned

Domenico into the hall and examined Teresa. "No rips, but the baby was small." He called over to Giovanna, "Did you deliver this baby?"

Giovanna shrugged apologetically. "*Non parlo inglese.*"

The doctor opened the door and called Domenico into the room. "Who's this?" he asked, pointing to Giovanna.

"My aunt."

"Did she deliver the child?"

"Of course."

"Ask her if she's a midwife."

"She is."

"Then why did you get me?"

"Mamma told me to." Domenico looked at the doctor like the man was an idiot.

"I'll never understand you people," he muttered. Turning to Domenico, he said, "Tell your aunt to go see the midwife Lucrezia LaManna at 247 MacDougal Street. She needs help. There are not enough people to deliver all these Italian babies."

"Okay. Do I tell Mamma anything?"

"Yes"—he snapped his bag shut—"tell her not to have any more children." The doctor left and with him went the stale smell of scotch.

Giovanna waited outside the fence at Brooklyn Union Gas. It was near quitting time, and she watched the men gather their tools and tin lunch boxes. A whistle blew and sweat-stained workers streamed out of the gate; Giovanna stopped the first Italian face she saw.

"Signore, do you know Nunzio Pontillo?"

"No." He turned quickly to another man. "Hey, is there a Nunzio Pontillo on this job?"

"No, no," protested Giovanna. "He was working here. My husband. He was killed on the job, almost a year ago. I want to find someone who worked with him."

The man sighed sympathetically. "I'm sorry, signora. Most of us are a new crew they brought in to line the tank."

Giovanna noticed another man who had stopped walking but hung back. For a moment they stared at each other. "And you, signore, do your remember my husband, Nunzio?"

The first man spun around to see whom Giovanna was talking to and exclaimed, "Oh, Nospeakada! He was here when the accident happened. I think he's the only one left."

"Did you know Nunzio?" Giovanna repeated.

"Signora, he hasn't spoken since the accident."

Giovanna didn't avert her gaze from Nospeakada. "Can you please help me?"

The other man noticed a foreman at the gate staring. "Signora, he can lose his job. It's no coincidence that the only guy left on the job is mute. It's best we all go."

"Here's my address." Giovanna pressed a scrap of paper into Nospeakada's hand. "Please, if you find your voice, I would like to talk."

The other man had already walked away and was motioning for Nospeakada to join him. Nospeakada glanced back at both Giovanna and the foreman and left.

With so many hours on her hands, she walked from Brooklyn back to the Lower East Side. It became apparent that here in America you would have to find beauty in different things, but she had a hard time getting past the filth. Nunzio had never written of it; his head must have been in the clouds. Grime seemed to cover everything and even hovered in the air. If Giovanna closed her eyes and thought of a color for New York, it would have been gray; the city dulled even the brightest blue skies, patches of grass, and fruit on pushcarts.

Through his letters, Nunzio had taught her to appreciate the lines and grandeur of New York's buildings, and she found beauty in their spires, angles, and in the shadows they cast. What she both hated and loved the most were the attempts at replicating the splendor of Italy in the tenements. She had seen Lorenzo's idyllic little paintings of Calabrian countrysides in the foyers of tenements. They made her heart ache at their nostalgic hopefulness, while her head laughed at the absurdity of these little landscapes in the dark. The paintings didn't amuse her as much as the burlap that was shellacked onto the walls with linseed oil in order to resemble linen in the dim light. What intrigued her most, however, were the plaster walls and wood trim painted to look like marble or granite. In this America, even if you didn't have something, you simply created its facsimile. On the surface, nothing would be denied you in America.

Giovanna observed that Italian-American immigrants fell into two categories—those who had completely embraced their new world and those who spoke only of returning to Italy. This schism made perfect sense; loyalty for Italians was often a much stronger characteristic than reason. However, the Italians who had wholeheartedly accepted America and cursed their homeland at every opportunity still took pride in their heritage. Giovanna was amazed that two of the most prominent statues in New York were of Italians.

Downtown, Domenico had taken her to the statue of Garibaldi in Washington Square Park, near the big arch to nowhere. "When he was a boy, your Zio Nunzio would ride his donkey and pretend he was Garibaldi," reminisced Giovanna, looking at the statue.

Domenico had looked at his aunt incredulously. "He had his *own* donkey?"

Another time, Lorenzo brought Giovanna uptown to see the new statue of Columbus at Fifty-ninth Street. Hundreds of Italians, mainly from the north of town, converged at the column on Sundays. Giovanna heard one well-dressed man exclaim that they should also put statues of Vespucci and Verrazano around the circle.

Returning home from her trek, she heard Domenico arguing with his father even before she opened the door.

"I can read and write. I speak English, what more do I need to know?"

"No! You stay in school. At least for a few more years."

As soon as Giovanna entered the apartment, Domenico tried to enlist her support. "Zia, tell Papa I should be a newsie like the other boys!"

"Domenico, I agree with your father. You're a smart boy who could one day write the papers, not sell them. But Lorenzo, what do you think, maybe he could work at Vito's Grocery in the afternoons?"

Domenico turned to his father. "Can I, Papa? I know Vito would give me a job."

"Fine. It's settled. But only after school and weekends."

Teresa was making sauce at the stove with the newborn slung against her chest. With every word of the conversation, Teresa's actions became louder and louder until her furious stirring and pot slamming woke the infant. Teresa's bitterness toward Giovanna had only grown after the birth of her daughter—she deeply resented feeling indebted to her capable sister-in-law.

Giovanna ignored Teresa, not knowing what else to do, and told Domenico about her visit to the construction site.

"Zia, you should hire a detective! They're not policemen. I read about them in comic books. They're called 'sleuths.'"

"Slu-eths?"

Giovanna tried over and over again to say the word, and each time her pronunciation was met with peals of laughter from Domenico and Concetta. This was not an easy word for an Italian tongue—she even let out a big, throaty laugh herself. It was an entertaining notion, but there would be no detectives. If there was something to find, Giovanna, with the blessing of Saint Joseph, would find it herself.

A few nights later, there was a light knock at the door. Family and friends didn't knock; they just announced themselves as they walked in. Hoping it was Nospeakada, she jumped up and opened the door without asking who was there. A stranger with dark eyes and thick lashes stood before her. She quickly closed the door to a wary crack.

Lorenzo moved behind Giovanna and asked, "Who are you?"

"I am Mariano Idone. Nunzio knew me as Pretty Boy."

They opened the door cautiously, and Mariano limped into their kitchen.

"Sit, Signore Idone," invited Lorenzo, pulling out a chair at the kitchen table.

"Nospeakada found me and gave me your address." Mariano quickly continued to fill the awkward silence. "I have a pushcart now. I can't do construction because of my leg."

Giovanna could see why he was called Pretty Boy, but the sparkle had been stolen from his eyes. Giovanna got the impression that if you rubbed him hard enough, you would find Pretty Boy underneath.

Mariano then told Giovanna, Lorenzo, and Domenico his version of the accident as Concetta helped her mother with the two youngest children. He began by recounting the supervisor's reluctance to follow instructions and oil the couplings from underneath. He described how when the disc didn't lower quickly enough, everyone was anxious, and then the supervisor was summoned to a phone call. He told them how after the call, the supervisor brought all the foremen and lead men together and of the decision among the lead men to be the ones to go under the disc. He began to cry when he recounted how a foreman had assigned the eight men to the interior and perimeter. And his tears became sobs as he described how Nunzio had saved his life, switching places with him and warning him and the others seconds before the collapse.

Everyone in the room was crying.

"You see, signora, I will forever be indebted to you and your family."

This was much more than Giovanna wanted to hear. Why couldn't this be Nunzio telling this man's wife the same story? She didn't need to know her husband was a hero. He always was a hero; he didn't need to die being one. In fact, for the first time, she was angry with Nunzio. Why had he done that? He knew she was waiting! She tried to calm down, but anger and sorrow boiled and exploded on Mariano.

"Why did you let him switch with you? You knew he was married! Why didn't you save him?" Her voice was so loud and hard that the children clung to Teresa.

"Giovanna, please, Signore Idone is our guest!" pleaded Lorenzo.

Mariano sobbed. "I was frightened, signora. I was frightened."

His honesty took the words from Giovanna's mouth. A heavy silence with muffled cries hung in the room. Mariano grabbed his hat and rose. Lorenzo put his hand on his arm. "Please, don't go. It is the shock of your story. There is more we need to know." Mariano looked at Giovanna, who looked away but motioned him back into his chair.

Lorenzo continued, "Signore, Giovanna said people seemed afraid to talk to her at the job site."

Mariano composed himself, grateful to talk about something that took the focus off his cowardice. "At roll call the day after the accident, the men were told that nosy reporters were asking questions that could stop the job. Everyone had to sign a paper saying they wouldn't talk about the accident. And they all were given a 'bonus' for their rescue efforts. I wasn't there. I was in the hospital, but two foremen came to my room."

Lorenzo was puzzled and asked, "Why did they care if anyone spoke of the accident? Accidents happen at construction sites all the time."

"I don't know. But Nunzio thought the way they were bringing the bottom down was crazy. Carmine Martello would know better. Nunzio and I spoke at lunch, but not much about the job. I think he spoke of these things with Carmine when they walked home."

Lorenzo remembered Nunzio mentioning a Carmine and thought that he had probably even seen him on occasion with Nunzio on Mulberry Street.

"Did they call him Saint Carmine?" Lorenzo asked.

"Yes, that's him," answered Mariano.

Giovanna thought of the story Nunzio had written in his letter about Carmine and the statue of Saint Gennaro. She had laughed when she read it and then said a prayer of forgiveness. She finally spoke. "Where is this Carmine?"

"I don't know. He never came back to the job. He didn't even get the money. Someone told me he had joined one of those traveling theater companies."

Giovanna felt sick and couldn't bear to hear anymore. She rose from the chair. "Thank you, Signore Idone."

Lorenzo was embarrassed and quickly asked if Mariano would like a glass of grappa.

Mariano turned to Giovanna. "Signora, when I lie down each night, I hear the sounds and feel the pain all over again. I have no money. I can only offer you the promise that if you ever need me, I will help you."

In the morning, when Lorenzo woke, Teresa grabbed his arm to keep him from getting out of bed. Whispering emphatically, she said, "Nunzio is dead! What good will all these questions bring? She'll bring the *malocchio* to this house! Giovanna should be working. And she needs to take a husband before she is too old and no one wants her. You must help her, Lorenzo."

Lorenzo considered his wife's words. Perhaps he wasn't helping Giovanna as he should. If she was busy, she might forget about searching for answers that didn't exist or didn't matter.

That night, after the children had gone to sleep, Lorenzo spoke with Giovanna. "I think now is a good time to get a job, Giovanna. Teresa has had a healthy baby thanks to you."

"I will do that, Lorenzo."

Lorenzo was startled. Even if Giovanna agreed with something, she wasn't so quick to admit it. So he stumbled on his next sentence. "Well, Teresa's heard of jobs at the shirt factory."

Giovanna had already decided to work, but she had other plans. "No. Tomorrow I will go see Lucrezia LaManna. The midwife."

Lorenzo stammered, "Okay then, it's settled."

TWELVE

Her decision to deliver babies in New York was a practical one. Initially afraid to deliver Teresa's baby, she found that she was capable of doing her job without opening her own emotional wounds. She would work as a technician.

Arriving at 247 MacDougal Street, Giovanna noticed it was a nicer building than most on the block. She asked some children on the stoop where to find Lucrezia LaManna. "Signora LaManna is on the top." Giovanna thanked them and marveled that even after a twenty-minute walk uptown, you still did not need to speak English.

She was taking the stairs in twos when she looked up and saw a woman waiting on the fourth-floor landing.

"Scusi, Signora LaManna?"

"Sì. Avanti."

Signora LaManna held her door open and Giovanna walked through self-consciously. It was the first apartment that Giovanna had seen in New York that wasn't crammed with extra beds and cloaked in darkness. It was small and modest, but natural light illuminated the freshly plastered walls. Signora LaManna sat behind her desk and motioned to Giovanna to take a seat.

Giovanna could tell that the signora was taken aback by her size. In Scilla, where everyone knew her, her height was accepted, but since coming to America, even people she passed on the street looked at her like she was a freak. For her part, Giovanna could not help but stare at the woman's face. The signora's refined features reminded Giovanna of her mother, Concetta, as did her grace. But Signora LaManna's worldliness also intrigued Giovanna. The signora's hair was streaked with gray and pulled near to the top of her head, rather than in the usual bun at the nape of the neck.

"The doctor sent me," began Giovanna.

Signora LaManna put on spectacles and picked up a pen. "Did he say how many months you were?"

Giovanna answered with both embarrassment and disappointment. "No, no, signora, I am not with child. I am a midwife."

Signora LaManna put down her pen and removed her glasses. "Una levatrice?"

"Sì."

"How long have you been in America?"

"Almost six months."

"Have you performed any deliveries in New York?"

"I delivered my sister-in-law's baby."

"Well," the midwife got up from her desk and moved to the kitchen, grabbing the espresso pot, "I don't know your name, signora."

"Giovanna Costa Pontillo. I am from Scilla, Calabria."

"Ah, so your family was starving, your husband came to work, and you followed him," stated the signora matter-of-factly.

Giovanna was taken, rather than taken aback, by her manner. "Not exactly."

The two women sat down at Signora LaManna's kitchen table and exchanged stories. Signora LaManna had been a doctor in Italy. She explained that when she came to America, she could no longer practice medicine, but of course she could serve as a midwife. She had accurately surmised that if she settled in the Italian community, she could use her medical skills in the tenements. There was no medical establishment there to care if she treated the sick children in the homes of her expectant mothers. Signora said it took her husband a while to agree to live near the Italian ghetto, but she prevailed by reminding him how easy it would be to get to the university by Washington Square, where he was a professor.

Hours later, when Signora LaManna was preparing lunch, Giovanna marveled at the circumstance. Here she was in New York and for the first time meeting a woman from northern Italy. Her mind swept back to being with Nunzio on the cliff and his dream for her to be a doctor.

When Signora LaManna returned to the table with food, both she and Giovanna were filled once again with questions. Giovanna found out the signora had a daughter, Claudia, who was studying art history in college, and Signora LaManna asked for details about Giovanna's search for information concerning Nunzio's death.

Soon after they got into their second round of discussion, a young girl appeared at the door, summoning Signora LaManna. The doctor turned to Giovanna. "We haven't yet spoken of delivering babies, but would you like to come along on this one?"

"Of course, Dottore . . . signora . . ."

"Please, I will call you Giovanna, and you will call me Lucrezia."

Giovanna was "interviewed" on their brisk walk to Hester Street. "Do you read and write, Giovanna?"

"Yes, fairly well."

"Good. I like to take notes on my patients."

Giovanna had never written a thing about a pregnancy. It seemed strangely academic to write about birth.

They reached the woman's tenement. "We'll have plenty of time to continue talking. This signora labors long and calls for me early," Lucrezia commented, starting up the stairs.

Three hours later, Giovanna sent the young girl, who turned out to be the woman's niece, to Lorenzo's home with a message explaining her absence.

"Giovanna, I think it best for you to work with me a while. I will introduce you around after I have confidence in your skills."

"Grazie, signora."

"Lucrezia."

"Lucrezia."

"As for money, I'll share with you what I get, but it is difficult to say what that will be. If they can pay, they pay. If you consider having little girls named after you payment, you will be wealthy indeed. Even though it is a northern name, there are many Lucrezias in Little Italy. Usually it is the fourth or fifth child, when they have run out of the names of grandparents."

"I see that a midwife's pay does not change when you cross the ocean," remarked Giovanna. Lucrezia laughed, "Yes, some traditions remain."

The woman was showing signs of needing to push. Lucrezia examined her and spoke to Giovanna. "She's ready. Why don't you do the delivery?" Lucrezia had been careful not to let the woman think a stranger was going to deliver the baby and risk losing her confidence for the birth, but the woman was at a stage in labor where her only thought would be pushing her baby out. Lucrezia continued to coach the woman but let Giovanna deliver the baby.

Lucrezia was impressed not only with how Giovanna birthed the child but also with the way she directed the action in the apartment. She gently shooed children from the room and suggested to the woman's mother that she prepare dinner and boil water to clean up. Lucrezia had learned much in medical school, but household management when delivering a child was not a subject they covered.

She also noticed that she would need to teach Giovanna more about rules of sterility and how to inspect the placenta for clues to the baby's health. But in their brief time together, she sensed that Giovanna would not scoff at new information. For all her confidence, she appeared to be an eager student.

Lucrezia planned to stay with the mother, but she suggested that Giovanna go home. "I'm sure your family is concerned. Tomorrow, come to my house at eight a.m., and we will make visits together. It is a busy time; I have seven women in their ninth month. You're skilled, Giovanna."

"I had a good teacher," replied Giovanna, thinking warmly of Signora Scalici.

"But more than skills, you have a healing touch. It's a gift."

Giovanna blushed. She said good-bye to the family and turned to Lucrezia. She tried to think of something to say that would convey her happiness at meeting her, but as was often the case, these types of words failed her, and she simply kissed Lucrezia's hand and left.

Giovanna felt triumphant entering her brother's apartment.

"Tell us, tell us everything!" Lorenzo exclaimed. "Have you eaten?

Teresa, get Giovanna her dinner. Sit, Giovanna. Tell me everything," implored Lorenzo, peeling a pear for the children.

Giovanna began to chronicle her day, but soon she dropped her reporter's tone and her excitement shone through.

"Working with a dottore! How wonderful!" Lorenzo practically shouted.

"Signora LaManna is not a doctor here in America."

"That's a technicality. Italy thought she was good enough to be a doctor, and she chose to work with you."

"I asked her for work."

"Another technicality."

Giovanna smiled at her brother's pride.

That night, Giovanna couldn't be sure, but she thought she heard Teresa crying in bed.

Opening what Lucrezia called her "little bag of tricks," Giovanna searched for honey. The bag had grown since she had discovered the herb shops in Chinatown. One day, in an exhausted stupor after a long delivery, she walked in the wrong direction and found herself standing in front of the most magnificent store with barrels of herbs of every scent and color. She walked up and down the rows; the herbs she didn't recognize on sight she rubbed between her fingers to smell. The proprietor watched her with interest; few non-Chinese came into his store. Seeing that Giovanna understood the herbs, he tried to explain those unfamiliar to her with pantomime and the three words of English they shared, *good* being one of them. After a few visits they had developed their own sign language. Giovanna became so accustomed to the signs that whenever she said "echinacea," her hand would instinctively circle her head, meaning for everything, and when she said "ginger root," she would gnarl her knuckles.

Taking the honey from her bag, Giovanna rubbed it on the stump of the baby's umbilical cord. Lucrezia did not scoff at her herbal remedies. In fact, she was interested and asked to be taught. Lucrezia had cut the mother an inch to allow the baby's head to be born. Giovanna whipped up a poultice of comfrey leaf for the mother's perineum and handed it to Lucrezia, who applied it to the perfectly sutured area.

Giovanna shared her homeopathic expertise with Lucrezia, and Lucrezia taught Giovanna about obstetrics and the illnesses that plagued the tenements, such as whooping cough, chicken pox, and dysentery. Because the need for medical care was so great and respect for Lucrezia so high, Lucrezia had no problem getting the prescriptions she needed, and she began to teach Giovanna much of what she knew about modern pharmacology.

With her new knowledge, Giovanna reflected back on her more difficult births in Scilla. If she knew then what she knew now, could things have turned out differently? Francesca Marasculo was foremost in her mind. Lucrezia had taught her to be wary of quick births and showed her the signs that signaled possible hemorrhaging and how to massage a uterus to help it to contract instead of allowing it to be an open door for the blood in a woman's body.

After one month of working together, Lucrezia had insisted that Giovanna should take on her own patients. Lucrezia showed Giovanna how to take notes and keep them in order, and on more than one occasion demonstrated their importance by using the previous information to help solve a current problem. Although they each had their own patients, they tended to work together on deliveries, when the other wasn't called away, simply because they enjoyed each other's company so much.

The two women became confidants. While Giovanna was serious and hardworking, she also had a quick, biting wit that amused Lucrezia to no end. Once, when Giovanna worried out loud that the relationship was too one-sided, with Lucrezia passing on all the advice and knowledge, Lucrezia exclaimed, "Nonsense! You teach me about all those smelly things in your old bag. Besides, you make me laugh."

After Giovanna met Lucrezia's husband, she understood her need to laugh. Signore LaManna fulfilled every southerner's expectation of an arrogant northerner. He was humorless, cold, and officious. Giovanna looked for signs in her older friend that would explain the mystery of their union, but she couldn't find them. For the first time, instead of feeling sorrow about Nunzio, she realized how lucky they were to have shared something so few people ever have. Memories of laughing together, running, and swimming flooded her mind. With all Lucrezia's gifts, she had not been given this one.

Giovanna spoke with Lucrezia of things she had never spoken with any woman. The difference in their age allowed her a certain freedom, and the fact that they were not family allowed her even more. Giovanna told Lucrezia of her problems with Teresa. She knew she frightened and intimidated her sister-in-law, but she didn't know how not to, and sometimes she was resentful that she should even have to try.

Discussion of her relationship with Teresa became a stepping-stone to other issues. While a mother rested between contractions, they often discussed in spirited whispers the role of women in Italy's north and south, Italian men, their perceptions of Americans, or the education of women. Lucrezia told her that she believed her own entry into university and medicine was destined when her mother named her Lucrezia after the seventeenth-century Venetian Lady Elena Lucrezia, the first woman to receive a university doctorate. After learning this fact, whenever Giovanna said Lucrezia's name, she felt it carried with it the strength of history.

In one of these conversations, Lucrezia questioned Giovanna about wanting children and marrying again. Normally, this was not the type of question a woman would ask openly; instead, it would be gossiped about by neighbors on a stoop. When Giovanna got over her initial embarrassment, she was relieved to tell Lucrezia about her failed attempts to get pregnant with Nunzio and her deep desire for children. As far as marriage went, all Giovanna could say was, "I could never love another as I did Nunzio."

Giovanna asked Lucrezia about her own courtship and marriage. Lucrezia wasn't very forthcoming, but Giovanna was able to piece together that Lucrezia's education set her apart and made her less of a marriage prospect. She had resigned herself to a life alone when she met her husband at the university. At first theirs was a professional relationship, but when Signore LaManna's fiancée broke their engagement, he asked Lucrezia to marry him.

Another recurring topic of conversation was Nunzio's accident.

Giovanna had told Lucrezia in detail about Mariano Idone's visit. Lucrezia filled Giovanna in on the conditions of workers and the world outside of Little Italy. She recounted stories she read in the newspaper about Italians being used as slave labor and the many deaths in the tunnels they were building for the underground trains. Lucrezia said her husband told her that Italians were dying at a greater rate than any other ethnic group building New York because there were so many of them, and because they didn't have the power to do anything about it.

"But your husband is an important man. He should do something about this!" was Giovanna's reaction.

"I'm afraid for him it is an issue of race," Lucrezia explained with embarrassment. Realizing that Giovanna didn't have a clue what she was talking about, she explained, "When you came into Ellis Island, did they ask you where in Italy you came from?"

"Yes."

"Well, it starts there. Actually, that is not true. It started before you got on the boat, but that's Italy's history."

"Lucrezia, please," intoned Giovanna, thinking that Lucrezia's tendency to digress was one of her few weaknesses.

"Italians entering Ellis Island are considered to be of two races. A race from the north and a race from the south. The northerners are classified 'white' and the southerners 'in-betweeners.' Of course, in Italy, the northerners simply call you peasants or Africans. My husband comfortably distances himself from the slurs, the accidents, the inequities, because he sees himself as a different race."

The image of Nunzio serving drinks at the Roman party flashed through Giovanna's mind. Shocked at Lucrezia's honesty, it confirmed her feeling that Lucrezia felt no allegiance to her husband if she was willing to share such embarrassing information. Everyone was worthy of contempt at the moment—the Americans, the northern Italians, and her fellow southern Italians—for accepting the injustice.

The new mother's husband arrived home to meet his infant son, his fourth. Lucrezia and Giovanna stepped into the hall to allow them a few moments of privacy. They leaned against the wall and continued their conversation. "Why have you stopped asking questions about Nunzio's accident?" asked Lucrezia.

"I don't know what or who to ask in the absence of this Carmine."

"Did you check the newspapers?"

THIRTEEN

"*Aspetta*, we have to turn right on Lafayette Street!" called Giovanna to Domenico, who was steps ahead of her on Grand Street. Domenico would no longer hold her hand and had a tendency to outdistance even Giovanna's long strides.

She was incredibly nervous. Nunzio had mentioned going to a library at school, but she had never been to one. She was filled with questions, not the least of which was what do you do when you get there? With her ten-year-old nephew as a guide, she tried to think of it as an adventure. And then came the more difficult part—she had to try to convince herself that she liked adventures.

As she stopped in the middle of the block, Giovanna's head pivoted from one side of the street to the other as she surveyed a large redbrick building on one side and a white columned row of buildings on the other. She looked at numbers, and Domenico looked at signs before they walked through the brick arched doors of the Astor Library on Lafayette Street.

Giovanna controlled her impulse to genuflect upon entering the building. She hadn't seen this much real marble and ornate carving since visiting the church in Naples where she prayed after Nunzio's departure. Domenico and Giovanna gazed in circles, taking it all in and looking for clues about what to do next. Carved wood balustrades surrounded bookcases on the right and desks on the left. A severe and squeaky-clean-looking woman sat at an imposing desk situated in the middle of the room. She didn't look approachable, but everyone else was engaged.

Giovanna nudged Domenico forward. It was one of the first times she had seen her intrepid nephew unsure of himself. On the streets of their neighborhood, he was king. Here, among the pages of history and leather-bound dictionaries, he was a street urchin. Giovanna poked his shoulder again, encouraging him to speak.

"Ma'am, we need newspapers."

"I believe you'll find those sold on the street, by boys looking like yourself." Before Domenico could protest, or, more likely, turn away, she added, "What kind of newspapers are you looking for?"

"One from September 1902."

"That would be an archival newspaper."

"Whatever you say, ma'am."

"What paper were you interested in?"

Domenico scratched his head.

"What do you want to find?" the librarian persisted.

"My uncle, her husband, was killed on a job. A lady said to look in the newspaper at the library."

The librarian, who appeared as if she wanted to ask a few more questions, simply said, "Follow me."

They walked for what seemed like blocks and then entered a room with shelves housing tall volumes. The librarian instructed them to sit at a desk that was so highly polished they could see their reflections in its surface.

"Do you know the date of your uncle's accident?"

Domenico looked up from the table. "September 2."

"Try this."

She heaved a huge book off the shelf. On the cover it read in gold letters, THE NEW YORK TIMES, SEPTEMBER 1902. Opening and leafing through the book filled with newspapers, she said, "It would be here in the beginning, September 3. If he perished on the second, you would look on the third." Her finger scanned the index, looking for obituaries, but before she got to O, her eye caught a headline on page one: FIVE MEN KILLED IN GAS TANK COLLAPSE.

"Young man, where was your uncle killed?"

"In Brooklyn."

Brooklyn Union Gas Company was cited in the first line. "And what was his name?"

"Nunzio Pontillo."

For the first time the woman paid attention to Giovanna. "Why don't you and your aunt come sit over here."

They followed her to a desk in the corner by a window.

She put the book down. "Do you read well, young man?"

"My teacher says I do."

"Well, it appears that the article about your uncle is right here. Are you going to copy it?"

"Yes." He took out a thick pencil and a scrap of paper that had wrapped yesterday's chestnuts.

"You'll need more paper than that." She left and returned with a few clean white sheets.

Domenico took his first look at the article, and his eyes widened.

"I will be back at my desk. But if you need something, you could ask that gentleman right there." She pointed to an old man hunched over papers and squinting through his glasses. "He's the archivist."

Giovanna, assuming they had moved for better light, didn't yet realize something had been found, and she had been amusing herself by running her hands over the gleaming wood and inhaling the smell of leather, ink, and paper in the lofty room.

"Zia, there is something here."

Giovanna looked at him distractedly.

FIVE MEN KILLED IN GAS TANK COLLAPSE. Domenico read the headline first in English and then translated it into Italian.

Giovanna snapped to attention, and her heart raced.

He read the subheadline: CRUSHED BETWEEN STEEL BOTTOM AND CONCRETE FLOOR. Domenico continued, "Then it says, 'THREE HOURS' WORK BEFORE THE LAST BODY WAS REACHED—1,764 RIVETS HAD TO BE CUT—SUPERINTENDENT MULLIGAN ARRESTED.'"

From the corner of his eye, Domenico saw his aunt begin to tremble.

Not far into the article was the list of the five men, their names, ages, and addresses. Nunzio's was the fourth name.

"Show me, show me," said Giovanna, who then ran her finger across Nunzio's name in the paper. Now she not only trembled but swallowed repeatedly while stretching her neck.

Painstakingly, Domenico translated each sentence. There were many words he didn't know, and whole sentences that he couldn't understand, but Giovanna kept motioning him on, saying, "Don't worry; write it down."

At one point, when Domenico was having a particularly difficult time reading, Giovanna's mind wandered to Scilla's chiazza. In her mind, she and Nunzio were under the juniper bush listening to Vittorio read the story of Nunzio's death.

It was nearly one hour before Domenico reached the part describing the accident.

"All went well until about 3 o'clock when Superintendent Mulligan, who was in sole charge of the operation, went to the telephone in the office of Taylor, Wood & Co. to send a private message. The bottom of the tank had been lowered six inches to twenty-six inches above the concrete floor. Eight men were in the space between the tank bottom and the concrete floor engaging in oiling the cups in which the pins of the jacks played.

"Suddenly, there was a creaking noise, and as three of the eight men darted from under the bottom of the tank, all slightly injured . . ."

"Mariano," thought Giovanna.

". . . the bottom gave a lurch westward, carrying away all the screw logs and laying all the jacks in that direction, and fell with a crash on the concrete bed just two feet and a half west from where it would have laid had the lowering been carried on as intended."

Giovanna could hear no more of her husband's death in this foreign place. She had already dug her nails into the polished wood of the table.

"Enough, Domenico. Just copy the sentences." Giovanna got up and paced the perimeter of the room. Her pacing made Domenico nervous. Once, his father had taken Concetta and him to the menagerie in the big park past the Columbus statue and he had watched in fear as a huge striped cat circled his cage without stopping. He looked up and saw the same dazed look in his aunt's eyes as she moved around the room. He copied the rest of the article as quickly as he could.

When at last he finished, Domenico couldn't keep up with his aunt as they made their way through the stacks of books; she was practically running. They sped past the woman at the desk, who tried not to show her interest. When they hit the sidewalk, Giovanna seemed to go even faster. Within minutes they were at Elizabeth Street.

"You go up, Domenico. I must see Signora LaManna." Before Domenico could say good-bye, his aunt was gone.

The moment Giovanna saw Lucrezia, all the bottled-up emotion spilled out into torrents of tears and sobs. When her tears were spent, Giovanna produced Domenico's thick lead scrawl and made espresso while Lucrezia sat at her desk and read.

A few espressos later, Lucrezia removed her glasses and looked up. "Giovanna, I think you should go to a lawyer."

Giovanna waited for an explanation.

"Did Domenico read this to you?"

"As best he could."

"Well, I will read it to you."

The reading and translation went much more quickly with Lucrezia, but it still took a long time. In the comfort of Lucrezia's home, Giovanna cried softly throughout.

"Giovanna, it reports that the superintendent was arrested. That act alone points to the fact that something was terribly wrong. It even quotes an engineer saying the jacks did not afford the necessary protection! They talk about an investigation. Are you sure there weren't any further articles about the accident?"

"Yes, the anarchist helped."

Lucrezia ignored the mistake and continued. "Giovanna, Brooklyn Union Gas is a big, important American company. I asked my husband to check, which he did reluctantly. It is run by James Jourdan, a Civil War general, and William Rockefeller is on the board of directors. It would be in Italy like having Garibaldi and King Umberto running the company."

Giovanna said nothing. Lucrezia went on, "Did they give you any money when Nunzio died?"

"Yes, a little. Lorenzo used it for his burial."

"Did he sign anything?"

"No. But I still don't understand why you say I should go to a lawyer."

"Because I think this company, or the construction company, made mistakes that led to your husband's death. They're responsible, but because they are so powerful, there has been no further investigation."

"But what can I do? I speak no English!"

"These companies count on you doing nothing! Without a family crying injustice, it's easy to divert a reporter."

"What do you think I should do?"

"Get a lawyer and sue them for the death of your husband."

Giovanna was silent.

"They are using Italians like donkeys to build New York. If they lose a few it doesn't matter. They can always get a new ass."

The harshness of Lucrezia's words set her pacing—stress and New York City's confined spaces had turned Giovanna's pacing into a habit. It was hard enough when Lucrezia spoke of Nunzio's accident in personal terms; making it political overwhelmed her completely. But what was she hoping to accomplish with all her questions anyway? She wanted justice. But what would justice be?

Her thoughts did not go much further. A woman was at the door announcing that her sister had gone into labor.

Lucrezia gathered up her things. "Come with me, Giovanna."

Giovanna was happy to go along because she didn't want to be alone. However, when they arrived at the woman's apartment she could tell something was not right. The laboring woman was moaning that the baby shouldn't be born. Seeing Giovanna's concern, the woman's sister explained that her brother-in-law had been killed building the Manhattan Bridge two months after his wife conceived their sixth child. Giovanna's head snapped up and looked at Lucrezia, who looked away, unable to feign innocence.

When the baby was delivered, there were no tears of joy from the mother, only laments and sobs as the mother wailed to her newborn, "How will I feed you?" Looking at the midwives she cried, "His poor brother, only eleven, works the job and returns home, his little body broken, and there is no food on the table."

Lucrezia and Giovanna said nothing to each other for the rest of the evening.

"Signore DeCegli, this is Giovanna Pontillo," Lucrezia said as they both sat down. They had walked up five flights in a Mott Street tenement to Signore DeCegli's office. They took their seats amid the piles of papers threatening to submerge his desk and file cabinets. A telephone sat on his desk. Giovanna hoped it would ring; she was fascinated by telephones and hadn't used one yet.

"Signora Pontillo, I reviewed the newspaper articles and death certificate that Signora LaManna brought to me."

The lawyer's Italian was perfect. So perfect that Giovanna sat up straighter and took her mind off the telephone. He was looking right at her, and she realized that this man was handsome. It was something she hadn't noticed about a man in a long while.

"I think there is no doubt that you have a case against the construction company. And although I am quite sure we could not win a case against Brooklyn Union Gas, it would be to our advantage to sue them as well."

Giovanna looked at Lucrezia, who motioned with her eyes to ask.

"What do you mean, signore?"

"What I mean, signora, is that I believe in all probability that negligence led to your husband's death, meaning that we can sue the company that is responsible."

"Signore, I have little to pay you."

"You do not have to pay me anything before the case is settled. I believe you will win your case and you will be compensated. My fee will come from your settlement."

Seeing Giovanna's puzzled look, Lucrezia stepped in. "Signore, we need to start from the beginning."

More than an hour later, when Signore DeCegli finished explaining the American legal system and Giovanna's options, he began asking questions of his own. Changing his tone, he said, "Tell me about Nunzio."

"He was my husband," murmured Giovanna, voice cracking, as if that said it all.

"Well, did he read and write?"

"Yes," answered Giovanna, indignant. "He was a maestro. An engineer."

"That will help. My guess is that if your husband had questions about the safety of this project, others did too. After we file, I intend to subpoena the supervisor and other workers."

"But they will say what the company wants them to say."

"Possibly, but generally I've found that Americans take truth in the courts seriously."

"What happens now, signore?"

"You wait while I prepare the case. It may take months. If I need anything I'll contact you, but don't be surprised if you don't hear from me for a while."

Signore DeCegli walked them downstairs. When the door closed, Lucrezia quipped, "It's a shame he was just married."

"Lucrezia, stop it. I told you I'm not interested."

Lucrezia let it go, but she was certain that she saw a flicker of disappointment in her friend's face.

FOURTEEN

"Wake up, Zia! It's Sunday! Can we go to the cemetery and stop for nuts? Please, Zia?"

Startled, Giovanna sat up groggily. But before she could answer, Teresa cut in. "No trips today. We're having company."

The children groaned and Giovanna, still sleepy, asked, "Who? The DiFrancos?"

Teresa was already ensconced in the kitchen. "No. Children, get dressed; I need your help. Giovanna, you will be here for dinner?" It was both a question and a command.

Giovanna thought Teresa was acting strange but decided to ignore it. "I will be here. Do you need help?"

"No, no. Concetta will help me. Don't you have to visit Signora Russo? She told me you were visiting her today."

"I do." It amazed Giovanna how her sister-in-law seemed to know all the business of the neighborhood. Teresa's body, even in the rare months that she was not pregnant, had become rotund. It was easy to envision Teresa as a bumblebee flitting in and out of the chambers of the hive that was Little Italy.

"Be back by three."

Usually when Teresa was out of sorts, Giovanna looked to Lorenzo for guidance, but Lorenzo had already left to paint bits of Italy in tenement foyers. Teresa busied herself with making the children's breakfast. After espresso, bread, and cheese, Giovanna left to escape the frenzy and tension.

Her quick exit brought her to an earlier mass than usual. Only old women, all widows, knelt in the pews. Giovanna wondered if they waited for the sun to rise and then hurried to mass because they had nothing else to anchor their lives. Even though she, too, was alone and dressed in black, she felt like an interloper and was threatened by the women. Nervous, she went to the altar to light a candle, but for the first time she didn't know for what she prayed.

It was too early to call on Signora Russo, and she avoided Lucrezia's house on weekends, when she was more likely to run into her husband, so she walked. Giovanna had grown accustomed to New York, but this morning the streets seemed extremely foreign and uninviting. She yearned for the narrow alleys of the Chianalea and her terrace, where she could sip her espresso and listen to the church bells before going to mass. Having walked all the way to Chinatown, she ended up on the herbalist's street. Giovanna thought she saw the proprietor inside and took a closer look through the locked door. The door swung open.

"Quick, quick," the proprietor motioned.

Giovanna understood that he didn't want to get caught selling on a Sunday. "No, no, I go," she answered.

"No, no, show you," replied the proprietor, waving her to the back of the store.

A wooden crate covered in Chinese characters was half unpacked.

"Good!" he exclaimed, taking a paper package from the crate. He carefully unfolded the paper to reveal what looked like a sea urchin.

He gripped one of the urchin's spines. "Good," he said, and then mimed pain.

Giovanna tried not to laugh when he contorted his face and moaned. He was very dramatic. Swallowing her smile, she shrugged her shoulders to indicate "How?" She half expected him to puncture her skin with it; she had learned about how the Chinese stuck needles into people. Instead, he went to the counter and ground the spine into a rough powder, and then added glycerin. Taking a small spoon, he showed her the proper amount and pointed to his mouth. Giovanna put a tiny bit on her finger and touched it to her tongue. At once she could tell that it had the power and qualities of an opiate.

"Good? Good?" the proprietor asked.

"Sì. Yes."

Giovanna doubted she would use it without knowing more, but in return for the kindness, she opened her purse to get a coin to purchase one of the exotic crustaceans.

"No. No. Sunday." Smiling, he waved her money away and rewrapped the urchin, putting it in her hand.

With her purse back in her bodice, and a strange Chinese sea urchin in her skirt pocket, Giovanna walked back up Mott Street, this time feeling more at home.

Her visit took longer than expected. Signora Russo was in her eighth month, and Giovanna was worried that this big baby, who was breech, was not going to turn. She decided to try performing a version—an external method to turn the baby. Taking out her stethoscope, a gift from Lucrezia, she had Signora Russo lie on her back and bend her knees. The hardest part of this procedure for Giovanna was being chatty, keeping the mother relaxed and distracted. With one hand on the baby's head and another on its culo, Giovanna gently turned the baby to the right. When there was no movement, she tried twisting the body to the left, and this time the baby turned a little. Waiting, chatting, and checking the baby's heartbeat between each movement, Giovanna slowly turned the baby to a transverse position. Signora Russo was starting to get nervous and feel pain, so Giovanna let her rest, holding the baby's head and culo in its new position for fear it would gravitate back to breech. "Even for babies, change must come slowly," she explained.

The woman's mother soon entered the apartment and provided the distraction Giovanna needed to continue. Twenty minutes later, the baby was in position.

"Signora, please stay and have supper with us," invited the mother, who was preparing their Sunday meal. The woman's kindness reminded Giovanna that she needed to head home.

"No, thank you, I must go. Signora, stay on your feet for the next hour. Go for a walk, let the baby settle, and send for me if you feel anything out of the ordinary."

———————

Teresa knew it was Giovanna coming up the stairs because no one else took the stairs in twos. She always wondered how Giovanna managed to do that in a long skirt. It seemed hard enough to get up the steep stairs without tripping on your hem.

Giovanna burst through the door, making apologies. "I'm sorry, my visit went longer than I thought." Her voice trailed off at the end of her sentence because she found herself face to face with a row of strangers. Almost at attention, there in front of her stood a man nervously holding his hat in his hand, with three children in their Sunday best lined up next to him.

"Buon giorno," mouthed Giovanna, but she was looking at Lorenzo for an explanation.

"Giovanna," said Lorenzo with more than usual flourish, "this is our friend Rocco Siena, from Scilla."

"Oh, *piacere*," said Giovanna, thinking the man's recent arrival to America explained this awkward formality. More relaxed, she added, "Welcome to America."

Two of the children giggled.

"Quiet! No, no, signora, we have been here a long time," interjected the stranger. "In fact, all my children were born in New York. I will introduce them." As if to make his point, he said all his children's names in English. "This is Clement, he's twelve, Frances is eight, and little Mary is four."

All the children gave her a big grin when their names were said.

"Well, let's sit," said Teresa. "You children can play in the hall or on the stoop. But don't go far, we'll eat soon."

Giovanna couldn't help but notice how uncomfortable her brother and sister-in-law were with their own friend.

"Signore Siena, I don't know any Sienas in Scilla," commented Giovanna, attempting to make conversation.

"Sì, signora, there are not many Sienas in Scilla. My wife, bless her soul, had much family in Scilla. She was a Bellantoni."

"Oh, of course, the Bellantonis," replied Giovanna.

Lorenzo cut in, "His wife was Angelina, daughter of Vincenzo and Mattia."

"Yes. Mamma knew them. They lived in San Giorgio, yes?"

"Sì," answered Rocco this time, "so did the Sienas. But we were sailors and often away." After an awkward pause, he said, "Your brother tells me you are a widow."

His question raised her worst suspicions, and she answered indignantly, "Yes, I was married to Nunzio Pontillo."

Lorenzo immediately started in on the sales pitch. "Giovanna, Rocco was given a medal by King Victor Emmanuel!"

Her reaction was to shoot Lorenzo a stony stare.

"He saved the king from drowning when their ship went down! Show her the medal, Rocco!" exhorted Lorenzo.

Giovanna politely looked at the medal only because the man was so embarrassed at being forced to produce it. A bronze disc nearly filled the man's palm, which was shaking slightly.

"Why were you on the king's ship?"

"I was a merchant mariner . . ."

Again, Lorenzo cut in enthusiastically. "The king wanted him to be in his Roman guard."

"And why didn't you?" questioned Giovanna skeptically.

"Because I wanted to start a new life in America with my family."

Teresa could see that Giovanna remained unimpressed and decided the best tactic was to keep things moving. "Lorenzo, call the children for dinner. Everything's ready."

Giovanna stood, as did Rocco. She did not need to work at avoiding his eyes because she was a head taller than him. Rocco's hair was wiry and going gray, as was his mustache, and although he was lean, his muscles were thick and gave him a stocky appearance. His laborer's hands looked enormous in proportion to his body. And now these big hands fumbled nervously as he tried to stuff the medal back in his pocket.

The commotion in the hall signaled the children's return. Unlike the adults, they were not having problems socializing, although Domenico was acting the tough guy because Clement was a working boy, and with his calluses came street status.

Even with the children's chatter, the awkwardness didn't go away. Giovanna was silently fuming. If Lorenzo and Teresa wanted her out of the house, why didn't they just tell her?

Teresa was the first to speak. "Rocco, who cares for little Mary?"

"Frances, of course. When Mary is old enough for school, Frances will work."

"I thought all children in America went to school," said Giovanna dryly.

"What does a daughter need to go to school for? America or no America?"

Giovanna wanted to hate him for this comment, but it seemed genuinely ignorant and not mean-spirited.

"And your son?"

"He's a big boy. We're in America to make money."

"Rocco and his family live in that new apartment building at 202 Elizabeth Street," bragged Teresa.

Giovanna knew the building; she had delivered a baby there. It was what they were calling "new law" tenements. They had more light, but the major improvement was that they each had their own toilet instead of a shared toilet in the hall.

Unimpressed, Giovanna changed the subject. "When did your wife, Angelina, pass, signore?"

"In childbirth, with Mary."

Her professional curiosity piqued, Giovanna only stopped herself from asking further questions when she caught Teresa's scolding look.

It was Lorenzo's turn to try to keep the conversation going. "Isn't it strange, Giovanna, we did not know Rocco in Scilla, but here in America, in this big city, we meet. Luigi and Pasqualina DiFranco introduced us."

With that, Giovanna knew that Teresa and her bosom buddy, Pasqualina, had dreamt up this scheme. Teresa believed in keeping her enemies close, so when she found out that Lorenzo had once loved Pasqualina, she made Pasqualina her friend and confidant.

"We're going back out," Domenico announced, as the children piled their plates in the washtub.

With the children out of the room and more wine in him, Rocco turned his focus to Giovanna. "Lorenzo tells me you are a levatrice," said Rocco.

"Sì."

"Working with Signora LaManna."

"Sì."

"She is a good woman."

"Sì." He was trying so hard, Giovanna softened a little. "Did she deliver your children?"

"Yes, but not Mary. My wife was already too sick by then and was in the hospital."

"Let's have our fruit," said Teresa.

"I have to go. I must visit a patient," interrupted Giovanna.

"You said you only had to see Signora Russo today!" Teresa protested.

"Well, this is sudden," replied Giovanna, grabbing her shawl.

"Signora, before you go," Rocco stepped forward, "can I ask you if next Sunday we can walk together?"

Unable to meet his expectant gaze, Giovanna instead looked over his head to Lorenzo's downcast eyes and Teresa's reddened face. She would have said or done anything to get out of the house at that moment. "*Va bene,* signore. But only if there are no babies to deliver."

She flew down the stairs, praying that Signora Russo would go into labor next Sunday, and almost tripped over Mary, who was sitting on the stoop.

"Signora, where are you going?" asked Mary, getting out of her way.

"I must see someone."

"Will you come visit us, signora?"

Giovanna was taken off guard and reached down to pat the child's head.

"Have you calmed down yet?" asked Lucrezia, pouring Giovanna another glass of wine.

"I have every right to be angry."

"Yes, you do," nodded Lucrezia, who had artfully defused Giovanna's rage by calmly agreeing with everything she said.

"He said you delivered two of the children."

"I did."

"What do you know about this family?"

"She was a good woman. He's a good man, hardworking, simple, but good."

"That doesn't tell me much."

"There isn't much more to tell." There was a pause, before Lucrezia continued. "Are you considering this?"

"Of course not."

"Why not?"

Giovanna looked at Lucrezia in shock.

"You told me you wanted children. You wanted to bring your own babies into this world."

"Yes, but not with just anyone!"

"Giovanna, do you believe you will ever love someone as you loved Nunzio?"

"I will never find another Nunzio. There is not another Nunzio," answered Giovanna indignantly.

"That's my point. If you want children, you only need to find a good man. And I don't need to remind you that at thirty-one, in all probability it will not be a young man without children."

"I don't believe you're encouraging me to do this!"

"I am not. I'm simply reviewing the facts and stripping the situation of your brother and sister-in-law's deceit so you can see it for what it is—an option. You can choose not to take this option, but you should not dismiss it out of anger."

While she recognized the wisdom in Lucrezia's words, she had a fiery confrontation with Lorenzo when she returned home.

"You are too young to be a widow! It is my job to take care of you!" Lorenzo yelled.

"Taking care of me is getting rid of me?"

"I want you to be happy, but you are as stubborn as a mule. If I had told you about this meeting, you would have never agreed to it!"

"Exactly."

"Yes, exactly. Please, Giovanna, you could live with me forever, but will that be living? I heard your promise at Nunzio's grave."

Giovanna looked at Teresa cowering in the back room. She wasn't so sure about the living with him forever part, but at that moment she started to forgive her brother.

FIFTEEN

Her prayers for Signora Russo were unanswered. The next Sunday, Giovanna dressed for her walk with Rocco. Teresa tried to encourage her not to wear black, and even offered her Sunday feathered hat, but Giovanna dismissed Teresa with an angry look. For an entire week there had been no banging pots or heavy sighs; Teresa practically tiptoed around her sister-in-law. While Giovanna had forgiven her brother, she had not forgiven Teresa. In actuality, Giovanna was grateful that Teresa had given her a solid reason to stop trying to be her friend.

"What do you think of him, Zia?" Domenico asked Giovanna, who was lacing her shoes. Not waiting for her reply, Domenico offered, "I like his son. The little girl is spoiled though."

Giovanna was amused at Domenico's tone of camaraderie and chose to play along. "The children should be in school. And you need not fault the little one. She never had a mother, and people try and make up for that."

"Are you going to marry him?"

"No, Domenico. I am going for a walk."

Giovanna asked Signore Siena if they could walk to the Brooklyn Bridge. It was her way of bringing Nunzio along. She made no attempt to shorten her strides as she often did when walking with other people and was impressed that the signore kept pace. Giovanna asked Rocco what he missed about Scilla. He replied, "L'America is my home." Rocco was in the "love it" group and, having pledged his loyalty to America, he did not allow himself sentimental thoughts of the home he left behind.

With Giovanna's occasional question and Signore Siena's one-word answers, Giovanna had plenty of time to assess the signore's appearance.

His clothes were clean, without holes, and made of good cloth. He was dark, and even the graying of his thick black hair did not soften his rough appearance. While there was no grace to him, he was respectful and politely nodded to people he knew along the way.

When they reached the Brooklyn Bridge, they rested on a bench. Giovanna asked him what he thought.

"What do I think of what?"

"The bridge."

"It's a bridge. It's a big bridge."

Perversely, Giovanna was pleased. There could be no mistaking this man for Nunzio.

Rocco seemed to be trying to say something, because he had taken off his cap and was twisting it in his hands as she had seen him do when they first met. He bit his lip, which caused his sizable mustache to move up and down.

"Signora. I don't ask you to love me. But I will be a good partner if you marry me."

They both stared out at Brooklyn. Giovanna marveled at the irony. Had Rocco Siena proposed by saying that he loved her, saying that he wanted her to love him, she would have dismissed the offer instantly. But this simple man had said exactly the right thing. She watched a tugboat pushing a tanker down the river and felt the breeze on her cheeks.

"I'll think about it."

Ten weeks later, Giovanna had grown marginally fond of Signore Siena, but she was falling in love with the children, particularly Mary. Giovanna had also begun to face up to the truth that in all likelihood she could not have her own children. After all, she was thirty-one, and she and Nunzio had tried to conceive without success. If she married this man, at least she would have a family.

Lorenzo and Teresa had not said a word on the topic, making it easier for her to consider the option. Lorenzo had written of the possibility to their parents, and yesterday she had received a letter, written by her mentor, Signora Scalici, on behalf of her family, assuring her that they would bless whatever decision Giovanna made. Signora Scalici couldn't help but add her two cents at the end of the letter, obliquely endorsing the marriage by writing, "I am told you are working with a woman doctor. A possibility like that would never exist here."

Giovanna didn't need to decide whether to marry Nunzio. It was a given. This, however, was a practical decision—to live her life alone or to create a family with a man she did not love but was beginning to respect. She thought of the lawyer, Signore DeCegli. Even if Signore DeCegli hadn't just got married, she would never have allowed herself to love him. A smart, handsome man threatened Nunzio's place in her heart.

Giovanna told Rocco on their next Sunday excursion that she would marry him. She reminded him of his promise that she did not have to love him. In return for this consideration, she said she would care for his children and treat them as her own. Rocco simply said, "Thank you." The only thing indicating his pleasure was the suggestion that they cut their walk short and go to Lorenzo's apartment, where his family was also gathered, to deliver the news.

Everyone, even the children, seemed to respect the difficulty of the decision and did not make a fuss. Instead they offered quiet congratulations and best wishes with polite kisses. The exception was Mary, who flung herself into Giovanna's arms and nuzzled her head into her neck.

Teresa insisted that everyone stay for supper. Giovanna sat opposite Rocco, taking a hard look at the whole of his face for what seemed like the first time. Panic rose in her chest with the realization that she had promised herself to this stranger. She said fervent, silent prayers that she had not made the wrong decision.

Giovanna and Rocco were married in City Hall. Alderman Reichter presided. Rocco had said, "We live in America; we will marry the American way." Giovanna wasn't sure there was an "American way" of doing anything but agreed, reasoning that a civil ceremony would further distance this marriage from her wedding to Nunzio.

Following the ceremony on the walk home, they stopped at the bench where Rocco had proposed twelve weeks before.

"So, the widow and the widower got married." Rocco put extra emphasis on "widow."

Giovanna had had to be coaxed out of her black dress that morning by Teresa, who had bought her a new one. "I'm sorry, but I will never forget him."

"No, don't be sorry. I know this. And I have decided that if we won't forget, then we should honor the memory of your husband and my wife," Rocco stammered.

Giovanna looked quizzically at Rocco, who stared at the bridge when he said, "If we have children, the girl will be called Angelina, and the boy will be Nunzio."

Rocco didn't see her smile because she, too, looked straight ahead and wondered what it was about this view that made this illiterate man say the right things. Covering his large, gnarled hand with her own, Giovanna touched him for the first time.

Cedar Grove, New Jersey, 1966

When my parents moved to the suburbs, my grandfather Nonno planted a gigantic garden and surrounded it with a six-foot fence. Every day, he would drive from Hoboken to garden with me at lunchtime. I was happiest within the big green fence with my grandfather. The neighbors complained because they thought it was going to be a chicken coop, but Nonno painted it green so it wouldn't be so noticeable among the manicured shrubs and sloping lawns.

"Nonno, she did it again," I complained, throwing a weed over the fence.

"Shake the dirt off the weeds before you throw them. Itsa good dirt."

"One of my friends came over to play, and she started screaming, 'She's not blood. Get her out of here! Tell her to go home.' No one wants to come to my house. They're afraid. Why can't Nanny be like you, or Thea's Yia-Yia?"

Nonno realized that he couldn't change the subject. He walked over to the two peach trees in the garden. "See this," he said, pointing to a gnarled spot on the trunk of one tree. "This is from the early frost a few years ago. It made the tree grow different. There are reasons for the way we are. Have patience with your grandmother. And remember, itsa been hard for her since your Big Nanny died."

"I don't like her, Nonno, she's mean."

"Anna, thatsa bad to say."

"You don't like her either. You fight all the time."

"Shesa tough, but I love your grandmother."

"Well, I don't."

Nonno put the small white Formica table in the middle of the garden and unwrapped two sandwiches. We sat in the dirt. I always tried to be quiet because Nonno didn't say much, but invariably I failed. I would chatter about the families who lived around our dead-end circle. Three Greek, two Italian, one Hungarian, one Polish, and one not anything. I always felt sorry for the kids who weren't anything. When people asked, "What are you?" they had to say, "Not anything" or, "I don't know." My grandmother had taught me how to figure out what people were by their last names. Nanny was real concerned with what people were.

The sandwich looked small in Nonno's hands, which were big and attached to even bigger forearms, one with a tattoo of a mermaid, the other with an anchor. The rest of Nonno wasn't so big. But he was tall enough, with brown eyes that sparkled.

"Nonno, tell me about the mermaids," I said.

"Again? Only if you promise no more questions."

"Deal."

"Okay, in the firsta World War I was in the blu marinos—you say 'navy' in English. The mermaids, they saved my life. After the torpedo hit, I wasa hanging onto a piece of wood. I think it wasa door from the submarine. I had no water, no food, so my head wasa no good. So I keep slipping off the wood, and every time that I sink into the sea, the mermaids push me back on the wood."

"How did you know it was mermaids?"

"Who else could ita be out there in the ocean?"

"Maybe Scylla."

"Scylla ate the sailors, no saved them."

"But maybe she saved you because you were from her town. It makes sense because the other men died. Maybe she wanted you to come back to Scilla."

"Ah, then I did a bad thing, because thatsa when I went to America to visit my aunt."

"Big Nanny?"

"Yes, Big Nanny."

"I still don't get how your mother-in-law is your aunt."

"For such a smarta girl I have to explain this again! My Uncle Nunzio wasa married to your great-grandmother."

"But how are you and Nanny cousins?"

"Because Nunzio and your great-grandmother wasa cousins."

I couldn't understand the family stuff no matter how hard I tried. So I went back to a topic I could understand. "Nonno, what are we going to plant there?"

"Strawberries. But we going to mix the sand ina the dirt."

Nonno nodded to the gate. "The *basanogol* needs caviar." Caviar is what Nonno called cow manure.

I unwrapped the dried figs Nonno had packed for dessert. In November, we would wrap the huge fig tree in Nonno's yard. I would stand at the base, squinting into the light, and hand Nonno the cloth and stuffing up through the labyrinthine branches. With one foot on the ladder and another on the tree, Nonno would rhythmically wind the cloth around each limb to protect it from the northeastern winter. He had named the broad, dignified tree Kate, for Kate Smith. He told me that sometimes at night he heard the fig tree singing "God Bless America."

Weeks later, I sat perfectly still on a wrought-iron kitchen chair cushioned in pink vinyl as Nonno cut my hair in the backyard. Minutes before, I'd been standing on the same chair to strain the tomatoes at the stove. Clippings of wavy dark brown hair fell in the dishcloth on my lap.

The kitchen window was open. My mother and grandmother were bickering so loudly as they prepared the Sunday meal that I didn't even try to talk to Nonno. My five-year-old sister, Marie, was on the patio, lost in her pretend world, puffing on a pencil. I wondered if my sister would get lead poisoning smoking those make-believe cigarettes and when she would have to strain the tomatoes. But my musings about Marie's health and the inequities of chores were interrupted by something I heard my mother say.

"Ma, come on. You can't still be getting nightmares. I mean, enough is enough. That was sixty years ago!"

My grandmother getting nightmares? She was the toughest person I knew. I noticed that my grandfather was paying attention as well.

"Be quiet! Forget I said it. Just give me the spatula," Nanny blurted.

Nonno finished cutting, and I got up, careful not to let any of the hair fall from the dishcloth. I went to the towering ash tree, the one that no one, including my big, towering father, could get his arms around, and scattered my hair all along the base. My grandfather had taught me that birds would use the hair in their nests. The first time I found a nest with my hair in it, I didn't miss my long hair anymore.

At dinner, we made it through a couple of courses to the fruit without a blowup, but there was tension in the air. My mother and grandmother were still aggravated with each other.

"Looka," said Nonno, picking up a discarded tangerine peel. "You want perfume?" He held the peel close to my neck and squeezed it between his finger, letting loose a spray of tangerine essence.

"Neat!" I was so excited I picked up a peel and squirted my mother.

"Stop that. Go get the milk and sugar."

"No fair. I got the fruit." I pointed to my older brother. "Make Michael get dessert."

My brother gave me a Three Stooges noogie on the head.

"Mom! He's teasing me!"

When I calmed down, my grandfather pointed to the sugar bowl, holding a cookie out of my reach. "*Zucchero.*"

"Zucchero," I proudly pronounced.

"*Bene.*" Nonno handed me the cookie.

"*Occhi.*"

"Occhi," I said, pulling my eyes sideways, cracking up my little sister.

"Stop that. Your eyes will stay that way!" reprimanded Nanny sharply. It was clear that whatever my grandmother was holding in was about to come out.

"And you!" she shouted, pointing at my grandfather. "Anna doesn't need to learn Italian. She needs to learn her times tables!" Nanny turned to my brother, sister, and me. "You think you'd have a meal like this in Italy? You'd eat misery, that's what you would eat! My father and mother suffered so we could live well here. It was all worth it. All of it!"

As soon as my grandmother's back was turned, Nonno poured a little wine into Michael's and my Howdy Doody cups.

"Come on, do your homework and maybe we'll play Pokerino later." My mother sounded both exasperated and tired.

For my part, I wondered if I would ever understand—or like—my grandmother.

PART FIVE

NEW YORK, NEW YORK
1905–1907

SIXTEEN

Giovanna's laughter was so loud and hard, the baby kicked her in protest. Rubbing her hand over her growing belly, she laughed and whispered, "Scusi." When she had realized five months ago that she was pregnant, it was the first time since Nunzio's death that she truly felt happiness.

Giovanna and Rocco were two of hundreds of people packed onto benches in the Teatro Villa Giulia on Grand Street to watch the star of satire and *macchiette*, Eduardo Migliaccio. Known as "Farfariello"—"The Little Butterfly"—Migliaccio had finished his opening song, and already Giovanna was laughing so hard, tears rolled from her eyes. The Little Butterfly pranced across the stage in a spangled skirt, shaking his ample bosom and buttocks. Since arriving in New York, Giovanna had taken advantage of all the theater opportunities, but the *opera buffa* was her favorite.

Rocco didn't really like satire, nor did he understand much of it, but he accompanied his wife because he was content to be with her. In the year since their marriage, he had grown fond of Giovanna. When Teresa and Pasqualina suggested he marry Giovanna, he readily agreed because he had already noticed her in the neighborhood and thought she was certain to be a good mother to his children. Little else entered into the decision. He was pleasantly surprised that, in addition to being all those things, she was a good companion and a good card player.

For Giovanna, the first few months were extremely difficult. She was uncomfortable around Rocco. Unlike Nunzio, he spoke rarely, and unlike her father, who also used words sparingly, you couldn't tell what he was thinking. But he had not interfered in her decisions about how to run her life and home. He only grumbled when she sent Frances back to school and said nothing when she brought Mary with her to visit patients.

Once she conceived, her feelings for Rocco changed. His status rose from "partner" to the more permanent "father of her child." They now had a bond beyond their marriage license. But sex with Rocco was perfunctory. It was quick, and Giovanna was grateful. And although she enjoyed the warmth that followed intercourse, she looked forward to the final months of her pregnancy when she could abstain and not be questioned.

Farfariello was marching across the stage with an enormous pasted-on mustache, a sash across his chest, and a saber over his shoulder, purloining Italian patriots. Next he became the "Iceman," "Issaman" to Italian-Americans, singing bawdy Italian folk songs. The audience knew this routine signaled the end of the show and were already on their feet, clapping and cheering. Farfariello's baritone stretched uncomfortably into a high note, and he exited stage right with a flourish. The crowd erupted into shouts and whistles.

Rocco protectively motioned his pregnant wife to sit for a few moments to avoid getting caught in the crush of the crowd, and they sat watching the stagehands while the audience filed out. Even before the applause ended, the stagehands had begun preparing for the next show.

A heavyset bald man struggled up a rope ladder to untie a drape from a truss. His younger counterpart called, "One more *cannolo* and we won't be able to hoist you up there!"

The man ignored him, but another stagehand joked, "Leave Saint Carmine alone. All he has is the cream in his cannolo and his *ammoratas* on Mulberry Street!"

Without saying a word, Giovanna rose and, stepping over benches, made her way directly to the stage. Rocco, concerned and confused, caught up with her.

"It's him!" she whispered to Rocco.

"Who?"

"Carmine. Nunzio's friend."

With her hands leaning on the stage, Giovanna called to the man on the rope ladder, "*Prego*, signore, are you Carmine?"

Without looking down, the man answered, "Why do you want to know?"

"Because I am—I was—the wife of Nunzio Pontillo."

Carmine stopped untying a knot and looked down. He didn't move.

"Saint Carmine, *che cosa fa?* What are you doing up there?" yelled one of the others.

Carmine climbed down the rope, slid off the stage, and turned to look at Giovanna, studying her face and scrutinizing her eyes. "Yes, yes, surely it is you."

They met in the cafe the next morning before the matinee. Out of respect for Rocco, they met with Lucrezia chaperoning. Though they knew each other only through Nunzio's letters, they reminisced as if they had known each other for years, their conversation punctuated by the stirring of their spoons in their espressos.

"Did you like that pasta pot drawing? He showed it to me before he mailed it."

"I laughed so hard. It was in that same letter Nunzio told me it was you who named the first foreman 'Linguine con Pomodoro'!"

Lucrezia was anxious to get to the heart of the matter. "Signore, Signora Siena is suing Brooklyn Union Gas and the construction company for negligence."

Carmine leaned back in his chair and whistled. It only took him a moment to recover. "Good! Good for you!" A lawsuit, while within the confines of the system, appealed to his anarchist tendencies. "What can I do to help?"

The older woman continued, "Her lawyer needs to prove negligence. He has eyewitness testimony, the police reports, and the press, but he still doesn't know precisely what they were doing wrong. Everyone said that Nunzio had doubts about the job and discussed them with you. Is that true?"

"Signora, you should consider becoming a lawyer yourself," commented Carmine, appraising her with an interested eye. Lucrezia flashed him a "stop the nonsense" look, and he continued, although Giovanna could tell Lucrezia was flattered.

"Yes, it is true. I'll tell you everything that I remember that wasn't lost to liquor and sorrow," answered Carmine dramatically.

Giovanna, with pencil poised, allowed Lucrezia to continue the questioning. Giovanna didn't understand much of what Carmine said about timbers and compromised metal and load ratios, but she dutifully wrote it all down.

"You see, signora, your husband was smart," said Carmine, tapping his temple with his finger. "He knew from the start that they were constructing that floor ass backwards, and then he knew that they were trying to lower it in a dangerous way."

"Did he tell anyone that?" asked Giovanna.

"Of course! And the foreman called him a stupid dago that should mind his own business."

Giovanna winced at the thought of her maestro husband being treated with disrespect. "Why didn't he leave the job?"

"Signora, I think you've been here long enough to know you do not leave a steady job with good pay. Besides, at first he thought that they knew something he didn't and it would soon all make sense. When it didn't, I think he figured the job was engineered by asses, but he didn't know it was going to kill him."

Carmine dug in his pocket. "Here, take these tickets to the show. I have to go, but I'm here for a few more days if you need to ask me anything."

"Carmine," whispered Giovanna as he rose, "grazie . . ." She tried to say more, to thank him for finding Nunzio's body, for his loyalty, but she could not. Since becoming pregnant, she couldn't control her emotions the way she usually could and did not want to chance crying in public.

"Say nothing, signora. It has been my honor," answered Carmine, sweeping his cap with a flourish. Giovanna could see tears in Carmine's eyes.

When Giovanna and Lucrezia reported on their meeting to Signore DeCegli, he insisted that they bring Carmine to his office to swear an affidavit. The lawyer felt he had to get what he could, even if it was the testimony of a dead man delivered secondhand by a traveling show-man. Unable to locate Supervisor Mulligan, who was no longer with the company, and certain that there was no complete set of blueprints for the project, although he had subpoenaed them months ago, Signore DeCegli felt he had little to make a case.

DeCegli was born in America. In fact, if he didn't say his last name, or had changed it like many of his colleagues had, he could "pass." He had been drawn back to his old neighborhood to practice in part because his parents were still there and in part because he believed that with a good lawyer, an Italian immigrant in the American justice system would be treated the same as any American. This case was forcing him to question his conviction.

Ironically, up until now, his belief hadn't been tested. By locating himself in an Italian community, most of his cases were Italians vs. Italians, because he was a civil attorney whose work consisted mainly of business disagreements and the occasional divorce. This was the first time he had come up against an American monolith and had to conduct anything resembling a criminal investigation. While he knew his unfamiliarity in these matters was not helping, he also knew that no amount of experience would get him past the closed doors and roadblocks. He felt stymied at every turn. Not wanting to risk the wrath of a giant, he had decided not to sue Brooklyn Union Gas and instead made the construction company, Taylor, Wood & Co., the sole defendant. But the giant was protecting its minion and had put all its legal and engineering expertise at the construction company's disposal.

From the workers he was able to track down and interview, he knew that they would probably have to be treated as hostile witnesses because they were so afraid. If Signore DeCegli ever had any doubt about whether this was a case of negligence, it was erased when he saw the fear that had been instilled in these men, and when he learned that his key witness had conveniently disappeared. It was rare that a man of the supervisor's stature could disappear without a trace. Even if Mulligan had left one afternoon months after the accident, never to return, as Taylor, Wood & Co. attested, it was clear the company had no interest in finding him or the files he supposedly stole. DeCegli's case was further encumbered by the fact that the murder weapon, the steel floor that had crushed Nunzio Pontillo, was now covered in thousands of cubic yards of gas and would never be seen again until the tanks were demolished during someone else's lifetime.

The greatest difficulty, however, was that without the qualified testimony of respected engineers, all the evidence was circumstantial. But the money to pay for expert testimony was only part of the problem. Signore DeCegli had approached a number of engineers on a speculative basis, and while they used the excuse of no payment upfront to turn down the job, the lawyer knew it was more likely because they were unwilling to go up against a giant. All of his testimony was from Italian laborers. Could he expect the same system that didn't value their lives to believe their testimony?

DeCegli was tempted to close the case but knew that if he did, the signora would somehow continue it on her own. That thought frightened him for two reasons: First, he had grown fond of the signora and feared for her safety, and second, given her determination and intelligence, she could possibly humiliate him by succeeding.

After reviewing the affidavit that Giovanna had compiled for the tenth time, Signore DeCegli saw something in "Pretty Boy" Mariano's story that ignited a spark. If they couldn't afford their own expert witnesses, they would use the experts at Taylor, Wood & Co.

James Wood, one of the principals of the company, was a former engineer known for his brash style and his ability to "get them up faster than anybody." Brooklyn Union Gas awarded Taylor, Wood the contract because they were under pressure to meet the demand for gas in the burgeoning city. DeCegli felt certain that it had been Wood on the phone with Mulligan that day.

James Wood walked up the five flights to Signore DeCegli's office in disgust. Not only was he furious that he had been summoned to New York in this preposterous matter, he was resentful that he was forced to pay the high hourly rates of the lawyer who huffed and puffed behind him. Answering the rap on the door, DeCegli welcomed them in. Heads rotating, disgust palpable, the men sat without being asked. The court reporter was not introduced and remained a fixture in the corner chair.

"Let's get on with this, shall we?" pronounced Wood, by way of introduction.

Seeing Wood's irritation and revulsion, DeCegli realized he had the upper hand and decided to lengthen the proceedings as much as possible in hopes of getting Wood to say something in anger that he would later regret.

DeCegli drew out the perfunctory questions. But when he saw the relish Wood took in reciting his credentials and that he was gaining strength from his belief in his own importance, DeCegli moved on to questions concerning the timeline and building of the gas tanks.

After a technical question, which Wood answered in arrogant detail, DeCegli quickly asked, "Did you speak with Supervisor Mulligan on the morning of the accident?"

"Yes."

"How many times before the accident did you speak with him?"

"I don't know, possibly three."

"And what was the nature of those calls?"

"This was two years ago."

"Yes, of course. Let me be more specific. Did Supervisor Mulligan express any concern about the procedure and safety of lowering this disc?"

"He was a man predisposed to worry. He left the company soon after."

"Yes, I know. However, he had been with the company for ten years. I suppose his worry was not worrisome until this incident."

"That is not a question, sir!" objected Wood's lawyer.

"Excuse me. What precisely were Supervisor Mulligan's objections to the method in which he had been instructed to lower the disc?"

"I don't remember."

"Sir, may I remind you, since the surroundings do not, that you are under oath."

"I told you, he worried a great deal."

"And I repeat, what was his worry?"

"That the disc would slip on its descent."

"And by slip, do you mean fall?'

"That was his assessment, not mine."

"If he was afraid of the disc falling, that would explain his reluctance to put men under the two hundred tons of steel, yes?"

Wood's lawyer interjected, "My client cannot suppose to know what this supervisor thought."

"You're absolutely right, barrister. That is why I need your client to remember exactly what he said."

It took more than a half hour of questioning before the court reporter was able to record Wood saying, "Supervisor Mulligan thought the disc was not secure enough for men to work underneath while it was being lowered."

DeCegli tried to hide his elation because he wasn't through with Mr. Wood yet. He got up and opened the window to allow the neighborhood sounds and smells to waft into the room.

"Mr. Wood, if your company wasn't responsible for this accident, who was?"

"I told you. Accidents happen. That's why they are called accidents."

"Is it your belief that there is nothing Taylor, Wood & Co. could have done to avert this particular accident?"

"I realize we have a language problem here." He exaggerated his enunciation saying, "There is nothing Taylor, Wood & Co. could have done to avert this accident." Waving his arm toward the window, he snidely added, "If they spoke English . . ."

Wood's lawyer jumped in. "Mr. Wood doesn't think any party is responsible for this accident."

"On the contrary, your client insinuated the Italians . . ."

"Don't twist my words, young man. I was commenting on the difficulty of working with these—your—people."

"If no one was responsible, why did you give the men money in exchange for not talking about the accident?"

"There was no exchange! We gave them money because they witnessed a tragedy and they worked overtime to find those bodies."

DeCegli pulled out the agreement that Mariano had signed. "It says nothing about overtime here. However, it does state that he agrees not to talk about the accident."

Wood's face reddened at seeing the document. "Because they are ignorant and say ignorant things! That's why. They could have said that one of their saints did it, or it was because of the evil eye, or something ridiculous that would have scared off the other workers!"

The attorney jumped in. "What Mr. Wood is saying, is that in order to protect future workers and his client, they asked the Italian workers not to talk about the accident."

DeCegli was momentarily stymied. This was the type of argument that would resonate with an American jury. Everyone was well aware of Italian superstitions.

"I need water," said DeCegli, getting up. "Can I get you gentlemen anything?"

"This has gone on long enough!" exclaimed Wood.

"I'll only be a minute," said DeCegli, leaving the room. He stood in the hall and assessed where he was. He had gotten Woods to say exactly what he wanted him to, but he had a feeling if he pushed him more, he could cement his case.

DeCegli reentered his office. "Excuse me, gentlemen. We're almost through. Carmine Martello, he was the laborer who was friendliest with Nunzio Pontillo and the one who found his body. Correct?"

"If you say so."

"Why, if your motive for this agreement was simply to avoid rumor and superstition, did you take the trouble to track down Mr. Martello in Pennsylvania? Surely he couldn't spread rumor and superstition in the Allegheny mountains about a Brooklyn construction job?"

Wood jumped out of his chair, indignant. "I'm tired of your innuendo! You people should be grateful! We let you into this country and gave you work, and you have the audacity to question us!"

His attorney tried to stop him, but Wood continued, sputtering, "If there was any problem on that job, it was hiring a pack of unskilled Italians and not losing more of them!"

DeCegli smiled. "Thank you, Mr. Wood. Thank you."

SEVENTEEN

Lucrezia swabbed Giovanna's head with a cool cloth. She was in her seventh hour of labor, and Lucrezia knew there were still many more to go. She told Rocco to take the girls to Teresa's apartment and to stay there. Clement would remain behind in case Lucrezia needed anything. Rocco left, awkwardly nodding good-bye to his wife and sternly telling Clement to come get him quickly if he was needed.

Clement settled on his cot in the kitchen and tried to rest as Lucrezia instructed. The apartment was spacious by tenement standards. It had two small bedrooms, a large kitchen, and a closet with a toilet. Giovanna labored on her and Rocco's double bed, above which she had hung pictures of the saints and her palms from mass. Borrowing from Sicilian tradition, she had encircled the bed with a *turnialettu,* a deep flounce of cloth to hide storage under the bed.

Lucrezia went to the sink for more water. The sink was also surrounded by drapery. Lucrezia smiled at the fussiness of this no-nonsense woman. It was hard to imagine Giovanna draping fabric or pinning religious medals on palm fronds and stepping back to see how they looked, but it was evident that she had.

While the labor was long, it was uncomplicated, and both she and Giovanna knew it. They simply had to settle in and wait for Giovanna's body to cooperate fully. Giovanna was far enough along in her labor that Lucrezia had stopped making feeble attempts at telling jokes and stories between contractions and instead was letting her rest.

When Giovanna was ready to push at four in the morning, she did so with an intensity and concentration Lucrezia rarely saw. Lucrezia slowed her down to prevent her from ripping, teasing, "I sound like you." When the baby's head was birthed, Giovanna bent forward, and during the next contraction she delivered the rest of her baby's body into the world.

At the first sound of the baby's cry, Clement, who had feigned sleep through the delivery, jumped up and called, "I'll get Papa!"

Lucrezia left the room, and in the quiet, Giovanna cuddled baby Angelina, examining every finger and every toe, crying with bittersweet happiness.

EIGHTEEN

1906

Elizabeth Street was bustling. It was late afternoon and the block was crowded with people selling, buying, and socializing, and with children playing among the barrels and boxes. Rocco looked at the few heads of cauliflower left in his cart; it had been a good day.

He surveyed the scene, and spying a short man with a beard, he called, "Fresh cauliflower! Only a few left."

Hearing Rocco's voice, another vegetable vendor looked up. "Cauliflower! Caul . . ." Rocco saw the vendor scrutinize the little man and change his call to "Fresh parsley! See the parsley!"

Yet another vendor joined in, louder than usual, "Parsley!"

Rocco looked around, confused. He hadn't seen parsley on the carts today. Turning to the vendor selling clams next to him, Rocco asked, "Do you see parsley?"

"Yeah, there's parsley right there," he answered, pointing to the short man with the beard.

"What are you talking about?"

"Petrosino, the sergeant in charge of the Italian Squad."

Rocco now understood the local thugs were being warned of the sergeant's not-so-undercover presence. "But why say parsley?" he asked the man.

"Ah, you Calabresi! *Petrosino*, in Sicilian, means parsley."

"Limonata!" shouted Giovanna, knocking on the door of apartment sixteen on the floor above her. Their building had five apartments per floor—two at the front, two at the back, and one small side apartment, which was where Limonata lived.

"Prego?" A young woman holding a nine-month-old—nearly the same age as Giovanna's daughter, Angelina—opened the door. "Oh, signora!" she said upon seeing Giovanna, sounding both pleased and relieved.

"Limonata, could you please be more careful! Your colored wash on the line drips onto my clean white clothes."

"Oh, scusi, signora, scusi."

The poor young woman looked like she was going to cry, and Giovanna at once regretted scolding her new neighbor who was having a difficult time coping. Noticing little spots of blood on Limonata's apron at her chest, Giovanna asked, "Are you having trouble again?"

"Sì, signora."

"Let me see." Giovanna entered the tiny apartment, which was crusted in dirt. The only thing sunny in this woman's life was her nickname, which she carried from childhood because of her love of lemonade. Her dull brown hair and slight body made her appearance even more nondescript.

"Have you heard from your husband?"

"No, signora. But he'll be back." Limonata had unbuttoned her blouse to reveal a cracked and bloodied nipple.

"I'll give you more aloe. Put it on every few hours. I see your cough is no better either. Did you go to see Signora LaManna like I told you?"

"No, signora, but I'll go this week."

Giovanna left saying, "You must go. And please, call me Giovanna."

When she heard Limonata's cough, she was grateful Angelina wasn't in the sling usually strapped to her chest. She reentered her apartment and washed her hands. Lucrezia's lectures about cleanliness had not been lost on her.

"Come, Frances, Mary, we'll go to the roof." They were doing the weekly wash, but the heat had become oppressive. Giovanna hoisted the clothes, washboard, and bucket. Frances picked up Angelina, and Mary carried the soap. They climbed the roof ladder, opened the hatch, and emerged onto the roof. An entire world was there to greet them. Many of their neighbors were already up there, and there were scores of others on the roofs of the adjacent buildings, playing cards, doing laundry, or simply trying to feel a breeze. One of their neighbors was spreading buckets of crushed tomatoes on a sheet stretched across a wooden frame, to dry into tomato paste. Giovanna felt a tinge of guilt for buying her tomato paste ready-made in the store.

"Please, Zia, can we go in?" squealed Frances and Mary upon seeing two children already swimming in the roof's water tank. Giovanna was tempted to say, "Only after you do your chores," but easily relented. It was hot. She could use a break herself. Taking Angelina from Frances's arms, she sat while the girls stripped to their petticoats. In only a handful of trips to a beach, Rocco had taught all his children to swim, proving he really was *Scillese*. Grateful that she could sit instead of stand guard at the tank, Giovanna relaxed but still kept one eye on the girls, knowing all too well how quickly children could, and did, drown in those tanks.

Unwinding strands of her hair from Angelina's chubby fist, Giovanna marveled at how dramatically a life could change. She was surrounded by children, sitting on the tar of a New York tenement rooftop, a rusted tank their ocean. Scilla's sandy beaches, sparkling seas, and dramatic cliffs were far behind her; instead, she faced a vista of crowded streets, pushcarts, and garbage, but it was a world cloaked in promise.

"TERROR IN ITALIAN SECTION. Here it is," read Giovanna from *Il Progresso*. "Rocco was lucky he wasn't hurt in the blast. His cart was right across the street from Paparo's store in front of the milliner's shop."

"Do you think they meant to murder Paparo's nephew, or was it just unlucky that he was there early?" asked Lucrezia.

"Evil is evil. Enrico the fruit seller told Rocco they sent Paparo letters demanding money. Paparo didn't pay, and he brought the letters to the police." Scanning the article further, Giovanna read, "'Detectives of Lieutenant Petrosino's Italian Squad are investigating the bombing, which they believe to be the work of the Black Hand.' What do you know of this Petrosino?"

As if on cue, there was a knock on Lucrezia's door and Domenico burst in.

"Zia, Zia, I saw him!"

"Catch your breath, boy. I can't understand you. Who did you see?"

"Petrosino!"

Domenico had listened attentively when Rocco had returned, still covered in ash from the bombing of Paparo's store, and described what had happened. He imagined himself a detective with the sleuthing he and Zia had done. And now, to know the most famous detective of all was this Petrosino—an Italian!

"Where did you see him?"

"On Elizabeth Street, near our apartment. He was dragging a man down the staircase and out of the house."

"How did you know it was him?"

"A crowd gathered when they saw him go in. I heard them talking, and I waited." Domenico had been building toward this moment, and with great drama he reenacted the scene.

"He drags the bum by the collar. You could hear his body bouncing on the steps. When he gets outside, he throws the guy against the brick and says, 'See this scum? This is the Black Hand you are all so afraid of! He is nothing. A common thief.' Then the crowd parts to let him through. He drags the guy down the street, calling, 'It's not like Italy here. You must work with the police. We can help you.' And then Petrosino turns, kicks the rat, and says, 'Andiamo, *schifoso.*'"

"Bravo!" exclaimed Lucrezia, clapping. Domenico smiled and bowed.

"What did he look like?" asked Giovanna, glancing at the picture of Petrosino in the newspaper.

"He was short, but big and strong. He had a black derby and overcoat. And his face had those dents."

"Smallpox scars," corrected Lucrezia, smiling. There was no doubt the boy did see Petrosino.

"Aren't you supposed to be at Vito's Grocery?"

"Sì, Zia. But I had to tell you. I saw the great Petrosino!"

"I'm sure a lot of people don't think he's so great. You keep your mouth quiet about him, you hear?"

"But Zia, he said not to be afraid!"

"That's easy for him to say."

Giovanna kissed Domenico and gently shooed him out of the apartment.

"Lucrezia, what do you think. Is he right?"

"I think it's true that the police here are not like the police in Italy. But this Petrosino couldn't stop Paparo's store from being bombed, could he? If you're marked by the Black Hand, it's like that expression you always use—what is it?—'between a rock and a hard place'?"

NINETEEN

1907

"Come on. You're doing a man's job. Have a man's drink," goaded Clement's co-worker in front of the Star of Italy bar. Clement couldn't admit that his hesitation had nothing to do with being fifteen but with being forbidden by his father to go into that particular tavern.

"I'll even pay for it so your daddy doesn't know," cajoled the worker, impatiently wiping sweat from his brow.

A beer would taste good; his throat stung from inhaling lime for ten hours, and he was broiling from the summer heat.

Even though his day pouring cement had ended, it was still bright outside, so Clement's eyes had to adjust to the dark, smoky room as he walked into the Star of Italy.

He tried to concentrate on his ale and his friend's banter, but eventually his curiosity got the best of him. He glanced around and saw some men gathered around a newspaper at a back table. They looked up suddenly when a thin, well-dressed man entered the bar.

"Vachris! What, no disguise today?" called a chinless brute as he closed the newspaper.

"Lupo, I know you gentlemen are too cunning to fall for that." The new arrival walked around the bar, taking in every detail. Seeing the paper, he commented, "Look, you even read newspapers now! Did you read that story about Mario Palermo?"

Silence greeted his question.

"Do you have anything to tell me about it?"

Gestures indicating "We know nothing" filled the room.

"It's a little boy, gentlemen. He's been gone ten days. I know it's not your turf, but the way I see it, you all know how to get to Brooklyn. Right, Tommaso?" Vachris directed his attention to a huge square-headed man.

"You tell your boss, Petrosino, that we don't get involved in Brooklyn and to stop breaking heads around here," yelled a voice from a smoky table.

"I hope we find that boy alive. Because if we don't, I won't be able to tell Lieutenant Petrosino anything."

Lieutenant Vachris surveyed the room and before leaving looked quizzically at Clement, who made an unsuccessful attempt to blend into his beer at the bar.

As soon as Vachris left, the square-headed guy picked up wood shavings from the floor, threw them at the door, and spat, "He's all talk, Lupo."

"I gotta help my father. Thanks for the beer," Clement said, bolting from the bar.

Hands deep in his pockets and walking quickly, he got half a block before he noticed his father staring at him from the opposite side of the street.

"Where were you?" Rocco sputtered.

"I had a beer."

"I saw you! I told you not to go there. It's filled with Blackhanders!"

"Papa, don't talk here," whispered Clement, turning and walking.

Rocco, an intensely private person, was not prone to public scenes, so he followed his son in silence. The second the apartment door closed, Rocco exploded.

Wanting to shield the girls from the anger, Giovanna gathered them in the bedroom.

"Papa, I'm sorry," pleaded Clement over and over.

"I'm afraid for you, afraid for all of us." Rocco was softening with Clement's apologies. "What happened in there?" asked Rocco of his son.

"There was this short guy, he didn't have a chin. He seemed to be in charge. They called him Lupo. This cop came in, a lieutenant. He asked about a boy who was kidnapped in Brooklyn. And there was this big guy named Tommaso."

"Clement, you trust no one, you hear? They're all bad—these men—the cops. Let them play their little games, and you keep your nose out of it."

Hearing Rocco's voice return to normal, Giovanna and the girls went back into the kitchen. "We'll eat in a minute," said Giovanna, stirring the pasta, "and we'll say a prayer for that boy before dinner."

"My eggplant is better," thought Giovanna with satisfaction. Having never eaten in a restaurant in America, she was at first intimidated when Signore DeCegli suggested that she and Rocco meet him at Saulino's at the corner of Lafayette and Spring streets. DeCegli signaled for more bread. It was apparent he was a frequent customer; the waiters addressed him by name. Their table was tucked into a corner, and despite the simple decor, the restaurant had an air of respectability.

Surreptitiously pointing with his fork at a short, pockmarked man eating alone, DeCegli whispered, "That is the famous Lieutenant Petrosino." Giovanna's head snapped in his direction and snapped back when Petrosino noticed her staring. "He is going to marry the owner's daughter, Adelina Saulino."

Rocco had no reaction to this or anything else that was said. He had not said a word and ordered by pointing to the cheapest meal on the menu. Signore DeCegli tried to encourage him to order something else, but he simply shook his head and pulled on his mustache. Enough time had passed that DeCegli tried again to connect with the man. "It's an honor to meet you, Signore Siena." DeCegli kept stealing glances at Rocco, incredulous that this was Giovanna's husband. They were a mismatched pair in every way that he could observe. But he had handled enough divorces to understand that in rough circumstances companions sometimes fared better than lovers.

Rocco folded and unfolded the napkin. He had only agreed to come because Giovanna couldn't eat with this man alone. This was uncomfortable business, another man's business.

DeCegli, too, was uncomfortable. He was about to tell Giovanna that the unthinkable had happened—an American company was offering her a settlement, but he couldn't help but question his decision not to go to trial. He had a stronger case than he ever thought possible. In court, though, Wood would be rehearsed. His deposition was far more damaging than anything they could get him to say on the stand. The politics of the case were up for grabs. In America's peculiar system, they could get a Judge appalled at the audacity of an immigrant challeng ing an American institution, or one who sympathized with the power- less. DeCegli contemplated feeding the story to one of the new breed of reporters who were making it their mission to expose the conditions in the immigrant communities. If they got public sentiment on their side, it could influence the trial. But it was a long shot.

DeCegli turned to Giovanna. "Signora, I am very pleased to tell you Taylor, Wood & Company has offered a settlement. They will pay you $1,700 now, $1,000 on January 1, 1909, and a final payment of $1,000 on January 1, 1910."

Rocco's look of discomfort turned into an incredulous expression.

"This is a remarkable victory, signora, and a testament to your per- severance and courage." DeCegli smiled warmly, but there was no ex- pression of relief or happiness on Giovanna's face. He tried continuing, "They have agreed to pay my percentage upfront, so you don't need to worry about making that transaction when you receive the payments. The total of $3,700 will be yours." He waited for Giovanna's look of triumph. Instead, she raised her hand, indicating she wanted him to stop speaking.

They ate in a stifling silence. Rocco stole an occasional glance at his wife, but for the most part he tried to remain motionless and control his fidgeting. He eventually broke the silence by calling for another bottle of wine.

DeCegli turned to Giovanna. "Signora, this is a major victory. How- ever, if you would like me to discuss other options, I would be happy to."

Giovanna looked at Signore DeCegli full in the face for the first time. "What I do not understand, and what I believe you can't help me with, is what it will mean to accept such an offer."

"Giovanna," said Rocco gruffly. What was his wife thinking? This entire business would be over, and they could establish a store. No more pushing the cart. They would own something!

"Rocco, I am not saying no. I must think about it. Of course, your feelings on the matter will weigh in my decision."

Rocco knew it wasn't true but was pleased at the generosity of the sentiment.

"I believe I should review your options," injected Signore DeCegli, hoping the facts would defuse potential family tension and make it easier for Giovanna to accept.

The lawyer went on to explain his thoughts about going to trial and how the other side would be better prepared. He chose not to mention that now, because she was a married woman, Giovanna's case didn't have the same sympathetic appeal.

He ended his review by saying cautiously, "A condition of the settlement is that you tell no one of the terms."

"This is family business. Why would we tell anyone?" interjected Rocco indignantly.

DeCegli turned to Giovanna. "You realize if you said anything, you would risk losing the second payment. There are four other victims, and they want to avoid lawsuits with them. That is the reason they want to pay it in three parts. It will extend beyond the statute of limitations."

Giovanna didn't bother to ask what that meant. That wasn't the issue. She took a long time to reply, during which Rocco drank another glass of wine. "Please take no offense, Signore DeCegli, but I would not view such a settlement as a victory." Giovanna looked away. The idea of trading Nunzio's life for money made her nauseous.

"Signora, I know of no other case where the family of an immigrant received a settlement for an on-the-job accident. You should be proud of what you've done."

In the awkward silence that ensued, DeCegli realized that she might never acknowledge the significance of this win. He changed the subject. "I suppose Petrosino is glum because of that poor boy . . . Actually, he usually appears that way."

Giovanna looked puzzled.

"I thought you would have heard. They found Mario Palermo's body."

Rocco squirmed in his chair thinking about Clement in that cafe. Giovanna crossed herself. "No, I hadn't heard."

Signore DeCegli apologized. "I'm sorry; I didn't mean to speak of unpleasant things. Well, for now, let's relax; we have two weeks to respond."

"I don't need two weeks, Signore DeCegli." Giovanna felt defeated acknowledging to herself for the first time that there could be no justice in Nunzio's death. "You can tell them we will take the offer."

"Yes, of course, she'll take the offer," echoed Rocco, relieved.

When Signore DeCegli got over his surprise, he too was relieved. But after toasting their triumph, he felt strangely let down.

"Lieutenant," saluted Detective Fiaschetti at the entry to Petrosino's office.

"Sit down, detective." Petrosino motioned to a chair.

"I got nothing on the Palermo boy, Lieutenant," announced the detective, who was dressed in street clothes and looked like the drunk he had been pretending to be. He was Petrosino's youngest detective and quickly responded to his lieutenant's look of disappointment by adding, "But Don Vito Cascio Ferro has come to town."

Petrosino's head snapped up. "I had him exiled after the barrel murder!"

"Well, he got back in and is looking quite the gentleman. Tailored suit, manicured beard and mustache. He was holding court in the Star of Italy with Lupo and his gang."

"He came to this neighborhood!" exclaimed Petrosino, indignant. "These thugs have no fear!"

Detective Fiaschetti removed a small notebook from his pocket. "He acted like a real professor, he did. Listen to this: 'Why break the bottle when you can skim off the cream? At this rate you'll soon have nothing left. Provide them a service, a protection service, and exact a fee.' And then he says, 'They'll thank you for it, and you won't need to deal with Petrosino.'"

Petrosino's face was red, and his hand was balled into a fist. Detective Fiaschetti quickly continued, trying to get the rest in before Petrosino's outburst. "Il Lupo treated him like God. Tommaso the Bull asked who they were providing these people protection from, and you know what Ferro says? He says, 'Why, thieves, of course!' and he and Lupo shared a big laugh."

Surf City, New Jersey, 1969

"I don't see anything," I moaned. Flat on our backs on redwood picnic benches, Nonno and I stared at the moon. We were outside our summer rental in Surf City, New Jersey. Across the street the bay lapped up on the shore.

"I no see nothing," agreed Nonno.

We could hear the television and the rest of the family talking inside.

"We have been told that in minutes Astronaut Neil Armstrong will emerge from the lunar module. But this is what it looked like when they touched down at 4:17 today . . ."

I could tell when things were really important because Walter Cronkite's voice wasn't perfect. They were replaying the landing. It was a scratchy recording, which made me think it already sounded like history.

"Houston, Tranquility Base here. The Eagle has landed!"

"Josie, put that disgusting book down and watch this," Nanny scolded my mother.

"Shut up, Ma. It's not disgusting. It's a bestseller."

"Nonno, let's go inside," I said to my grandfather.

"Why? So we can heara them argue?"

"We can hear them anyway, and I want to see it."

I squeezed onto the couch as my sixteen-year-old brother pontificated. "Right now, some guy in Vietnam is getting blown to bits, but we don't have to see it because they're landing on the moon."

"Michael, where's your patriotism?" My father was seething.

I was depressed. My grandfather thought the landing on the moon was a Hollywood movie; my brother thought it was a trick to make people forget about the war; my father only cared about my brother's hair being too long; my mother was distracted by some book about the Mafia; and my grandmother was mad at my mother for reading the Mafia book. I looked to my little sister to share this moment, but she was crying about her sunburn.

Walter Cronkite touched his ear. *"I believe we are going to hear the president talk to the astronauts."* Soon President Nixon's voice filled the airwaves. *"Neil and Buzz, I am talking to you from the Oval Office . . ."*

"Eh, itsa Tricky Dick," kidded Nonno.

I giggled, but my father shushed me.

". . . As you talk to us from the Sea of Tranquility, it inspires us to redouble our efforts to bring peace and tranquility to earth."

My brother scoffed. My father was aggravated and said he and my mother should have gone dancing at the Seashell. My mother didn't hear any of it because she was absorbed in *The Godfather*.

The next day, we camped on the beach with umbrellas, towels, chairs, and coolers—suburban nomads exercising our tribal instincts. Since it was the weekend, there were first cousins, second cousins, pretend cousins, and the numerous *gombadas* who were all called Aunt or Uncle regardless of whether they were relatives.

"I'll take two," I said to my grandfather. We were playing poker under the fringed umbrella.

"Due," replied Nonno, dealing.

I glowered at the men playing bocce.

"What, are you blind? Red's closer!" shouted my cousin.

"What a bunch of *gedrools*! Do you believe this, Frankie? These kids can't take losing to a bunch of old guys," my father called out to my uncle.

"Why do they play if all they do is argue?" I asked Nonno.

"Thatsa part of the game." Nonno didn't look up from his hand.

"Yeah, well I can play better than any of them."

"Now you playing poker."

I heard my father yell, "Michael, you look like a girl, and you throw like a girl!"

My mother still had her nose in that book.

"Josie, they say there's a character in there that's got to be Sinatra. You were close with Sinatra's cousin, what do you think? Was he in with the Mob?" asked one of my aunts.

Nanny tugged on her bathing cap. "I'm going swimming if you're going to talk about those people."

"Ma, we're not going to discuss it." My mother put down her book.

"I'm going in anyway," Nanny announced.

I watched my grandmother dive into a wave. She didn't swim like the other old ladies, who waded into the ocean and patted their broiling arms with the cold water. Nanny pushed through the whitecaps and swam far out with powerful strokes.

Nonno saw me watching her and said, "I taught her to swim when she wasa little girl."

"I thought you met when she was in high school?"

"No, one time she came witha your Big Nanny to my home in Italy. She wasa only three years old and had these biga dark eyes."

"Josie, what happened to the letters they sent?" My aunt interrupted my mother's reading again.

"My father burned them when she couldn't sleep one night."

"What are they talking about, Nonno?"

"Nothing. You pay attention to everything buta your cards. See! I gotta full house."

Six months later, Nonno died. The phone call came in the middle of the night, and when I heard my mother wail, I knew what had happened. I spent the rest of the night under my bed shivering and crying. My world was shattered. I wanted desperately to bond with my grandmother in grief. She allowed me to hug her, but it only lasted for a second.

PART SIX

NEW YORK, NEW YORK
1908

TWENTY

"Frances, please help me," called Giovanna, trying to lift a crate of cucumbers. With the first payment from Nunzio's settlement, they were lucky enough to rent a basement at 242 Elizabeth Street, only a block from their apartment. Giovanna was free to work each day with Rocco, and their efforts were paying off.

There had been a long line at Siena's Fruit and Vegetables when word swept through the neighborhood that they had broccoli rabe for a good price. It was late in the day, and Giovanna was only now getting to stack some of the fruit and vegetables. Rocco was tending to the horse and cart that enabled him to go to a distributor in Brooklyn for their produce.

"Frances, Mary, you girls head home with Angelina and put water on for the pasta. I'll be closing soon."

"Sì, Zia," obeyed Frances, taking Angelina's hand and bundling her up for the frigid weather.

"Buon giorno," greeted a man, tipping his hat to the girls who passed him on the stairs. The man, face covered in black moles, entered the store and looked around.

"What can I get you?" asked Giovanna.

"Signora, is your husband here?"

"No."

"Well, I'll come again then." He smiled, tipped his hat, and left.

Lieutenant Petrosino, holding the *New York Times,* waited outside the commissioner's office. He paced the anteroom, practicing what he was going to say. He had no problem talking about police business, but when he had to say something personal, he was afraid his English would fail him.

"Joe! Come on in here. Sorry you had to wait," called the commissioner, sticking his head out his office door. Commissioner Bingham was as tall and thin as Lieutenant Petrosino was short and squat. His graying hair and perfectly groomed mustache gave him a dapper appeal that conflicted with his authoritarian presence.

Petrosino remained standing, knowing full well that if he sat down it would only be a matter of minutes before the commissioner was up and circling the room, pounding on his mantel for emphasis, or surveying the street from his second-floor window.

"Commissioner, I want to thank you," said Petrosino, pointing to an article in the newspaper.

"Oh, Joe, don't be silly, you don't have to thank me. Those dandies don't know a thing about police work. I'd like to see those prissy-ass aldermen on the street for even an hour."

"Well, even so, my men and I want you to know how important it is to us to have a commissioner who understands that sometimes you have to teach a lesson with your fists."

"Don't you worry, Joe. If they bring it up again, I'll say the same thing." With his finger in the air he reenacted his speech. "I am the police commissioner! I am responsible for everything my men do! Petrosino is one of our best detectives. Of course he has to use force now and then!"

The lieutenant rewarded him with one of his rare smiles. "Bravo!"

Bingham finally sat down. The office had changed little since Teddy Roosevelt was police commissioner. "So tell me, what's on your mind, Joe? I know you didn't come here just to compliment me on my oratory."

Petrosino took his seat opposite the massive mahogany desk and waved a stack of papers. "Commissioner, I've read this new immigration law, and it wouldn't get a spider out of its web. We have more Italian ex-cons in New York City than in all of Italy! We have to get the Italian government to help us."

"That's not going to happen." The commissioner was picking lint off his trousers.

"They get back in! Remember Don Cascio Ferro, who we exiled after the barrel murder?" Petrosino asked. Bingham nodded. "He's back! My men found him, and we threw him on the next boat, but not before he rallied the hoodlums here. Commissioner, can't we go to the president?"

"Joe, as much as Teddy respects you, this isn't something he can take on. We'll have to go it alone. But I want you to know that I'm working on it, and I'll explain it all to you at the proper time." Bingham could see Petrosino's question forming and preempted him. "I promise you that you and I together will smash this band of criminals and anarchists your native land has given us." Bingham spoke with such drama that Petrosino knew it had been rehearsed and that it signaled the end of the discussion.

"Commissioner, I knew I could count on you. And you should know that even with all its loopholes, I'll use this new law to get rid of all the blackmailing schifosi we can."

Petrosino turned toward the door, and the commissioner patted him on the back. "That's right, Joe. We'll get your *shevosee,* and the world will know about it."

Siena's Fruit and Vegetables was a basement store, which meant that Rocco often saw his customers' feet before he saw their faces. He could tell the man now walking down the stairs was not coming to buy figs or any other produce by the artificial swagger to his steps. The bell rang as the door opened. Rocco continued to stack zucchinis, but out of the corner of his eye he could see a man looking around the room.

"You've got a really nice store here, Signore Siena. You don't want anything to happen to it. After all, you know how rough this neighborhood can be," said the man, who had black moles on his face.

Rocco didn't say anything, but his motions became louder. He threw a sack of potatoes onto the counter.

"Didn't I see you after the bombing of Paparo's store? What a shame, and less than a block from here," jeered the moled man.

Rocco slammed a crate to the floor.

"But for only fifty dollars a week, we'll make sure you stay safe."

"Disgraziato! Get out of here before I kill you with my own hands!" Rocco shouted.

"Signore," the moled man tipped his hat, "I will return."

It took only a week for the man with the moles to return. This time, he ignored Rocco and addressed Giovanna. "Signora, possibly you're not aware that we offered your husband protection for a small fee. It is a wise business investment."

"How dare you speak to my wife! Out!" Rocco's face contorted in rage.

The man backed out of the store, but his demeanor changed. "Signore, remember that the hard heads of the Calabresi can be broken. Good day, signora."

"Rocco, what was that about?"

"*Niente.*"

"Answer me, Rocco."

"It's a lazy mafioso who wants money to 'protect' us. Don't you have to get home?"

"Mary won't be home for another half hour, but I'm leaving," said Giovanna indignantly, gathering up Angelina. "I want to know if he returns. This is *our* store, Rocco."

As soon as they entered the apartment, Angelina began banging on the piano that was Giovanna's only indulgence from the first payment of Nunzio's money. Mary and Frances were both taking lessons, and although they played poorly, it still brought Giovanna great pleasure to hear music in her home. The dough that she had made that morning had risen, and she punched it down with more force than usual and formed it into two loaves, placing them on the stone marked SIENA.

"Angelina, why don't you go upstairs and see if Carmela is home?"

"Sì, Mamma," chirped Angelina, going out the door.

Giovanna leaned backwards out the open door, hands covered in dough, watching Angelina walk upstairs and knock on the neighbor's door. Limonata opened the door in an apron. The past two years had changed her from a wisp of a girl into a weathered woman with dyed blond hair who copied American fashions. Limonata's "husband" never materialized, and she survived on handouts from various boyfriends and from whatever Giovanna sent over.

"Limonata, can Angelina stay by you while I get dinner made?" Giovanna called.

"Of course! Come, Angelina."

"I'll have fresh bread later."

"Grazie, Giovanna—you're too kind," Limonata said, going back into her apartment.

Without Angelina's banging, Giovanna weighed the options. Later that night, she encouraged Rocco to pay them the money. "You saw Paparo's store. Do you want that to be us?"

"*Loro brutti puzzolenti mafiosi!*"

"All the curses in the world won't make them go away."

"I'll take care of it."

"How? You can't be there every hour! So don't pay the fifty dollars, but pay him *something.*"

It was overcast. Giovanna scanned the skies on the short walk to the store, deciding how much produce to place outside in the early spring air. Angelina clung to her hand. At nearly three, Angelina walked everywhere, but had a hard time keeping up with her mother's long strides.

Giovanna fished in her dress pocket for the store key. The bell clanged loudly when she opened the door.

Angelina ran to her favorite spot behind the counter and picked up a folded piece of paper that was on the floor. "Mamma, who made this drawing?"

Giovanna snatched it from her and looked.

"*Beware. Give the money or everything will be destroyed. La Mano Nera.*"

Beneath the words was the imprint of a thick hand in black ink.

"What does it say, Mamma?"

"Niente, niente." The bottom few feet of Rocco's horse and carriage were visible through the window. Giovanna panicked and stuffed the paper down her dress.

Looking into Angelina's face, she instructed, "This is nothing. Go help your papa."

Her heart pounding, she watched Rocco through the window lift the crates of fruit off the cart while Angelina picked up the pieces that fell along the way. Giovanna still looked shocked when he entered.

"Cos'è successo?" asked Rocco, confused. His wife never stood still or looked frightened.

Giovanna didn't have the strength to hide the letter. She took it from her dress and handed it to him.

The drawings were for the benefit of illiterates like Rocco, whose face turned purple. He slammed the paper and his fist onto the counter.

"What have you decided?" asked Lucrezia, handing back the letter to Giovanna.

"I want to pay something."

"And Rocco?"

"He says he will sleep in the store—he threatens to kill him with his own hands."

"See, if you were still a midwife you wouldn't be blackhanded, because they would know you had no money." Lucrezia's stab at levity failed, so she continued. "What about bringing the letter to Petrosino?"

"You saw what happened to Paparo's store! They brought the letter to Petrosino. Besides, Petrosino may be Italian, but he's still the police. Rocco would never allow it."

"What about DeCegli?"

"For what reason? So he can negotiate the payment?"

"Do you want me to talk to my husband?"

"No! Lucrezia, please say nothing. Forget I told you!"

It was possible the thief was smarter than Giovanna thought, because the next time that he visited, only Giovanna was in the store. Rocco had sworn to spend every minute in the shop, but Giovanna knew that was unlikely for a man who had spent his entire life outside.

"Signora, is your husband here?"

"No." Giovanna used her foot to feel under the counter for the wood pole that Rocco had spiked with nails.

He turned to go. "Let him know I was here, I have business with him."

"You want money from him."

The man turned back around. Giovanna could tell he wasn't comfortable dealing with a woman, but the mention of money was too strong a lure.

"How much do you want?"

"Fifty dollars a week for protection."

"That's too much. We don't have that kind of money."

"But, signora, I see your business. It's a good business. Surely you want to protect that."

"We can pay ten dollars."

"For you, signora, I will take the ten dollars. And when your business gets stronger, you'll want more protection."

He stood there staring, and Giovanna realized the *stronzo* wanted the money now. She grabbed ten dollars from the cash box and put it on the counter.

Taking the money, the thug said, "Today is Friday. I'll see you next Friday, signora."

TWENTY-ONE

Lorenzo noticed that Rocco had not said one word throughout the entire Sunday dinner. His comments were always rare, but usually he at least complimented Teresa on her meal. Giovanna and Rocco had not exchanged words or glances, but that, too, wasn't out of the ordinary.

"How are piano lessons going?" Lorenzo asked the girls.

His stepnieces answered excitedly, but he barely heard them. Instead, he studied his sister.

Giovanna did not notice Lorenzo's scrutiny because she was focused on avoiding eye contact with her husband. Rocco still had not spoken to Giovanna. On Friday, when he counted the money at the end of the day, Giovanna was forced to tell him about the payment. Rocco hadn't known where to direct his rage. One minute he was yelling at Giovanna, the next he was cursing the lazy schifosi. He swung his spiked wood at the invisible enemy. Giovanna had let him rant and didn't debate the issue. But after having spent her first day since the letter arrived not looking over her shoulder or jumping at every sound, she also knew that on the following Friday she fully intended to pay the thief another ten dollars.

While Rocco was furious, he was even more frustrated. Frustrated that he couldn't protect his family and frustrated that another man's money put his wife in this position of power.

On Friday, Giovanna took the ten dollars from the cash box and laid it on the counter when the Blackhander arrived. A short, fat bug of a man was with him this time. The moled man pocketed the money and commented, "I take it you've had no problems, signora?"

Giovanna waved her hand, both ignoring and dismissing him.

"Good day, signora. And good day, little signorina." The fat man smiled at Angelina, revealing a mouth of mostly missing teeth.

Rocco had invented a hundred reasons not to be in the store that day. He didn't trust that he wouldn't kill the blackmailer and put his family in danger. Besides, if his wife wanted to pay them, let *her* do it.

Giovanna cranked the awning down and struggled to get the barrels back into the store. Taking the day's diminished proceeds, Giovanna locked the door and headed home. She was alone because Frances had already picked up Angelina at closing time. Remembering that she hadn't gotten milk, she turned the corner onto Mulberry Street. A shiver ran down her spine when she realized she was being followed. She ducked into a fish store, pretending to shop, but when she turned around, she bumped into a short man wearing a derby.

"Signora, I am sorry I frightened you, but I didn't want anyone to see me go into your store."

Giovanna looked down and recognized the man's pockmarked face.

"I am Lieutenant Petrosino of the Italian Squad."

"I know who you are." Giovanna continued to scrutinize the fish.

"We can help you, signora. The police are not like they are in Italy. We can be trusted."

"I don't know what you're talking about," Giovanna said coolly, while inside she was panicking. Who could have told the police?

As if in answer, the lieutenant said, "I've seen suspicious men going into your store. Did they send you letters?"

"You must be mistaken, signore." Noticing glances in their direction from the other customers, she ignored him entirely and worked her way in among the women at the counter jostling for service. "Pescespada!" she called, and a moment later she was relieved to see that the lieutenant was not in sight. But when she exited the store, her swordfish wrapped in paper and tucked under her arm, he was there.

Petrosino walked quickly to keep up with her. "Signora, give us a chance. You are not trapped."

"Signore, I am Scillese. I have been trapped between a rock and a hard place my entire life." Turning back onto Elizabeth Street, Giovanna changed her tone. "I'm sorry, but you seem to have me confused with someone else." Lieutenant Petrosino held back and let her go.

"Zia! Swordfish!" squealed Mary when Giovanna walked in the door.

"But, Zia, I already made chi chi beans!" exclaimed Frances, wiping her hands on her apron and looking older than her twelve years.

"Well, tonight we'll have chi chi beans and swordfish."

Rocco, who was already home, looked at his wife suspiciously. Giovanna was glad they still weren't speaking.

A tall, thin man walked into Siena's Fruit and Vegetables. Giovanna recognized him as her neighbor, the cafe owner of 226 Elizabeth Street. "Signore Inzerillo," greeted Giovanna. "What can I get you?"

"Actually, signora, I came to see if I could be of assistance to you."

Giovanna looked skeptically at the dignified-looking man, who sported the thickest mustache she had ever seen.

"I've heard that gentlemen outside the neighborhood have been blackmailing you for money."

Stunned, Giovanna stared at the man before saying, "Is there a sign on my door that I didn't see?"

Pietro Inzerillo laughed. "Signora, little goes on in this neighborhood that's unnoticed."

It sounded too real to be amusing. "What is it you want to tell me, signore?" asked Giovanna.

"It's what I want to do for you. I've been here a while, and I hate to see fellow shopkeepers fall prey to these animals. Unlike the police, I know who these men are. I can influence their actions."

"And why would you do me this favor, signore?"

"Because you are my neighbor. I can offer you real protection. Not like the extortionists who only want your money. I will see to it that no one touches your family or store."

"Signore, are you offering to protect our store for a fee?"

"I am offering you a security service."

"How much does this security service cost?"

"As you're a new store owner, I would give you the lowest rate of thirty dollars per week, and I will have a man guard your store each evening."

"What if they come back?"

"I assure you, you will never see these men again."

Giovanna believed him. She didn't trust him at all, but she weighed her options: soon the moled man and his short, fat counterpart would demand the fifty dollars per week, and there was no doubt in her mind that they would indeed bomb her store. If she went to the policeman, someone in her family could be killed. If she paid the cafe owner thirty dollars a week, she always knew where to find him, and he would *have* to make good on his offer of protection.

"And if someone is not here each night or these men or other men come back, we can terminate our agreement?"

"Absolutely, signora. You are hiring me for a job, and unless you get the service, you do not pay. In fact, there is no need to pay me now. You'll see that you won't hear from these men, and I'll come see you next week."

Before the week was out, Giovanna felt forced to explain to Rocco the arrangement she had made with Inzerillo.

Rocco raged. "I can protect my own store! I don't need a Sicilian cafe owner to protect me! Thirty dollars a week? Are you crazy? That's all our profits!"

Giovanna couldn't stop Rocco when he stormed out of their store and headed down the block to Café Pasticceria. It was only eight stores down, so Giovanna watched Rocco stride into the cafe. She half expected him to be thrown out, but only a few minutes later Rocco walked back looking satisfied.

"He said he understood and that it was my decision. He also apologized for doing business with you. Go home. I will take care of this."

Giovanna bristled at the order, but she was sick of fighting.

From that point on, Giovanna no longer went to the store. Rocco was there continuously; the only time the store was vacant was during his trips to the produce distributor in Brooklyn. The children brought him his meals at the store, and he slept on a cot in the back room. Homemade weapons were hidden in every corner, and he hung mirrors in strategic locations so that no part of the store was hidden from his eye. Rocco was waiting. Even while helping customers or carrying boxes, he was waiting. He considered having Clement go to Brooklyn to get the produce so he would never have to leave, but he was afraid Clement would be ambushed. Instead, he put bars on the windows and doors for those rare times he was away.

The moled man and his sidekick visited the week after Rocco told Pietro Inzerillo he would not need his services. Rocco was ready, and before they even had a chance to get down the stairs, Rocco ran at them, brandishing the wood bat he had spiked, and the men ran off shouting curses. They got two more letters, but Rocco didn't even bother to have Giovanna read them to him.

When Rocco received the third letter, he lost his temper completely. He took all three letters, ran up the steps to the street, and threw them on the ground after igniting them with a match. Stamping on the burning letters, he shouted, "See this? This is what I think of your threats! May you burn in hell!" His rage and the fire cooled at the same time, and he noticed that life on Elizabeth Street had come to a halt as people stopped to watch. A woman crossed herself, and down the block he saw Pietro Inzerillo look at him and nod.

Rocco, confident that his defiance was witnessed, hoped it would incite the blackmailers. He was anxious to catch the rats red-handed with their weapons or bombs. He had decided to kill them.

With more free time than usual, Giovanna tended to travel farther when shopping and even brought Angelina to her old friend's store in Chinatown. It was during one of these visits that Giovanna once again bumped into Lieutenant Petrosino.

"Please, I told you, we have no problems." Giovanna continued to walk up the block, Angelina's hand clutched in hers.

"Is that why you are no longer in the store and your husband sleeps there?"

"This is none of your business."

"Signora, you appear to be an intelligent woman, so I am going to tell you a story." Petrosino, glancing at Angelina, spoke quietly. "Before there was the Italian Squad, there was a shooting on Mulberry Street. Me and another detective went to investigate. A young man was sprawled dead on the corner. An older man was standing over him, horrified. We asked, 'Who did this?' He said, 'I know nothing.' Then we asked him, 'Who is this man?' and he replied, 'I don't know.' Later that day we found out he was the dead man's father." Petrosino looked at Giovanna for a reaction.

"What does this story have to do with me, Lieutenant?"

"Signora, this fear is laying ruin to our people! A man denies his own son? Look, I know you are a strong woman, a brave woman. You would have to be to sue a big American company."

Giovanna's head snapped in his direction, her eyes flashing both anger and fear.

"Of course I know about it, signora. I'm a detective after all. But please, don't fool yourself into thinking no one else knows. It is probably one of the reasons you are being blackmailed."

Petrosino felt terrible when he saw the look of betrayal and bewilderment in Giovanna's face. "I'm sorry, signora, for upsetting you. Please don't blame anyone you know. It could have happened a hundred ways. Think about it. The payment went to a bank, didn't it? One of the clerks could have whispered something to someone. And besides, do you think it would have gone unnoticed that an immigrant won a case like this?"

From Giovanna's expression, Petrosino realized that he should end the conversation, but he also saw that he had got her thinking.

The next time Rocco saw the moled man and his fat accomplice, they were standing across the street from his store before dawn. He rode up in his cart laden with fruit. These were not the type of men to wake early. Rocco stopped the horse, jumped from his cart, and instead of running into his store, he grabbed a piece of wood and ran across the street toward them. Rocco swung at the tall moled one first.

"He's crazy! Pazzo!" shouted one to the other.

As the tall one ducked and attempted to throw a punch, out of the corner of his eye Rocco saw the fat one check his pocket watch. He dropped the board and ran toward his store. He was twenty feet from the entrance when the window blew.

Giovanna was stirring polenta when she heard the explosion. Not stopping to put on her coat, she ran down the steps to the street and was nearly run over by the No. 9 hook and ladder leaving the garage across the street. The smoke was exactly where she feared it would be. Most people were running away from the scene in shock and horror; she ran against the current of the crowd. The buildings opposite the store had had their windows blown out. For one brief moment she thought they had escaped being the target, but running forward, she saw policemen disappear into a cloud of smoke in front of their store.

Tripping over barrels, glass, and what she thought was a piece of their awning, she tried to make her way through the black smoke. She ran into a policeman who attempted to pull her back, but Giovanna broke away. Covering her face with her apron, she stumbled upon two policemen crouched over a man.

"He's alive," shouted one cop to the other. "Let's get him out of the smoke."

Giovanna followed them, and by the time they reached the opposite side of the street, she could see it was Rocco.

"Is the ambulance coming?" asked one cop of the other.

"Yeah. I'm going in to check the rest of the building. It shouldn't collapse because it blew out—probably not dynamite—but I want to make sure."

Looking up they saw Giovanna. "You his wife?"

Giovanna stooped over Rocco, examining him. He was unconscious. She checked his pulse, surprised to find it strong, and inspected his cuts. He was covered in blood, but the wounds appeared superficial.

"*Dell'acqua, per favore. Acqua*," implored Giovanna to the remaining cop.

"Lady, the ambulance is coming."

"Acqua."

"Could somebody bring water? I think she wants water."

A fireman came over with a bucket. Giovanna dipped her dress into the water and wiped the blood from Rocco's face. She then dripped water into his mouth; Rocco coughed.

"*Aiutami, aiutami.*" She motioned to the cop for help. Together they lifted Rocco and leaned him against the building. His eyes opened and closed.

A car pulled up. "Jesus Christ, that's Commissioner Bingham," the cop mumbled to himself. Turning to Giovanna, he said, "Lady, I'll make sure the ambulance gets here. Just wait. Okay?"

Giovanna nodded and watched him run off to join the other policemen gathering around the black car. At the same time, she saw Lorenzo galloping toward her.

"What happened? Giovanna, is he alright?" Not waiting for an answer, he said, "Madonna! I had a feeling this was going on. Let me get help."

Lorenzo returned with an Italian-speaking police detective. By now Rocco was conscious and even was trying to stand. Giovanna forced him back down.

"I saw them. I fought them," he stammered.

"You saw who?" asked the cop.

Turning to the unfamiliar voice and realizing it was a policeman, he stopped. "Nothing. I saw nothing."

"It is not a good time to talk to my husband. I want to get him to a doctor."

"Of course, signora."

On the other side of the block, Commissioner Bingham strode up to Lieutenant Petrosino exclaiming, "Jesus, Joe, what happened?"

"They wouldn't pay the protection money, and they wouldn't let us help. They're new store owners." Petrosino nodded toward Giovanna and Rocco.

"So it wasn't an attack on the precinct in any way?"

"I don't think so, Commissioner. I think it was a mistake. A little too much explosive."

Bingham lowered his voice. "Well, let's not tell anyone else that. We'll get more support if people think they tried to go after us. Any idea who did it?"

"I don't think it's Lupo. Too inexperienced."

Giovanna sat at Rocco's side in the hospital, and Clement paced the room. Rocco insisted that he could go home after having his cuts and bruises tended to, but he also had broken ribs, and Lucrezia and Giovanna forced him to stay. The harried doctors didn't look like they cared if the poor Italian stayed or went.

As devastated as Rocco was, he was grateful that Giovanna had not left his side and was ministering to him with devotion.

"Is there anything left?" Rocco asked his son.

"Nothing. Papa, why didn't you tell me? I would have left my job and worked with you!"

"Why, so you could lie here, or worse?"

They stopped talking at the sound of people approaching. Two men walked into the room. While not in uniform, they were clearly detectives. Lieutenant Petrosino followed a moment later. Having not told Rocco of her encounters with him, Giovanna tensed. Petrosino sensed her discomfort and ignored her.

"Signore Siena, you are a lucky man. It may not seem that way at the moment, but you are. I am Lieutenant Petrosino, and this is Sergeant Crowley and Detective Fiaschetti."

He was greeted with silence.

"The explosion in your store not only destroyed your business, it rocked our police headquarters. The commissioner is most anxious to know what happened. So are the newspaper reporters. What should I tell them, signore?"

Rocco shrugged. When Petrosino continued to wait for an answer, Rocco mumbled, "It blew up."

Gripping the bed rail to contain his anger, Petrosino blurted, "I was hoping for once someone would get so mad they wouldn't be afraid!"

Taking a minute to compose himself, but not hiding his exasperation, Petrosino continued. "Va bene. I know you are frightened, but it is not as if you remained safe without the police involved. Signore Siena, had you entered your store, you would have been blown to bits."

Petrosino, seeing the fear on everyone's faces, softened his tone. "Every time you say nothing, you make them stronger. Rotten scum like this makes us all look bad. With your cooperation, we can put them in jail and honest, hardworking people like yourselves will not have to live in terror. Please, tell us what you know, signore."

Rocco turned his face to the wall.

The lieutenant waited and then spoke. "Okay, I will tell you what *I* know." Petrosino leaned on the iron bars of the bed. "At approximately five twenty this morning, a bomb was set in the front of your store near the counter. I noticed that you had bars on your windows, signore, indicating that this has been going on for a while, although now those same bars are twisted like limp spaghetti. Do you want to know how they got in? I'm not certain, but my guess is that they had a key to your back door. They were careful to do damage only to your store by using a bomb instead of dynamite. You see, dynamite forces the explosion down, and this type of bomb explodes out. But, while they are ruthless, they are not always expert. The bomb was bigger than they needed, and its force shook half the block."

Petrosino walked to the other side of Rocco's bed and looked him straight in the face. "That is all I know, although I can guess much more. I imagine they came to you for money; they might have even called it 'protection money.' That is their new tactic. Being an honest man, you probably refused to give it to them. Or," he said, "you didn't give them enough." Petrosino put his derby back on.

"Signore, you just lost your hard-earned store. I don't pretend that I can make everything right, but we can put these criminals behind bars by working together. You get better, signore, and we'll talk again." He turned and tipped his hat to Giovanna. "Good day, signora."

For days, Giovanna did not go out. She did not want to run into Petrosino. Avoiding her neighbor Pietro Inzerillo was more difficult. Sure enough, her first time out of the house, she had to listen to him express his condolences and say, "If only I was allowed to be of service to you."

They sold the horse and cart so that Rocco could set himself up as a street vendor once again. If passing the boarded-up store was not reminder enough of the tragedy, the back-breaking work of pushing the cart didn't allow him to forget.

Rocco and Giovanna argued long and loud after Lieutenant Petrosino's second "chance encounter" with them on the street. Giovanna's feeling was that they had nothing to lose, so why not cooperate in hopes of seeing justice served. But Rocco's mistrust of the police led him to believe that something even worse could happen if the police were involved. Giovanna was beginning to like Petrosino and trust him, and in spite of Rocco's suspicions—and vows to kill the Blackhanders himself—she could tell that he, too, liked the little lieutenant.

A month later, Giovanna announced, "Rocco, I will work with Petrosino. You never have to be seen with him. If they are watching at all, they'll be watching you."

After more than four years of marriage to this man, she was learning the signs. He didn't say yes, but there was no tirade, which meant that Giovanna could proceed as she wanted without Rocco having to bruise his pride by acquiescing.

TWENTY-TWO

In just one meeting, Lieutenant Petrosino realized that he would not be the only one asking the questions. If Giovanna was going to help, she made it known that she was going to have to understand the situation, and on that first morning, Giovanna's education into the ways of the Black Hand began.

Petrosino admitted to himself that Giovanna intimidated him. She towered over him, and when she asked questions, her blue eyes were so penetrating that it seemed she would instantly know if he was hedging or not telling the truth. Ruthless crooks were easier to deal with, yet despite his discomfort, he had grown to like this big woman who now sat at an oak table in his cramped precinct office.

Giovanna was poring through stacks and stacks of identification cards. On the front of each card were two photos—a profile and a full-face shot. On the back were words and numbers that were gibberish to Giovanna, and not only because she didn't speak English.

After more than two hours of scrutinizing each photo, Giovanna walked over to Petrosino's desk. "Lieutenant, I have found an important similarity about these Blackhanders."

Lieutenant Petrosino responded to her solemn expression. "Yes, signora, please tell me."

"They are all ugly." Giovanna slapped her face in an expression of ugliness. *"Brutti, tutti sono brutti."*

It was the first time Giovanna heard the lieutenant laugh, and it escaped like something that had been in hiding.

"Sit, sit, signora," Petrosino said, still chuckling and motioning to a chair in front of his desk.

"What does all this say?" Giovanna asked, pointing to the card's back.

"It's the Bertillon measurements; it's how we identify the criminals. Although now there's a new method. You put black ink on fingers and make prints. Each one is unique—like a little map."

Giovanna remembered the black-ink handprint on one of the letters and silently cursed Rocco for destroying them. Pointing at the titles on the card, she asked, "But here, what do these words say?"

"Height, weight, head length, outer arms, trunk, forearm . . ."

"Are you arresting them or making them new suits?"

Once again, the lieutenant chuckled.

"Who's that ugly one?" asked Giovanna, pointing to a photo pinned to Petrosino's wall.

"That is 'Il Lupo.' In English, 'The Wolf.'"

"He looks more like that kind of dog without a snout. What is that?"

"A bulldog! Yes, you're right! We've arrested Lupo many times but have never been able to keep him in jail."

"I think my stepson saw him in the Star of Italy."

"I'm sure he did. It's one of his haunts. My affair with Lupo began in 1902. He murdered a man, but we didn't get the evidence we needed. Then in 1903, I had proof he was involved in the barrel murder I told you about, but he was mysteriously cleared by the jury. Later that year, he was arrested for kidnapping, and again they let him go."

"How does this happen?"

"Influence and fear. He pays people in high places, and if the case makes it to a jury, he frightens them. They think he will have them killed or curse their entire family with the evil eye. He's worked hard on creating a reputation as someone with powers. His newest trick is he is pretending to be a respectable businessman with a grocery store on Mott Street. Not unlike your neighbor Pietro Inzerillo."

"Do this Lupo and Inzerillo work together?"

"Sì. Inzerillo was arrested for the barrel murder with Lupo, and they're often together. Now that you've seen his picture, I wouldn't be surprised if you notice Lupo in Inzerillo's cafe."

Giovanna gagged on the thought that she had come close to engaging a murderer to protect her store, but she forged on. "So why do you think that Lupo wasn't involved in the blackmail of my store?"

"I didn't say that exactly. I doubted Lupo was involved, based on the sloppy explosion. But even if he was, I have nothing to go after Lupo with. You didn't exchange money with Inzerillo, and he presented his offer with no threats. I could never prove blackmail."

"So the only thing to do is find the moled man and fat bug?"

"Yes, signora, many crimes lead to Lupo. But hundreds more do not. There are thousands of Italian criminals in New York. There are so many of them that shopkeepers are being blackhanded by three different crooks or gangs at the same time."

"But why so many?"

"When criminals get out of jail in Italy, the police make their life miserable, so they bribe their way onto ships. Usually they arrive in New York with the name of another criminal in their pocket. That thief gives him food and shelter in exchange for swindling shopkeepers since no one will know the newcomer's face. When the job is done, if we are investigating, they just go to another city."

"And the Americans can't stop them getting in?"

"We're trying, signora. The American laws are loose, and only now is the Italian government starting to cooperate with us."

A noticeable change took place in the lieutenant's demeanor. He had been speaking forcefully, and with this last question he looked defeated, so Giovanna changed the topic.

"Ah, there is a pretty face!" exclaimed Giovanna, pointing to a picture of a woman on his desk.

Giovanna swore she saw Petrosino blush. "This is my wife." He turned the picture toward Giovanna. "My Adelina."

Giovanna could tell he had more to say. "Any children?"

"In November we will have our first," he said with both embarrassment and pride.

"Bravo!" Spying a gold-embellished certificate from Italy on the wall, Giovanna asked, "What's that, Lieutenant?"

"After King Umberto was assassinated, I tracked down the anarchist in Paterson who pulled the trigger."

"You are a hero, Lieutenant!" exclaimed Giovanna, sincerely impressed.

"Unfortunately," said Petrosino puffing up, "the second part of the story does not go so well. You see, at the same time I was doing my undercover work to get this killer, I discovered a plot by the anarchists to kill the American president. I went to my old friend Vice President Roosevelt. He was the police commissioner when I started on the force, and I warned him, but they didn't take the threat seriously."

Giovanna stared blankly at the lieutenant, and he realized she didn't know what he was talking about.

"The American president, McKinley, was assassinated in 1901, signora."

"Oh, I was still in Italy, Lieutenant."

Petrosino saw that Giovanna was embarrassed and went back to the issue at hand. "So, beyond ugly faces, there were none that looked like your two Blackhanders?"

"Not completely. If I take the eyes of one and put them on the cheeks of another . . ."

"Signora, see here on the card, it says, 'remarks.' This card says, 'tattoos on both arms.' Look for the word 'mole' in English. It's written like this." Petrosino wrote the letters in lead pencil. "You might not see the moles so well in the photograph, but it could be in the notes."

"M-o-l-e. Va bene. Lieutenant, you said that when the crime is done, sometimes the swindlers leave town. So, if I find the names of these crooks and they've left, can you still get them in another city?"

"It's complicated, signora. In America you can change your name every day with no penalty."

"So it is hopeless."

"No, signora, not at all. Difficult, yes. Hopeless, no. So," sighed Petrosino, taking the stack of photographs from her and handing her another, "I'm afraid you must look at more ugly faces."

Lucrezia read and translated into Italian as dramatically as the text was written. "'The skull and crossbones flag of piracy is gone from the seas. But in our cities flourishes the Black Hand, a symbol every bit as significant of greed and cruelty—even more an emblem of cowardice and treachery. The scoundrels who lurk behind the terror of the Black Hand wax fat and daily grow more arrogant in their contempt for American law and order.'"

"What are you reading from?" Giovanna asked Lucrezia.

"It's *Everybody's Magazine*. I got it from my husband and thought you'd be interested. You haven't told me much about your dealings with Petrosino."

"There's not much to tell. Read more."

Lucrezia leafed through the article. "Here's the part about the name that I was telling you about. 'Back in the Inquisition days in Spain, there was La Mano Nera, a secret society that fought the government and the church. It passed, and the secret societies of southern Italy were its heirs. Twenty years ago, a false report was raised in Spain that La Mano Nera had been revived. The story lingered in the brain of a *New York Herald* reporter and one fine day he attempted to rejuvenate waning interest in a puzzling Italian murder case by speculating as to the coming to life of the Black Hand among immigrants in America. The other newspapers seized on the idea eagerly and kept it going.'"

"Petrosino said there is no organization, that it is a bunch of thugs."

"Well, apparently this writer agrees with him. 'The terror of the Black Hand now is tremendously increased by its mystery. The mystery will never be revealed, because there is nothing tangible to reveal. The police have not been battling with a complicated and secretly united murdering graft machine, but with individual produces of the opportunities for criminal education afforded by southern Italy for hundreds of years.'"

"Let me see that," said Giovanna, taking the article from Lucrezia. A copy of a Black Hand letter was reproduced on the page and, because it was written in Italian, she read it herself.

"These people got a much longer letter than we did! Listen, 'This is the second time that I have warned you. Sunday at ten o'clock in the morning, at the corner of Second Street and Third Avenue, bring three hundred dollars without fail. Otherwise we will set fire to you and blow you up with a bomb. Consider this matter well, for this is the last warning I will give you. I sign the Black Hand.' This is definitely not from the same scoundrels. Even the drawing is different."

"Yes, detective," smirked Lucrezia.

Giovanna ignored her. "You know, Lieutenant Petrosino told me two

Russian Jews used the name Black Hand to scare money out of a real estate dealer."

Lucrezia recognized Giovanna's intellectual interest in all this and asked, "Giovanna, tell me, what do you hope will come of all this?"

"I don't know, Lucrezia. I'm beginning to realize that they might not find the brutti lowlifes who did it. But it doesn't matter. How can I sit back and do nothing?"

"I suppose I'll continue to have no help in the next few months delivering babies?"

"If you need me, you get me."

Lucrezia muttered, "I'll take that as a no."

Giovanna and Lucrezia squeezed into a courtroom bench. The chambers were packed with expectant onlookers and reporters. Lieutenant Petrosino had told Giovanna about the case of Signore Spinella, a tailor who confessed to his priest that he was receiving Black Hand letters. The priest, against Spinella's wishes, went to the police. The detectives watched Spinella's store and, soon enough, they saw a man enter who they were sure was a crook. When the man left, they questioned the frightened tailor, who finally admitted that indeed this man was blackmailing him.

Now the blackmailer was on trial, and Giovanna, after persuading Lucrezia to accompany her, came to see American justice at work.

The tailor was a slight man, and his nervousness on the witness stand was evident. The poor man had to be prodded again and again by the prosecutor to tell his story. Finally, the prosecutor asked, "Is the man who threatened you in this room?"

The tailor was silent and anxiously glanced around the courtroom.

The prosecutor posed the question again even more dramatically. "Is this the man who threatened you?" he shouted, pointing to the defendant.

But the tailor wasn't looking at the defendant. Instead he saw a man leaning against the wall slowly draw his finger across his throat.

"No, I don't see him here," blurted the tailor.

Gasps filled the courtroom.

"Isn't this the man who threatened you?" shouted the prosecutor, now thumping on the defendant's shoulder.

"No, that's not him," mumbled the tailor.

The man leaning against the wall quickly left while the judge gaveled the room silent. In desperation, the frustrated prosecutor asked again and again, until the judge pronounced the case dismissed.

Giovanna was stunned. She looked at the tailor disdainfully, but when she saw him rejoined by his weeping wife and children, she sighed knowingly. She could see the disgust on Lucrezia's face but couldn't read it. At times like this, Giovanna suspected that Lucrezia's contempt for the uneducated, poor immigrants surfaced. Or was she frustrated with a system that couldn't protect them? Giovanna herself could not answer the question.

Petrosino's cough rattled his chest and the office walls.

Giovanna wiped the perspiration from her own forehead with a handkerchief she had woven and embroidered with the initials G.C., because if she used either of her married names she felt like she was betraying someone. The heat in the room was oppressive.

"You must see a doctor, Lieutenant," counseled Giovanna. "Sometimes summer brings the worst lung illnesses."

"My wife agrees," answered Petrosino, drinking water.

Following her experience in court, Giovanna lost some of her enthusiasm for finding the blackmailers, but she still met regularly with Petrosino, from whom she continued to learn more about this secret society that was in actuality neither secret nor a society. She now knew that the role of Sicily's Mafia or the Camorra of Naples was limited to aiding and abetting the criminals in their travels between the countries. She agreed with Petrosino that Lupo's gang hadn't been involved in the blackmail of their store. All the signs pointed to one of the small gangs of blackmailers that came and went in Little Italy. She decided that if Rocco had killed their Blackhanders, that might have been the end of it. At least until the next one came along.

"Keep your eyes on Inzerillo's cafe, signora. The Wolf has disappeared," said Petrosino between coughs.

"What? Lupo is gone? What of his store?"

"He claimed bankruptcy. He took what money he had and left his creditors behind."

"So, Lieutenant, this is good news, yes? At least he is gone."

"No, signora. It only means I don't know where he is." Petrosino punctuated his sentence with his wracking cough, which would not stop.

"Lieutenant, there is no need to wait. You should see the doctor," said Giovanna, standing. She handed him his derby.

Petrosino, not having the energy to fight, took his hat and left.

Two weeks later, when word reached Giovanna that Petrosino was home with pneumonia, Giovanna asked Lucrezia to go with her to visit him. Carrying homemade chicken soup and a variety of herbal remedies in the July heat, they walked to his apartment at the corner of Lafayette and Sullivan. Fiaschetti, the young barrel-chested detective who had accompanied Petrosino to the hospital after the bombing, stood guard outside the door to his apartment.

"Signora! What are you doing here?"

"I brought soup."

"I'll be back in a minute."

Lucrezia gave Giovanna a look that said, "What did you get me into?" She wasn't accustomed to being left waiting in hallways.

"Signora Petrosino said to come in," announced Fiaschetti upon returning.

A pregnant Adelina Petrosino greeted them at the door. "How kind of you to come."

"I am so sorry the lieutenant is ill. This is my friend Signora LaManna, who is a doctor."

Adelina looked at Lucrezia sideways and said, "Thank you, but the doctor has been to see him. He will be fine if he rests."

In the uncomfortable moment that followed, Giovanna and Lucrezia stole glances at the large but modest apartment.

"Adelina, who is there?" called Petrosino from the bedroom.

"I'm sorry, I didn't get your name."

"Signora Siena."

Adelina walked into the bedroom and spoke to her husband. When she returned, she said, "He would like to see you for a minute."

Giovanna, nudging Lucrezia to go with her, walked inside.

Lieutenant Petrosino was propped up on pillows. His face looked drawn, but in Giovanna's quick assessment, she decided he would recover.

"This is Dottore LaManna, my friend."

"It's an honor, Dottore."

"Signora LaManna, Lieutenant."

"Signora Siena has told me all about you, Dottore. So I assume she brought you here to see if I will live."

Giovanna laughed. "Oh, you'll live alright, but only if you are tied to this bed."

"I will tell you this confidentially: the one good thing about my illness is I think it made everyone feel guilty enough to allow the commissioner to expand the Italian Squad."

"Congratulations, Lieutenant!"

"I'm not sure much will happen in my absence."

"You rest, Lieutenant. Even I am taking time off. I'm going to Scilla with my daughter in just one week. It has been a long time since I've seen my family."

"Good for you, signora! I suppose it was doctor's orders," he commented, winking at Lucrezia.

"I can see what a perceptive detective you are," answered Lucrezia, smiling.

Saying good-bye to Adelina at the door, Giovanna could not help but notice that Adelina was carrying well and the pregnancy appeared healthy.

Cedar Grove, New Jersey, 1973

"'Put money into one loaf of the bread and deliver to Rossi. Make the loaf darker than the others.' Mamma! How much money do we have?"

"Five or six dollars."

"I mean all the money!"

"But, Pop, I only have one more year and then I'll be a teacher."

"What can we do? You know what happened to little Marisa."

"I could talk to Lieutenant Petrosino."

"This is a private affair. Private business."

"This isn't Sicily, Papa. Here the police are on our side. Lieutenant Petrosino, he's Italian like we are."

"No! I told you! No!"

The clicking of my grandmother's knitting needles was bothering me, so I turned up the TV. It was Sunday afternoon, and I was watching an old black-and-white movie. A baker in the movie had decided not to pay extortion money after his daughter cried, and now the bad guys were breaking into his store. I cringed. It was a horrible scene. They had the guy tied to a chair and were cracking eggs over his head before they put him in a brick oven.

"Does it go this way or that way?" asked my grandmother, turning around the paper on which I had drawn a peace sign.

Without turning away from the TV, I flipped the peace sign right side up. "This way."

"Do you like the orange?"

"Yes, I like it." I tried not to show my exasperation at being interrupted again because she was doing me a favor by knitting a patch for my jeans.

As politely as possible, I turned my attention back to the guy from McHale's Navy who was playing an Italian cop.

"That's so loud," complained Nanny.

"You keep talking."

"Turn it down. What are you watching anyway?"

"Some old movie about the Mafia."

"You shouldn't watch that garbage."

"I know, I know . . ." I was familiar with my grandmother's feelings about anything that was Mafia-related.

I was relieved. The good guy in the oven was saved and the Italian cop was interrogating him as he was brought out.

"Who did this to you?"

"Lupo and two others."

"Are you sure it was Lupo?"

The half-finished orange peace sign attached to Nanny's needles dropped to the floor. My grandmother tentatively rose from the crushed velvet La-Z-Boy and walked toward the TV, stopping before she got too close. She leaned sideways to look at the picture, acting as if she got too near the television it could hurt her. Nanny watched and listened for a few moments before gasping in air and clasping her hand to her mouth. For a second she seemed rooted to the checkered linoleum.

"Turn it off!" she shouted, before storming up the den stairs into the kitchen. I heard her continue up the second set of stairs leading to the bedrooms.

My grandmother was not beyond throwing a fit, but this seemed odd. I was torn between wanting to finish watching the movie—now the baker's daughter was being attacked in a dark hallway—and my curiosity about why my grandmother was acting so weird. It didn't occur to me to be concerned; Nanny wasn't the kind of person who evoked worry or sympathy. Even at the worst of times, she was strong and eerily detached. Eventually, curiosity and guilt won out.

Nanny was in my room sitting on the edge of the bed.

"Did you turn that off?" demanded Nanny without looking at me.

"Yes," I lied. "What's the matter? I'm sorry if it was too loud."

"I told you not to watch that garbage."

"Nanny, not all Mafia stuff is garbage. You act like the Mafia's not real or something."

"Don't tell me! I know what's real and what's not!"

"Why are you screaming?"

"Because you don't know what you're talking about. Go do your homework!"

"I did it already. What's the big deal? It's a dumb old Mafia movie!"

"It's not the Mafia, it's the Black Hand!"

"Same thing."

"See! You know nothing!"

"They just said it! The movie's based on a true story, a cop named Petrosino fighting the Mafia."

"They killed him."

"Who?"

"The policeman, Petrosino."

"Did you see the movie?"

"No."

"Then how do you know he gets killed?"

She didn't answer.

"How do you know he gets killed, Nanny?"

That night, I left Nanny with my sister and went to the local pizza parlor parking lot to hang out with my friends. I had decided not to tell anyone, but that lasted about fifteen minutes.

"I'm telling you, Thea, my grandmother was kidnapped."

"That's so cool," Thea marveled.

"I don't think she thought it was cool. She was only four."

"How did they get her back?"

"I'm not sure. I think they paid a ransom or something. She didn't tell me much."

"Was it, like, Al Capone?"

"No, it was the Black Hand. They came before the Mafia."

"You gotta get her to tell you more."

"I don't think that's going to happen."

———

A few months later, my mother was stunned at my enthusiasm for attending the family reunion picnic. She kept looking at me out of the corner of her eye. It baffled me that my mother knew so little about the kidnapping. "That's so long ago. What do you care?"

Unlike my grandmother, who was stonewalling me, my mother honestly didn't have the information and didn't seem interested. But for me, it had become an obsession. I replayed scenes from the past, looking for clues. There was the obvious—Nanny yelling to get the strangers out of the house when my friends came to visit—but I needed to know more to be able to make sense of it all. For the first time, I truly tried to understand the tangled web of my family. It wasn't easy. Nanny and Nonno were cousins as well as husband and wife, and they weren't the only ones. Our family tree had so many diagonal lines it looked like it was covered in netting. I missed Nonno every day, but now I felt desperate for him.

There wasn't a hamburger or hot dog in sight at the family picnic. Trays of lasagna, eggplant parmigiana, swordfish, clams on the half shell, steamed mussels, calamari salads, veal rollatini, stuffed artichokes, and more covered the redwood picnic tables. The tuna casserole and noodle salad brought by the few cousins who had married non-Italians were politely put on a separate picnic table and went untouched.

I decided that Uncle Cakey, Nanny's younger brother, would be my best source. Nanny's older brother, Clement, and sister, Frances, were both dead. Aunt Mary lived in Wildwood and wouldn't be coming, and Aunt Etta was a lot younger than Nanny, so I figured she didn't know much.

Uncle Cakey was immediately drafted for a game of bocce, so I had to wait. When the game and bickering about whose ball was closer ended, I brought Uncle Cakey a glass of wine and steered him far away from my grandmother.

"So, Uncle Cakey, were you born when Nanny was kidnapped?"

"You know about that?"

I tried to sound nonchalant. "Yeah, of course."

He looked at me skeptically but answered. "I was born when they had your grandmother."

One of the old cousins walked by. "Dominick, my great-niece here wants to know about when they took Lena."

Dominick looked older than Uncle Cakey but was taller. He pulled up a folding chair.

"Yeah? Who's your mother?"

"Josie. I'm Angelina's granddaughter Anna."

"You look like her."

Cousin Dominick squeezed my face and gave me a kiss. "How old are you?"

"I'm sixteen . . . I saw this old movie about a cop named Petrosino."

"Oh, yeah, Petrosino, I knew him. I wanted to be a policeman."

"Did he help when my grandmother was kidnapped?"

"No, he was dead by then. I still remember his funeral. It didn't matter that he was Italian—everyone came. I had a friend who worked for him. Detective Forseti, Fachetti—something like that."

"So what exactly was the Black Hand?"

"Thugs. Black rats. You know they even tried to get money out of Caruso when he came to New York. My friend the detective got them that time."

"So was he the one that got Nanny back?"

"No, your great-grandmother got her back. I helped her, you know. She was smart, your great-grandmother. And strong. I loved Zia Giovanna. My father, Lorenzo, didn't live long like she did, but my mother, Teresa, God rest her soul, had eleven children and died at ninety-two."

"How did Big Nanny get her back?"

"Does your grandmother know you're asking all these questions?"

I lied. "Sure. But what does it matter?"

"Because you don't talk about it, that's all. Cakey, did you tell her about how people would wait around the block for our ice cream in Hoboken? If you want to hear old stories, that's what you should know."

"See this muscle?" Uncle Cakey jumped into the conversation by flexing his biceps. "The longshoremen didn't have muscles like this! We had to lift barrels of ice and rock salt. Even your grandmother had muscles from carrying the cream and condensed milk."

"Lena!" Cousin Dominick called Nanny. "Tell your granddaughter about our ice cream."

Nanny walked over, effectively ending my investigation. Within minutes Uncle Cakey was recounting in detail how they made the lemon ice.

"You cut the tits off the lemons . . . the barrels would go into rock salt . . ."

"Remember Mamma would say, 'Don't let Uncle Lorenzo buy the lemons! He's an artist. He always picks the lemons that look good, not the ones with the thin skins that you need.'"

Nanny actually chuckled at the memory, but I began to tune out. I was plotting my next move, because although I'd gotten a few answers, I ended up with more questions.

PART SEVEN

SCILLA, ITALY
AUGUST–DECEMBER 1908

TWENTY-THREE

Returning from the mountains, Angelina jumped down from her grand-father's shoulders and ran through the door of her grandparents' house in Scilla.

"Domenico, she'll soon bleat like a goat!" chided Concetta.

"My American granddaughter needs fresh milk!" he said proudly, leaving the milk and cheese on the table. Domenico was enraptured with Angelina. Her complexion and hair were far darker than anyone in the family, and he treated her like an exotic jewel.

Giovanna and Angelina had arrived in Scilla three weeks before. For the final leg of their journey, Cousin Pasquale had picked them up by boat from Reggio. As they sailed north past the beach of Marina Grande, turning the corner around the castle into the Chianalea, Giovanna had to stop herself from diving in and swimming to her parents, who waited on the dock.

Giovanna's initial euphoria over being back in Scilla was replaced by torrents of tears. Her mother's presence allowed her to be a vulner-able child, and she didn't leave her side. Days later, when the sobbing stopped, melancholy set in. Everywhere she looked evoked memo-ries, and always those memories included Nunzio. Her sadness was complicated by the guilt she felt for only thinking of Nunzio. It was days before it occurred to her that Rocco, too, came from Scilla. She forced herself to walk to the address where he said he grew up. The tiny stone house stared back at her, as foreign and impenetrable as her husband.

Nunzio's family, including his mother, Zia Marianna, all lived within a few feet of her own mother's house, and his family was with them each day. Angelina particularly liked playing with the children of Nunzio's sister, Fortunata. The girls treated her like a porcelain doll and giggled when Angelina spoke in an Italian that had been bastardized by English. Fortunata's twelve-year-old boy, Antonio, took Angelina fishing and taught her to swim. Antonio looked so much like his Uncle Nunzio that at first Giovanna found it unnerving; he didn't have Nunzio's red hair, but he had his handsome face and tall, thin build. He also had his uncle's curiosity. After a while, Giovanna not only took comfort in the boy's presence but fantasized that Antonio would marry Angelina and her grandchildren would have Nunzio's blood.

"How beautiful, Nonna!" squealed Angelina, running her fingers over the embroidered flowers on the white dress.

"Let's try it on," said Concetta, slipping the dress over her grand-daughter's head. "There. You're going to be the prettiest girl at the feast!"

"Will there really be fire in the sky, Nonna? That's what Nonno said."

"For once your Nonno isn't telling stories!"

"Thank you, Mamma," whispered Giovanna to her mother. There were times in New York that Giovanna thought she would never see an-other proper Feast of Saint Rocco, the patron saint of Scilla. But tonight she would walk in the procession with her daughter, and, as usual, her father would be one of the men to shoulder the statue of Saint Rocco through the streets.

"Look at Nonno!" pointed Angelina, giggling. Her grandfather came down the stairs in his blue shirt and red neck scarf.

"You're getting too old to carry the statue, Domenico," chided Concetta.

"Too old! Who carries our granddaughter each day on his shoul-ders?!" he said, tickling Angelina.

At the church, Domenico went with the men to retrieve the ten-foot statue for the procession. It was to be carried, as it had been for more than a hundred years, from the church, through the streets of Scilla, borne on an ornate litter atop the shoulders of twenty men. The band of the City of Scilla, dressed in uniforms with sashes across their chests, followed the statue and all the men of the Saint Rocco Society. Behind the band walked the population of Scilla.

"Antonio, why does Saint Rocco point to his knee?" Angelina asked her cousin, who walked beside her.

"Shhh, Angelina."

"Where did you get that cap?" she whispered, ignoring him.

"Your mother gave it to me. Now be quiet," reprimanded Antonio.

"Okay, but how much farther?"

"Soon we will be at the chiazza, and you will see the fireworks," assured Antonio.

Angelina was half asleep on her mother's shoulder when they finally reached the chiazza, but with the first explosion she was wide awake. Giovanna watched the reflection of the fireworks and the wonder in her daughter's eyes. It was the first time during this trip to Scilla that she was creating a memory instead of evoking one.

"The boat's coming in, Angelina. Let's see if they caught the last of the swordfish," said Domenico to his granddaughter.

It was difficult for Domenico to no longer be able to fish. He kept hoping that the pains in his arms and legs that kept him from sailing would go away, but when the second swordfish season without him at sea came and went, he realized that this was the curse of old age.

From the front door of the Costa home to where the boats docked was less than twenty feet. Angelina watched the boat that looked like a strange insect rowing back to shore.

"Nonno, why is the man up in the air?"

"To look for the swordfish. He calls to the others when he sees one. They are smart, these fish, and they feel you coming. You must sneak up on them. The man at the front, he throws the spear on the caller's direction."

The boat neared the dock, and the man on the pole waved. Angelina realized it wasn't a man at all, but Antonio. The person holding the spear was Antonio's father, Giuseppe, and his other two sons, Salvatore and Franco, were at the oars. Angelina jumped up and down and waved.

From the door to the house, Giovanna watched with a smile on her face, pleased that Angelina and Antonio genuinely liked each other.

Within thirty feet of the shore, Giuseppe called, answering Domenico's unasked question. "Nothing, Domenico. We netted a few fluke, that's all."

Domenico helped them reel in the boat by winding the chain and pulling the boat onshore.

"What can you see up there?" Angelina asked Antonio.

"Everything. Dolphins, fish with bright stripes, the mermaids . . ."

"Mermaids! Take me to see the mermaids!" Angelina exclaimed.

"The mermaids won't show themselves if they know you are looking."

"Antonio! Stop filling her head with nonsense and help me with this net," scolded Giuseppe.

"Antonio sees everything but the swordfish!" joked his older brother Salvatore.

In October, the issue as to whether, and when, Giovanna would return to New York hung in the air. Her parents wanted to ask, but they didn't, far too content to have their daughter and granddaughter with them. It was Angelina who brought it up at the dinner table. "Mamma, when will we see Papa?"

Her question was greeted in silence. Eventually, Concetta spoke. "You know, Giovanna, with some work we could fit everyone here."

"He would never come here. He belongs to America."

The silence continued throughout dinner and the remainder of the evening. Giovanna knew she must decide. She had just received a letter from Rocco in Frances's handwriting. The letter said that Mary missed her and wanted Giovanna to meet her new teacher. Giovanna knew this was Rocco's way of asking her to come back.

Giovanna had not told her parents anything about the bombing of the store. She could sense that as much as they wanted her to stay in Scilla, deep down they believed she must return to New York. Had she told them, Giovanna knew they would have been worried and conflicted. She realized that with Nunzio gone, all that was left was duty. If she stayed in Scilla, she would still not have her love—but she also would not have her honor.

That night, Giovanna wrote to Rocco telling him that she and Angelina would return to New York City within the month. But she also wrote that her return was based on the understanding that with the next payment from Nunzio's settlement, they would move away from Elizabeth Street.

TWENTY-FOUR

Antonio climbed into bed after the long Christmas weekend. Christmas had fallen on a Friday this year, and for three long days he had not gone fishing.

It had been a particularly large Christmas dinner. His family had been joined by Zia Concetta and Zio Domenico, and his neighbors, the Cubellis, who had just returned from l'America. Antonio's father, Giuseppe, would punctuate Signore Cubelli's sentences with "Did you hear that?" every time he described the horrors they had to endure in l'America. Much to his father's displeasure, in the two months since Giovanna and Angelina had returned to New York, twelve-year-old Antonio never missed an opportunity to voice his determination to go to l'America.

"Did you see my Zia Giovanna in l'America?" Antonio asked Signore Cubelli.

"L'America is big, Antonio!" chided the signore. "We were in a place called Pennsylvania. I worked from morning till night in a factory, never seeing the sun. The padrone would take our wages and put them in a bank. He said that our money would grow. I should have known not to believe something so stupid! Vegetables grow! Fungus grows! When the factory closed, so did the bank—with all our money in it!"

"Did you hear that, Antonio?" shouted Giuseppe.

"Giuseppe, let the boy eat," reprimanded Fortunata, protecting her son. She knew her husband's admonishments about l'America to be futile. Theirs was destined to be a divided family. There were few men left in Scilla for her daughters to marry, and it was only a matter of time before they received marriage inquiries from friends and family who had already immigrated to America. As for her sons, she knew the older boys, Orazio and Raffaele, would stay in Scilla; they already had their own families and boats. But she speculated that her younger sons, Salvatore, Franco, and especially Antonio, would be lured to the shores of l'America by the torch-wielding siren.

Twisting and turning on the straw mattress he shared with Salvatore and Franco, Antonio reached out and grabbed his cap given to him by Zia Giovanna. It was of fine wool, but most impressive was the hat's silky lining. Fantasizing about his future in America and the fine suit he would wear, he fell asleep.

A hand shook Antonio's shoulder. Even without light, he could tell his parents were up earlier than usual. It meant that they were rowing the women to Messina for work before going fishing and that his father was anxious to cast his nets after three days of rest. He heard his nephew crying to be fed, and Antonio watched his mother and sister-in-law shush him. They were waiting to feed the baby on the boat since the combination of milk and the lull of the gentle waves would put him back to sleep.

After dressing quickly, he headed outside to help his father. His older brothers, Orazio and Raffaele, were readying the boat that they shared next to their father's slightly larger skiff. His brothers' wives climbed onboard, babies at their breasts.

The men worked in silence. Only the sound of the chains unwinding from the great spools and releasing the boats into the sea cut into the predawn darkness. The chill of the December morning increased the family's efficiency, and soon the two boats set off on a particularly placid sea just before five in the morning.

Giuseppe's boat was full. Antonio, his older brother Salvatore, and his younger brother, Franco, had gone fishing with their father from the time that each of them turned six years old. Today, even the boys' two older sisters were aboard. Fortunata thought that the wealthy woman in Messina would have even more work for them after the Christmas holiday.

"I'll row," said Giuseppe, uncharacteristically, to his sons. Antonio noticed that his father kept looking around as if a storm was approaching, but the sky was clear and the sea calm. His brothers also seemed to be studying the cliffs and the water.

"Papà, che cosa fa?"

"Niente, Antonio." The unnatural tone in Giuseppe's voice made Fortunata look up at her husband.

"It is nothing. The birds and fish are just skittish today."

Giuseppe raised his oars and turned away from his wife. He looked across at his older sons who silently shrugged in answer to his expression. They were two hundred yards from shore, heading south into the strait of Messina.

Giuseppe dipped his oars back in the water. A slow, growling noise made him scan the skies again. Still nothing, but before he had time to register his confusion, the rumble grew in decibels until it was louder and more resonant than the thunder of the worst storm.

Pulling the oars in, Giuseppe pushed his family off their seats to the bottom of the boat. Barely a second later, the boat rose out of the sea as if a mighty underwater power had lifted it skyward. They were atop a mountain of water and, for a second, Giuseppe was certain that he even saw the sea's bottom below them. The boat stayed on the wave as it collapsed. The initial rumbling roar turned into the sound of a thousand bombs bursting and was quickly followed by a torrential rain.

The sea was swelling in every direction, and Giuseppe managed to get his oars back in the water. Yelling to his sons to do the same, he struggled to see their boat through the sheets of rain. The explosive noises gave way to ear-splitting cracks. Giuseppe caught glimpses of Scilla. It was as if God was a sculptor and was swinging his hammer at a chisel in the cliffs. Crashes and a sinister hissing followed the cracking of the rock. Straining to see, Antonio pulled himself up and squinted over the edge of the boat and watched in horror as much of Scilla collapsed.

After the first few houses in the Chianalea fell like sand, the dust and smoke from onshore obscured most of what could be seen beyond the pelting rain and hail. The boat was violently spun around, but not before Antonio saw parts of Castello Ruffo fall into the sea. Farther across the strait in Messina, they could see nothing but flames.

As they cascaded over a swell, Giuseppe stood straining to see through the rain and black smoke filling the strait. Looking up, Antonio saw horror on his father's face. Giuseppe yelled to Orazio and Raffaele to catch the rope that he threw in the direction of their boat. Muttering prayers, Fortunata kept trying to raise her head, only to have it pushed down again by her husband. Giuseppe grabbed one oar and shouted to Antonio and Salvatore to grab the other. "Hold tight the oars, sons!" he shouted. Antonio struggled against the rain and wind to raise himself from the floor of the boat onto the seat. Grabbing the oar and sitting upright, Antonio saw what his father had already seen. A fifty-foot wave, as tall as the cliffs that were now dust, was heading west in the strait for Messina.

Giuseppe had tied his boat to his sons' boat. Antonio knew that this was not safe and that it meant that his father thought they had no chance of staying in their boats. It was a desperate attempt to keep his family within reach. They were north of the strait and would avoid being swept into the tsunami, but when it hit Messina, they would have to survive its aftermath.

"Listen to me," shouted Giuseppe to his boys. "Hold tight to the oars and push back on the swells. Keep your oar to the wave, when it shifts, you shift."

"Sì, Papa!" screamed Antonio, pulling the oar toward him. Young Franco was pushed to the bottom of the boat, and Salvatore was frozen in fear. "Do you understand, Salvatore? Salvatore!" There was a flicker of recognition.

"Fortunata, no matter what, don't let the children up!"

Sounds collided and smoke momentarily cleared when the tidal wave smashed into Messina. The entire port of Messina disappeared. The wave receded, and the sea rushed through the streets and buildings as if they were pebbles on the beach. Giuseppe and his sons braced themselves and watched in horror as the catastrophic wave pulled back over thousands of years of civilization.

The sky became pitch black from the momentarily extinguished flames so they couldn't see the first wave to crash into them. The two boats were thrown at one another. Antonio emerged from the wave coughing, and in a second his father was shoving his own oar into Antonio's hands. Through the slaps of water on his face, Antonio could see glimpses of the sinew of his father's arms dragging his sisters-in-law and their babies into the boat. His brothers' boat was nearly severed in half and was starting to pull down on their boat. Having gotten their wives onboard, his brothers were using the rope to pull their way through the foam. As soon as Orazio and Raffaele reached the boat, Giuseppe cut the rope loose, and what was left of his sons' boat disappeared beneath the foam.

Raffaele and Orazio each grabbed an oar and shared the seat with Antonio and Salvatore. Giuseppe moved to the prow shouting instructions to his oarsmen.

"Don't fight, ride them!" rasped Giuseppe. "Here comes one to the left. Use your oars to stay in the boat. Steady!" The boat rode the crest of the wave and was delivered hundreds of feet northwest. Giuseppe said a prayer of thanks because his goal was to get as far north of the strait as possible. His relief was short-lived. They were hit by another wave, knocking them back and nearly overturning the boat. Giuseppe continued to shout instructions to his sons, whose arms strained against the oars.

When they emerged from under the last wave, Giuseppe tried to get a sense of where they were. They had stayed north, but they were farther west, off the coast of Sicily. South of him in the strait, he could see the fires of Messina and for the first time the ruin of Reggio. It was like two bonfires had been set facing each other on the coasts. A cloud of smoke hung over Scilla, but he saw only isolated flames.

Two waves approached from both the east and west, and he shouted to the boys to row toward the end of the western wave in hopes of skirting up its back to avoid being caught in the collision. Just in time they flew down the back of the wave and only caught the backlash of the force of the two waves smacking together.

Antonio wasn't sure if he was crying or not. Seeing his mother and sisters drenched and screaming at his feet frightened him more than the waves. They clung to the bottom of the boat, sputtering for air between waves. Antonio prayed to his patron saint. He thought of his grandparents, cousins, and many aunts and uncles onshore in Scilla. Were they alive? The thought of reaching them gave him renewed strength, and he listened to his father's instructions even more intently.

His sisters-in-law kept the two infants breathing by clasping their heads between their breasts so that they could find air when waves swept over the boat. After the collision of the last two waves, Fortunata saw her infant grandson pushed up against the side of the boat, crying next to his unconscious mother. Fortunata wasn't sure whether Raffaele's wife had been knocked out or had swallowed too much water, but she pumped her chest and blew into her mouth, not calling to the others for fear Raffaele would release his oar. Pumping and breathing, she prayed for the break in the waves to continue. Torturously long minutes later, her daughter-in-law began coughing up water, and Fortunata was able to raise her to a sitting position. She propped her against the side of the boat and put her grandson in her daughter's arms.

After the tidal wave hit Messina, it crossed over the strait, slapping back at Reggio. The waves continued back and forth across the strait, each time lessening in height and intensity.

They were now able to ride the waves without being completely engulfed by each swell. For the first time, Giuseppe could think instead of simply react. Where was his family better off—on land or sea? What if there was another tremor? He looked at the others instead of the sea for the first time and saw that his young daughter-in-law was nearly unconscious and many of his children white and weak from enduring the constant onslaught. Deciding that they couldn't endure much more, he planned to navigate the boat back to the eastern side of the strait, toward the northernmost point in Scilla.

Battling shifting currents and crashing waves, they inched toward Scilla. Hours later, Antonio's arms burned from the exertion. But the pain in his muscles wasn't nearly as excruciating as the sights and noises that were growing more discernable from the coast with each dip of their oars. They could hear before they could see. Cascading stone, crumbling brick, and the crashing of half-collapsed buildings. Exploding gas and water mains. The closer they got, the more horrific the sounds became, and they were no longer anonymous. There were screams, moans, and calls for help. After fighting for their lives, the devastation they were beginning to see through the smoke, the agony they heard, and the smell of ruin signaled that a worse fate awaited them onshore.

PART EIGHT

NEW YORK, NEW YORK
DECEMBER 29, 1908–SEPTEMBER 8, 1909

TWENTY-FIVE

DECEMBER 29, 1908

"Terremoto! Terremoto in Sicilia e Calabria!" The Italian newsies ran down Mulberry and Elizabeth Streets, abandoning their usual corners.

"Messina destroyed!"

"No news from Reggio!"

"Earthquake followed by tidal wave!"

"Thousands dead!"

Before the newsies were done trumpeting headlines, church bells began to toll. If the residents of the Italian colony were not awoken by the sound of their neighbors' footsteps running downstairs to get the paper, the chorus of pealing bells roused them. The newsies' canvas bags were quickly emptied, and people grouped around the nearest person with a paper. Those who couldn't read or were too far from the newspaper beseeched the readers, "Tell us! Tell us!" Their pleadings were met with loud admonishments to be quiet as the reader, hands shaking, tried to get through the front page.

Often when they finished or reached a sentence that spelled doom, the reader collapsed, unable to tell their family and neighbors of the catastrophe. Weeping summaries were reduced to "Gone, they are all gone!" Then the others would also collapse, and each doorway was littered with knots of people moaning "No!" and praying aloud to the saints.

Frances had run downstairs for the paper and had scanned it on her way up before handing it to her stepmother. She knew her father no longer had family in Italy, but she had quickly read enough to know that this was horrible news for her stepmother.

Giovanna laid the paper on the kitchen table, spreading it out in full. Unable to sit, she stood over it, gripping the sides of the pages. Her daughter, husband, and stepchildren watched in silence as her chest heaved and her pale skin turned blotchy, but with a steely concentration she continued reading. An emotional earthquake was taking place. The surface of her body showed only the faintest signs, but the pressure building up beneath was visible. Frances was sure her stepmother was going to split in two. Instead, it was the paper that was torn in half from the stress of Giovanna's grip. Leaving the ripped paper on the table, Giovanna ran to her bedroom.

"Giovanna! What is going on?" asked Rocco.

"Messina is destroyed. Probably Reggio too. An earthquake and a tidal wave. They could all be trapped. I'm going to find them," she said, throwing things, including the little money they had saved, in a bag.

"Stop this! You can't go there. Even if it was possible, it would take weeks, and by then . . ."

Giovanna flashed Rocco a look of determination and grabbed her bag and rushed to the door. When she opened it, Lorenzo was standing there with a look of terror on his face.

DECEMBER 30, 1908

After a day of grieving, Lorenzo knew that the only thing to do was to go with Giovanna to the shipping lines. The ticket office was crowded with hundreds of Italians, each being told the same thing. There were no tickets, and even if they could get to Naples, there was no way to get to the stricken area. Only first-class tickets aboard the *Lucania* were on sale. In desperation, immigrants handed money and scraps of paper bearing family names and locations to wealthy Italians boarding the *Lucania,* begging them to send word of their families.

"Giovanna, I know that man!" exclaimed Lorenzo, pointing to a man ready to board. "I painted a mural in his import office."

Lorenzo fought his way through the crowd, calling the man's name. The well-dressed signore heard the call and turned.

"Signore, I am Lorenzo Costa. Can you help us?" The man's face was swollen and red, and he looked at Lorenzo with a dazed expression.

"Remember, signore, I painted your mural? Of the Strait of Messina?"

"Oh, sì, sì." The man continued to stare at Lorenzo.

"Signore, please, can you send word of my family? They are in Scilla, Calabria."

"But I hope to go to Messina. My wife, my children, my parents, they are all there. I . . .," he said, pounding his chest, "I sent them. I sent them for Christmas. I sent them to their deaths. May the saints be with your family, Signore *Artiste*." The gentleman turned and left.

The scene at the cable office, which was their next stop, was no different. Crowds of Sicilians and Calabrians jammed the small office and the street. A clerk, standing on his desk, tried to yell over the din of the crowd. "You can place a cable, but it won't get there. There are no telegraph or telephone lines in the area. Try again in a few days."

Most of the crowd, including Giovanna and Lorenzo, waited in line anyway to send their futile missives, even prepaying for the reply they wouldn't receive. The line was long, and the crowd exchanged newspapers while waiting. Today's story was longer, covering many pages and featuring maps and photographs of Messina and Reggio before the disaster. Giovanna was given a *New York Herald* and was about to pass it on when she saw much of it was written in Italian. Leaving Lorenzo in line, she went outside to read.

100,000 DEAD IN MESSINA,
REGGIO'S LOSS IS 45,000 IN STAGGERING CALAMITY

SHIPS RUSHED TO STRICKEN SECTIONS WITH FOOD AND TENTS

HELPLESS, HOPELESS SURVIVORS OF THE TERRIFYING SHOCK BECOME
SHRIEKING MANIACS AND ADD TO THE TERROR OF
THE SCENES BY ENDING LIVES ALONGSIDE VICTIMS' BODIES

Try as she might by praying feverishly, Giovanna could not stop visualizing her parents trapped beneath rubble, dead—or worse, in pain and unreachable. To have her fears expounded upon in the ink of a newspaper was too much to bear. She forced herself to scan the article, looking for mention of Scilla, but she did not find it. Even the map didn't show Scilla. But it did show the neighboring towns of Bagnara and Palmi, and it said that hundreds of bodies had been found. She shivered at the thought that Scilla was closer to Reggio and Messina than either of these two places.

"It is sent." Lorenzo lifted his sister off the crate by her hand. "Did you find out anything more?" Wordlessly, she showed him the map and pointed out all the surrounding cities that had been destroyed. He looked at the paper but said nothing.

"I heard someone say that people are going to the Consul General's office," mumbled Lorenzo. "Let's try."

Arriving at Consul General Massiglia's office on Lafayette Street, they were greeted by mayhem. People were fighting to get in the door and yelling, "Give us transport!" "Release the names of the dead!" The Consul General's underlings moved through the crowd, telling them the little they knew and trying hopelessly to quell the anxiety and assure people that when they received information it would be quickly disseminated. Lorenzo shrugged in desperation. There was only one place left to go.

Lorenzo and Giovanna stepped into Our Lady of Loreto on Elizabeth Street. Every candle was lit, and the church was crowded with weeping women—and even with men, who were unaccustomed to the surroundings because baptism and death were often the only occasions that brought an Italian man to church.

Looking around, Giovanna felt a pang of guilt for not coming here first. She surprised herself at how practical she could be sometimes. Kneeling before the altar, she took a stick from the tray and placed it in an existing flame. There were not enough candles in all the churches of New York for the victims. Each candle would have to carry the burden of many souls. More than fifty times she put the stick in a flame, saying the name of the person for whom she prayed, starting with her mother and father. After lighting their candles, she lit one each for Nunzio's mother, Zia Marianna, Nunzio's sister, Fortunata, and her husband, Giuseppe Arena, and their children. Because her mind was clouded with smoke and grief, she aided the process of inventorying her loved ones by imagining the faces of her friends and family in her trip down the aisle to marry Nunzio. She lit a flame for each soul and prayed to Nunzio to save them or receive them in heaven.

Lorenzo was also mumbling prayers not far from where Father Longa was trying to comfort the many families surrounding him. Giovanna knew Father Longa came from Messina and wondered how he had the strength to comfort others when his own family's fate was unknown. She decided Father Longa was either blessed with this diversion or had a higher calling.

DECEMBER 31, 1908

It took Angelina a day to figure out what was happening, but when she did, she was inconsolable. Her Nonna and Nonno, who had lavished her with attention in Scilla, might be buried in rocks, drowned in a gigantic wave, or burned in a fire. Everywhere she went, adults were talking or reading the paper. And if she didn't understand what they said, she could understand the grief of women who sat in doorways with their aprons thrown over their heads, wailing and rocking.

When she wasn't thinking about Nonna and Nonno, she was thinking about Antonio and his brothers and sisters. How could that same calm, beautiful water that Antonio taught her to swim in swallow people up? She heard one lady reading that the survivors were going insane and walking around naked. Frances said that meant that they were crazy. Was Antonio crazy, with no clothes on?

That morning when she woke up, her mother was already kneeling beside her bed praying. Angelina started crying again, but she tried to muffle her sobs with her pillow. The only time her mother cried was when she saw Angelina cry, and she didn't want that to happen. Seeing her mother cry was worse than imagining all those horrible things.

When Rocco came home from work, earlier than usual, he looked at the sad expressions on his children's faces and his wife still on her knees in prayer and said, "Come, children, let's all go for hot chestnuts and visit your cousins. It's New Year's Eve."

Mary, with Angelina clinging to her hand, whispered to her father, "I don't want to leave Zia."

"Zio Lorenzo will come sit with her."

Rocco sensed that his wife didn't want him around and was only finding comfort with her brother. Her grief and anxiety were far too great for him to resent her feelings, so he tried to stay out of her way.

The door closed on Giovanna's solitude; her shoulders slumped in relief, and she laid her head on the bed. Her mind wandered to the New Year's Eve she spent as a voiceless widow traveling in the bowels of a boat to a foreign land. Six years later, worse than sailing away from the land and people she loved, she might have lost them completely. The memory of the pink icing on that little girl's finger burned in her throat.

JANUARY 1, 1909

The first day of the New Year brought confirmation of Giovanna's worst fears. The headlines of the *New York Herald* were each more horrifying than the one before.

IN ONE INSTANCE THE GROUND OPENED AND FROM A
CHASM EIGHTY FEET WIDE THERE SPOUTED BOILING WATER
IN WHICH THOUSANDS WERE SCALDED TO DEATH

CLOUDS OF CROWS MYSTERIOUSLY ATTRACTED TO THE
STRICKEN DISTRICTS ADD TO THE TERRORS THERE

HUMAN BEINGS FIGHT WITH DOGS FOR FOOD

Scanning the first page, she ignored details while desperately looking for the word *Scilla*. Turning the page, her search ended, for there was the name "Scilla" staring back at her. A box listed all the affected cities, their populations, and the number dead. Number six on the list was Scilla. But while all the other cities listed a number dead, or said "hundreds dead," in Scilla's column it simply said "in ruins."

Giovanna stayed at the table staring. Rocco looked over her shoulder; the chart was easy enough to figure out even for an illiterate. His gnarled index finger pointed at *"in rovine"* across from Scilla's name.

"What does this say?"

"In ruins."

"Let's go for a walk."

"No."

"I'll take the children for a walk. Do you want me to get Lorenzo?"

Giovanna didn't answer. The children, who were just waking up, gathered around Giovanna and the newspaper. Their father tried to shoo them away.

"Come on, get dressed. We're going for a walk." Rocco even roused Clement who was still sleeping.

Rocco and the children were nearly out the door when Lucrezia knocked. She carried holiday pastries, a *New York Times,* and her doctor's bag. Rocco waved her in, and, motioning to his wife, gently shook his head. He tipped his cap in farewell.

"Giovanna, it's me, Lucrezia." She sat at Giovanna's side, and Giovanna actually took her hand and held it.

Lucrezia used her other hand to fish in her bag. She pulled out Humphries Pills No. 17, which, although advertised for depression, Lucrezia had found to be a good sedative.

"Here, take this," she said, putting the pill in Giovanna's mouth and getting up to get her a glass of water. "Before I speak further you should know that my husband said they could be exaggerating the devastation to get more aid. But there was more news of Scilla today."

Giovanna nodded and pointed at the chart in the newspaper in front of her. Lucrezia looked at it. "Yes, that's what the *New York Times* had. There was something else, too. It said two priests from Scilla escaped because they were in the vault of a church that resisted collapse."

Giovanna's eyes flickered. This was the first news of Scilla that was not abstract. She tried to think which church had a vault.

"It also said that Scilla was completely destroyed. Even the rock of Scylla has completely disappeared." Lucrezia's voice lowered. "The priests think they are the only survivors."

For the first time in her life, Giovanna fainted. Lucrezia had a difficult time getting her to the bed. Once conscious, Giovanna was still drowsy because the sedative had begun to work. In spite of this, Giovanna pushed up from the bed.

"I must tell Lorenzo!"

Lucrezia gently pushed her down. "He knows. I saw him before coming here. He asked me to take care of you. You need to sleep." Lucrezia lay down beside Giovanna and held her friend, who gagged on her tears before falling into a deep sleep.

Hours later, when Giovanna woke, Lucrezia was at the stove stirring soup. "I made you broth. If you feel up to it, there is a special service at the Church of the Most Precious Blood on Baxter."

For once in her life, Giovanna's preference was not to be alone. This tragedy extended beyond her family, and she felt the need to congregate. "I'll go."

Lucrezia miraculously made Giovanna's family reappear and got them ready for the service.

The mass, led by Father Bernardino Polizzo, was packed with people clad in black and heartbreak. Giovanna clutched Angelina's hand. At least she had her daughter and stepchildren. From the number of single men in the church, she surmised that many of their wives and children were sent home during the last year when times in New York had become even more difficult. These men were probably all that was left of their families. She also noticed that Italians of all classes were in the pews. Tragedy was more common in the lower classes, but it had enveloped them all.

Angelina was tugging at her mother's hand. In tired exasperation, Giovanna asked, "What is it?"

"Mamma—Nonna and Nonno are still alive."

Giovanna squeezed her daughter's hand a little too hard and whispered, "Angelina, I told you what we read today."

"But he told me!"

"Who told you?"

"Saint Rocco." Angelina pointed to his statue on the altar. "I was praying to him, and he told me that they are safe."

Giovanna, who usually believed in miracles, could not accept this. Instead, she cradled her child and said sadly, "You keep praying."

JANUARY 2, 1909

In what was now a ritual, the day started with the papers. For the first time, there was a list of confirmed dead, city by city. And there it was, *"Scilla, 2,800."*

"That means 2,200 are still alive!" Giovanna thought with elation. It was the mathematics of tragedy, where every number becomes disconnected from the horror and pain of the life it represents. Giovanna found her thoughts consumed with macabre fractions. "If my parents are alive, then these three people are dead." But complicating matters was the disclaimer at the bottom of the chart: "This list does not include the deaths that may occur in hospitals." With this in mind, it was no longer simple math.

She began to add all the numbers for each city and then realized the total was already listed at the bottom: 164,850 confirmed dead. Who were the unconfirmed dead? Was that like not being baptized?

The sound of trumpets and drums from the street saved her from her thoughts. Clement ran to the window and reported. "There's a band and lots of people and carriages behind it." The entire family went to the window to see carriages decorated with Italian and American flags and signs asking for contributions for the earthquake's victims. The first carriage was draped with banners reading IL PROGRESSO and was followed by men in thick overcoats and sashes.

Giovanna squinted to see the people in the carriages. They appeared to be important Italians—they had medals pinned to their chests in addition to the sashes. She was certain that one woman, whose picture she had seen in the paper, was an opera star. Young girls carrying tin boxes were at the sides of the procession, darting in and out of stores and vestibules to collect contributions. The carriages were already piled high with cans of food, medicine, and clothing.

Angelina watched a man at a fish cart unbutton his shirt, rip it from his body, and throw it on the carriage, leaving him bare-chested in the January wind. Women and children crossed themselves as the procession passed and ran into their apartments to get what little they had.

Giovanna quickly moved through the apartment picking up whatever she could and putting it into a basket. Thrusting the basket and coins into her stepson's hands, Giovanna shouted, "Here, Clement, run down with this." She was nearly drowned out by the sound of the band that was under their window and the weeping on the street when the procession passed.

JANUARY 3, 1909

"Rocco!" called Giovanna, running back into their apartment with the newspaper. "Rocco, here look!" Her husband was still in bed. She sat on the edge of the bed and read to him. "'Physician gets no word from Italy. Dr. Bellantoni sends messages and money but obtains no reply.' And he is from Scilla! Is this Bellantoni related to your Angelina?"

"And if he is? What can he do?" Rocco asked.

"He is sending messages everywhere. Listen to this: 'In his efforts to obtain some word from the stricken district, the physician has sent messages to the Italian government and has appealed to the Italian Consul in this city, but all efforts so far failed to obtain any results.'"

"He is my wife's third cousin. But I don't see how he can help. He hasn't been able to help himself."

"Can I go see him?"

"I will go with you."

It was a long trip to Dr. Bellantoni's home, north on Amsterdam Avenue. His was an imposing brick house with a doorway framed in etched glass and brass hardware.

"Is it all his?" asked Giovanna, surveying the building.

"I think so," answered Rocco, removing his cap and using the knocker.

A maid answered.

"I am from Scilla, here to see Dr. Bellantoni."

Hearing "Scilla," the maid hurried them into the foyer and scurried off to get the doctor.

They heard the doctor's quick footsteps before they saw him. A short, rotund man practically lunged into the room to greet them. He looked quizzically at Rocco.

"I am Rocco Siena—Angelina's husband. This now is my wife, Giovanna."

"Yes, yes, of course. I knew I recognized you. Have you brought news?" he added anxiously.

Giovanna's heart sank. In thinking of herself, she hadn't considered that their visit would raise his hopes. She said gently, "I'm sorry, Dottore, we know nothing. We were hoping you might know something more."

Dr. Bellantoni's disappointment was palpable, but he responded graciously. "Please, come in," he instructed, leading them to the sitting room.

Under different circumstances, Giovanna would have memorized the brocades, the enameled globe, and gilt frames. Instead, she sat down awkwardly and Rocco followed.

"If I remember correctly, Signore Siena, you no longer had family in Scilla."

"True. But my wife, Giovanna, all her family is in Scilla, and we've had no word."

"And their names?"

"I am a Costa. Our other family names are Pontillo and Arena."

"I remember. You are in the Chianalea, yes?"

"Sì."

Dr. Bellantoni looked uncomfortable. "I have received no word on individuals. But I do know the devastation in Scilla was great. Particularly in the Chianalea."

"Yes. We also heard this." Giovanna tried to hide her pain upon hearing the Chianalea singled out. "We were thinking, Dottore, that perhaps when you send your messages, you could add my families' names. I only know how to send a cable, and the paper mentioned that you've been in touch with the government."

Dr. Bellantoni's face flickered with the recognition of how they got here, and he also seemed to notice for the first time their Sunday best, which was far from the best. "Oh, yes, the paper. Yes, of course. I will do what I can."

There was nothing left to say. After a moment of uncomfortable silence, the doctor said, "Can I invite you to share my Sunday meal?"

Rocco stood and answered before Giovanna could. "Thank you, Dottore. But the children are waiting at home to be fed."

Giovanna also rose. "Dottore, I am so sorry that we have bothered you."

"No, no, it is no bother. We must help each other in this time of crisis. Please, wait a few moments and I will get you a carriage."

"That is not necessary."

"It's my personal carriage. I insist."

All heads turned on Elizabeth Street when Giovanna and Rocco alit from a private carriage. On the ride downtown, Giovanna thought how hospitable New York could be when you had means.

JANUARY 11, 1909

Lucrezia had insisted that she needed Giovanna's help, but Giovanna knew it was only to get her out of the house. In the last week the only time she had left the confines of her apartment was to check the telegraph office, which she did as religiously as she lit candles in church.

She imagined that Lucrezia also wanted to tell her all about the concert she went to last night at the Metropolitan. Scores of singing sensations performed to raise money for the victims of the earthquake, including the great Enrico Caruso. Already, Giovanna could see the headlines announcing, MORE THAN $15,000 RAISED as she made her way down the street. With a stab of resentment, she imagined Lucrezia's husband accompanying her to the opera. It allowed him to show his concern for the heathens and still wear white gloves. Giovanna quickly chastised herself; it was unkind of her to question the charity of others.

She decided to stop by the telegraph office before going to Lucrezia's. The clerk was just unlocking the door.

"You're early this morning, signora." He went to the in-boxes and leafed through the stack of cables quickly because he had become accustomed to no replies from the hundreds of telegrams he was sending to Italy.

Giovanna's head was turned when the clerk doubled back through the stack.

"Giovanna Costa Siena, correct?"

Giovanna spun around.

"Yes. You have an answer."

After all this waiting, Giovanna couldn't take the envelope from the clerk's hand.

"Open it for me."

"Signora, I am only allowed to read your missive if you are illiterate."

"I can't read." At that moment she wasn't lying.

"Va bene," he said, eyebrow raised, and slit the envelope with a silver knife. It took an eternity to unfold the paper.

"*Concetta and Domenico Costa, Marianna Pontillo, the Arena Family. We live.*"

In the dead of winter sweat poured between Giovanna's breasts as she ran from Little Italy in search of her brother. She arrived at his job site, telegram waving in her hand. Lorenzo dropped his shovel and ran to her, knowing this would not be how she would announce their parents' death. They embraced, crying and laughing, and then knelt on the frozen ground and prayed.

TWENTY-SIX

Rocco packed up his cart in the dim winter light. Snow was falling, and he was anxious to get the cart back before it accumulated. Giovanna stood at the apartment window and watched it fall. After seven years in New York, she still found snow a novelty. Her husband cursed it, but she looked forward to the first few hours when the soot of New York was blanketed in clean white crystals.

From the window, she had already seen Rocco turn the corner with his cart, heading to the garage. Knowing he was this close to home, she went to the stove, put the pasta in the boiling water, and stirred the chi chi beans in garlic and olive oil with her wooden spoon. The heat of the stove felt good. It was bitterly cold, and she had given away her warmest sweater the second time there was a collection for victims of the earthquake.

The girls were doing their homework and the table was set, so she went back to the window, pulling a shawl around her body. Rocco had just stepped aside to let a carriage pass, but it stopped in front of their building. She saw Rocco hurry toward it and realized it was Dr. Bellantoni's carriage. The door opened and a man exited, but even from three flights up it was apparent that it was not Dr. Bellantoni. This man was thin and in clothes much like theirs. Rocco shook the man's hand and escorted him into the building. Giovanna looked around her apartment to see if there was anything she could straighten up and opted instead to set another place at the table.

"Giovanna! There is someone here with news!" announced Rocco, coming through the door.

In the weeks since receiving the telegram, most of Giovanna's time had been spent speculating about what had happened. After the initial elation of finding out that her loved ones had survived, she was filled with questions that went unanswered, despite her numerous letters and cables. It was difficult for Giovanna even to greet this man without first demanding information.

"Good evening, signora. I am Enrico Bellantoni, a cousin of Dr. Bellantoni. Until last month, I lived in Scilla."

Giovanna stared at the man, hoping to recognize him, but didn't. The man perceived her anxiousness and kept talking.

"I was in Naples for work when the earthquake hit. It took a week, but I returned to find I had no home. I saw the many cables from Dr. Bellantoni and decided to contact him. His family, like mine, is all gone." The man crossed himself, and Giovanna realized her body had been blocking the entrance to the apartment and she hadn't invited the man in.

"Signore Bellantoni, please, come sit and eat with us."

The children had learned to be incredibly quiet since the tragedy struck. They assembled at the table, eager to be included in hearing the details firsthand.

"It's a simple meal, Signore Bellantoni."

"It is hot, signora, and in this weather that is all that matters. And, please, call me Enrico. There are few people left on this earth who can."

"So, Dr. Bellantoni sent you?"

"Yes. I was able to make contact with him when I was in Italy, and I told him the devastating news. He sent money for me to come to New York and also gave me the names of your family members to look up before I sailed."

The man hungrily slurped at his soup.

"Your husband told me that you've already received the wonderful news that your family is alive." Although Enrico Bellantoni tried to sound positive, there was no escaping the underlying message of 'but my family is not.' "I found your family before coming here, and I have much to tell."

The pasta remained untouched in Giovanna's bowl as Enrico did what no newspaper, cable, or rumor had been able to do. He told her what had happened to her family. Enrico was not a good storyteller, but some stories tell themselves. The children's eyes widened with each detail, and the only other noise in the apartment was the scraping of shovels outside.

"Your parents are alive because they live under Santa Maria di Porto Salvo. The church couldn't save itself, but it saved your parents. The foundation of the church remains, but nothing else."

"The murals are gone?!" exclaimed Giovanna.

Enrico practically snorted. "Signora, not only are the Scillese practically wiped out, so is our history! Do you not know the extent of the devastation? Pieces of Castello Ruffo are in the sea. Scylla's rock that inspired Homer is gone! Do you think because your family is alive, Scilla is not devastated?"

Giovanna felt terrible. "I'm sorry, Enrico, I didn't mean . . ."

"No, no, it is me who should be sorry. I apologize. Sometimes I think I will lose my mind, and it will be a blessing."

Rocco rose from the table and got more wine, which he poured into Enrico's glass, muttering, "Drink, drink."

"Yes, the murals are gone, but your parents' house is intact with practically no damage. They were sleeping at the time, and thankfully they stayed in their house, because if they had come outside they would have been in greater danger—much collapsed around them."

Thinking of Nunzio's house only a few yards away, Giovanna asked, "And my aunt Marianna Pontillo?"

"She was trapped for two days."

Giovanna stifled her gasp.

"Your father and a few other men heard her cries and dug her out."

"Is she alright?"

"I didn't see her. She was in the hospital that the French made from tents. But your mother thinks she will recover. Her house is gone, though."

"And Marianna's daughter, Fortunata Arena, and her husband, Giuseppe?"

"This story I heard even before I knew it was your family! They were in a boat, all of them, on their way to Messina, and they managed to survive."

Mary dropped her spoon. "But how?" In Mary's mind, their boat was teetering on the top of the gigantic wave like a magic carpet.

"I can't tell you how, little one. No one wants to speak of survival." He turned to Giovanna. "They are living with your mother. Their house was not totally destroyed, but the top floor caved in. When I called on your mother, Giuseppe Arena and his boys were out digging through the rubble of their neighbors' homes looking to find the bodies to bury. Your cousin, she had no interest in speaking about what happened. Her daughters-in-law were there, and they lost their families."

Giovanna brought her cold, full plate of pasta to the sink. It was hard to stay in her seat. She had to fight her instinct to rush to the nearest dock, sail to Italy, and dig with her hands if she had to.

"My brother will sail for Scilla. I must go with him."

"Signora, your mother was clear with me. She said to tell you she forbade you to come. Disease and pestilence are sweeping the area, and she said you and your brother could do more for them by staying here. The armies are beginning to show up, and they will do the digging and rebuilding."

Giovanna put her head in her hands and cried at her helplessness. Mary and Angelina went to her side.

"Zia, you can't go. I don't want you to get sick," whispered Mary.

"Mamma, don't cry," pleaded Angelina.

"Enrico," said Giovanna, wiping her tears, "there are many more people I must ask about. Maybe you know them. The midwife, Signora Scalici?"

"Signora Scalici brought me into this world. No one has found her."

Giovanna twisted and knotted the napkin in her hand. "Father Clemente?"

"He survived, but then died in the hospital."

"My cousin Pasquale Costa?"

"Where did he live?"

"South of my parents in the Chianalea."

"In the stretch beneath the castle?"

"Yes."

"Signora, that entire enclave of the Chianalea and the people in it are gone. There is no trace. Even the land is in the sea."

Giovanna quickly did the death calculations. That would mean Zia Antoinette was gone and Pablo Caruso. She took deep breaths, forcing herself to be mindful that this man's losses were far worse than her own. Grief would come later. "Enrico, what will you do now?"

"The good doctor has been kind enough to invite me to live with him. I have nothing left in Scilla. Nor does he."

Seeing Giovanna's expression, he realized he had once again made her feel guilty. "Signora, it has been a privilege to bring you this good news. I am sincerely happy that your family has survived. But, as I know, it is not so easy in this circumstance to be among the living. I will pray for your family as I pray for mine."

Clement spoke for the first time. "Signore, are you related to my mother, Angelina Bellantoni?"

"A third cousin, yes."

"Did anyone from my mother's family die in the terremoto?"

"Most everyone."

These were distant relatives that the children had little knowledge of, but the news brought the disaster closer to home for her stepchildren, who had never even seen Scilla. Giovanna thought about how tragedies knitted themselves into your soul when there was a connection—no matter how tenuous. If you walked down a street where a murder had occurred, or studied a country where there was a famine, all of a sudden the horror became your own. She watched ownership of this earthquake creep over her stepchildren's faces.

Giovanna went to her bedroom and took two palm fronds that had been braided into crosses off the wall. "These are from Scilla's Feast of Saint Rocco this past August. Please take one and give the other one to Dr. Bellantoni."

TWENTY-SEVEN

FEBRUARY 1, 1909

The thousand-dollar payment from Nunzio's settlement did not arrive on January 1. In fact, Signore DeCegli had to remind the attorney to send it. They had never seen the first check; it had gone directly to the bank to pay for the store. Giovanna stared at the check with three zeros and tried to figure out the safest way to get it to Scilla. With Lieutenant Petrosino's warnings ringing in her ears, she decided to ask Signore DeCegli's advice. Signore DeCegli assured her that Bank Stabile on Mulberry Street would transmit it safely, and he accompanied her there. She was not the first Italian to be sending money home, but Giovanna couldn't help but notice the clerk's expression when he saw the amount.

"I do not want to send this unless you can tell me that it will go directly to my family," stated Giovanna.

"I assure you, signora, we can do that. We have already sent a great deal of money to Messina and Reggio."

"But this isn't going to Messina and Reggio; it's a small village."

"I understand, signora, and we will get it there safely."

Signore DeCegli stepped in. "I suggest that we prepay a reply for her family. This is my card. Certainly, if it does not arrive in due time, I could be called for assistance."

Taking the card, the banker said in an offended tone, "Sir, we are a reputable institution."

At the door, Giovanna thanked Signore DeCegli.

"I assume you will no longer be moving, signora."

"No. We'll have to wait." Giovanna's voice carried with it the conviction she felt. When she buried the swordfish mustasole at Nunzio's grave, she promised to watch over all that Nunzio loved in Scilla. The earthquake left Nunzio's mother and his sister's family without homes and in need of medicine. Now Nunzio would provide for them. While her plans to move her family to a safer place were scuttled for now, tonight she would go to sleep knowing that her family in Italy would have shelter and food.

Feeling at peace for the first time in a long while, Giovanna headed home. At the corner of Prince and Elizabeth streets, she nearly careened into Lieutenant Petrosino.

"Lieutenant!"

"Good day, signora. How fortunate! I wanted to speak to you. But not here. Can you come to my office?"

When they had settled into chairs at his desk, Petrosino said, "I heard the good news about your family!"

"How is it that you know everything?"

"When will you understand that this is my job!" chided Petrosino good-naturedly. "In all seriousness, signora, I am so happy your family survived."

"Thank you, Lieutenant. But that isn't why you asked me here, is it?"

"No. I have a question. Do you know Manzella's store, two doors from you?"

"Of course. He just closed his shop."

"He filed for bankruptcy. I was suspicious and questioned him. It turns out that for three years Lupo had been extorting money from him."

"But Lupo's gone! Do you believe Manzella?"

"I believe him, because this was something he had no intention of telling. What it means is that Lupo left town with a lot of money— Manzella's cash and his creditor's money."

"Does this make you think Lupo was behind the bombing of our store?"

"No, no, I didn't say that. It might. It might not. But this is your block, signora, so I want you to keep an eye out for the bulldog-faced wolf and watch Inzerillo."

"What of Manzella?"

"He's looking for work. If we ever find Lupo, we'll prosecute him."

It was clear that Petrosino was preoccupied and didn't want to take this conversation further. As he walked her down the stairs, Giovanna asked, "And your little girl, how is she?"

"Oh, signora, she is beautiful! She's two months old today. And when she sees her papa, it's all smiles!"

"And your wife, is she well?"

"Sì, thank you for asking."

At the door, Giovanna commented, "I saw in the papers that you now have a secret service to fight the Black Hand."

"Yes, signora. Even though the Board of Aldermen wouldn't fund it, Commissioner Bingham got it funded privately. We also have the Italian government's cooperation. We can begin deporting all the criminals who have taken haven here."

"Should I begin working on our case again, Lieutenant?"

"Well . . . yes, yes, of course, signora. You come see me. If I am not here, be sure you work with Lieutenant Vachris. There are new photos for you to review."

"I'll do that, Lieutenant. *Arrivederci*."

Giovanna watched the little man turn back up the stairs into his headquarters at 19 Elizabeth Street.

FEBRUARY 7, 1909

Clement was between jobs and helping his father. It was difficult to find construction work in the winter.

Rocco took advantage of their time together and lectured Clement incessantly. "When you're my age, you won't push a cart, or even build someone else's building. You will have your own business. Your own house. You can't have another man own you. Work every day and save your money for these things. You hear me, Clement?"

"Yes, Pop."

"Pop? What's Pop?"

Clement smiled. "Papa." Clement's Italian had become Americanized.

"See that, you speak good English. You need to speak English. In fact, from now on you only speak to me in English."

"Papa, you don't speak English."

"Don't you worry about me. I understand."

"Okay, if that's what you want. I'll speak English."

"*Che?*"

Clement smiled and switched back to Italian. "Papa, don't you worry. I'll become a rich American."

"Va bene. You see that stronzo across the street with the brown coat? No, no, don't be so obvious!"

Turning his head back to the cart, Clement muttered, "I see him."

"He's been watching us. He's another Blackhander."

"What would they want with us? We have nothing left."

"I heard they even harass pushcart sellers."

"Let me get him first," seethed Clement.

"No! Clement, I want to cut these rats to their knees, but I don't want you or your sisters hurt. I've heard too many stories from your stepmother about how they get you back. We will watch him, as he watches us."

"But what will we do?"

"Your stepmother says the lieutenant has a secret service that will send them all back to Italy soon. For now, we will try to be invisible."

Lieutenant Petrosino, his expression dour, was uncharacteristically slumped in the chair opposite Commissioner Bingham's desk.

"Joe, I'm sorry it has to be you, but there really isn't anyone else qualified to do this job. Who else could work the system and the informants to get these records?" cajoled Commissioner Bingham.

"I understand, Commissioner; it's just that my little girl will grow so much in the three months I'm away." Lieutenant Petrosino lowered his face to hide his emotion.

"You're a good man, Joe, and a good father. That little girl will have much to be proud of. Let's go over the details."

Bingham settled into his chair. "We have promises from the Italian government to hand over the criminal records. And we have promises from our own government to deport the thugs when we have their records in our hands." He took out a steamer ticket from a leather portfolio on his desk. "You sail the day after tomorrow on the *Duca di Genova*—first class, I might add. You'll travel as a Jewish businessman with the identity of Simone Velletri. In this folder I have letters of introduction for the Italian Minister of the Interior and the head of Italy's police forces, Francesco Leonardi."

While Petrosino inspected the letters, Bingham joked, "Joe, I know how much you love that watch," pointing to the gold chain across Petrosino's pocket. "But I don't think a gift from the Italian government thanking you for arresting criminals would be a good thing to carry."

Petrosino managed a little laugh. "Yes, I think I'll leave it at home."

"I want you to stay home with Adelina and the baby tomorrow. We'll spread the rumor that you've had a relapse of pneumonia and on doctor's orders you are leaving town to convalesce. Only members of the Italian Squad will know your whereabouts."

"And my Adelina, of course."

"Of course. We'll take good care of her, Joe. Now, do you have your list in order?"

"Yes, Commissioner. And it starts with Lupo."

"Lupo's been here more than three years, Joe."

"I know, Commissioner, but my brother works at Ellis Island, and we found proof that he traveled to Italy last year under an alias."

"You are clever! How many names do you have on that list anyway?"

"It's up to seven hundred, sir."

"Joe, you'll need an army to dig up that many records."

"Imagine, Commissioner, if we could deport them all."

Commissioner Bingham stood. "Imagine, indeed. We'll be heroes, Joe."

FEBRUARY 12, 1909

Giovanna stared at her mother's writing on the envelope. At last, the proof that she needed. Tears welled in her eyes as she slit the letter open.

Dearest Giovanna,

We received your generous cable with 1,000 US dollars.

Giovanna breathed a great sigh of relief and continued.

I only hope that you have not sacrificed everything to send it. This is a fortune.
Zia Marianna will also be writing to you, but I can say without a doubt that this
money has saved her life. Her health was so fragile and her despair was so great
that your father and I feared she would die. This gives her hope of establishing
a home again. The same is true of cousin Fortunata and her family. Everything
that you said in your letter that Enrico Bellantoni told you is true. So many of our
friends and family are gone, but we live. I don't know why this is, and I question our
fortune each day. We that remain live all together in our home. It's probably hard
for you to believe, but fourteen of us live here now. Zia Marianna remains in the
French hospital. Each day, we work at rebuilding houses. Soon Fortunata's family
will be moving back into their home. The armies removed the bodies and much of
the debris. They never found your Zia Antoinette's and Signora Scalici's bodies.
Pasquale's body was found only last week. It was his rings that identified him. You
know how he loved those rings! People work night and day rebuilding and cleaning,
but I worry that when the work is done, we will look around only to see a Scilla
that is empty. Please do not come here. The money you sent will help more than
you'll ever know. Give my love to your brother and all my grandchildren. Mamma.

FEBRUARY 28, 1909

Bingham paced his office. He had spent the entire week questioning his
decision to tell the press of Petrosino's mission. Those dandy aldermen
were all over him and he needed to prove he had taken decisive action.
But he hadn't expected the story to be picked up by the *International
Herald.*

"Come in," called Bingham, answering the knock on his door.

Lieutenant Vachris entered and instantly Bingham could read his
anger.

"Sit down, Lieutenant. I hear you wanted to see me."

"Yes, Commissioner. Why? This mission was . . ."

"Not so secret, truth be told, Lieutenant. I had word that more than one person on the ship recognized Joe, and these Blackhanders are not so stupid."

"But still . . ."

"Unfortunately, Lieutenant, you cannot separate police work from politics and, in this case, politically it was the necessary thing to do."

Vachris literally bit down on his lip.

"Commissioner, with his cover blown, he's a sitting duck. Send me over to help him."

"Lieutenant, it's impossible for you both to be out of the country. Besides, in a few weeks his mission will be completed. From what Joe said in his last cable, when he returns we should have plenty of penal records to deport these thieving blackmailers. You get the men ready for his return, because when he does, Lieutenant, it's going to be an old-fashioned roundup."

TWENTY-EIGHT

MARCH 13, 1909

Louis Saulino, Lieutenant Petrosino's brother-in-law, ran up the steps at 300 Mulberry Street into police headquarters and grabbed the first policeman he saw.

"Calm down, sir," assured the officer. "It's another reporter with a good imagination. This isn't the first time there have been rumors of your brother-in-law's death."

"Why would he come to my sister's home at two in the morning?"

"Because he's a muckraking reporter, Mr. Saulino. Wouldn't we have heard if something had happened to Lieutenant Petrosino? Please, go to your sister and tell her it was a cruel joke."

After being told the same thing by the desk sergeant, Saulino left headquarters. The day was just dawning, and the newsies were hitting the streets. He hadn't gone a full block before he heard the first newsboy shout, "Famous detective murdered!" He snatched a paper and sprinted back to police headquarters.

"Do you still think it's a joke?" he shouted, waving the newspaper in front of the desk sergeant's face. "Some joke, Sergeant!"

Bingham was in Washington, so a call was placed to Deputy Commissioner Woods, rousing him from bed. Newspaper or not, the men in police headquarters and at Petrosino's precinct on Elizabeth Street refused to believe the report and waited for official word. At ten o'clock that morning, they received their cable:

"Palermo, Italy, 12 March 1909 Petrosino killed revolver center city tonight killers unknown martyr's death Consul Bishop."

APRIL 12, 1909

Giovanna dressed for Lieutenant Petrosino's funeral. Her grief over his murder became personal when the detective from the Italian Squad knocked on her door with two tickets to the mass. Up until that point, she had successfully treated it as the death of a public figure that she read about in the newspapers.

"Signora, I got you these," offered young Detective Fiaschetti. "I believe the lieutenant would have wanted you there."

Taking the tickets from the officer's hand, Giovanna felt her throat tighten. Given all the tragedy she had endured, she should have been able to shake her head and say a prayer for the slain policeman. At thirty-six, she had lost a husband, a business, and been uprooted from her home, which was in ruins and served as a tomb for dead friends and family. Yet somehow Giovanna had maintained her faith that good would prevail. But with Lieutenant Petrosino's murder, she knew she was burying the last shreds of her idealism with the little lieutenant.

Moments passed before Giovanna could look at Detective Fiaschetti. "Grazie," she mumbled. "You're kind. I would like to attend."

When she closed the door, Rocco, who had been sitting at the table, was ready with the comment she expected. "This is no business of yours."

"This death is everybody's business," she snapped, but she quickly softened. "There will be thousands of people there. Rocco, there is no need to worry."

"I will not go with you!"

"I will have my nephew accompany me then."

It was Domenico, practically in tears, who had delivered the news to Giovanna nearly a month before. In the days that followed, she was riveted to the newspaper each morning. Domenico would arrive before school to read her the American papers, and she would read him *Il Progresso*. She had grown from a young girl anxiously awaiting the arrival of a newspaper in Scilla to a woman in New York who was drowning in news. They had to wait if Rocco had not yet left to get his cart because he had forbidden any discussion of Petrosino or the Black Hand. Giovanna thought Rocco was like a small child who hides his head under a pillow and thinks he's invisible because he can't see. But she also had to admit that her way, Lieutenant Petrosino's way, had not brought justice—only tragedy.

It wasn't until Giovanna saw the pages upon pages devoted to Lieutenant Petrosino in the American papers that she realized how important this man was. All of a sudden their meetings took on an even greater significance in her mind. There was, of course, speculation as to who was responsible for the Petrosino murder, and she searched her own memory, reviewing their many conversations for clues. She thought with rage of the article trumpeting his "secret" mission and had to stop herself from running to the commissioner's office and hurling blame. Her anger was only slightly abated when she read that it was possible Petrosino's killers actually traveled to Italy on the same ship as Petrosino, and that most criminals were well aware of his mission. In the month since he had been slain, people on both sides of the ocean had been arrested, but each of the many suspects was released because they had no evidence.

She could not help but think of Petrosino's widow and infant girl. How would Adelina be today among all this pomp and circumstance, unable to bury her husband in private? After that horrible article in the *Herald,* she didn't allow Domenico to buy that newspaper anymore. The paper had congratulated itself on being the first to learn of Petrosino's death and told of how its reporter had arrived at Mrs. Petrosino's house in the middle of the night to announce the news. They did not even allow time for her husband's spirit to visit her.

Giovanna adjusted her hat and looked at her face, one section at a time, in the tiny mirror hanging near the bed. A moment later, Domenico came through the door with the ubiquitous newspapers. "Today, they listed all the Black Hand bombings. Your store is here."

"Let me see."

Domenico pointed to 242 Elizabeth Street.

Giovanna scowled. "Let's go."

They were fortunate to have tickets, but they still had to stand in the back of Saint Patrick's Cathedral on Mott Street. The sermon was in English, except for a brief bit that Pastor Lavelle said in Italian, so

Giovanna concentrated on her rosary while Domenico stared at the uniforms and the important people who filled the church. To the left of the center aisle were Mayor McClellan, Commissioner Bingham, and assorted other men whose bearing announced their position. One hundred schoolchildren sang from the cathedral's choir loft, but their angelic voices were not enough to drown out the sobs of the women and the noises made by the men clearing their throats to stifle tears.

The Easter decorations had been removed and only resurrection lilies remained on the altar. The mass was beautiful, but it didn't comfort Giovanna. It was a disillusioned woman who stood in the cavernous cathedral. She had put her faith in a man, and that man had been murdered. She wasn't thinking that his death was God's plan, or that the lieutenant had died a martyr. Instead, she was thinking that her only duty in life was to protect her family. Nothing else mattered.

Petrosino's coffin was carried out of the church and placed in the hearse. The delegations from sixty Italian societies were ready, drawn up with bands at intervals. The mounted police led the procession, followed by the fire department and the street cleaners, which was where Lieutenant Petrosino had begun his career. At least a thousand police followed on foot, along with five open carriages filled with flowers, the hearse, and the black carriages carrying his family. The clear air resounded with Chopin's funeral march and the Italian funeral march in turn. When the last of the regiments joined the parade, Giovanna and Domenico followed with the other civilian mourners.

The neighborhood streets, windows, and fire escapes were filled with tearful residents shouting benedictions and tossing flowers. When the procession made its way out of the Italian colony, Giovanna expected that the crowds would thin and it would be easier to walk, but this was not the case. On Fifth Avenue, every foot of sidewalk was thronged with mourners and even the flags at the luxury hotels were at half-mast. Because of the crowds, it took four hours for the funeral procession to reach Fifty-seventh Street and Second Avenue. There, everyone on foot disbanded, and the carriages and the hearse continued alone across the bridge to Calvary Cemetery.

"Domenico, here is a coin for the trolley. Go to Vito's. It is late, and your mother will be angry with me."

"Are you going there, Zia?"

Giovanna nodded.

"I thought so." Domenico kissed her cheek and left.

By the time Giovanna got to the cemetery, Petrosino's coffin had already been laid in its grave. No one was there except one policeman standing guard and the gravediggers who continued shoveling dirt to fill the hole.

In the quiet, Giovanna leaned against a tree and wondered what to make of all this. Here was an Italian man buried with all the honor of a king, but he was indeed being buried. If Lieutenant Petrosino was so important and so loved, why hadn't they given him the help he had asked for? She remembered the lieutenant telling her that out of the 285 arrests made in one year, "where we had them dead to center," there were only forty-five convictions. He tried to explain the American legal system, but he eventually shrugged in frustration and said, "It doesn't matter. These criminals have friends in City Hall who look out for them." But wasn't it City Hall who gave the Italian detective this regal funeral? The only thing she knew was that she must return to her neighborhood, where Italian criminals were free to prey upon their brethren.

She was exhausted—and probably pregnant. Her period was late, and now, after this trek, Giovanna looked down at her swollen ankles. Knowing there were only a few more hours of daylight, she released the half-wilted flower nearly stuck to her hand and went to pray at Nunzio's grave.

TWENTY-NINE

APRIL 20, 1909

Domenico Costa watched the Star of Italy from behind the pole of the gas lamp. He knew that if anyone caught him lingering there, including his cousin Clement, he would get a beating. He, like everyone in the family, had been forbidden to go near Black Hand haunts or discuss them. But Domenico couldn't help himself when he saw five policemen enter the building with their nightsticks raised. Although it was only April, it was hot and they wore their summer uniforms, each with a single row of gleaming brass buttons down the front.

No one knew who the enemy was anymore. Since Lieutenant Petrosino had been killed, the police were angry. It wasn't just the Italian Squad; loads of policemen were coming around and banging heads for no reason. Some of the very same store owners who were victims of the blackmailers' swindling were being questioned and knocked around by the police.

Domenico had learned not to defend the police. A lot of self-satisfied people, including his Uncle Rocco, were running around saying, "See! They do nothing for us! They got the lieutenant killed, and now they take it out on us!" But the way Domenico saw it, they were avenging the lieutenant's death. He was proud that the Irish cops were angry that the little Italian detective had been killed.

The cops pulled two skinny men out of the Star of Italy by their collars. They made a big show of dragging them down the street to the precinct. Domenico vaguely recognized them and was pretty certain they weren't Black Hand. He pulled a stub of a pencil and his little black book from his pocket and made a note of the arrest. The book was only two inches wide, enabling him to slip it in any pocket and keep it out of view of his family. He had seen Lieutenant Petrosino making notes in a book like it and begged Zia Giovanna to find him one, which she had done last Christmas. Precious few pages were left, because it was nearly filled with notations of the suspicious faces attending Lieutenant Petrosino's funeral. Zia had told him about the cards at the police station, and although he couldn't weigh or measure the suspects, he described them, dutifully recording the date and location he had seen them.

"What are you looking at, you little hoodlum?" A hand under his arm nearly raised Domenico off the ground, and he ended up face-to-face with a ruddy-cheeked policeman.

"Nothing, officer. I was just standing around."

"We'll see about that. Come on then."

Tight in the officer's grip, Domenico spied Frances down the block. She nearly dropped the bread she was carrying as he called out in Italian, "Tell Zia to come to the police station."

"Speak English, boy."

"Yes, sir."

Domenico crossed himself in thanks that there was a chance that Zia would make it to the police station before his mother and was again relieved to see they were headed to the Italian Squad's precinct at 19 Elizabeth Street. Once inside, he scanned the room for familiar faces.

"What do you have here, Rafter?" asked the desk sergeant.

"He was watching the arrest at Star of Italy. Probably a messenger."

"No, sir, officer!"

Yanking him by the collar, Officer Rafter reprimanded, "I'm not talking to you!"

"So what did you see, kid?" asked the desk sergeant.

"Two black rats being taken away." Domenico had heard Lieutenant Petrosino use that term.

A cop not in uniform, but one Domenico recognized, smiled. "Really? You know this?"

"Well, I don't know . . ."

Giovanna swept through the door, breathless. "Cos'è successo?"

"Signora, is he yours?" asked the detective in Italian. It was Fiaschetti, the barrel-chested policeman who had brought her the tickets.

"Sì. My nephew. A good boy."

"I thought I recognized him. The way he was acting, the officer thought he was a lookout."

"No, no, detective. My nephew, he wants to be a policeman."

"Officer Rafter, we can let him go. He's just a boy who wants a badge."

"I want to be like Lieutenant Petrosino," piped in Domenico.

"Keep your nose out of police business, boy, or you could end up just like Lieutenant Petrosino," growled Rafter.

"What did he say?" asked Giovanna of Fiaschetti.

"Nothing, signora. Take the boy home."

MAY 27, 1909

The sound of the knife on the barber's leather strap was relaxing to Rocco. He tilted his head back and closed his eyes.

The barber leaned closer to Rocco's ear as he cranked up the seat. "Are they bothering you again, Rocco?" he whispered.

Rocco put up his hand, waving the question away.

"They're everywhere lately. Not just one gang, but five. They come in almost every day. I can't even put out a barber's pole for fear they'll think I have extra money. Francesco, with the lady's shop, he said he's afraid to buy a cash register because they'll think it's filled with money."

Rocco waited until the barber was done shaving his upper lip. "Shut up, Luigi. I don't want to hear this. Everything is fine."

"Are you afraid that your ears will be cut off, like the poor garlic seller last week?"

"*Smettila!*"

"After the Italian detective's death, the police came in, beat up the neighborhood, and left."

"I said, basta!"

"Va bene. But it isn't going to go away." He threw a hot towel over Rocco's face.

JUNE 11, 1909

Mary and Frances heard the school bell ring and hurried to get their books. The back entrance of P.S. 21 was just diagonally across the street.

"I have to do some shopping; I'll walk you down," said Giovanna, grabbing her basket. Taking Angelina's hand, she followed her step-daughters down the stairs.

Giovanna and Angelina waved from the base of the school steps as Mary and Frances bounded into the building. The school principal stood next to them, speaking with a mother whose daughter hid in the folds of her skirt.

"Ma'am, she will never learn English unless she attends school every day."

The woman smiled and shrugged.

In frustration, the principal turned to Giovanna. "Could you translate?"

"My English no good," stammered Giovanna, but nudged her three-year-old. "Angelina, help."

"Alright, then," said the principal, looking down at Angelina in both amusement and exasperation. "Little girl, will you please tell this woman that it is important for her daughter to come to school every day."

Angelina, who acted much older than her years, turned to the woman confidently. *"Signora, è importante che vostra figlia venga a scuola giornalmente."*

"Sì, ho capito."

Angelina turned to the principal and, relishing her role, translated. "The lady said she understood."

"Then ask her why her daughter is absent so much."

"What's *absent*?"

"Not in school."

"Perché spesso vostra figlia non è a scuola?"

"Ha solamente un vestito."

"Because she only has one dress."

"I don't understand."

"Non capisce."

"Devo lavare il vestito ed a volte non è asciutto di mattina."

"Oh," exclaimed Angelina, now understanding herself and turning back to the principal. "She has to wash the dress and sometimes it isn't dry in the morning."

The principal put his hands on his hips and let out a big sigh. "Tell the mother that before next year starts, I will get her a second dress—and I want her daughter in school every day."

Angelina translated and the woman smiled.

"She said thank you."

"You're a smart little girl," said the principal, patting her head. "Thank you very much."

"Can I come to school? I'm almost four."

"Soon . . ."

An explosion nearly rocked them off their feet. It was followed by a series of small exploding noises. The children's screams of *"La Mano Nera!"* rang out from the open windows.

Within seconds there was the sound of chaos—chairs scraping, yelling, and stampeding feet. The principal looked around and, seeing nothing, ran into the building, shouting, "Stay in your classrooms. Everything is alright!" But the principal's admonishments were drowned out by the children's screams and their teachers' efforts to control them.

Through the door, Giovanna saw children running down the stairs and falling over one another. The only way to help was to keep them flowing through the door. With Angelina clinging to her back, she held the door open and shouted to the children to keep walking, but not to run.

When the children saw no black smoke or cascading bricks, they began to calm down. The stampede stopped, and teachers lined the students up and inspected them for injuries. Giovanna spotted Mary and Frances and sighed in relief.

Up the block, two policemen were speaking with Father Salevini and a short man whose face was covered with ash. The father's hands were gesticulating wildly. Giovanna moved closer to the principal, knowing the officers would report to him. When they strode up, she instructed Angelina to listen.

"What did they say?" she asked her daughter.

"They said the man was getting the bombs and firecrackers ready for Saint Anthony's Feast on Sunday, and some of them went off."

Giovanna sighed, softly shaking her head.

Angelina tugged on her mother's skirt. "Mamma, are we going to the feast?"

JULY 21, 1909

Rocco bent to the crate to get more fruit for the cart. His hand shot to his back and he winced. Mondays were difficult, especially after such a big Sunday meal and a little too much wine. He mopped his brow with his handkerchief and squinted up at the sun to guess the time. Instead, he found himself staring into the face of the big square-headed man whom he knew had been watching him on and off for weeks.

"Ah, so the rat has finally come for the cheese?" exclaimed Rocco.

"It's true then! I heard you were not so right in the head."

"You should have also heard that I have no money, since your fellow schifosi bombed my store."

"I know nothing of your store. Only that you seem to have a good pushcart business that needs to be protected."

"Protected from you."

"This is the price of business."

"I'd rather my cart blow up and watch melons rain down on you, you big oaf!"

"*Vaffanculo*, you stupid jerk. You had your chance." The man kicked Rocco's cart as he walked away, spilling fruit to the street.

THIRTY

AUGUST 15, 1909

Angelina held Mary's hand as they climbed the stairs to the elevated train. Watching her older brother and sisters' excitement made her even more eager. It was hard to put a smile on Clement's face, but even he was beaming.

Giovanna carried a big basket with their meal, which competed with her growing belly. Rocco, whose birthday was the excuse for this extravagant outing, toted a woven bag with their clothes for bathing, and bottles of wine and water.

"How much did it cost?" Angelina asked Mary after their father walked away from the train ticket window.

"One dime each. But I think you're free, so that would be fifty cents."

"I hope we still have money for Dreamland."

"Don't worry, Angelina, this is going to be the best day of our lives," said Frances.

The train went over the Brooklyn Bridge, which Angelina thought in itself was worth the ten cents. Once over the bridge, Angelina felt devilish peeking into second-story bedrooms and seeing men in collarless shirts reading the paper. Soon they were riding into more open space, where detached houses competed with big signs advertising the buildings of tomorrow. The meadows became marshes, which stretched to the sea. And then, in the distance, they saw the strange shapes of Coney Island.

Although it was early morning, the train was packed, and Angelina clung to Giovanna in the throng of weekenders jostling to get off. "First, we'll swim," announced Giovanna, steering her family to the beach and the bathhouses.

Angelina could see the excitement in her mother's eyes. From their trip to Italy, she remembered how much her mother loved the water. The color of this ocean was more gray-blue, and the waves larger and louder, but it was the closest vision to Scilla they had seen. As they looked away from the shore, instead of seeing cliffs and lemon groves, they saw blinking lights, waving flags, and grand, fanciful buildings.

For twenty cents, they were given a small tent to change in and a place to leave their clothes. Giovanna had begged and borrowed bathing costumes for everyone. It was most difficult to find something to fit herself. Rocco had forbidden her to go swimming in her condition, but she had every intention of at least wading in the surf. Clement was the first to spring through the flap of the door and run to the ocean, his father's warnings chasing him. Within minutes, Frances and Mary followed, as did Angelina, clinging to her mother's hand.

Angelina's shoulders lifted to her ears when the first wave washed over her feet. The water was cold. Her brother and sisters were already in, squealing with delight as they jumped over the waves. Inch by inch, Angelina made her way farther into the ocean without releasing her grip on her mother's hand. She watched her father swim far out toward the horizon until he was just a speck. "Mamma! Papa is going to disappear!"

"No, he's just showing off because he's fifty-three today," Giovanna said, smiling.

With each passing minute the beach became more crowded. When they arrived, it had been fairly empty, but now, wherever they turned, they bumped into someone.

Rocco walked out of the waves, panting but invigorated.

"Papa, you swim like a fish!" shouted Angelina.

Her father smiled, looked at the sky to check the position of the sun, and announced, "Let's eat our meal."

Giovanna spread out a tablecloth on the sand and emptied the basket of food. Before long, they were eating fried eggplant, olives, and fruit.

"Mamma, it doesn't matter if I spill my food down my front! I can just go swimming!" exclaimed Angelina, with peach juice running down her chin.

By four in the afternoon, the allure of the boardwalk was too great. Rocco and Giovanna couldn't bear the children's pestering any longer. "Va bene," said Rocco, "we'll go. But listen to me—we each get to do one thing. You can tell the others of your adventure."

"I know what I'm doing!" screamed Frances. "The slide in Dreamland!"

In the cabana, they dried themselves and brushed the sand off before slipping back into their Sunday best. They strolled the boardwalk, jostling elbows with every type of New Yorker and, for once, not feeling out of place. Everyone was so caught up in the sights and sounds around them that there was no time to look disdainfully at the immigrants and the poor. The crowd was equalized by the din of music from around the world and the promise of thrills.

Since Frances was the only one quite sure of what she wanted to do, they headed to Dreamland, walking down the Bowery. "This Bowery is sure different from our Bowery," commented Clement, looking at the signs advertising curious exhibitions, restaurants, and music halls.

"See it as it happened! The great Johnstown Flood!" yelled a barker, directing his call at them. After he took a closer look, he shouted, "Italians! Come right this way for the Fall of Pompeii, only ten cents!"

Giovanna asked the children what the man was saying. "I have no idea," answered Clement, speaking the truth.

"Guarda, Zia, there it is!" exclaimed Frances.

A gigantic angel, her wings forming a great arch, was the entrance to Dreamland. Inside, it was a city of fantasy. A great tower rose above a lagoon. Across the water, a mountain of slides were filled with obstacles that bumped and turned the shrieking riders until they reached the bottom in a breathless but exhilarated mess. At the other end, another man-made mountain of jagged peaks loomed, pierced by a train car weaving in and out of its slopes.

The children were unable to contain their excitement. They looked in every direction, speaking at once in Italian, English, and squeals of delight. Angelina clung to her mother, dazed. Rocco, too, looked either overwhelmed or simply dumbfounded. Giovanna took charge.

"We'll go to the slides for Frances."

At the sight of the long stairs and thousands of people, they were unwilling to allow Frances to go alone, so after negotiating with Clement, they agreed that this didn't count as his choice but that he should accompany his sister.

The wait wasn't nearly as long as Frances's and Clement's detailed descriptions of climbing the stairs, the fear in their bellies at the top, the push off, and each obstacle, twist, and turn along the way to the bottom, where they both tumbled head over heels. Giovanna cringed at seeing Frances upside down in her dress, but there were women far older who were doing the same thing with no one much noticing or caring.

"On the way up, I heard these boys talking about a Trip to Mars at Luna Park. That's where I want to go!" shouted Clement.

"Va bene. But first we will walk around here," answered Rocco.

"Mamma, look!" Angelina spied a miniature railroad that circled Dreamland. Children and adults, looking ridiculously out of scale, were stuffed into its little cars. The puffing engine enthralled Angelina, but none of her siblings could be persuaded to go on the ride, and her mother's big belly would never fit. On the verge of tears, she turned to her father. "Papa, it's your birthday, don't you want to ride with me on the train?"

Rocco, not generally a pushover even with his daughters, looked at Angelina and said, "Let's ride the train."

Giovanna and the children hid their laughter as the train circled round. Seated behind Angelina, Rocco had his knees nearly drawn to his chest. His embarrassment was washed away with Angelina's kisses and exclamations of joy when the ride ended.

"To Luna Park!" directed Clement.

The entrance to Luna Park was decorated with moons and half-moons of light. It was even more grandiose than Dreamland. They walked into a little Venice complete with gondoliers but flanked by pagoda-like structures. Frances let out a huge sigh upon seeing the Helter Skelter slide at Luna Park and worried that it might be better than the one at Dreamland. They wove their way through the crowds until they reached the Trip to Mars by Aeroplane. Clement got in line, and the family sat down on a bench nearby. Giovanna was grateful for the rest, but all too soon Clement came back.

"There were these boys on line who've been on everything here! I asked them which was the best and they said the Musical Railway near Dreamland."

"Clement, they're making fun of you! A musical railway! That is something Angelina would like!" growled Rocco.

"Papa, I only have one choice. Please let me see about this ride. They say the Trip to Mars is only *medza menz*."

"Okay, but we're not going back to Mars if you don't like this railway!"

Giovanna looked at Clement's excitement. For years now he had functioned as a man. It was wonderful to see him acting like a boy again. Giovanna got up off the bench, and they headed back toward Dreamland. From the size of the line at the Musical Railway, it appeared that the boys were right. Mary decided to make this her ride and went off with her brother. The sunlight was infused with the warm glow of early evening. They found an open bench; Angelina sat on Frances's lap, and Giovanna sat beside them. Rocco waited for Clement and Mary at the ride's exit. Nearly an hour later, the trio walked back to the bench. When Mary saw Giovanna, she broke from her father and ran to her, flinging herself into Giovanna's arms.

"Zia! We were in a train car, and it was completely dark, and then the train car fell straight down in the dark. I thought we would die!"

Rocco and Clement reached the bench. "Oh, Mary, don't be a baby!"

"You screamed, too, Clement, right before that beam almost took our heads off!"

"It was great, Zia. Don't listen to her."

Mary still clutched Giovanna, who caressed her head. "We never did have a treat after dinner, and I saw something for us to try. Let's go."

Giovanna led them to a stand selling ice cream on a wafer that you could hold and eat at the same time. Rocco counted out six nickels. Leaning on the rail by the water, they all laughed at the sight of one another licking the ice cream. "Mary, guarda! Don't lick too hard, it will fall off!" cautioned Giovanna. Clement was the first to make it down to the wafer and took a bite. "It's good!" he pronounced with melted ice cream running down his chin. But it was Giovanna who seemed most taken with these new concoctions.

As they licked their cones, they surveyed the boardwalk's goings-on. A barker in front of what was supposed to be a funny show did nothing but stand on a pedestal and laugh. Next door, a man outside a menagerie mimicked the sounds of wild animals to call attention to the attraction, roaring one minute and screeching like a bird the next.

A painting of a saint outside an attraction prompted Giovanna to ask Frances to translate the sign. "The Temptation of Saint Anthony," answered Frances. "The man keeps saying, 'See Saint Anthony avoid temptation!'"

"Giovanna, if you want, I will go with you."

Giovanna was surprised at Rocco's interest, but she figured it out when she saw the predominantly male crowd lined up for the "show." Her curiosity got the best of her, though, and after threatening Clement with his life if he or his sisters moved from the spot where they left them, Giovanna and Rocco joined the crowd, paying ten cents each to see the Temptation of Saint Anthony.

They entered a small room where a curtain was drawn to reveal a large oil painting of Saint Anthony on his knees, praying. The man who sold the tickets disappeared behind the painting and in an exaggerated but disinterested voice, began to tell of the life of the saint. Within minutes, men were grousing under their breath, and a second panel was revealed picturing a blonde clad in scanty garments. In a few more minutes, the murmured complaints started again and the blonde was replaced with another painting, this time of a brunette in slightly less clothing. Saint Anthony's life story conveniently ended after the third panel, of a near-naked redhead, was put in place. Giovanna was too amused to be offended and left simply shaking her head. "At least he knows a bit more about Saint Anthony," she thought.

Waiting like obedient soldiers, the children asked for an explanation of their parents' adventure. "It was nothing you haven't heard in church," remarked Giovanna, putting an end to further questions.

The sun was setting, and the electric lights were switched on. The sky began to swirl with color both natural and man-made. Cacophonous music drowned out the pounding of the surf. Rocco once again counted his money. "I have an idea. Before we go home, how about we all go on that Ferris wheel." The girls hugged him, and Giovanna smiled at the sight of her serious husband having fun.

By the time they got through the long line at the Ferris wheel, the sun had set but the sky was ablaze. It didn't seem possible that in darkness there could be so much light. The attendants opened the door to the car, which could have fit twenty people, but closed it after the family of six entered. They inched up into the sky as each car was unloaded and refilled, and then, the gigantic wheel began to turn in a slow, continuous motion.

The dancing lights of Luna Park, the view of Dreamland, and the searchlights on the sea left them breathless. Angelina wanted to stay on this Ferris wheel forever and squeezed her eyes shut trying to lock in the memory. When she opened her eyes, she saw her mother smiling at her and her father puffed-up with pride as they circled in the New York night.

"Happy birthday to you, happy birthday to you ..." Angelina's voice trailed off in the salty night air.

THIRTY-ONE

Rocco decided to bring his cart back an hour early to leave time to change for the Feast of Saint Rocco procession. Usually, his name day was the only day of the year he took off, but this year with their troubles, he decided to work.

It was hard maneuvering the cart through the throngs of people—and animals. Sheep were being led through the streets to be raffled off later that night in one of the many backyard celebrations. Because the Sicilians and Calabrians wouldn't gather together, there were competing holy rituals throughout Little Italy. Nearly any alley would take you to a shrine and backyard fire escapes festooned with decorations. At each shrine, a statue of Saint Rocco, typically owned by the local tavern, along with hundreds of candles and flowers, sat atop a makeshift altar covered in bedsheets.

Rocco had sold most everything he had because people bought more generously on feast days to prepare large meals. So when he was cleaning up, it didn't take long to notice a piece of paper in his cart. Unfolding it, he saw a drawing of a knife and a black handprint, but also something else—a crude drawing of a Ferris wheel with a car falling into the ocean.

The realization that they had been watching his family out of the neighborhood immobilized Rocco. He was frozen in fear, and for the first time he didn't immediately rip up a Black Hand threat—and for the first time he wanted to know what it said.

"It says bring the money, five hundred dollars, on Tuesday the twenty-fourth to the Garibaldi statue in Washington Square Park," read Clement.

"Five hundred dollars! They are crazy!"

"Papa, how did they know we went to Coney Island?"

"How? I don't know!" Rocco spit. "You trust no one."

"Maybe we should pay."

"Pay with what? We don't have five hundred dollars!"

"If they took the time to follow us to Coney Island, they're not going to go away."

"That's why I'll kill them."

"Papa, you're old . . ."

"Look at these muscles . . ."

Clement interrupted, "Papa! These are thugs."

"Then what, Clement?"

"Give them something until I find out who's behind this."

"No! You're not getting involved! I knew I shouldn't have shown you this! I want you to go far away! Do you hear me? Even if you go to Pennsylvania and work in those mines."

"Pop, you still have to decide what to do."

"I'll give them something. And if you try to get involved, I'll kill you myself."

AUGUST 29, 1909
HIGHLAND, NEW YORK

"How long you going to stay in the woods up here, Lupo?" asked Tommaso.

"It's not the woods. It's a cheese farm. Can't you see that, you jerk?"

"Lupo, you're not a country boy."

"Give me the ink and shut your mouth."

Tommaso pulled a large bottle from the sack around his shoulder. "How they doing in there?" asked Tommaso, pointing to the barn where two men were printing two-dollar bills off counterfeit plates.

"With this ink they can finish and we'll get rid of everything."

"But what if you get another order?"

"We're not taking no more orders. The cops, and not the kind we own, are poking around. Secret police from Washington. Do you have the money from Siena, the fruit seller?"

Tommaso the Bull put a twenty-dollar bill on the table.

"Twenty? We told him five hundred!"

"Lupo, those two punks who were working the street got their money and then blew up their store. He's only got a pushcart."

"No brains! Since when do you think you have brains? You listen to me. You think I'd demand five hundred dollars from a guy with a pushcart if I didn't know better? Huh? His wife, she sent a thousand dollars to her family in Italy after the earthquake. I got it direct. And how come those two morons knew they had money before we did? Get the five hundred dollars! And make it a regular payment!"

"I need money to get back."

"Walk, you idiot!"

"Come on, Lupo, just give me a couple of those," he said, pointing to a stack of counterfeit two-dollar bills.

"You really are an idiot. Here," said Lupo, throwing a five-dollar bill on the table. "You owe me change."

SEPTEMBER 1, 1909

Her belly was getting even bigger, but all out front. "It's a boy," thought Giovanna, rubbing her swelled stomach, "Little Nunzio." She made a strong espresso at the stove for Rocco while he dressed. In the predawn quiet, Giovanna wondered what was bothering her husband. He was even quieter than usual and avoided her eyes. In bed, he turned to the wall. He acted as if he couldn't bear to be near her, or the children for that matter.

"No bread. Just espresso," barked Rocco, coming to the table. Not taking the time to sit down, he threw back the thick black coffee. Mumbling *"Ciao,"* he left.

Rocco was leaving the house earlier and coming home from work later. He was exhausted, but his anger and stubbornness kept him going.

After he had given them money, they'd left more notes. This time he didn't ask Clement to translate and instead went back to ripping the notes into shreds. He told Clement all was well after he paid them twenty dollars.

When Giovanna sent the second payment to Scilla, he'd been relieved they weren't moving as he'd promised her they would. Life was dangerous on Elizabeth Street—but it could be worse somewhere else. Now, in idle moments, he spent his time counting the months to the next and final check, and he paid more attention when he heard people talking about places like Newark and Hoboken.

Rocco wheeled his cart into his regular spot. He eyed everyone who passed suspiciously and made a habit of patting his pocket to check on the presence of his knife. Today was a dull day, moisture clouding the dawn light. Only a few other vendors were setting up this early. Rocco methodically stacked his fruit into small towers on the cart. Across the street, the pepper seller alternated his greens and reds even though it was more practical to keep them separate. There was great pride and competitiveness in the display of produce, but Rocco was distracted. Lately his towers didn't have their usual aesthetic appeal—nor were they engineered well.

After creating a tower of pears, they suddenly began to tumble. He lurched forward to stop them from falling into the street at the exact moment he felt something drop behind his back. A split second later a thunderous thud caused Rocco to fall over his cart.

The noise and the sight of Rocco and his cart collapsing frightened the other vendors, and they fled. A woman screamed, *"La Mano Nera!"* and crossed herself. Within seconds Rocco was up, knife drawn, looking for the assailant. Instead, he saw a huge rock on the sidewalk where he had stood.

SEPTEMBER 4, 1909
HIGHLAND, NEW YORK

"Those idiots! They're lucky he moved. I said, 'Get the money,' not 'Kill him!' " fumed Lupo.

Pietro Inzerillo swatted at the flies circling his head. "Tommaso said he's Calabrian *gabbadotz*."

"The fruit seller may be stubborn, but Tommaso's stupid. You're sure they have the money, yes?"

"Twice she's received big payments, and she has more coming. It's a settlement from the gas company Brooklyn Union," answered Inzerillo, continuing his war on the flies.

"She got money from them? She's smarter than us. We're up here knee-deep in cow shit, and she sits home and gets fat checks from the Americans for nothing."

Lupo stormed around the barn while Inzerillo fanned himself with hay. There was a look of resolve on Lupo's pug face. "I'm going to give this one to Leo."

SEPTEMBER 8, 1909

"Commissioner Baker, it was an extremely successful mission," Lieutenant Vachris and Sergeant Crowley reported, standing at attention in the new police commissioner's office.

They had just returned from nearly three months in Italy. The Italian government was embarrassed by Lieutenant Petrosino's murder and had fully cooperated in collecting the penal records that Petrosino had uncovered. Lieutenant Vachris's eyes roamed the room. All traces of Commissioner Bingham, who had been replaced during their trip, were gone. The new commissioner didn't invite them to take a seat.

"I'm glad to see you two men home alive. We couldn't afford another screw-up over there."

Vachris was pretty sure he didn't like this man. "We were advised not to go into Sicily. They felt sure we would be killed. But with the Italian police, we were able to secure the records of seven hundred criminals. Seven hundred! Just about everyone from Lieutenant Petrosino's list and more."

Crowley jumped in. "Commissioner, if we could get more help on the Italian Squad, we can have most of these criminals deported within the year. The Italian colony would be free of crime."

"It's the best way to avenge Lieutenant Petrosino's death," added Vachris.

"I don't think we're ready to move that quick, men."

"But, sir, if the crooks are here three years, we can't get rid of them! Some of them will pass the three-year mark in just a few months." Thinking he'd made his argument clear based on the commissioner's silence, Lieutenant Vachris continued, "Detective Crowley and I figured out a plan to round them up . . ."

"I don't think you heard me, Lieutenant. I said we're not ready to move on this yet."

"But, Commissioner, look!" exclaimed Vachris, leafing through the papers in his hand. "In two months, these men will reach three years: Vincenzo Sapio, Tommaso the Bull, Alfonso . . ."

"We can pick them up right now," Detective Crowley interrupted before the commissioner could.

"There's more to policing in this city than the Italian Squad. This is one neighborhood, gentlemen! In fact, I need you both elsewhere, and I've arranged for your transfers to other departments."

"You can't . . ."

"I am the police commissioner, and I can. I suggest you take your transfers gratefully. I order you to not breathe a word of your mission or these records, which I will take for safekeeping. When we're ready, we'll deal with them."

"Will we be ready after the election, Commissioner?" sneered Vachris. Flipping through the records, he added, "Is it their votes or their fists that the alderman requires?"

"Vachris, I'll let that go with a two-week suspension, because I am sure you're tired from your trip. However, if I find out you have discussed this mission or its results with anyone, you'll be discharged from the force. Am I understood?"

Scilla, Italy, August 1978

I had been in Italy a month and was getting frustrated. No matter how many frescoes, bronzes, and cathedrals I saw, I wasn't satisfied. It took me a while to realize that I was looking for something I would never find in the splendor of the northern cities. I was trying to find Nonno's Italy. I needed to see where he fished for swordfish. I wanted to connect all those stories that he told me as a child with places that weren't imaginary.

"Nanny, I'm in Italy." An international call was a backpacking extravagance, but I was confused.

"What? I thought you were still in school in London."

"The term is over. I'm traveling. So, Nanny, I can't find Scilla on the map."

"You're going to go there?"

"If I can find it."

"Look in the toe. It's spelled S-c-i-l-l-a."

"No wonder. I was looking for S-h-e-i-l-a-h."

"That's Irish."

"Do we still have family there?"

"No, there was no work. They'll all be gone by now."

"Did you ever visit?"

"I went with the cousins' club in 1970, after Nonno died. It's beautiful there. But I was also there when I was a little girl. I went with my mother, just the two of us. That's when I first saw your grandfather . . ."

It took ten trains to get to the toe of the boot. The sea was a gorgeous turquoise that glowed in the early evening light. Land was visible across the water, and from all my staring at maps, I knew it was Sicily. The way my family spoke of Sicilians, it was hard to believe they came from the same country, let alone only a mile or two across the water. A mountain was also visible across the strait, and it was smoking. The difference between the civilized north and seismic south couldn't be more obvious.

There was only one pensione in town. It was called "Le Sirene"—"the mermaids"—and sat on a beautiful white sandy beach. The room was sparse. Tile floors, stuccoed walls. Over the bed was a picture of Saint Anthony. I tried to remember from catechism class what he was the patron saint of. His claim to fame wasn't visually obvious, like Saint Lucy, who was always shown holding her eyeballs on a plate. I had to look it up: "patron saint of those searching for something."

Hunger pangs struck, and I picked the restaurant with the swordfish on the sign. Inside, the walls were lined with old fishing pictures. I was stunned by how all the men's faces resembled my relatives. I stared harder hoping to actually recognize Nonno in one of the photos.

"What are you looking for?"

The man next to me spoke English.

"Well, my family was from Scilla."

"Thousands of American families were from Scilla." The man sounded bored, like he heard this all the time. From the way he stopped to talk to waiters, it was apparent he was the owner of the place.

Obligingly he asked, "What's your family's name?"

"Arena."

"Ah, Arena. You know what Arena means in Italian? It means 'sand.' There are nearly as many Arenas from Scilla as there are grains of sand on this beach."

"The town doesn't look that big."

"You Americans are so literal." Seeing I wasn't going to give up, he asked disinterestedly, "Do you know anyone who would have lived here in my lifetime?"

"My grandfather's name was Anthony, I mean Antonio."

"Half the boys are Rocco and half are Antonio. I'm Antonio."

"Well, I had an Uncle Sal who came back and forth from America."

"Salvatore Arena?"

"Yes."

"Tell me about this Salvatore." Antonio looked expectant.

"Well, he was pretty bad . . . ."

"What do you mean, 'bad'?"

"He was the black sheep. He gambled; he drank . . ."

"Salvatore Arena! He was my father's best friend! Salvatore," he said, shaking his head. "Sit down. Sit down."

Antonio led me back to my table and called for wine.

"You know, you have family here," he said. "Salvatore's two children—Cosmo is a fisherman, and he lives with his sister, Rosa, and her family."

"Where's their house?" I asked, practically standing up.

"In the Chianalea with all the fishermen. It's too late to go there now. Meet me here tomorrow morning, and I'll take you."

The next morning, Antonio was waiting outside the restaurant in his car. We drove less than a minute before he pulled over and parked.

"We have to walk from here. Cars don't fit in the Chianalea."

We wove our way down stone staircases and through narrow streets. Occasionally, I had to flatten myself against a wall to allow a scooter through. In the breaks between the houses, I could see the water. At a large opening between buildings, where five or six boats were drawn up on shore, a man sat repairing a net.

Antonio called in Italian, "Cosmo! Cosmo! This is your cousin from America."

"Che?"

"Questa è tua cugina."

Cosmo walked over, looking confused. Antonio explained that Cosmo's father and my grandfather were brothers. Cosmo nodded, and I smiled. I saw an older woman walking toward us holding groceries in netted bags. She stared at me for a moment, dropped her bags, and ran over.

"You're family. You're family," she said repeatedly in Italian while stroking my hands. When Antonio confirmed what she already knew, my cousin Rosa cried and kissed my face.

"Ciao, I have to get back to the restaurant," called Antonio, walking off.

I panicked. "But Antonio, you can't leave. My Italian is terrible."

"You'll manage; it's your family," he answered from farther down the alley.

I looked at my smiling cousins and understood they needed to feed me.

For five days, I was fed and feted. There were more cousins, some distant, but all insisted that I eat with them. At these meals, with the little bit of Italian I knew, and lots of drawings, I learned about my grandfather's life in Scilla. They showed me where my grandfather caught his biggest swordfish, where my great-grandmother Fortunata got her water at the public fountain, pictures of all the Arena brothers and sisters, and old postcards from America.

On the second day, Rosa took a key off her wall and said we were going to Nonno's house. She stopped in front of a small building a few doors down and behind her own house.

"This is where my father, Salvatore, and your grandfather Antonio were born and lived," explained Rosa.

I was practically shaking as I entered the vacant house. There was little inside, but it was easy to imagine that nothing had changed since Nonno was born there eighty-three years ago. When I asked why no one lived in the house now, Cosmo, whom I had the easiest time communicating with, explained that there was no water or electricity. He also said something about how they had tried to fix the house after an earthquake, but that the repairs hadn't lasted.

On my last day in Scilla, I walked past a stone house that looked like it was built into the foundation of the church above it. We had walked past this house many times, and I had noticed that it seemed older than all the other buildings.

"This was your great-grandmother Giovanna's house," said Rosa.

I was so focused on my grandfather's life in Scilla that I hadn't asked about Big Nanny's house and family. This house was also vacant, but no one could remember who had the key. Cosmo explained that Big Nanny's house was one of the oldest houses in the village because it wasn't destroyed in the same earthquake that had made Nonno's house uninhabitable.

"The fisherman's church above it was ruined—that's a new church, built in 1910. But your great-grandmother's house, because it's built into the cliff, survived. Her parents lived in the house alone after their children went to America. No one has lived here since they died."

"What do you know about my great-grandmother?" I asked, my mind instantly going back to the blue sparkling dress in the coffin.

"Your great-grandmother was my second cousin," answered Cosmo. These conversations were difficult enough to understand in English, never mind in a foreign language. When Cosmo drew a family tree, I understood. I knew Nonno was related to Big Nanny, but seeing it explained in boxes and lines made sense.

"There are still stories in Scilla about your great-grandmother. She left before I was born, but because she was a midwife, the tales got passed down."

"Who was her first husband again?"

"Nunzio, my great-uncle. He was killed in a construction accident in New York."

The family in Italy seemed much better than the Americans at passing down family history and keeping track of who was who.

When I tried to leave, I was told I couldn't. "The Feast of Saint Rocco is only two days away! Cosmo will carry the saint!" exclaimed Rosa.

I knew it wasn't negotiable. So for the first time, I left my notebook and questions back with the mermaids and Saint Anthony and swam out into the Strait of Messina.

PART NINE

NEW YORK, NEW YORK
SEPTEMBER 11, 1909–DECEMBER 8, 1909

THIRTY-TWO

SATURDAY, SEPTEMBER 11, 1909

Angelina squirmed as Giovanna took the rags out of her hair. The night before, Giovanna had wrapped Angelina's wet locks in rags to make perfect ringlets, which now sprung free.

"Happy birthday, my beautiful big four-year-old girl!" cried Giovanna, taking Angelina and kissing her. "Your Nonna and Nonno won't believe how much you've grown in a year when they see your picture."

"Will it hurt my eyes?" asked Angelina.

"No, not at all. And when we're done we'll eat pizza at Lombardi's, just the two of us."

"Mamma, I love you!" exclaimed Angelina, hugging her mother.

"That's not all. Tomorrow, your cousins will come for Sunday dinner and we'll have a party."

Angelina practically danced all the way to the photographer's studio on Grand Street. Her white dress bounced around her, but whenever it was in danger of touching a building or another person, she protectively held her dress close so that it wouldn't get dirty. The ringlets were nearly gone, but her hair shone.

Once inside, a kindly man with a waxed mustache stood her on an elaborately carved oak chair. A screen painted with a landscape was the backdrop. Angelina kept fussing with her dress, frustrating the photographer, who was trying to keep her hands still.

"I think she should hold something," he mumbled to Giovanna.

Looking around his studio, he grabbed a flag that he had gotten at a parade. The photographer liked to put American objects in the portraits, knowing they would impress the sitter's relatives in Italy.

"Here, Angelina, I want you to hold this flag."

It worked. Angelina, statue still, held the little white flag that said ERIN GO BRAGH. Giovanna shuffled behind the photographer's umbrella as he covered himself with a big black cloak. A muffled voice came from beneath the black fabric.

"Angelina, don't move anything, not even your face. Pretend you're a doll, and look right here at the camera. You're going to hear a pop and see smoke, but stay still."

"*Cosí bella*, Angelina!" exclaimed Giovanna.

"*Uno, due, tre ...*"

THIRTY-THREE

SUNDAY, SEPTEMBER 12, 1909

The early morning sun streamed through the stained glass, making colored patterns on the pew that Angelina used as stepping-stones for her fingers. Her mother was kneeling, so Angelina's fingers walked behind her mother's back to tickle Mary, who sat on the other side. Mary gave her a stern look. Rebuked, Angelina leaned against the pew and clasped her hands in prayer. Squeezing her eyes shut, she whispered, "God, please make this mass over, and bless Mamma, Papa, Mary, Frances, Clement, and everyone who is going to visit me today. It was my birthday yesterday. But I guess you know that. Grazie. Amen."

Giovanna stirred a pot on the stove. "Angelina, you're making me crazy. Only five minutes ago you asked what time it was."

"Mamma, that was more than five minutes."

"Mary, see if there is something in that room to amuse her." Giovanna needed Mary and Frances to help with the preparation of the meal; otherwise, she would have sent one of them outside to play with the anxious Angelina.

"Can I put my dress on, Mamma?" pleaded Angelina.

"No, it's too early. It's at least two more hours before anyone will arrive."

"Come on, Angelina. Take a look at this," encouraged Mary, showing her one of her schoolbooks. It was not often that Mary let her touch her books, and Angelina jumped at the opportunity.

Giovanna peered over her stomach and down at her swollen feet. She would have to remember to sit down as much as possible. Sprinkling the table with more flour, she leaned into the dough, which was nearly up to her elbows, when there was a knock at the door.

"Frances, please."

Frances opened the door to their neighbor Limonata and her daughter.

"Ciao, Giovanna. I hear you are already so busy. I'm taking Carmela for a walk. Do you want me to take Angelina with us?"

Giovanna looked at Limonata with surprise. It was not like Limonata to take a walk or to make such an offer. She was even wearing Sunday clothes and a hat. Maybe things were looking up for her.

When Giovanna didn't answer right away, Limonata stammered, "We'll go for a banana. I know you love bananas, right, Angelina?"

"Yes! Yes! Can I go, Mamma, please?"

Giovanna noticed that Carmela had not let go of her mother's hand nor looked up from the floor.

"Carmela, are you feeling well?" Giovanna asked.

"Oh, she's fine," answered Limonata, before Carmela could open her mouth.

"Please, Mamma, can I go?"

Giovanna looked at Angelina's excited face and silently chastised herself. Where was this reluctance coming from? Only minutes ago, she couldn't get Angelina out from beneath her feet, and now her neighbor was offering to take her for a walk.

"We'll just go for an hour," said Limonata.

"Mamma, should I put on my dress?"

Giovanna hesitated and said, "Don't change now. When you get back."

"Okay, then. Let's go," mumbled Limonata, taking Angelina's hand.

"Wait," said Giovanna. "Angelina, give Mamma a kiss." Angelina jumped up and her mother bent down. "Please, Limonata, only an hour. All our family is coming for her party, and she'll need to change."

Limonata led the girls to the stairs. "No problem, just a walk and a banana."

Seeing Limonata's smile, Giovanna felt guilty for her initial hesitation and called down the stairs after them. "Limonata, if you and Carmela would like to join us, you're welcome for dinner."

Limonata didn't turn around but said, "Grazie, sì, sì."

"We're walking far, signora!"

"We're going to my brother. He always has a banana."

"You can get a banana on Mott Street."

"But today is Sunday."

"Oh." Angelina seemed to take notice of the silent Carmela's clothes for the first time. "Carmela, you have so many things on, aren't you hot?"

Before she could answer, Limonata did. "She has a cough, she must stay warm. See, here we are already."

A tall, skinny man with a droopy eye was waiting in front of a butcher store on Delancey Street. "Angelina, this is my brother." Angelina didn't see a banana and looked around his back in case he was hiding it. Noticing her looking, Limonata said, "He's going to take you to get the banana."

"But I have to get home for my party!"

"Oh, not far," mumbled Limonata.

The man took Angelina's hand, and she pulled it away, clinging to Limonata.

"No, no, Angelina, you go with my brother."

"Aren't you coming?"

"I have to go to the dentist to have my tooth pulled. He'll go with you."

"I don't want the banana. I want to go home."

"Come on, I'll take you home," said the brother.

Limonata was already halfway down the block with Carmela racing to catch up, so Angelina reluctantly took the outstretched hand of this man.

Angelina shouted to Limonata, "Can Carmela come with us?"

Limonata didn't look back or answer, and when Carmela turned around, she yanked her daughter's arm forward.

"Come on, kid. I'll get you the banana and take you home on the train."

"The train?" This sounded good to Angelina. She couldn't walk any farther and wanted to get home soon.

"Forza," ordered the man.

"Where's the birthday girl?" asked Teresa, bursting through the door with her three little ones, as the older children, including Domenico, squeezed around her to get in the tenement.

"Our neighbor Limonata took her for a walk, but they're late. I asked her to be home long before now."

"She probably couldn't get them out of the park," said Teresa, setting down a package and a tray of stuffed calamari, her specialty.

Lorenzo eventually made it up the stairs. "Ciao, *sorella mia!*" He took a look at Giovanna and asked, "What's the matter?"

"What's the matter? She's seven months pregnant and cooking in the heat," answered Teresa.

Lorenzo squinted at Giovanna who replied, "No, nothing. I'm just upset that Angelina isn't back yet."

"Don't worry. She'll be upstairs any minute."

Angelina looked at the tall, dark, thin man buying the tickets for the El. He didn't look at all like Limonata, who was short and pale. Turning away from the kiosk, he shouted in a thick Sicilian accent, "Come on, kid," over the roar of an approaching train.

The train was practically empty. After sitting down, Angelina moved a seat away from Limonata's brother. "This train will take us to Elizabeth Street?" she asked.

"Yeah."

Angelina stared out the window. In a few minutes they were heading over the Brooklyn Bridge.

"This isn't the way to my house. This is the way to Coney Island." Angelina stood up from her seat. "We're going the wrong way!"

The only two other people on the train looked up at the little girl. The man pulled her back into her seat.

"This is another way. You don't know this way. Sit down." He looked at the people and smiled, relieved to hear that they were speaking

English. They smiled back. When the train pulled to a stop, Angelina jumped back up.

The man took her arm and pulled her into the seat with a forced smile on his face. He said through gritted teeth, "Stay in this seat." His voice was tough, his grip firm, and his droopy eye looked even more frightening from below.

Angelina began to cry, and when the doors to the train closed at the stop, her cry turned into a wail.

The two other passengers stared once again, and the man smiled and shrugged, trying to communicate, "What's a father to do?" This time the passengers didn't smile back but turned away.

"Look, stop crying. We'll get off soon and I'll get you the damn banana."

"I don't want a banana. I want to go home!"

With the passenger's eyes upon them, the man turned to Angelina and, using a sweet tone of voice, said, "If you say another word, or cry again, you'll never go home."

The table was piled with meatballs, lasagna, stuffed calamari, eggplant parmigiana, olives, and artichokes. A large number four cut from paper hung from the ceiling. The adults sat around the table, silent. Giovanna stormed out and went upstairs to bang on Limonata's door. Rocco called to her, "Giovanna, you knocked ten minutes ago. We would hear them come home!" Giovanna, wringing her hands on her apron, walked back downstairs into the apartment. Rocco looked at his wife and said, "Okay, everyone, let's eat. Call the children. When she gets home, she'll eat."

Lorenzo quietly obeyed, taking a plate and filling it with food. Soon the apartment was noisy again as the children bounded up the stairs and hungrily dove on the table. Teresa helped them fix their plates while Giovanna remained in the hall watching the door.

"We're getting off," growled the man, grabbing Angelina's hand. He no longer pretended to be nice—the other two passengers had left the train, and they were alone. She noticed they were leaving the train before she could see Coney Island, but after they had passed most of the houses. Angelina bit her lip. She was trying so hard not to cry; she wanted to go home.

"Where are we going?"

The man didn't even bother to answer her anymore.

"I can't walk so fast," she pleaded, wiping her eyes on her shoulders so he wouldn't see the tears.

"Are the signora and Carmela going to be here?"

"Yeah. Keep walking."

At the base of the stairs to the El there was open space in every direction. The man pulled her down the one paved street. Every few hundred feet, a house or store faced the road. That road led to another with even fewer buildings. Two buildings faced each other—a ramshackle wooden house and a small brick office with a sign in the window. The man led her to the door of the house and knocked. A short man answered and hurried them into a small room with a black stove in the middle of the floor. Two women and four children, all smaller than Angelina, stared at her.

"What are we doing here? Who are these people?" asked Angelina, with the tears she couldn't control streaming down her face again.

The short man ignored her and talked to Limonata's brother. "Bravo. Any problems, Leo?"

"Idiot!" spat Leo, slapping the man's face. "What did I tell you about names?"

Angelina became even more frightened. "I want to go home. Take me home," she screamed, turning her plea to the woman.

The tall man named Leo grabbed her arm. "What I told you on the train is the same here. If you cry, or scream, or don't listen, you'll never go home again. You be quiet, forget everything you hear and see, and you'll go home."

"Get her in the room, " the short guy growled to one of the women, still angry and embarrassed by Leo's rebuke.

The men and older boys were out searching the streets. Before they left, Rocco's last words were, "Talk to no one, and if anyone goes to the police, I'll kill you with my own hands."

Giovanna had already tried to get into Limonata's apartment via the fire escape, but the window was locked and so dirty she couldn't see anything inside. Finally, she heard the sound of the super opening his door, and she flew down the steps.

"Limonata borrowed my beer pitcher. She's not home. Can you open the door?"

"You know I don't like to do that. Can't you wait?"

"How am I supposed to get beer for this crowd?"

"Alright, I'll be up in a minute."

Giovanna paced in front of Limonata's door until she heard the super's heavy footsteps and keys jangling on his way up the stairs.

"I'll wait here," mumbled the super at the threshold to the apartment.

Giovanna was trying extremely hard to act as if nothing was wrong as she walked into Limonata's apartment. But even in the late afternoon light she could sense that something was not right. Limonata had little in her two rooms, but now there was even less. Giovanna glanced around the kitchen. The shelves were empty, there was no cloth on the table, and the pot was missing. But it was the bedroom that confirmed her worst fears—the clothes rack was empty. She had been breathing deeply to calm herself, and her breath turned into an inhaled scream.

The super came in and looked around. *"Puttana!"* He kicked the table and turned to Giovanna. "You're screaming because she took your beer pitcher! I have to tell the big man she left without paying last month's rent!"

The woman led Angelina into a small room with a little window. Quickly, she pulled a thick piece of dark muslin over it, blocking the view of the brick office across the street.

"Why did he take me here?" Angelina openly sobbed now that she was out of sight of the men.

"I know nothing. But you listen to them and stop your crying. I'll get you something to eat."

"I can eat at home. Here, see, I stopped crying. He said if I didn't cry I would go home," asserted Angelina, pushing past the woman to the door. The woman grabbed Angelina's arm, flung her back in the room, and quickly closed the door behind her. Angelina heard the lock click as she lunged for the doorknob.

The sound of Rocco and the men returning reached the kitchen before they did. Giovanna knew they hadn't found Angelina and not only because their trudging footsteps told her so.

"She's gone. Limonata's gone, Rocco!" The door was not even fully opened when Giovanna began shouting. "Nothing is left in the apartment. I know what this means. Did they come to you again, Rocco? Did they? Did you not tell me? Did you not pay them?"

"Giovanna, stop it. People will hear!"

"What people, Rocco? My brother? Your children? You're a fool, Rocco! A stupid, stubborn fool! You should have paid them the money!"

"Be quiet!"

"I will not be quiet! They have my daughter!" shouted Giovanna, collapsing into a chair and desperately trying to get her breath.

"Send one of the boys for Lucrezia," instructed Teresa.

"No! No, don't get her. Don't get anyone. We'll take care of this!" growled Rocco. "Listen to me. I want everyone in this room now," he commanded with a ferocity even his children hadn't seen before. The children in the other rooms squeezed into the kitchen. "Angelina is fine. She has gone visiting. Do you hear me? She is visiting. That is all you know. And if anyone," he looked straight at Teresa, "says anything different to anyone outside of this room, they will have blood on their hands. Now, go home and remember—Angelina is visiting relatives!"

THIRTY-FOUR

MONDAY, SEPTEMBER 13, 1909

Hollow-eyed and silent, Giovanna and Rocco sat at the kitchen table. Neither had changed nor slept. Rocco had spent most of the night walking the streets looking for the square-headed man who had come to his cart. The children, bleary-eyed themselves, woke up slowly. Mary filled the coffeepot, and Frances lit the stove to toast the bread.

Clement slid into a chair next to his father. "Papa, what do we do now?"

"You put on your clothes and go to work. Even you, Frances. See if you can get sewing work from the signora down the street. Or ask Zia Teresa about factory jobs."

Mary stood at attention, waiting for her assignment. When her father didn't address her, she asked, "Papa?"

"You go to school. People will be suspicious if we take you out of school, but Frances should have been out long ago."

Rocco had heard from Teresa that Giovanna hadn't spoken for many months after her husband's death; he wondered if it was going to happen again. Giovanna hadn't said anything since last night, and she didn't protest when Rocco ordered Frances to work. He was thinking it might not be a bad thing for Giovanna to lose her speech—but then she spoke.

"Mary, I'll get piecework for you to do after school."

Rocco assumed this was Giovanna's way of saying she approved of what he was doing. He was grateful for this little bit of recognition.

Rocco got up. "Let's go. I'll take Mary across the street and tell the principal it is time for Frances to go to work."

Giovanna remained seated as the family bustled around her. While her body and lips were motionless, her mind was reeling. Her husband's solution to everything was to work. While she was grateful he at least took action, did he really believe that the money the children brought in would make a difference? She wanted him and everyone else out of the apartment so that she could leave before Teresa showed up.

Last night, Rocco described the big man who had come to his cart, and Clement said that he was the same man he saw in the Star of Italy and that his name was Tommaso. Giovanna was anxious to walk through the neighborhood. There had to be something she could find that Rocco didn't.

The moment that everyone was gone, Giovanna removed the clothes she had been wearing since the day before, washed her face, and dressed. In the hall she heard the calls and burdened footsteps of the iceman. The doors on the second floor were opening and closing. Looping string through the buttonholes on her skirt to accommodate her belly, she was knotting it together when outside her own door the man called, *"Issaman!"*

"I need no ice," answered Giovanna, opening the door a crack. But instead of a block of ice on his shoulder, the iceman held out an envelope.

"Signora, a man downstairs asked me to bring this to you since I was coming up."

Giovanna did not move to take the envelope from the iceman's outstretched hand.

"Who gave you this?"

"I told you, a man outside."

"What man? Show him to me?" pleaded Giovanna, flinging open the door and running to the window.

The iceman reluctantly went to the window and looked. "I don't see him. I made two deliveries before I came to your door. Signora, are you going to take this?" he asked once again, stretching out his hand.

"Sì, sì." Giovanna glanced at the envelope. "What did he look like? Big chest and square head?"

"No, short, a mustache." The man got frustrated. "I don't know, signora. You put two hundred pounds on your shoulder, and the only thing you notice is that your back hurts."

The frantic expression on Giovanna's face finally caught his attention. "Signora, what's wrong?"

His question stopped Giovanna's mind from racing, and she tried to cover, "No, no, nothing." Walking him to the door, she said, "I was hoping it might have been word from a woman whose child I must deliver. Thank you." She closed the door. The sweat from Giovanna's hand had already stained the envelope. Lifting the flap, she removed a coarse piece of brown paper.

Giovanna steadied herself against the wall at the confirmation of what she already knew. She moved in fruitless circles from the window to the table. Reading about the earthquake had given her experience at feeling powerless, but this was worse. Her child was frightened, maybe hurt, or worse, and there wasn't anyone running to rescue her. It was like the type of nightmare where you try to move but nothing happens. Both she and Angelina were imprisoned.

When she caught her breath she took in the words of the note. Four thousand dollars! Disgraziati! What made these thieves think that they had such money? What could she possibly put in the envelope to satisfy them?

TUESDAY, SEPTEMBER 14, 1909

Angelina awoke from her second night spent on the floor. She was able to figure out that there were two women, two men, and two sets of children in the little house. One of the women, the younger one, had brought her rags and hay that she had used to cover the cold floor tile. The hay was the only thing she had to amuse herself with when she was locked back into the room before the men came home for supper. Doll-like shapes that she had braided and twisted from the straw the night before were lined up against the wall.

She could hear them eating breakfast. She didn't understand all the words because they spoke in a thick dialect that sounded like the Sicilian neighbors on her block. Picking up and braiding more straw, she had nearly tuned them out when one of the men thundered, "What do you mean you went together to the market!"

"There was too much to carry!"

"*Merda!*" Angelina heard a hard slap.

"What if she screamed and someone had heard her?"

"She didn't scream."

"How would you know, you weren't here! Only one of you goes shopping and the other stays here with the children. *Capisci?*"

Angelina's silent tears began to flow, although this time it was not because she was frightened but because she was mad at herself. She hadn't thought to scream. Why hadn't she screamed? What a stupid girl she was! She wasn't smart like the principal said! If she had screamed, someone in that office across the street with the blue shade could have heard her. She pinched herself in anger and frustration. She had lost her chance to get away.

"And don't you let the bambini play with her! They could tell someone!"

"Who would they tell? You won't let us out!"

Angelina heard another whack and then crying. She drew her knees to her chest and slid as far as possible into the corner.

Looking down from her window, Giovanna saw three women from the building talking outside the front door. Their building had no stoop, making it difficult to congregate, so conversations didn't last long. She quickly grabbed her basket and headed downstairs.

"Buon giorno," greeted Giovanna, opening the door.

"Buon giorno," answered the women, who, because of Giovanna's midwife status, treated her respectfully.

Not one to stop and chat, Giovanna used her own pregnancy as an excuse. "Those stairs are getting difficult," she complained, rubbing her belly.

"Can't one of the children do the shopping?" the neighbor asked.

"Between work and school, they don't have the time. I was going to ask Limonata to help me," fished Giovanna.

"You know that she up and left without paying the rent?" exclaimed the other woman.

"I heard she was gone. Did anyone know she was going?" Giovanna asked as nonchalantly as possible.

"Who knows? I never liked her. No father to that child. She said he died, but with all those boyfriends, who could believe her!"

"Maybe she left with her boyfriend," offered up Giovanna. "Wasn't she seeing a man with red hair?"

"No, that was ages ago, signora. Her latest was dark with a lidded eye. He looked like a dead fish!"

"Oh, I think I did see him. He was heavy, yes?"

"No, that must have been another one. This one was tall and bony.

Like a mackerel. I heard her call him Leo."

"Well, if you see this Leo or Limonata, will you tell me? She left with my beer pitcher!"

"That puttana!" exclaimed one of the ladies. "I saw you give her food, signora, and she stole from you!"

Giovanna could feel her eyes welling up and her body quaking. "Sì, well if you hear . . . buon giorno," she stammered, rushing off to her nonexistent errands.

Giovanna saw that Inzerillo took notice when she entered his Café Pasticceria. Pretending to look at the pastries, she waited until there was no one else near the counter.

"Signore, I was wondering if I could get your advice."

"Why, of course, signora." Inzerillo motioned someone into the back room, which was quickly emptied of four men holding cards.

Closing the door behind them, he asked, "What can I do for you, signora?"

"Signore, I need to communicate with some men who I do not know. I need these people to understand a few important things." Giovanna paused, trying to gauge whether his expression registered any recognition of what she was saying. But he was either clueless or playing it smart.

"Go on, signora."

"I need these men to understand three things. First, they must know that I do not believe you can ever work with the police. Second, they should know that there is no money under my mattress, but I will get what I can. And third, signore, they must understand that if anything ever happened to anyone in my family, I would hunt them down and slit their throats."

"Signora, I assure you that I have no knowledge of what would prompt you to deliver such a message. But without putting anyone at risk, I will do my best to find these men and communicate this information."

"One of the men might be large with a squarish head. Another, short with a mustache. And perhaps one is tall and skinny with a lidded eye."

"Don't worry, signora, I will find them," assured Inzerillo.

It had taken every bit of Giovanna's strength to say her piece without breaking down. She felt her facade crumbling, and she wanted to collapse into this man's arms, who she knew was a murderer. With her last ounce of fortitude, she said, "Grazie, signore," and got up quickly to make her exit.

"Signora," Inzerillo called. Giovanna stopped but did not turn, not trusting that she could control her tears. "Signora, you did the right thing by coming to me. I will see that your message is delivered."

WEDNESDAY, SEPTEMBER 15, 1909

Giovanna started the day by buying the paper, for while Rocco's weapon and solace was work, Giovanna's was information.

After scanning every headline for anything relevant, Giovanna went back to page one. PEARY GETS TO NORTH POLE. Giovanna bristled with resentment at the irony. Some man had managed to find the end of the earth, and she couldn't find her daughter.

Picking up a pencil, she copied the note she had written to the kidnappers for the fifth time, making sure it was perfect.

In this envelope is $507. This is all the money that we have in the world. You are mistaken if you think we have more. Please take it and return our daughter and we will never speak of this. She is only a little girl, please.

She would deliver the note tonight. With Angelina's birthday dress in her lap, she prayed that all would go well and this would be over. She had picked up the dress yesterday and hadn't put it down since. Initially, she held it to her face, searching for a scent of her daughter—the sweet smell of her skin after her bath or the soft whisper of her breath. There was no vestige of Angelina to be found.

At supper she didn't eat a thing and picked up the plates from the table before the others finished. Rocco and Clement rose to put on their boots.

"Why are you getting dressed?" Giovanna's blue eyes narrowed.

"Don't be ridiculous. You're not going there alone."

"We spoke of this! We can't frighten them!"

"They'll only see you. But Clement and I will be near in case you need us."

"If this is what you wanted, you should have told me earlier! What makes you think they're not watching! If they see you leave they'll think you're meeting the police."

Rocco wondered where his wife had learned to think this way. "Okay, Clement and I will go to the roof and leave from another building," he said, continuing to put on his shoes.

"If I wanted to watch the front door of a building, I would watch it from the roof."

"What do you want?" Rocco shouted in exasperation.

"To do this as we planned. I'm in no danger. There's no money for them without me."

Rocco knew she spoke the truth, but he couldn't let her leave without protection. He went into the bedroom and called Giovanna to join him. Closing the door behind her, he went to the bottom drawer of their one bureau, where his two extra shirts were stored, and from beneath the shirts drew out a pistol.

Giovanna stifled a gasp.

"After they threw the rock, I got it from Clement's friend. It cost practically nothing."

Staring at the gun in disbelief and confusion, she quickly became practical. "How does it work?"

"You cock it here and pull the trigger. There are three bullets."

"I won't need this, Rocco, but thank you." Giovanna took the gun from his hand and floundered for somewhere to put it. Rocco lifted her blouse and tucked it into her waistband. "It won't show; the baby will hide it."

"You're right," replied Giovanna, looking down at herself. "I should go."

"Giovanna, I love you." The words hung in the air. Rocco had never said it before. Giovanna was taken aback. Despite the emotion of the moment, she believed he meant it.

She stroked his face as affectionately as she could manage. "Thank you, Rocco."

They opened the door, and the children who had been leaning

against it eavesdropping jumped back. All three studied Giovanna's waistline in awe.

Giovanna took her red shawl, wrapped it around her shoulders, and said, "Do not follow me. If I am not home by ten o'clock you can come looking for me."

Mary was crying, and Giovanna hugged her at the door. "I am perfectly safe, and we will get your sister back."

By the time she had walked three blocks north, her body heat had warmed the metal of the gun, and the envelope had settled into position within her corset. Heading toward Washington Square, she planned her route to avoid the streets near Lucrezia's apartment. They hadn't seen each other since the kidnapping, and there was no way she would get past her without revealing something.

Checking the time, she saw that she still had half an hour and only a few blocks to go. She was east of the park on Broadway and Bond. She slowed down, wanting to time her arrival to a few minutes before eight, and said a prayer of thanks that the moon was nearly full. Her hope was to get a good look at the man so she could find him again and trail him.

As she approached the park, she saw Garibaldi's back, hand to the hilt of his sword, at the ready to unsheathe his weapon. She allowed herself the fantasy of Garibaldi springing to life and slicing up the kidnapper, scaring him into bringing her to Angelina. At that moment it occurred to her that she could put Rocco's gun to the man's head and demand to be taken to her daughter. Adrenaline pumped through her body thinking about it, but when she played the scenario out in her head, her initial euphoria was dampened by the thought that there would surely be other gang members among the trees, or that the bagman wouldn't even know where Angelina was hidden. The kidnapper's rules would have to prevail.

Reaching the statue, she leaned back on the base. She didn't see anyone waiting or suspiciously idle. She was looking down, pretending to tend to her swollen feet, when a legless beggar rolled toward her.

"Scusi, signora, you have something for me?"

"*Vai*, go, go." Giovanna brushed him away with her hand.

"I believe you have something for me. An envelope."

Giovanna was so stunned that she stared down wordlessly at the crippled man who was atop a piece of wood with wheels attached.

"Signora, in two seconds I will be gone."

Giovanna bent toward the man and swiftly took the envelope from her blouse. The second she placed the envelope in his hands, the cripple put his knuckles to the paving stones and launched his body away.

"Wait!! I must talk to you!" Giovanna called after him fruitlessly. He sped around a group of people strolling through the park, and in seconds the beggar bagman was nowhere in sight. She walked aimlessly through the park, looking around trees and bushes, hoping against hope to see Angelina. Instead, there was emptiness. There was no sign of her daughter, no money clutched to her bosom, and no one to follow. Giovanna felt consumed by her own naïveté and terror.

THURSDAY, SEPTEMBER 16, 1909

The front door slammed, and Angelina waited anxiously for her own door to open. When it didn't happen quickly enough, Angelina moaned through the door, "Signora, please, please, the men are gone. I'll be good."

"Stop your begging." The door opened abruptly. "Okay, out." Angelina moved around the older woman's skirts. Halfway out the door, she grabbed her. "Get your chamber pot. No reason you can't empty it yourself. I'm not your slave."

"Sì, signora." Angelina headed back into the room for the bucket that was her toilet. "Where do I empty it, signora?"

"So, the *principessa* has never emptied a chamber pot?"

"No, signora, we have a toilet."

"Yes, of course, you're a principessa. It's only pee. Throw it out the back door."

Angelina opened the back door and squinted; she couldn't see. Her first glimpse of sunlight blinded her. Before her eyes could adjust, the other woman pulled her back in by the shoulder and shut the door. "What are you doing?"

"The signora told me to empty the pot."

"Are you crazy?" The woman turned to the other. "You'll be beaten again if she goes outside."

"They are such big shots! But who has to feed her and take care of her? And where is this fortune? Where?"

Angelina cowered against the wall. She feared the anger would spill over to her. The woman who was yelling looked older, although they were nearly identical.

The four children said little. They would often just sit and stare or become amused by the simplest of things. During the first few days they would poke her, giggle, and run away. As dismal as the company was, it was much better than being locked alone in the room, so Angelina did everything she could to please the women. She didn't cry. She barely made a noise, and she helped with the two littlest children.

After her outburst, the woman calmed down and went about her chores. The oldest child, a boy nearly her age, was drawing on the kitchen wall with a charred piece of wood. The first day, when she had asked the child's name, the younger woman smacked Angelina's face, so she knew to tug on a sleeve to get attention. Not wanting to share, the boy pointed to another piece of wood, and Angelina settled herself next to him and began writing her letters. His curiosity got the best of him, and when he asked what they were, Angelina was thrilled with the opportunity to play teacher. For the next hour she forgot her fear, hunger, and sadness.

THIRTY-FIVE

FRIDAY, SEPTEMBER 17, 1909

Giovanna had spent all day Thursday pacing the small apartment waiting for word. The second she heard a sound in the hall, she would throw open the door, only to startle a neighbor. At the call of the iceman, she ran to the window and asked if he had anything for her.

"I have a big block of ice."

"No, I mean an envelope."

"Signora, I am the iceman, not the postman."

Today, Rocco had left the house at dawn, only to return minutes later. Handing the letter to Giovanna, he said, "It was in my empty cart."

Giovanna shook and wept. Rocco tried to comfort his wife, his large hands patting her shoulders.

"What about going to that lawyer and getting the rest of the money?" asked Rocco.

"I tried, yesterday. Signore DeCegli became suspicious. He showed me in the contract where it said that the money can only be paid on the dates in the agreement."

WEDNESDAY, SEPTEMBER 22, 1909

Padre Luongo exited Our Lady of Loreto and was surrounded by a gang of children tugging at his vestments. Mary noticed the group from afar and watched them come toward her. One little boy was shouting, "Padre, Padre, it's my birthday!" The priest stopped, dug into his robes, and produced a gleaming nickel, which he placed in the boy's hand. The children surrounded him and then ran off together in the opposite direction.

The priest, now alone, passed Mary. She ran a couple of feet to catch up.

"Padre, you give all children a nickel on their birthday?"

"If they ask."

"It's my birthday, Padre."

"Well then, here's a nickel for you. Happy birthday, my child."

Mary made the sign of the cross. The priest smiled at what he thought was her piety.

"Please, God, forgive me, but I know you'll understand," Mary muttered.

SATURDAY, SEPTEMBER 25, 1909

Giovanna cleared the dinner table and retreated to her bedroom. She dropped to her knees before the shrine she had created of candles flanked by statues of the blessed mother and Saint Rocco. Balanced on the top of the largest candle was a prayer card depicting Saint Anthony, patron saint of the lost. From the moment Giovanna knew Angelina had been kidnapped, not an hour went by that she didn't beseech Saint Anthony for the safe return of her daughter.

A knock at the door interrupted her prayers. She heard Rocco tell her upstairs neighbor she was resting. Giovanna remembered that this was one of the women on the stoop.

"No, no, I'm awake," declared Giovanna, coming out of the bedroom.

She brushed past Rocco and into the hall with her neighbor. "Excuse me, signora, we just ate and the kitchen is a mess," apologized Giovanna, closing the door to the apartment.

"See, you're a good, proud woman, not like that puttana, Limonata. That's why I stopped by. I saw that boyfriend of hers, Leo!"

"Did you see Limonata?" Giovanna blurted.

The neighbor's gossipy tone and expression changed at Giovanna's outburst. "No, signora levatrice . . ."

"Oh, I am sorry. I didn't mean to startle you. It's just that . . . we're finding she took more than the beer pitcher."

"Really! Well, he claims that he doesn't know where she is. He acted like he didn't even know her. He was going into an apartment, so I waited and asked someone if he was living there with a woman and a young girl. But they said he was a boarder in the building."

"Where was this apartment?"

"Sixty-six Hester Street. But don't bother, signora. She's not there, and that Leo is a mean one. He scared me. The only reason I stayed to ask questions is our super offered a few dollars if we got him Limonata's address."

SUNDAY, SEPTEMBER 26, 1909

Giovanna waited on the east end of Hester at Mulberry Street and Rocco at the west end at Baxter. They arrived before sunrise, and with the dawn came rain.

After an hour, Rocco ran through the rain toward Giovanna, shielding his head with his coat. Reaching her, he grumbled, "We don't even know if he has anything to do with this. I should just go and knock on his door. I'll beat him if he doesn't talk."

Giovanna answered with little patience. "If he's involved he may say nothing, and then we'll never know where she is! If you follow him, he can lead you to her, Rocco. Just do what we planned!"

As Rocco walked back in frustration, Giovanna wiped her eyes. It was going to be extremely difficult to spot this Leo in the rain. Another hour passed. She could see Rocco pacing.

The first man to exit the building was stocky. It was the fourth man who'd left the building that matched the description. He was using a piece of cardboard as an umbrella, so Giovanna couldn't see his eye, but he was tall, skinny, and dark. Rocco noticed him, too, and took pursuit. Giovanna swept into the building, shaking herself off in the vestibule.

At the apartment on the right, she listened at the door. It sounded like a family was eating breakfast. At the apartment on the left, she heard nothing but knocked, calling, "Limonata!" She did the same thing on the second floor, and an apartment door opened.

"Signora, can I help you?" asked a woman.

Flustered, Giovanna quickly composed herself. "Oh, yes, I'm a midwife."

The woman glanced at her stomach, confused.

Giovanna forced a little laugh. "Sometimes even midwives have babies."

The woman smiled.

"No, I seem to be getting forgetful with this pregnancy, and I've lost the address of a woman I was attending to on this block. I thought this was the house."

"There's no Limonata in this building, signora. It can't be this house."

"Oh, grazie. You know, I just saw a man exit that looked like the father. Tall, lidded eye?"

"No, that must have been Leo. He's a boarder who lives on four."

"Now I'm not only forgetful, I can't see so well!"

"You're wet. Do you need a cup of tea?" offered the woman.

"Thank you, signora. But I really must find her."

Giovanna sat at their apartment window waiting and watching for

Rocco. In the distance she saw a man running through the rain. He crossed the street in the middle and headed straight for their building. Giovanna's heart pounded. Surely this meant news. Had Rocco found Angelina? Was Rocco dead? She paced in front of her door and opened it before the man reached her landing. Breathing deeply, she tried not to let her anxiety show. She recognized him, but from where? When his entire face lifted, she knew the dramatic mustache and hazel eyes.

"Signora! The photos have been ready but you haven't picked them up," exclaimed the photographer, taking a package from inside his jacket and handing it to Giovanna. "After all, they are paid for and I wanted you to have them."

Giovanna stared at the package.

"Signora, are you going to take them?" The man was still holding out his hand.

She gingerly took the photographs wrapped in brown paper and tied with string.

"Don't you want to see them?" asked the man with a hint of pride.

Trying to control her tears, Giovanna stammered, "I'll open them with my daughter. She's out with her father. Thank you. Thank you for delivering them." The photographer was left standing outside the door.

Two hours later, Rocco arrived home. He looked away from his wife's pained face and mumbled, "I lost him."

THIRTY-SIX

TUESDAY, SEPTEMBER 28, 1909

There was nothing else for her to pursue, so Giovanna watched Leo's apartment from the corner of Hester and Mulberry day and night. She had become so accustomed to not seeing him that she nearly missed him when he stepped out of the door. Leo looked up and down the street before heading west away from Giovanna.

In three short blocks he was on Lafayette and then turned left to the Canal Street Station of the underground railway. Keeping her distance, she saw him descend the stairs to the uptown platform. Hundreds of people mobbed the station, and Giovanna was reminded that the big American Hudson-Fulton parade was scheduled at one o'clock on Fifth Avenue.

Fumbling for change, she got a ticket and waited at the opposite end of the platform. She didn't think the man had noticed her, but cursing her height and size, she pulled her gray shawl tight and high around her in an effort to be less conspicuous.

In seconds, a train thundered into the station. Giovanna stiffened. She was so focused on her pursuit of Leo that until that moment she had forgotten that the only other time she had ridden the underground railway, she vowed fearfully never to do it again. She entered the car adjacent to Leo and remained standing where she could see him through the car window. The train went all the way to Rector Street before he exited. At street level, he checked his pocket watch and headed to Trinity Church.

Entering Trinity's cemetery, Leo sat on a bench under an oak tree. Giovanna lingered at the outskirts of the graveyard, pretending to look at the church. The sky was blue and the day was warm. The next time she took a glance, another man, this one considerably better-dressed, sat beside Leo. His hands, noticeably untouched by labor, opened his newspaper in front of a face framed by groomed sideburns. In the same motion, the man laid an envelope on the bench between himself and Leo. Leo nonchalantly picked up the envelope and walked away.

He didn't go far. He leapt up the steps of a tall building next to the cemetery. Through the glass doors Giovanna could see a long, narrow marble corridor with ornate carvings on the ceiling and Leo waiting at the rear bank of elevators. When he stepped into an open lift, Giovanna hurried into the building. The door to Leo's elevator closed, and Giovanna watched the numbers light as the lift ascended.

"Can I help you, ma'am?" questioned a guard, eyeing her suspiciously.

The words were foreign, but Giovanna knew he wanted to know where the Italian woman was going. A board with names and numbers faced the elevator. Giovanna picked one with an "Esq." at the end, like Signore DeCegli's name. She pointed to the name on the board, smiling.

The man's eyes narrowed. "Mr. Schmidt, the attorney. That would be the nineteenth floor."

Giovanna smiled and continued to watch the numbers. The elevator stopped on the eleventh floor. She waited anxiously for the car to come back down. When the doors opened, a number of people streamed out, and Giovanna was about to get on when she saw Leo at the back of the car. He didn't exit the elevator, and she didn't enter. The doors closed again. This time it went down to a floor labeled "TP." Another elevator opened and Giovanna entered, motioning down to the elevator operator. In seconds she was down a floor in time to see Leo exit the building's back doors onto Trinity Place.

She didn't follow immediately because when the elevator door opened, she thought Leo might have seen her face. She followed him down Trinity Place back to the Rector Place underground station, keeping farther behind than before. As Leo entered the uptown train, she stepped in the car behind him.

Was he trying to lose her? Or was he trying to avoid being followed?

If someone was watching him, then they must also be watching her, and for the first time Giovanna was as afraid of what was behind her as what was in front of her.

On the train she could see Leo's shoulder through the car window. Her ankles were swollen, and the veins in her legs were throbbing. Mercifully, Leo didn't get out right away. He exited at Bryant Park, walked upstairs, and switched to the Sixth Avenue El.

The parade had already started. Throngs of people clogged the sidewalks. She had never seen such a large crowd in her life—this was a hundred times the size of a feast—in Scilla or New York. When they reached the last stop at Fifty-eighth Street, she saw the tops of floats half a block long squeezing down Fifth Avenue.

Trying not to be distracted by the pageantry, Giovanna followed Leo east to Fifth Avenue. The streets were so packed with exuberant crowds that Giovanna no longer had to worry about keeping her distance, but instead was trying desperately not to lose Leo in the multitude.

"Get your souvenir programs here!" shouted a man, holding a sack like a newsboy. Leo flipped him a nickel and, rolling the program under his arm, headed downtown at Fifth Avenue, parallel with the parade.

To get through the crowd, Giovanna walked on the innermost portion of the sidewalk, but between her height and the immense size of the floats, she was able to see an old ship manned by people in costume sail down the street. On its side was painted HALF MOON. Teams of horses pulled the floats, and each horse was covered in a red blanket stitched with an *H* and an *F*.

"We've got the line of march. Learn about the floats!" shouted a barker who blocked Giovanna's path.

Maneuvering around him only led her into a gang of kids on the corner holding up crates, yelling, "Get yer own grandstand here, only fifteen cents. Keeps yuh three feet off the sidewalk!"

In between the floats marched bands from every nation, and men, puffed chests adorned by sashes, walked in formation behind their flags. Sometimes the music of one band stepped on the toes of another, and the crowd reacted to the clash of cultures by sticking their fingers in their ears.

Leo checked his pocket watch, slowed, and turned to view the parade. Giovanna reacted by stopping abruptly, and someone pushed into her from behind, unleashing a string of angry words. The words were foreign, but the meaning clear. Mumbling "Excuse me" in heavily accented English, she pressed into the crowd, watching the parade with one eye and Leo with the other.

Walking more slowly, she became aware of the dampness in her shoes. The pain in her feet was such that she knew the moisture was blood.

A passing float elicited cheers and hats were raised in salute. Giovanna recognized the figure that was part of this tableau—he was the white-haired first president of America who was in Mary's schoolbooks. He stood on a building's balcony, and below, on what was made to resemble an old street, people waved flags.

Leo continued down Fifth Avenue, picking up his pace, and Giovanna struggled to keep up. As they neared Forty-second Street, the crowd became so dense it was nearly impossible to get through. Large columns lined the streets, and a massive grandstand faced the festivities. Leo bullied his way through the throng toward the grandstand, and Giovanna followed in his wake. When he reached it, he hovered there. Giovanna stopped at a safe distance and immediately heard complaints. She played dumb and smiled, excusing herself in Italian.

"Look! That's probably why she pushed her way to the front. There's an eye-talian float."

Hearing the unmistakable "eye-talian," Giovanna took a second look at the approaching float, which was preceded by an Italian band. A man dressed as Garibaldi stood in front of a small house and a sign that read STATEN ISLAND.

The entire section of the grandstand near where Leo stood erupted into cheers. If the standing ovation they gave the float was not proof enough that these dignitaries were Italian, their red, white, and green sashes confirmed it. Following the float, men from the Italian societies marched with crossed American and Italian flags, and the grandstand cheers grew even more thunderous. An older man with a sash across his chest, graying hair, and a pockmarked face strode past Leo. A split second later she saw the man with the sash holding the envelope that had been left at the bench in Trinity's cemetery. Leo was already moving out of the crowd.

She hustled to catch up but was caught in a surge of Italians leaving the grandstand. Bounced from body to body, Giovanna could feel him escaping. She tried to cut under the grandstand but was stopped by a policeman who held her there until a group of dignitaries passed. She nearly tripped free when the policeman lifted his arm, but there were no straight lines of pedestrian traffic anymore; people were crisscrossing the side streets and sidewalks, and after nearly six hours of following him, she could no longer see any part of Leo.

WEDNESDAY, SEPTEMBER 29, 1909

After wrapping her bleeding and swollen feet in chamomile-soaked rags, Giovanna put on an old pair of Rocco's boots, the only shoes that would fit. Once again, she tucked the gun into her ballooning waistband.

Giovanna bought a paper in front of 111 Broadway, the building that yesterday Leo had entered and then exited out the back. The newsstand didn't have Italian papers, so she bought the one with the most pictures of the parade, thinking she would save it for Angelina. Near the same time as yesterday's exchange, she sat on a bench diagonally across from the one under the oak tree where the man had sat with Leo. A leaf fluttered onto Giovanna's shoulder, and she almost jumped out of her skin. Looking up, she realized that the trees were changing color and that she hadn't noticed—she was spending all her time looking, but not seeing.

Like clockwork, the businessman entered the cemetery with a paper under his arm, and Giovanna snapped back to attention. He strode directly toward the same bench, but it was taken. Without skipping a step, he continued on to the next bench, which was directly opposite Giovanna.

Giovanna jerked the newspaper in front of her face in surprise and embarrassment. It hardly mattered, because within a few moments she could see that, unlike yesterday, he was not on the lookout for anything and that droopy-eyed Leo was not in sight.

Although she didn't exactly blend in, at least there were other women in the park, Giovanna knew that it was unacceptable for unescorted ladies to eat in restaurants, which explained why so many office workers were eating lunch in the cemetery. Clusters of women sat on the grass, leaning against gravestones and chatting.

The man with the sideburns concentrated on his reading, turning the pages slowly. A steady stream of people walked through the cemetery heading to a grave that was covered in flowers. Leaning to one side, she tried to get a look at the name on the grave, squinting to make out the letters. Someone moved and she saw the inscription, ROBERT FULTON. It was impossible to escape this Fulton. If only Angelina was so easy to find.

Precisely twenty-five minutes later, the man stood up to leave. Giovanna put her paper in the netted shopping bag she'd brought along and followed him. While the man might not have noticed her, many of the office workers out for a lunchtime stroll on Broadway raised an eyebrow at her appearance. Rocco's worn boots didn't help. She did her best not to make eye contact with anyone as she walked in the man's path north on Broadway to Chambers Street. He turned left, away from City Hall, and entered a storefront painted red, white, and blue. Giovanna crossed the street and took the pencil and book that Domenico had given her from her bag and recorded the words on the sign: ELECT GAYNOR MAYOR AND TAMMANY HEADQUARTERS.

Although those words meant nothing, the gaiety of the signs, the colors, and the lack of merchandise communicated to Giovanna that it had something to do with voting. She had been in the country long enough to know that Americans treated elections like a holiday, or a party, and even "the eye-talians" were welcome. At similar storefronts in the Italian district, they were always being invited inside. Giovanna fixed the stray hair that was cascading out of her pins and tugged at her skirt, pulling it lower to cover Rocco's boots, before crossing the street and entering the storefront.

"Can I help you?" asked a young man in suspenders behind a counter. The man from the church cemetery sat at a desk in one of the offices beyond the counter. A handmade sign with his name was tacked to the door.

"*Voto*," mumbled Giovanna. Looking past the young man, she tried to memorize the name on the sign.

"You're a woman. You can't vote. You want your husband to vote?"

Giovanna shrugged.

"Does anybody in here speak eye-talian?" shouted the young man over his shoulder.

"No, send her to the precinct on Mulberry Street."

"Lady, here," said the young man, taking a flyer depicting a proud portrait of William Gaynor. "Go here. They'll help you." He wrote a Mulberry Street address.

Once outside, Giovanna took the little black book and wrote down "Edwin Reese," the name outside the man's door.

Heading to the Battery, she saw throngs of people and a brass band lined up along the bulkhead. Everyone was facing the water and waving American flags. She passed the El to get a closer view. People were looking up, and there was an air of anticipation among the crowd. She followed the pointing fingers and shouts until she saw a speck in the sky grow larger; when the wings became visible, she heard it as well. A flying machine headed toward the Scylla in the harbor. Uproarious cheers greeted the aeroplane, and the crowd thrust signs with portraits of two men, labeled WRIGHT and CURTISS, into the air.

The aeroplane circled Lady Liberty, looking like a fly the statue would soon swat with her upraised arm if it got any closer to her face. Many in the crowd stood with their jaws agape at the spectacle; little children jumped up and down, and a number of people couldn't contain their tears of excitement. The crowd, swept up in the moment, began to sing with the band, "America, America, God shed his grace on thee, and . . ."

Giovanna also started to cry. "You, the American Madonna! Men build machines to fly around your head! Find her! Please, I beg of you, find her . . ."

THURSDAY, SEPTEMBER 30, 1909

"Pietro, you said this woman was going to behave. This crazy lady is following me. I had to move yesterday!"

"Leo, I said she wouldn't go to the police." Pietro Inzerillo played with the brim of his hat. He hated coming out to Brooklyn. He hated Leo. And he hated that he had to be involved in this when there was more pressing and potentially more lucrative business going on upstate.

"Tell Lupo we should kill the kid and forget it," Leo pronounced.

"Lupo said if we keep getting money to keep her alive."

"Since when does Lupo care about a couple hundred bucks?"

"Sometimes it takes money to make money," answered Inzerillo cryptically.

"What are you talking about?" Leo was agitated.

"Nothing, Leo. Calm down."

"That *strega* needs to just come up with the money."

"Maybe she doesn't have it," commented Inzerillo, who was beginning to believe Giovanna.

"Are you kidding? Lupo said she sent a grand to Italy. And besides, everyone knows how cheap and stubborn her husband is. Those other guys had to blow up his store. They have it."

"Well then, Leo, I'm sure you'll get it," commented Inzerillo, getting up.

"Make sure that crazy strega knows that if she follows me again, I'll kill her and the kid."

SATURDAY, OCTOBER 2, 1909

The festivities of the Hudson-Fulton celebration had made it to the Lower East Side.

"Zia, I need another pin here," instructed Mary.

"Mary, let me finish with Frances first," said Giovanna, wrapping the skirt around her stepdaughter's waist. "There."

Frances swung around, swirling the skirt. "Is this really what Italian girls wear?"

"I would wear skirts and blouses like this, but only for special holidays."

"Zia, I need a pin!"

"Mary, patience!"

"The teacher said we had to meet in front of the school on Mott Street at noon."

"That's nearly an hour away. Patience."

Giovanna had spent the entire morning making the girls costumes and replaying her conversation with Inzerillo in her head. By reprimanding her for following Leo, Inzerillo had confirmed that Leo was one of the culprits.

"If Clement was still in school, he could have played the slide trombone," moaned Mary.

"Is Papa coming?" asked Frances.

"You heard your father say he'd be there."

"I know it's early, Zia, but can we go?"

Nodding her head, Giovanna watched the girls descend the stairs, trying to conceal their excitement. How strange this was, seeing her stepdaughters off to a parade. All of New York, including her own family, was celebrating as if nothing was wrong, as if Angelina wasn't being held captive by criminals in this festooned city.

At one o'clock Giovanna headed for Mulberry Bend Park. Already the streets were jammed, and she could hear instruments being tuned in the distance. In the center of the park was a small stage decorated with flags surrounded by empty, roped-off benches.

Regiment after regiment of schoolchildren arrived until the park and benches were packed. Each child carried a little furled flag. A bugle sounded. The children fell silent. At the second blast from the bugle, all the children whipped American flags over their heads, converting the park into a waving sea of patriotism that was greeted by thunderous cheers. At a third signal, the youngsters recited the "Pledge of Allegiance" and then, accompanied by the school bands, they sang "The Star-Spangled Banner."

With this homage to their adopted homeland complete, the performances began. The first featured a Jewish girl dressed as an Indian doing a dance to attract the attention of an Indian buck, played by an

Italian boy. Giovanna was certain he was Italian by his appearance, and she knew the girl was Jewish when she stopped midperformance to shake her fist at the bandmaster and scold him in Yiddish.

After the Indians came the Dutch. As each school finished, a file of policemen escorted the children, giddy with pride, home.

Last on the program, Italian girls dressed in costumes from southern Italy mounted the platform. The crowd had thinned, and Giovanna was able to maneuver to a bench with a perfect view of Frances and Mary. The boys on trombone struck up a tune, and the dance started.

Giovanna was clapping when a woman handed her an envelope. "Signora, your husband said to give this to you. He had to leave."

Giovanna recognized the paper at once. But Rocco would never give this letter to someone else to deliver.

"Where was my husband?" Giovanna quizzed the woman.

"Over there," she said, pointing. "I don't see him now."

"What did he look like?"

"Signora, you don't know what your own husband looks like?" chided the woman.

"It wasn't my . . ." Giovanna stopped. "Yes, of course," she said, jumping up and quickly surveying the crowd.

Every face looked familiar, but none familiar enough.

"Have you lost something, signora?" asked a man whom she had seen seated with the dignitaries.

Until that moment Giovanna didn't realize how frantic she appeared.

"Oh, I'm trying to find my daughter."

"Was she in the program?"

"Sì."

"Signora, you have no need to worry. She was escorted back to her school."

"Giovanna, is something wrong?" Rocco appeared by her side.

She slipped the envelope into her skirt pocket.

"No, no, this kind gentleman was telling me that the children were walked back to school."

Giovanna read Rocco the letter in the bedroom.

You think you so smart following us? You want your little girl cut into little pieces? It matters nothing if you know who we are. Tell the police, and she's dead. Tell anyone, and she's dead. Put the money—all of it—in an envelope. You (the mother woman) should watch the parade tonight at the southwest corner of 14th street and 5th. Hold the envelope in front of you. Beware! Do not try and be smart or leave! Or else!

Rocco left to see what Lorenzo could contribute. He returned with $40 and with what they had earned over the last two weeks; it only totaled $159. Knowing this wouldn't be enough to satisfy the kidnappers, Giovanna grabbed her shawl and left the apartment.

Circling the block, she looked at her neighborhood in a new way—as a thief. She tried to figure out how to reach into cash boxes or pockets but could think of nothing that wouldn't get her seen or arrested.

Desperation mounting, she was about to go to Lucrezia when she remembered Pretty Boy's pledge to help her family whenever she needed him. It took two hours to find Nunzio's former co-worker, but when she did, Mariano handed over $130 without question.

Standing at the designated corner, Giovanna held the envelope to her chest. It held $289.

Rocco and the children insisted on going with Giovanna, but she was able to persuade them to remain at a safe distance and not be seen. They stood on the east side of Fifth Avenue near Thirteenth Street.

"I think it's coming," said Mary, jumping out into the street.

"Don't do that again, Mary!" shouted her father. "You stay in the crowd!"

Clement tried to catch sight of his stepmother on the southwest corner of Fourteenth Street. "She's still there, Papa," he reported.

The first of the electric floats passed. They held elaborate scenes of heroes and fantastic creatures. Marchers holding colored flames walked at the edge of the floats.

"I don't get this," commented Clement with one eye on a float and the other on his stepmother.

"A girl at work said it was a German parade about myths and legends," offered Frances.

Sure enough, a band marched by, playing what Rocco called "oom-pah" music. It was followed by another float covered in thousands of colored lights that illuminated the smoke from the torches. The clouds of colored smoke made it nearly impossible to see Giovanna. Clement strained to see through the haze. He was not only checking on his stepmother, but he was there with strict instructions from Domenico to get a description of the person who took the envelope. Lorenzo had forbidden Domenico to go with them after Rocco had come by earlier in the day to ask for more money. It broke Lorenzo's heart that he had already given all the money he could spare and some he could not.

A break in the floats cleared the air, and clowns came stumbling down the street. One clown clutched a "North Pole" that was captioned I GOT IT. Another clown played a stringless violin, while yet another rode a bicycle with no tires. They were flanked by a line of clowns on either side who jostled the crowd, tilting hats and honking noses. The line of clowns blocked Rocco's view of Giovanna, and soon the clowns were in front of them, one tugging at Clement's suspender. Ripples of laughter flowed through the crowd as various people were picked on. When the clowns passed, Rocco looked to Giovanna. It was Clement who noticed first.

"She's not there. Zia's gone."

A policeman stopped them from crossing the street. They ran behind the crowd on the sidewalk heading south, assuming Giovanna had followed the flow of the parade. At Tenth Street, Clement spotted her running through the crowd on the opposite side of the street, as they were doing. At every block, they attempted to cross the street, but each time a policeman caught them and sent them back.

The parade ended at Washington Square Park, and it was here that they were finally able to catch up with Giovanna.

"It was one of the clowns. He took the envelope," Giovanna sputtered breathlessly.

"Zia, come, we must find a place to sit," said Frances, alarmed at her stepmother's breathing.

Rocco and Clement escorted Giovanna to a bench. They were silent; the only sound was Giovanna's breath slowly returning to normal.

"Every clown was dressed the same. What made you think you would find him running like that! Besides, you risk her life if you follow them!" Rocco was both angry and worried.

"It wasn't Leo. The clown was too short. But he could have led us to her . . ."

They sat in silence for a long time. "Let's go home," Rocco said, lifting Giovanna to her feet.

THIRTY-SEVEN

MONDAY, OCTOBER 4, 1909

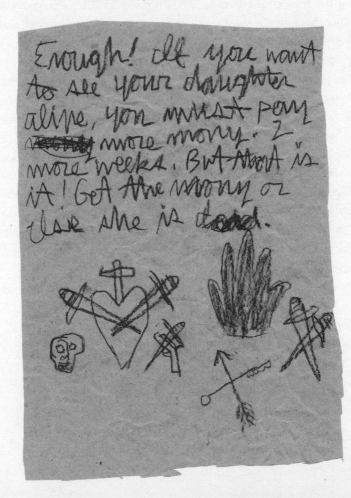

Giovanna knew they wouldn't be satisfied with what she had given them, but even though she expected the threat, it didn't make it any less terrifying. The only positive sign was that they were once again given two weeks to get the money, but that meant two more weeks that Angelina was in their filthy hands.

Her heart was palpitating, and it set the baby to kicking. Everything was outside of her control, even the movements within her own body. Panic rose in her chest, and she bolted from her chair with nowhere to go. The walls of the tenement were closing in on her, and she had an inexplicable urge to get to the roof. She needed air; she needed the freedom her daughter and unborn baby didn't have.

Opening the door to the hallway, she nearly knocked over Lucrezia.

"Giovanna! Where have you been? I came to check on you."

Giovanna stared into Lucrezia's face. Every muscle in her body wanted to relax, weeping into her arms. She wanted Lucrezia to hold her head, stroke it, and tell her what to do.

"Giovanna? Is something the matter?"

Giovanna froze.

"Let's go inside your apartment. Come on, dear."

The movement back inside and loss of eye contact with Lucrezia helped Giovanna to compose herself.

"I'm fine, Lucrezia. Just a little dizzy."

"Lie down. I wonder if it's your sugar." Lucrezia went to her bag and withdrew all sorts of instruments and elixirs. Listening to Giovanna's heart, she looked around and asked, "Where's Angelina?"

Caught off guard, Giovanna answered, "I sent her to her grandparents." Seeing Lucrezia's perplexed face, she added, "I've been exhausted with this pregnancy."

"But, Giovanna, so soon after the earthquake? There's disease."

"No, no. It's nearly a year. They say it's fine."

Giovanna could tell that Lucrezia was skeptical either of the soundness of her decision or of her truthfulness.

"Your blood pressure is way up. Giovanna, why didn't you call me? You're not well."

"It's just a bad day, Lucrezia. Really. I overdid it watching these American festivities."

"Lie back down."

Giovanna obeyed, and Lucrezia propped pillows beneath her head. She then went to remove Giovanna's shoes.

"No . . ." protested Giovanna, but it was too late. Lucrezia had seen her raw feet.

"Did you march in the parades? What on earth have you been doing? Giovanna, really, you know better! I don't understand this at all."

"It's nothing. Stop fussing."

"I'm surprised you're so interested in all this nonsense."

Giovanna remained silent.

"My husband says this Hudson-Fulton celebration is a ploy to get all the new immigrants interested in voting before the elections."

"I doubt it. It would have been cheaper to pay everyone double what they normally do for voting. They even dressed the horses."

Lucrezia laughed, relieved at a sign of her friend's humor. "I didn't see it, but I read in the paper that during the naval parade, Hudson's boat, the *Half Moon*, rammed into Fulton's *Clermont*."

"On purpose?"

"They say it was an accident, but if you ask me, it was the ghosts of these two men's egos at work. And they say women are jealous!"

Giovanna laughed a real laugh, and Lucrezia continued, encouraged.

"And did you hear what happened in Brooklyn?"

"No," answered Giovanna, not at all surprised that Lucrezia had all this information.

"They lost thirty-five of the fifty-four floats that were supposed to be in the parade."

"That's not possible!"

"It's like losing the elephants at the circus! You can get up if you want. Your heart rate is normal now."

Giovanna swung her legs over the bed. "Lucrezia, I'm fine, really."

"Giovanna, I would hope after all our time together that if you had anything to tell me you would feel free to do so."

"Sì, sì . . ." Giovanna couldn't look Lucrezia in the face. "I'll walk out with you. I was on my way to get things for dinner."

When they parted, Giovanna felt far worse than she had before. Her anxiety had lessened, but it was replaced with a heavy, broken heart.

THURSDAY, OCTOBER 7, 1909

Hands over her eyes, Angelina tried to imagine the sights and sounds from the Ferris wheel. *"Happy birthday to you. Happy birthday to you..."* The room was pitch dark and her lids were shut tight and covered, but no matter how hard she tried, she couldn't pretend. Something crawled up her skin. Trembling and shaking, she tried again. *"Happy birthday to you. Happy birthday to you..."*

SATURDAY, OCTOBER 9, 1909

"I heard something!" Teresa entered the apartment nearly breathless and handed over a baby each to Mary and Frances.

Giovanna jumped up and closed the door. "Sit, Teresa."

"Don't get excited..."

"Just tell," beseeched Giovanna.

"I overheard these drunken men talking about all the new greenhorns Il Lupo had working for him. They said that they were the ones who bombed the Bank Pati where the teller was killed."

"And?" asked Rocco.

"That's it. That's what I heard," replied Teresa.

"Are you crazy? You get us all excited, and you tell us nothing!" Rocco shouted.

"Rocco! Stop! Do you think we will just happen to hear where she is? Teresa was right to come. This could be helpful," said Giovanna.

SATURDAY, OCTOBER 16, 1909

An early light snow was falling, the first of the season. Giovanna was nearly oblivious to it, sitting at the window looking for signs or signals. Everyone was at work, including Mary, who had insisted on going with Frances.

It was two weeks to the day and she had not received instructions. No crude drawings and misspelled words. No sign of Leo or the phony

cripple. Every few days she dropped into Inzerillo's cafe to beg him
to persuade the kidnappers not to harm Angelina and to let him know
they were working hard to get the money. She assumed that once again
word would come via Rocco because it was fairly easy to drop a piece
of paper unseen into his cart, and so she hoped and half expected to
see Rocco hurrying toward their building.

Instead, a moment later, her heart leapt when she saw Lieutenant
Petrosino. Clutching her chest, she didn't move her eyes off him and
quickly debated whether to tell her old friend. For nearly ten seconds
she was certain Petrosino was alive and his death had been staged.
But when he came closer she could see that all this man and Petrosino
shared was their stature and a derby. His face held none of the determination of the little lieutenant.

When Giovanna calmed down, she poured herself a glass of wine
and went back to her position at the window. She remembered the first
time she saw Petrosino in Saulino's restaurant. He looked so depressed,
and the lawyer DeCegli said it was because a little boy who had been
kidnapped was found dead.

Maybe her dead friend was trying to tell her something, because
the memory ignited a spark, and seconds later she was off her chair,
wrapping herself in a thick shawl, and out the door. The kidnappers
were right. It was not enough to know who they were. She needed to
know their secrets.

Giovanna went to the library, and the same librarian who had helped
her and Domenico find articles about Nunzio's accident directed her to
articles about kidnapping in the Italian language newspapers. She left
the library with a name and address in Brooklyn.

It was a dress shop. Giovanna hesitated before the door, and when
she saw someone from inside looking at her suspiciously, she brushed
the snow from her shawl and entered.

"Is Signora Palermo here?"

"Why? I can help you," answered a small, stooped woman standing
behind the counter.

"I wanted to speak with the signora."

"What about?"

"I prefer to speak directly to her."

"I would need to know why."

Giovanna noticed the sorrow around the woman's eyes and decided to speak frankly.

"It's a private matter. But I believe the tragedy in the signora's life can help me avoid a similar fate."

The woman wordlessly retreated to a back room. The door opened, a young woman exited, and the stooped woman from behind the counter beckoned to Giovanna. "Follow me," she instructed.

Giovanna found herself in a storeroom lined with dress racks, and she was invited to take a seat at a small desk. The woman seated herself and moved a dress form out of the way. "I am Signora Palermo."

"Yes, I thought so. Thank you for speaking with me."

"I am not speaking with you yet, signora."

"No, but I hope you will. No one knows what I am going to tell you, but you will have no reason to talk to me unless you hear the truth, and even then, I can only appeal to your sympathy."

It was obvious even to a stranger that this burst of emotional honesty was out of character for this woman, who the signora realized was pregnant. Glancing at Giovanna's feet, the woman slid a crate beneath them. "Talk, signora."

"My daughter has been kidnapped."

The woman's eyes closed momentarily, and she inhaled deeply. "Do the police know?"

"No!" Giovanna reacted like the woman had made a suggestion, and she only relaxed when Signora Palermo replied, "Thank God."

"I do not understand why you are coming to me. My Mario is gone. We could not get him back." Tears welled in her eyes even before she said her dead son's name, and in seconds she was trying to stifle deep sobs. Giovanna reached for the woman's hand. Seeing Signora Palermo's grief triggered the emotion that Giovanna was suppressing, and the strangers ended up crying in each other's arms.

It was a long time before Giovanna said anything. But eventually she asked, "Signora, do you know who kidnapped your son?" Seeing the fear on the woman's face, Giovanna added, "I swear on my daughter's head, no one will know, no one, what you tell me."

"Why do you want to know then?"

"Because, signora, the only hope I have of finding my daughter is to know their crimes. I must make her safe return more valuable than ransom."

Signora Palermo stared a long time at Giovanna and then began. "Even my husband does not know my suspicions, because if he did he would try to kill them himself, and I would lose a son *and* a husband."

"I understand, signora. Please, I promise you. No one will know we've spoken, not even your husband."

"There was a man. He kept coming and asking for money. My husband was proud and sent him away, week after week. Then a different man started coming—a large brute. I think I heard another man call him 'The Bull' once. This man, too, even though he was frightening, was sent away by my husband. The next time he came he was with a tall, thin man with a droopy eye. I saw the *cafone* look at my Mario, and I pleaded with my husband to pay, but he refused. Two days after their visit, Mario was gone."

The signora was crying so hard she fought to catch her breath. Knowing it was the same kidnappers, and that they were truly capable of killing, paralyzed Giovanna.

"They sent us letters and asked for a lot of money. We didn't have that much money. We were supposed to look for a man with a red handkerchief, but we didn't go because we had only a few dollars. Instead, my husband went to the police; it was all we could do, signora! Two days later they found my Mario's body."

Giovanna, consumed by fear, held and rocked the woman, wiping her face with her sleeve. "Did you ever see these men again?"

"No, but another man came to the funeral. He told my husband if we spoke to the police again he would kill us." Stopping and looking at Giovanna, she wailed, "Signora, Mario was my only son! So I decided to tell the police about the man who defiled my son's wake. We spoke with the dead policeman, you know, the famous one, and he said only a wolf with no fear would come to my boy's funeral."

The trip home from Brooklyn felt like the longest Giovanna had ever taken. Time seemed to expand as it did on the boat to America. She was now certain that Il Lupo was behind Angelina's kidnapping and that his accomplice Leo had murdered at least one kidnapped child. She revisited every word of her conversations with Inzerillo, knowing that her messages were indeed going straight to the source.

Her thoughts churned. Inzerillo had children! Yes, that was it! She would kidnap one of his children and return the child in exchange for Angelina. It took only a few stops on the El to find the flaws in this plan. Giovanna had learned that kidnapping was a crime of mind games and strategy. If she took Inzerillo's child, for the plan to be effective, they would have to believe that she was capable of killing the child. Additionally, it would prompt all-out war, and none of her stepchildren, nieces, or nephews would be safe.

Giovanna climbed the stairs to her apartment, not knowing her next move. She was relieved to see Frances and Mary already preparing supper and said a prayer of thanks for her stepdaughters, even though at the moment they were acting awkward. Rocco was also home and making their tenement even smaller by pacing its perimeter. Needing to put her feet up, Giovanna decided to take a few minutes to lie down and think about the conversation with Signora Palermo. Teresa's information about Il Lupo's gang and the bombing at the bank was also ringing in her ears.

"Where's Angelina's dress?" called Giovanna from the bedroom. It was missing from where she kept it under her pillow.

Frances and Mary exchanged looks in the kitchen.

"What does it matter? She can't wear it," answered Rocco, already defensive.

"What do you mean?" Giovanna yelled, louder than she ever had in her life.

Rocco was already putting on his jacket. "They came collecting clothes for the people of the earthquake. We had nothing left to give."

"You didn't have to give anything! We gave plenty! How, how could you?" Giovanna wailed with pain. "If I hadn't sent the money to Scilla, we could have moved! We would have been far away from the schifosi. Because of the earthquake they have my daughter!"

Rocco slammed the door on the way out, leaving his daughters to comfort Giovanna. Mary and Frances expected their stepmother to be upset, but they hadn't expected her to fall completely apart. They didn't realize her rage was fueled by fear. Giovanna now knew who the kidnappers were and what they were capable of—and she was terrified. She lay on the bed, alternately clutching and punching a pillow. It was hours before she stopped blaming herself, the terremoto, her husband, and Lieutenant Petrosino for Angelina's abduction. Frances and Mary had given up trying to console her and had sent for Teresa.

Teresa entered the apartment alone and began ministering her magic. Had she been a Costa by blood, it could have been said that she took after Zia Antoinette. But it was under the tutelage of her own mother that Teresa had become versed in the curses, rituals, and prayers that she was to master.

To release her sister-in-law's demons, Teresa heated glass cups. Putting water around the rims, she placed them on Giovanna's back, and with the suction they created, she captured the bad spirits. After this cleansing, Teresa took olive oil and made the sign of the cross on Giovanna's forehead over and over while murmuring prayers. When she stopped, she spat twice on Giovanna's head.

"That will take the pain away," announced Teresa. "And soon you will sleep."

Giovanna, weak from raging, submitted to all Teresa's ministrations without resistance. Teresa sat by her bed, occasionally patting Giovanna's hand and commanding her to sleep while she recited prayer after prayer.

Whether it was something Teresa had done, or exhaustion, Giovanna slept through the following day.

THIRTY-EIGHT

Giovanna woke with a plan. If she couldn't kidnap Inzerillo's child, she would hold information hostage and demand her daughter in return. Lupo was an experienced thug. He would make the best business decision.

Teresa's evil eye remedies inspired part two of the plan. Although these schifosi were living in New York, they were still peasants from Italy. Guns were less frightening than the evil eye. Her size, presence, and the fact that she was a midwife, already made her suspect. It would be easy to play the part of a witch.

Giovanna turned the corner onto Bayard Street and entered another world. The signs were Chinese, women scarce, and the smells pungent. Heading toward her friend's shop, she was shocked to see a small group of white men and women, dressed extremely well, being led down the sidewalk by an older Chinese man. They were laughing and taking in the sights. Steps from her they entered what she knew from her many walks in the neighborhood to be an opium den. Had she not been on a mission, she would have waited and followed them out of curiosity. It never occurred to her that she, too, looked out of place.

The proprietor of the herb shop waved her in with a genuine smile. It appeared even more crowded than normal, piled high with crates, bins, drying plants, and mysterious jars. So many smells competed for attention that they canceled each other out and instead created an air laden with possibility. Seeing her belly, the herbalist assumed she wanted something to bring on labor and went for a raspberry leaf and blue cohosh tincture. "No, no," Giovanna said, looking for a piece of paper and a pencil. This would be a challenge. He handed her brown paper and a stub of pencil lead. She drew a hand, and then she drew bumps on the hand and pantomimed scratching.

"No, no problem," said the proprietor and he scurried away. Giovanna had a feeling he would return with the exact opposite of what she wanted and tried to think of the way to communicate that she wanted something that would cause, not cure, a rash.

"Good, good?" He returned with aloe and arrowroot powder in his hand.

Giovanna picked up the lead and drew nettles. Whether her drawing was bad, or there weren't nettles in China, she didn't know, because the herbalist was stumped. Giovanna realized she was trying to be too specific. She drew a skull and crossbones and scratched at her skin.

"Yes, yes!" His euphoria at getting the clue was quickly replaced by confusion. The Italian lady always bought healing herbs. He doubted himself until he produced an oil-like tincture that after inspection produced a triumphant nod from Giovanna.

Still skeptical, the herbalist made all sorts of cautionary gestures that Giovanna greeted with reassuring smiles. On her way out, he took a look at her big belly and called her back in for what Giovanna thought would be a final warning, but instead he handed her raspberry leaf tea.

WEDNESDAY, OCTOBER 20, 1909

From her post at the window, Giovanna absentmindedly scratched her hand. Looking down she was pleased to see little red blisters. When she had returned from Chinatown she had put a small dot of the tincture on a piece of paper. She waited until the next morning to handle the paper, which looked like it was stained with fish oil. Less than a day later the poison had produced a rash. If she got such results with this small amount, surely the scoundrels' hands would be covered.

Mary opened the door with a bang of her hip. Her arms were filled with two primers and a writing notebook sent from school so she could study in the evenings. Relieved to have the company and the diversion, Giovanna leaned on the windowsill and lifted herself out of the chair.

"Don't get up, Zia. I can get you something."

"No, I need to move. Why all the books?"

"My teacher sent them so I can practice my writing. They were in the foyer."

"Let me see, Mary." Giovanna walked to the kitchen table where Mary had left her books and opened the top one. A handmade envelope fell out.

Mary was busy removing her coat and boots, so Giovanna turned her back to her and said, "Mary, I must lie down." The letters were frightening enough; she didn't want Mary to be further traumatized by knowing the threat had been placed in her schoolbook.

"See, Zia, I told you not to get up! I'll make you tea."

"No, no. I want to sleep. Do your schoolwork."

On the bed with her back facing the kitchen, she quietly opened the envelope.

It was when she put the letter back that she saw a dark brown lock of Angelina's hair at the bottom of the envelope.

SUNDAY, OCTOBER 24, 1909

"Zia, I can't find my hat!"

"Look under your coat, Mary."

Rocco had gone for his morning coffee, and Clement was still asleep, giving Giovanna the little bit of privacy that she needed. Opening her bottom drawer, she grabbed the gun, but also a knife—a kitchen knife that she had spent the better part of Saturday sharpening. It had occurred to her that it was probably foolish to sharpen a knife that she had no intention of using, but she wanted it to gleam.

She placed the knife into a makeshift sheath and attached it to her waistband next to where she tucked the gun. "Scusa, bambino." Giovanna wondered for a quick second what Zia Antoinette would have said about the future of a baby that had spent its last months in utero cuddled up to a knife and gun. Saying a quick prayer to Zia Antoinette to reverse its effect, she headed to the door.

Earlier that morning, she had told Lorenzo that she needed Domenico's help moving the piano. It was nearly true—she had sold the piano, but it wouldn't be moved until that evening. Giovanna had already taken Domenico for coffee and explained her plan. His eyes widened, and he sat straighter than Giovanna had ever seen him. She made him promise to stick to her scheme, which would not put him in touch with the kidnappers, but she thought herself insane to be involving her nephew and added this to her list of sins.

"Let's go, girls." Giovanna grabbed a purse and dropped in the envelope marked FOR THE BABY JESUS. With the sale of the piano it held $224.

Frances and Mary noticed that their stepmother was on edge, but that had become normal. They tried to keep pace with her as she walked north on Elizabeth Street to Our Lady of Loreto. They were early and stood aside to watch the parishioners from the nine o'clock mass exit.

Mary mimicked her stepmother by scrutinizing every face. When they entered the church, Giovanna walked down three rows and nudged the girls into the pew.

"Zia, we always sit up front!" exclaimed Mary, tugging at her hand.

"I don't want to walk that far. Sit, Mary."

The church was cool, but Giovanna was already sweating and fanning herself with the pages of the missal.

"Are you okay, Zia?" asked Frances, looking at her. "You sure you don't want to go home?"

"No, no. Just pray. Pray to Saint Anthony." Frances knew what praying to Saint Anthony meant.

Little bits of the priest's sermon on the paganism of the American holiday Halloween drifted in and out of Giovanna's consciousness. His voice rallied when he warned parents not to let their children dress in costume on next week's Sabbath. His admonishments interrupted Giovanna's calculation of the number of minutes until the first collection of offerings.

Finally, four ushers, one on each side aisle and two in the center, walked from the back of the church to the altar. They waited there, hands crossed over the stick of their rattan baskets, for the priest to announce the first offering. Giovanna studied their faces. They were all good family men she recognized from the neighborhood, but with a stab to her heart she remembered Limonata's deceit, and once again they became suspects.

The ushers began to weave the baskets in and out of the pews collecting contributions. After the last row, the ushers would walk to the vestry room off the church foyer, empty the money and envelopes, lock the door, and then walk back down to the altar for the second collection.

The ushers were now only five rows in front of her; a hymn drowned out the beating of her heart. Her face was completely flushed, and she saw Frances staring at her—it would work in her favor.

When they reached her row, Giovanna lifted her arm noticeably and dropped the envelope in the basket. Without looking, she monitored the ushers' movements. There were three more rows behind her—slide the basket in and out, in, out, in, out. Six steps to the vestry. Open the door. Empty the baskets. She heard the coins cascade into a strong box. Now they'll close the door. Six steps back inside the church, footsteps on marble. Start gasping.

"Zia, what's wrong?" asked Frances, concerned.

"I'm fine. I just need air. You stay here." She fanned herself on the way out of the church.

Domenico stood at the open door and nodded his head in the direction of the vestry, meaning the crook was inside collecting the payoff. Giovanna went outside to the alley entrance while Domenico stayed at his post. At least two minutes passed. Was there another exit? She was beginning to panic when she saw Domenico nod, indicating the man was coming. There was an alley on either side of the church. If the Blackhander came her way, she could easily pull him in. If he went in the other direction, she would have to run to reach him before he passed the alley. Domenico nodded again, this time to the left, indicating he was exiting on the side opposite Giovanna. His nod gave her the precious few seconds she needed.

A foot before the alley entrance she flung out her arm, grabbed the man's neck from behind, and dragged him into the alley. She held him so tight he was choking. He tried to pry her arm from his neck until she drew the blade to his chin. His hands dropped, and for a moment Giovanna was unnerved when she looked into his face and realized it was the "cripple" from Washington Square.

"Be quiet. Say nothing or I'll slit your chicken neck," Giovanna hissed.

Everything about the man quieted except his eyes, which he desperately tried to roll backward in an attempt to see his attacker. Giovanna's enormous belly was pressed so tightly against his back that she knew he must feel the baby kicking. He was so short that his head was pulled back onto her breasts.

"Listen, clown, I know who you are and I know who your boss is. You tell him this. You tell him that there are three sealed envelopes waiting to go to the police, the mayor, and the newspaper with details about the killing of Mario Palermo and the bombing of Bank Pati. If anything, *anything*, happens to my daughter, to me, or to anyone in my family, someone has been instructed to deliver these letters. The evidence will hang you all. Do you understand, cafone?"

The man tried to nod but couldn't move his head in Giovanna's death grip. "If you understand, stomp your foot."

His foot stomped.

Giovanna slowly let go, and by the time he jerked around to face her she had her gun pointed at him. "Go. Take the money. And take the message."

The man was frozen.

"Go, you phony cripple, go!" Giovanna commanded, knocking him in the head with the gun before he fled. "*Va al diavolo!*"

After tucking the knife and gun back into her waistband, she re-pinned her hair, took a few deep breaths, and exited the alley, practically falling to the steps of the church. No sooner had she got there than she realized Domenico was gone. "I knew it! I should not have trusted him!" her voice screamed in her head.

The recessional hymn sounded on the organ; the priest was the first to exit the church. "Signora! Are you alright?" He hurried to Giovanna on the steps.

"Sì, Father. It's difficult with the baby, that's all."

"Zia!" Frances and Mary came running.

"Girls, you shouldn't leave your mother."

Giovanna defended them. "No, no, Father, I didn't want them to miss mass."

"God would forgive them. Children, take your mother home to bed."

"Clement's not here. He went with Papa to the cafe," greeted Frances from the stove, where she was frying meatballs, as Domenico walked into the apartment.

Giovanna slumped in relief. Her wait for Domenico had been interminable.

"Zia almost fainted in church, Domenico," announced Mary.

"Girls, go ask Zia Teresa if we can eat together at her house. I'm too exhausted to have the meal here."

"Mary can go, Zia. I'll finish this."

"No. I don't want her walking alone. Go."

"Va bene." Frances reluctantly grabbed Mary's hand, and they left.

Giovanna said nothing. She waited for her nephew to speak.

"I followed him."

"I told you not to do that."

"You told me many things, Zia. I listened to most."

Giovanna sighed. Zia. Only Aunt. There was no one to call her "Mamma." Even her stepchildren called her Zia. She looked at Domenico with the loss that she felt and said, "You could have been killed."

"Zia, that man was too scared to wipe his ass, let alone kill someone! Where did you learn to talk like that? *I* was frightened listening to you!"

Giovanna smiled but turned serious again. "Where did he go, Domenico?"

"I'm a failure as a detective." Domenico's voice cracked. "I was so close to him leading me right to her. Then I lost him. I lost him, Zia."

"They are experienced in knowing how not to be followed. You can't blame yourself."

Although his aunt's words were kind, Domenico heard the disappointment in her voice. "Zia, I only know that he went to Brooklyn. Where in Brooklyn, I don't know, because that's where I lost him."

"That's more than we knew yesterday."

Domenico's head was bowed dejectedly. He looked like a little boy.

"Did he see you?" asked Giovanna gently.

"No, I don't think so. And I don't think he knew someone was following him, which makes my losing him all the worse."

"No, Domenico, we did good today. Angelina is safer tonight, I think."

After a few moments of silence, Giovanna asked, "Domenico, how did the schifoso get into the vestry? Did he jimmy the lock?"

"No, it was open."

"Open? Who was the last usher out? Describe him."

"Thick, shiny black hair. The fish seller."

"Molfetti?"

"I think that's his name."

THIRTY-NINE

WEDNESDAY, OCTOBER 27, 1909

Triumphantly, Giovanna noticed that there were no drawings of dripping knives or misshapen guns on the letter.

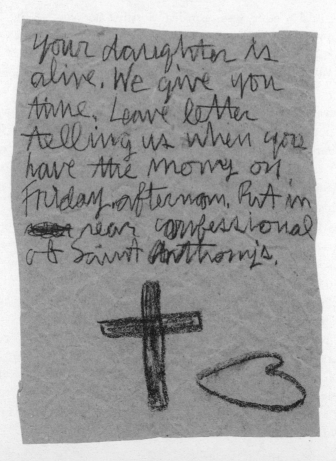

FRIDAY, OCTOBER 29, 1909

How do I know my daughter is alive? Ask her what she did on her birthday and give me the answer. If you give me this word, I will give you more money.

Giovanna took out the poison tincture and with an eyedropper carefully edged the paper and the envelope with little drops. Hours later when it was dry, she put on her gloves and, wrapping herself in her shawls, headed toward Saint Anthony's church.

SATURDAY, OCTOBER 30, 1909

Molfetti's fish store was crowded. Jostling her way to the front, Giovanna's eyes fixed on Molfetti's hands filleting a flounder. They looked red.

"Signora, what are you doing down here?" asked a woman next to her.

Giovanna had delivered the woman's baby but couldn't remember her name. It amazed her that if you went an extra few blocks in the neighborhood to buy something, people noticed.

"It's my stepson's birthday. I wanted to get a nice piece of fish."

"He does have good fish," agreed the woman, sounding privileged that this was her local fish store.

As if to explain the redness, Molfetti thrust his hands into a tub of ice water and, on closer inspection, Giovanna could see there was no rash.

"Good luck to you, signora," said the woman upon leaving.

"Good luck?" replied Giovanna, preoccupied.

"Sì, with the baby!" nodded the woman, smiling at her stomach.

"Signore Molfetti," greeted Giovanna at the counter.

"I'm sorry, signora, I seem to have forgotten your name," replied Molfetti.

"Oh, you probably don't know it," said Giovanna cheerily. "I'll have that piece of flounder," she indicated, pointing.

As Molfetti wrapped the fish, she continued, "It's just that I recognize you from church; you're an usher, yes?"

"Yes, of course, that's where I've seen you," commented Molfetti, handing her change.

"Signore, you should make a point of locking the vestry door," whispered Giovanna emphatically as she turned and left.

SUNDAY, OCTOBER 31, 1909

"Can I dress up tonight?" asked Mary.

Giovanna was making the morning espresso. "We'll see."

"Sometimes they give you a penny instead of a treat."

"Then I suppose your father would consider it work." The priest's sermon came to mind. "And God will forgive us."

Mary had wanted to be an Indian during the Hudson-Fulton celebration, and Halloween gave her a second chance. She borrowed a costume, and before setting out, Giovanna braided Mary's hair and put rouge from Aunt Teresa in stripes on her face. At Prince Street, Mary headed west.

"Where are you going?" questioned Giovanna. "We know more people the other way."

"But they have more money in these neighborhoods."

Giovanna smiled at her stepdaughter.

"Stay on the street when I go in the store, Zia."

It took Giovanna a few stops to get what Mary was up to. She heard Mary's loud "Trick or treat!" and when someone presented her with a candy she politely shook her head and pointed inside her mouth to a phantom rotted tooth. Giovanna would see Mary's feathers nod thanks when she was instead offered a penny.

An hour later, Mary shook her little burlap bag. "Not bad, Zia, and there's a bunch more blocks we can go."

"Except next time, you take the candy. You deserve it." Giovanna bent down, hugged Mary, and got a stripe of lipstick on her shoulder. Her only thought had been how this trauma would affect Angelina, but now she was reminded that, to a lesser degree, everyone in the family would have scars.

At nine thirty, Giovanna had to convince Mary it was time to go home. They met Rocco and Clement on the stoop returning from selling sweet potatoes to the chilled trick-or-treaters.

"Papa! I got many pennies!" Mary held up her bag.

"I think you made more than we did, Mary!" answered Rocco, winking.

When they opened the door, Frances was pacing the little kitchen, holding an envelope.

"Angelina is alive."

Giovanna tore the envelope from Frances's hand.

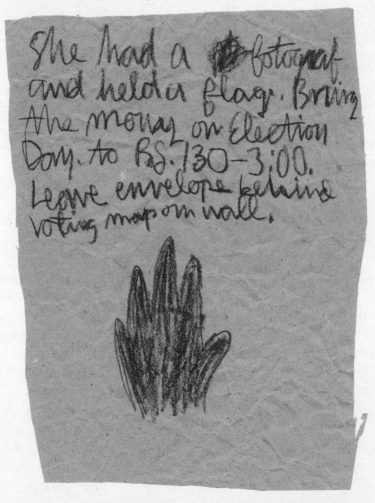

"Frances! How did you get this?" shouted Rocco.

"I was on the stoop. Someone in a mask came up to me, handed me the envelope, and said 'Trick or treat.' I didn't know, I didn't know." Frances broke down in tears.

"Frances," said Giovanna embracing her, "There's nothing you could have done."

"The children can't be alone. Ever," commanded Rocco.

MONDAY, NOVEMBER 1, 1909

"Lupo, you're crazy. Why did you want to meet here?"

"Because, Pietro, I want them all to see me," Lupo said expansively.

Lupo and Inzerillo were having dinner at Delmonico's on Beaver Street. The restaurant was filled with local politicians making last-minute plans for the morning.

"I still don't get it."

"They need to think I'm more involved in the election tomorrow than I really am. The feds are all over us for counterfeiting, and we need the locals' protection."

"But there's a warrant for your arrest, Lupo."

"Pietro, who would arrest me tonight?"

"I understand that, but next week? They'll be forced to."

"I've got it worked out. They want me for fleeing bankruptcy, but instead, I'll become the victim. I'll go to the police and say I was black-handed. By the time they finish the investigation, I'll be gone."

Inzerillo couldn't help but laugh. "Shrewd. What about the Manzella case? There's a warrant out for your arrest on that one, too."

"I have a few days; I'll deal with Manzella."

"Well, then," smirked Inzerillo, "a toast to your return."

"And to All Saints Day!"

After clinking wine glasses, Lupo asked, "What's the story with the fruit seller?"

"Every few weeks they come up with more money."

"Good. Tell Leo not to do anything stupid. We need the cash."

"He said the Gallucci brothers were hysterical the other day, claiming the kid's mother was a witch and knew too much."

"The Galluccis are greenhorns. You've talked to her, what do you think?"

"She's smart. But she's not going anywhere. She's desperate to get that kid back."

"Then tell Leo to keep the greenhorns in line."

"I have. And I will."

"They should be working the election tomorrow. Everybody we have should be working."

"They'll all be out. What about you?"

"I'm going to keep my eye on Leo. I want to make sure he's not been taking advantage of my absence."

TUESDAY, NOVEMBER 2, 1909

Giovanna got out the dropper to add black magic to her note.

Take this $155 and give me my daughter or I will tell Edwin Reese that in addition to being involved in elections you are kidnappers. Or instead, I could threaten Edwin Reese that I will tell his secret to the newspapers. You think your skin is on fire now? Return Angelina, or your skin will fall off the bone!

Much of the election hoopla had escaped Giovanna. She knew the basics: there was a party called Tammany, and their candidate was William Gaynor, and a party called Fusion, and their candidate was Otto Bannard. Earlier, there was a newspaperman named Hearst who was going to run, but didn't. And everyone said voting didn't matter on the Lower East Side because the Sullivans were in control.

But she did know that a man named Edwin Reese who worked in an election office had given an envelope, probably containing money, to one of the scoundrels involved in Angelina's kidnapping. And now the Blackhanders wanted the next payment dropped at the poll.

It was pouring. An American flag hung outside in the rain at P.S.

130, as did all sorts of men with buttons covering their coats. On another corner, under umbrellas, stood three well-dressed ladies draped in sashes that read, VOTES FOR WOMEN.

Giovanna could barely walk anymore her legs were so swollen. She entered the school, shook the water from her shawl, and lumbered painfully to the gymnasium. She surveyed the setup and the faces, especially people with ribbons pinned to their chests, and headed to the precinct maps on the wall.

"Signora, can I help you?" asked a man in Italian who was accompanied by a policeman.

"My husband wants to vote, but he can't read. I came to find out where he has to go," answered Giovanna.

The official's voice changed. "Let me help you, signora. Where do you live?"

"At two . . . at 236 Elizabeth Street."

"That wouldn't be here, that would be at P.S. 21."

"Grazie, signore, but I think I'll take a look anyway to check for my brother." Thankfully, the man was pulled away and Giovanna had just enough time to slip the envelope behind the map.

FORTY

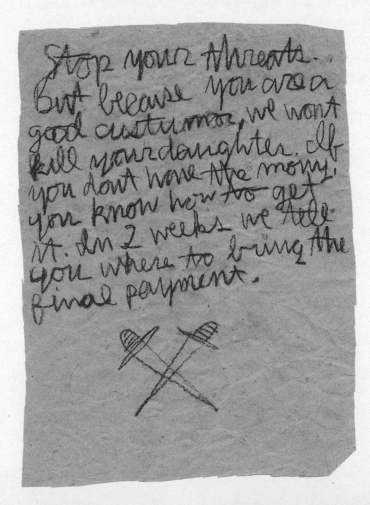

FRIDAY, NOVEMBER 5, 1909

"Zia, there's loads of people outside the Elizabeth Street police station," announced Mary, coming through the door after work. Giovanna was confined to bed. Lucrezia wanted to put her in the hospital, but Giovanna wouldn't allow it.

"Go to Zio Lorenzo's house and get Domenico to go with you and find out what's happening."

It was nearly an hour before Domenico and Mary returned.

"It's the Chinese, Zia. I saw Detective Fiaschetti, and he told me it was something called a tong war. Somebody got killed in August, and now the other gang killed someone in revenge."

Giovanna, who had raised herself on her elbows, fell back onto the bed. Domenico entered her room and half closed the door. "There's more, Zia."

From Domenico's expression, Giovanna could tell that it was serious. With great difficulty she once again lifted her upper body from the bed. "Go on," she instructed.

"You're going to think this is a joke, Zia."

"Any joke now would be a cruel one, and you're not cruel, Domenico."

"Detective Fiaschetti told me that Lupo came to the police station today to make a complaint. Lupo said he was blackhanded at his store on Mulberry Street and that's why he went out of business."

"Lupo? Here?"

"Yes, Zia."

"Didn't they arrest him?"

"No. The detective said something about needing to get a complaint in order."

"Lupo, on Elizabeth Street? And they let him go!"

"Zia, maybe he isn't involved."

"Maybe."

"But imagine, Zia, he said he was blackhanded!"

"Domenico, do the police still play games in the settlement gym with boys from the neighborhood?"

"I think so."

"I want you to go, Domenico. We need information on Lupo, but I don't want anyone to see you go into the police station."

"I'll try, Zia, but I don't think anyone other than Detective Fiaschetti would talk to me." Secretly, Domenico was thrilled. This gave him the permission he needed to snoop around.

SUNDAY, NOVEMBER 7, 1909

It must be Sunday—they never let her out on Sunday when the men were home all day. But she couldn't hold it in anymore. The bugs had bitten her badly, and her stomach ached, and the dark of the room was frightening. They had boarded up the window when the winter came; she couldn't even see the blue shade across the street anymore. The only light in the room came from a little window high in the door. She tried to stifle the sobs. When she cried, they shouted and called her names. But today she couldn't stop. The more she tried to choke down the tears, the louder she cried. Chairs scraped on the floor, and she cringed against the back wall, but even the threat of the men hurting her couldn't stop the sobs. They had been meaner lately, ever since they got rashes and tore at their skin.

The window to her door blackened, and she could see the face of an animal.

"Stop it or il lupo will get you!" they called in rough voices. They bounced a stuffed bear up and down. "We said stop the goddamn crying or we promise il lupo will get you!"

"Stupid men," thought Angelina. "It's a bear, not a wolf."

MONDAY, NOVEMBER 8, 1909

Rocco sent for Lucrezia. It was the second time in two days that he'd become frightened his wife was going to die. She still wouldn't go to the hospital. Medically, Lucrezia couldn't explain why Giovanna was delirious, but she supposed that if Giovanna spoke to her honestly, the reason would become evident. All Lucrezia could do was sedate Giovanna, and her secrets.

FRIDAY, NOVEMBER 12, 1909

"Leo, she's a witch! Let's get rid of the kid!" fumed the younger of the Gallucci brothers.

"Stop moaning," commanded Leo, who had met them on a street corner.

"You're not the one whose skin is blistered. I'm going to be scarred!" said the older Gallucci brother.

"You got a rash, that's all," dismissed Leo.

"Then how come she knows about it?"

"Because she's probably following you, you idiots. I told you to be careful."

"Leo," said the younger brother, trying to play the reasonable one of the two, "we need to tell Lupo everything this crazy lady knows."

"You want to get killed? You think Lupo would be happy knowing we were followed?"

The older Gallucci looked skeptically at Leo. "What's going on here, Leo? Who's Edwin Reese anyway?"

"How should I know? She's nuts. Lupo said to not touch the kid if we keep getting money. And that's what you'll do."

SUNDAY, NOVEMBER 14, 1909

"Come on, girl, see the snow."

The woman was holding the door to the room open. Angelina's eyes tried to adjust to the light, but she was blinded by the glare on the snow.

With the other children next to her, Angelina gazed out the door, her hands shielding her eyes. A few feet already blanketed the ground, and it was still snowing.

"America is brutta," scoffed one of the women.

"I like the snow," replied the other.

"But you can't go out. You can't move."

"Where can we go with this kid anyway?"

"It won't be much longer."

Angelina always tried to listen to them but had a hard time with their accents, especially when they spoke quickly, as they were doing now. But she guessed that the conversation had something to do with her, and she tried to make herself invisible.

"Mamma, can we go out?" pleaded one of the children.

"Let them go," said the younger woman.

"I'll light a fire. They won't last but a few minutes."

She opened the door and shooed the children out, leaving Angelina behind.

"Signora, please, can I go, too?"

Ignoring Angelina, she turned to the other woman and shrugged. "She can't run away, she'll sink in the snow."

"Va bene. Go, go," she commanded, pushing Angelina out the door and closing it.

The other children giggled, trying to walk. Angelina threw herself into a drift. Her skin always felt like it was on fire. The snow stopped the itching of the bug bites and put the fire out. She was clean in the snow; it didn't matter to her that she was frigid and shivering. Opening her mouth, she gulped in great swallows. She rubbed her hair and scalp, which also felt like it was aflame, in the icy crystals. Rolling back and forth, back and forth, she cooled and cleaned her body until a strong pair of hands gripped her waist.

A wet slap landed on Angelina's face. "What are you, pazza? You can't get sick. We didn't feed you all these months for nothing."

"Get her inside," shouted the other woman from the door.

The women stripped off her clothes in front of the fire. It was the first time they had been removed, and her petticoat was nearly shredded. Hanging her clothes near the flames, they shooed her naked into her room and slammed the door.

MONDAY, NOVEMBER 15, 1909

A savage wind whipped at the windows of 202 Elizabeth Street. After two days of snow it was beginning to rain, but rather than melt the snow, the rain covered it in a crust of ice.

The baby was coming. Giovanna wanted to hold out as long as she could before calling Lucrezia; she was worried that the more time Lucrezia spent in the apartment the greater the risk that someone would slip and say something. Finally, she could wait no longer, and Rocco left to get the midwife.

The weather was too horrid to send the children down the block to Lorenzo's apartment. Instead, everyone, including Rocco, huddled in the children's tiny room and left the kitchen and bedroom to the laboring woman and midwife.

Lucrezia didn't see the same kind of determination in Giovanna's labor that she had with the first baby. Although that could be explained by the sedatives and two weeks in bed, she figured it had more to do with the unspoken horror that had made Giovanna construct this strange altar in the bedroom topped by Saint Anthony. Lucrezia found the story about Angelina being in Italy hard to believe. But the idea that Angelina had been taken from Giovanna was also too terrible to fathom.

Because pain makes truth harder to hide, many times in the middle of a contraction Giovanna wanted to confess to Lucrezia the inner torment that had nothing to do with pushing this baby out of her body. She longed to birth her baby and her secrets at the same time. The pain of needing Lucrezia so badly was indistinguishable from the labor. But between contractions, it didn't matter. Lucrezia was not family. No longer could they trust anyone who was not of their flesh and blood.

It was nearly dawn when her son emerged. Her long, difficult labor had mimicked the storm raging outside the windows. Giovanna had been so certain that the baby was a boy that she was taken aback by Rocco's surprise and excitement. After Lucrezia had cleaned the child and the birth area, the children crowded around the bed. From the moment Lucrezia put the fair boy in Giovanna's arms she was heartened. No one was trying to replace Angelina. At the foot of her bed, the candles on her makeshift altar flickered. At least twice in the night they had gone out, and she had begged Lucrezia to relight them.

"So, children, this is Nunzio," announced Rocco. Giovanna smiled at Rocco for remembering his promise, but she had prayed to Nunzio and the angels all night long and knew what she must do.

"No, the child will be called Anthony," Giovanna whispered.

TUESDAY, NOVEMBER 16, 1909

"Domenico, come see our new brother," greeted Mary when Domenico stepped in the door.

Domenico was so anxious to speak with his aunt that he hardly glanced at the infant.

"Zia, they arrested Lupo today. He's in the city jail."

Once again, Giovanna was left wondering what this would mean for her daughter.

"Do you know on what charges?"

"For blackhanding a shop owner named Manzella."

WEDNESDAY, NOVEMBER 17, 1909

"Lupo had this all planned. There's nothing to worry about, Leo," reassured Inzerillo.

"You should of told me is all. I was real surprised," complained Leo.

"Leo, speaking of telling each other things, Molfetti stopped by to see me and said that the fruit seller's wife knew that he unlocked the vestry door. How did she know that, Leo?"

"How should I know?"

"You said the Gallucci brothers were nervous she knew too much. What else does this woman know, Leo?"

"I told you, she knows my name, and she knows what those idiots look like. That's all. Hey, we're getting the money aren't we? Just like I told you."

"That's right, Leo, you're getting the money and you need to get more. With Lupo in jail, we need cash." Turning to leave, Inzerillo warned, "And Leo. Nothing can go wrong, Leo."

FORTY-ONE

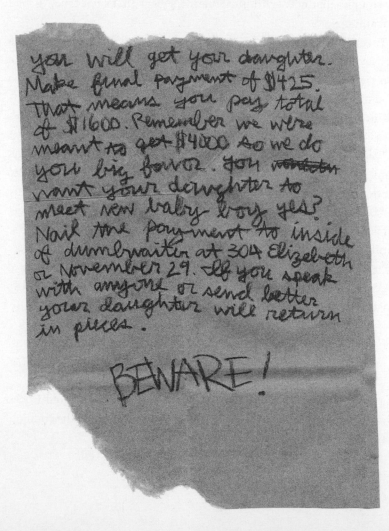

you will get your daughter.
Make final payment of $425.
That means you pay total
of $1600. Remember we were
meant to get $4000 so we do
you big favor. You want you
want your daughter to
meet new baby boy yes?
Nail the payment to inside
of dumbwaiter at 304 Elizabeth
on November 29. If you speak
with anyone or send letter
your daughter will return
in pieces.

BEWARE!

"Congratulations, signora. I hear you have a son," greeted Inzerillo, ushering her into the back room.

How bizarre these meetings were, thought Giovanna. It was like they were two leashed dogs that, if untethered, would tear each other apart.

"Thank you, signore. His name is Anthony." Giovanna wondered if this godless creature would understand the significance of her son's name.

"Sit, please, signora," directed Inzerillo.

"I heard that Lupo is in jail. I must admit, I thought he was behind my troubles, but now with him in jail it's clear that's not true," fished Giovanna.

Inzerillo tried to hide his surprise and interest in what Giovanna was saying. "You're right to assume I know Lupo, signora. And you're also right to assume that he knows nothing of your troubles. He's a good man."

"In a way, I wish he was involved, signore. I get the feeling that he's a reasonable man and would understand that we have no more money."

"Signora, I was told that these men were going to ask for a final payment. Surely, knowing that this is the last payment will inspire you to get the money."

"Listen, signore. We do not have this money. I will find a way to get it if you can promise that there will be no more demands and my entire family will be together and safe."

"Signora, you forget that I am only a messenger, but I promise to use all my influence to make this so. You have acted honorably and so must these thieves."

FRIDAY, NOVEMBER 19, 1909

For the first time in a long time, Giovanna sat down and told Rocco what was going on. She avoided the details and focused on the contents of the last letter.

"How do we know this will really be it?" Rocco asked.

"We don't."

Rocco looked at his wife out of the corner of his eye, realizing she was holding something back, but he was too debilitated by this process to ask questions. "But we don't have the money. Lorenzo's given us everything he has," said Rocco, frustrated. "And no matter how much we work between now and then, we couldn't earn it."

"Maybe my parents have money left from what I sent them," offered Giovanna.

"Even if they did, it would never get here in time."

"I could ask Lucrezia." Giovanna couldn't believe she suggested it, but she meant it.

"Are you crazy? If she went to the police now, all this would be for nothing. If we ask someone outside the family, it has got to be someone who won't be suspicious of why we need the money."

Impressed with Rocco's thinking, Giovanna said, "That rules out Signore DeCegli." In her mind she was going through the possibilities. Were she to ask Mariano again, it would raise suspicions or questions.

"I'll get the money," resolved Rocco. "I'll get it."

Rocco saw in his wife's eyes how grateful she was, but for the first time, he also thought he saw love.

SATURDAY, NOVEMBER 20, 1909

"Some of the guys at the station said you kept asking for me down here," greeted Detective Fiaschetti, throwing a ball at Domenico.

"Detective! You came!" Domenico hadn't spent so much time playing ball since he was a little boy.

"Why did you want me to come? There's other guys around," commented Fiaschetti, pointing to the handful of cops who were playing with the kids.

"Well, you're Italian. There's not many Italians and, besides, you knew the great Petrosino!"

"Your name is Domenico, right?"

"That's right, detective. I was hoping you could tell me stories about Lupo."

"Why do you want to know about him?" Fiaschetti asked suspiciously.

"He's a famous crook. And didn't Petrosino want to catch him, and now you have him in jail?"

Fiaschetti looked hard at Domenico. "You're the one who wants to be the detective, right?"

"That's me," answered Domenico.

"Come on, sit down over here," directed Fiaschetti. They leaned against the gym wall. "Lupo is being brought to court on Monday for blackhanding a shopkeeper named Manzella. If you're so interested, why don't you come?"

"I will!"

"Domenico, I have a few questions for you."

"Okay." Domenico put on his most innocent face.

"Some of the detectives have noticed that things aren't so normal around your aunt's house."

"What do you mean, detective?"

"One of your cousins is missing, the others were taken out of school—and your aunt seems to be walking all over the city."

"It's nothing, detective. Angelina is in Italy with her grandparents. My aunt was having a hard time with the new baby so they sent her there. And my uncle, he thinks everyone should work," explained Domenico dismissively.

"Good job, Domenico. You just might become a detective."

Domenico looked down to hide his smile.

"Look, son, you tell your aunt that I'm here for her if she needs me."

MONDAY, NOVEMBER 22, 1909

Hours before she expected him, Domenico burst through the door. "Zia! Manzella didn't show! It was a mistrial."

Giovanna shook her head, understanding Manzella's fear and hoping that it was fear, not death, that had kept him from the courthouse.

"Lupo got up from the defendant's seat the moment the judge said, 'You're free to go,' with a huge smile on his face. Then Lupo is surrounded by cops, including Detective Fiaschetti, and they walk him away in handcuffs. The reporters told me he was arrested again on counterfeiting charges."

Domenico's tone changed. "But, Zia, this reporter started asking questions about Angelina. He said, 'I heard your cousin is missing.'"

"How does he know?" Giovanna gasped, gripping Domenico's arm.

Domenico let out a yelp and rubbed his arm. "When I told him it wasn't true he said a librarian told him you were looking for articles on kidnapping."

THURSDAY, NOVEMBER 25, 1909

"Come, Giovanna. Teresa is making an American turkey; you need to get out," pleaded Lorenzo.

"No thank you, Lorenzo. I'll stay here."

"Giovanna, I wish there was a way to help you."

"You've done what you can."

Lorenzo rubbed his face as he often did when he was nervous. "Sometimes I think I should have found a way to send you back." He paced the tiny kitchen. "We forced you to stay here with Rocco."

"Go back? So I could have been killed in the earthquake? So I could scratch plaster from the walls to add to the flour? It's not your fault, Lorenzo. And besides, I wouldn't have had Angelina and Anthony."

Lorenzo shuffled around awkwardly. Giovanna tried to ease his guilt.

"It was the money I sent to Scilla. Someone told them. But even so, they blackmail people with nothing. There is no understanding evil."

"Are you sure you won't come? Please?"

"No, no. Lorenzo, how many pounds is the turkey?"

"I don't know, I think fifteen," answered Lorenzo, puzzled.

Giovanna calculated. Turkey was expensive this year, thirty-two cents a pound. That was nearly five dollars that could have been ransom money.

"I'll send Rocco and the children," replied Giovanna, thinking she would at least save money on their own supper and her family would eat a little meat.

"Va bene, but I wish you would come," said Lorenzo, kissing his sister and the top of the baby's head good-bye.

FRIDAY, NOVEMBER 26, 1909

"Release Lupo," ordered the lieutenant.

Fiaschetti rolled his eyes. "Why?"

"There's not enough evidence. It was a flimsy arrest in the first place."

"Then why did we do it?"

"Look, we know Lupo's involved in counterfeiting, so the police chief wanted to prove he was doing something about it to impress the feds. But his friends in City Hall said to let him go."

"He's a wolf, but he's slippery as an eel. We'll never keep him more than a couple weeks," moaned Fiaschetti.

"I don't know," reasoned the lieutenant, "it seems different now. The chief announced today that any cop who uncovers evidence of Lupo's counterfeiting will be made a first-grade detective."

Fiaschetti whistled. "Murder, extortion, that's one thing, but when you start messing with the money, that's serious."

"Come on, get Lupo out of here."

SATURDAY, NOVEMBER 27, 1909

"I got the money," said Rocco, coming in the door.

Two weeks before, when Rocco said he would get the money, Giovanna believed him, and something in their relationship changed. He finally became her partner, and she found herself looking at him in an entirely new light. Had he failed, she would have been crushed, not only because they wouldn't have the final ransom payment, but because she would lose the new warmth she felt for him.

"Rocco, from where? You don't have to tell me if you can't."

Rocco sat down beside her. "From Dr. Bellantoni."

Giovanna kissed Rocco with tenderness. She knew that asking another man for money was, for him, the greatest sacrifice.

SUNDAY, NOVEMBER 28, 1909

"The baby is so strong, Giovanna!" exclaimed Lucrezia, examining him. "But I'm surprised you didn't name him Nunzio."

"You must need to get back for Sunday dinner," remarked Giovanna, changing the subject.

"No, I have time. I want to take a look at you, and besides, my husband is away at another conference."

Giovanna could hear in Lucrezia's voice that there was more to this, but she didn't ask questions, fearing that one confidence might lead to another. She laid baby Anthony on one side of the bed, where he poked at the air with his arms and feet, and stretched out on the other for Lucrezia's examination.

"Did you see the papers today?" commented Lucrezia, filling the awkward silence.

"No." Giovanna wished she had so she could have more of an answer, but Lucrezia good-naturedly continued on while Giovanna said a prayer of thanks that Lucrezia had the kind heart not to be meddlesome.

"Last night at the Metropolitan, Caruso sang *La Traviata* with Toscanini conducting. Two Italians snuck up the fire escape and got into the balcony to hear the concert. I suppose that isn't uncommon. But what was funny was that an Irish policeman discovered them, and instead of arresting them on the spot, he locked them in a closet so he could hear the rest of the performance!"

"I hope they heard it, too!" responded Giovanna with a forced laugh. "Did you go?"

"No. My husband left on Friday."

"So why didn't you go alone?"

"Ah." Lucrezia shrugged her shoulders. For a split second Giovanna wanted to follow up the shrug and comfort her, but once again she stopped herself.

"I'll be going. You're doing well."

"Thank you, Lucrezia. I'll come visit when the weather is better."

"You do that," answered Lucrezia with resignation, knowing full well that she wouldn't see her friend anytime soon.

FORTY-TWO

MONDAY, NOVEMBER 29, 1909

This is it. Here's the final payment. I want my daughter returned immediately. If you delay, next it is your coglioni. *They'll start to itch, blister, and fall off.*

Giovanna allowed Rocco to take the final payment to the arranged spot in the dumbwaiter at 304 Elizabeth Street.

TUESDAY, NOVEMBER 30, 1909

A loud rap at the door startled Giovanna. It was them. It had to be them. She flung the door open. Instead, she looked into the faces of two even more startled settlement workers.

"Buon giorno, signora. Many people in this area are getting consumption and we have come to teach your family how to avoid becoming ill . . ."

WEDNESDAY, DECEMBER 1, 1909

When Giovanna returned home from buying bread, there was another booklet about consumption in front of the door. She picked it up with difficulty because Anthony was in the sling at her chest. Inside, as she tossed it into a pile of papers to be burned, a note fell out.

In seconds, Giovanna was in Inzerillo's cafe, the gun in her waistband at the ready.

"We need to talk!" ordered Giovanna, walking into the back room without stopping.

Closing the door, Inzerillo hissed, "What do you mean coming in here this way for all to see!"

Giovanna grabbed the gun and put it to Inzerillo's head. "Is it better they see you dead?"

"Signora! Put that away."

"Not until you sit down and listen," she said, locking the door.

"Okay, I will listen."

"Read this," she ordered, thrusting the note in his hands.

Inzerillo read it. "I agree this is most unfortunate."

"It's more than unfortunate, you crook. It's suicide. I know now they are playing with me, and I am done playing. Here's your message, disgraziato." Giovanna felt liberated by dropping all pretense with Inzerillo. "My daughter is to be delivered safe and unharmed to me immediately. If not, letters will be sent to the police and newspapers. These letters will give evidence that Lupo and his gang were involved in the Bank Pati bombing and the kidnapping and murder of Mario Palermo. They will tell how Leo took money from Edwin Reese for the elections, and, finally, they will have evidence of Lupo's counterfeiting. If anything happens to my daughter, to me, or to anyone in my family, people unknown to you have been told to deliver the letters."

Inzerillo remained seated and silent. The only sound was Giovanna's labored breathing. Eventually, Inzerillo said, "That is quite a message, signora."

"That's only the half of it. You'll all be braying at the moon in jail with the curse of the malocchio. Lupo thinks he can cast the evil eye? He'll learn what a midwife can do!"

"Signora, because you are so upset, I am going to ignore the fact that you keep implicating Lupo and me in this crime. We have not touched your daughter. But because I am a man of honor, I will deliver your message and use my influence to see that your daughter is returned immediately."

"I want word by tomorrow. If not, the letters will be sent and the curses cast."

"How much longer do we have to keep her?" nagged the older Gallucci brother's wife.

"There is nothing out here. We're going crazy," chimed in the younger woman.

"Shut up!" yelled the older of the two kidnappers.

"Shhh, someone's at the door," whispered his brother.

The older brother drew his gun and motioned their wives and children into the bedroom. The younger brother, gun also drawn, opened the door.

"Lupo! Pietro!" Putting his gun away, the younger brother said, "We didn't know you were coming."

The older brother lowered his gun but kept it in his hand, saying skeptically, "It's dangerous for you to be here."

"Dangerous? What's dangerous is trusting you," growled Lupo, barging through the door.

"Lupo, what are you talking about?" asked the younger brother in a panic.

When Lupo and Inzerillo seated themselves at the table, the brothers calmed down.

"What's going on?" asked the older brother.

"That's what we came here to find out," answered Inzerillo. "It seems that the fruit seller's wife knows more than she should."

"We told Leo! After she grabbed me in the church, we told Leo to tell you everything she said, but Leo thought you'd be angry we were followed," whined the younger brother.

"Grabbed you in the church . . ." repeated Inzerillo.

"And Lupo, she's a witch! She gave me the rash that caused these scars. My brother too!"

Seeing Lupo's disgusted expression, the older brother retrieved Giovanna's notes. "Every time she sent money, she sent letters. We have them here," he said, handing them to Lupo, who passed them to Inzerillo without looking at them.

While Inzerillo read the notes, Lupo interrogated the men, ending with, "So, what did you do for Edwin Reese?"

"We don't know an Edwin Reese. The first time we saw his name was in the witch woman's letter. We asked Leo, but he said she was crazy."

"Shit for brains. Shit for brains," muttered Lupo.

"So what do you want us to do, Lupo?" asked the younger brother. "If she knows so much, do we kill them both right away?"

"You'd have to kill the entire family. Others too."

"Is that what you want?"

"No, you idiots, that's not what I want. I just got out of jail. The feds are watching me. It took four hours to get here. I don't need dead bodies and letters pointing to me."

"Lupo, this has been going on a while," reported Inzerillo, handing Lupo the notes from Giovanna.

Standing up to face the brothers, Lupo ordered, "The kid is going back. Don't shave, and wait for instructions."

Angelina, hearing the men call someone Lupo, decided that the wolf had come for her. She was too tired to be afraid, and instead, unconsciously, she scratched an *L* on her leg over and over till it bled. Seeing the blood-red *L*, she wished she knew how to spell because then, when they found her, they would know who had killed her.

"Leo, I give you a job, and it's not enough that you fuck it up so bad. Who's Edwin Reese, Leo?

"Lupo, I got your share right here!" sputtered Leo, trying to break free of Tommaso the Bull's grip on him.

"Leo, you do a couple of kidnappings and you think you're a big man. You move in on election money."

"I told you, Lupo, I got the money for you."

"I don't like not knowing things, Leo."

"Lupo, I was doing you a favor . . ."

"You're trading on my name, Leo. Do you think those politicians would have anything to do with you if you weren't working for Lupo?"

"Of course not, Lupo. Lupo, tell Tommaso to let me go and I'll show you the money."

Lupo nodded to Tommaso, who kept his eye on Leo as he went to his jacket.

Pulling out an envelope, he handed it to Lupo. "Here. There's sixteen hundred dollars in ransom money. And Lupo, that family didn't have a stack of money somewhere. I found out they're waiting for another payment. Because of me, we got that much," bragged Leo. "And here," he continued, taking out another envelope from his jacket, "seven hundred dollars for getting out the vote."

Lupo took the money from the envelopes and fanned it in front of his face. "You know, Leo, that's lots of exposure for a little over two grand.

Sloppy, very sloppy."

"Lupo, I know things didn't go perfect. But you gave me two idiot greenhorns!"

"I want you to return the kid. Deliver a letter right away telling them the girl will be back within the week. After you deliver her, tell the Gallucci brothers to clean the place out. No clues. Give them this," Lupo peeled off bills totaling three hundred dollars, "and tell them to go to Chicago. I never want to see them again."

"With pleasure," smirked Leo.

"I'll settle with you when the kid is returned. Now get out of here."

When Leo left, Lupo gave orders to Tommaso. "When the kid's returned, make sure it's common knowledge that Leo did the job, and then make him disappear for good."

THURSDAY, DECEMBER 2, 1909

The note was slipped under their door while they were sleeping.

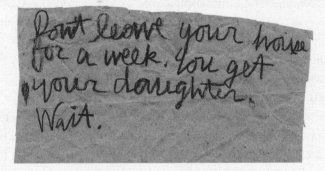

FRIDAY, DECEMBER 3, 1909

"A week! Why a week?" questioned Giovanna of Inzerillo in his back room.

"You're a formidable foe, signora. They have to be sure that they won't be ambushed by the police or greeted with one of your curses."

"If they are playing with me, signore, even your family will not be safe."

"Enough with the threats, signora. I give you my word that your daughter will be returned within the week."

"Your word." Giovanna stopped herself from spitting.

SATURDAY, DECEMBER 4, 1909

Scratching the scab of the *L*, Angelina watched the blood trickle down her leg. She scratched off another scab and watched that rivulet join in with the first at her ankle. Stretching out her other leg, she scratched scabs off her thighs and held imaginary races to see which line of blood would reach the floor first.

SUNDAY, DECEMBER 5, 1909

Two days of waiting felt like two years. Baby Anthony was held so tightly that he was nearly crushed. Giovanna began to believe that perhaps Saint Anthony did send her this child, because he was the only thing keeping her from shooting Inzerillo.

When another note came, Giovanna's disappointment was crushing, but at least it had a specific direction.

MONDAY, DECEMBER 6, 1909

The bell tinkled when she walked into Donatello's store, minutes after it opened.

"May I help you?" asked the woman clerk.

"Yes, I need a coat for a four-year-old girl."

"These here should all be around the right size with plenty of room for growth."

Thinking of the red shawl she wore the first time she delivered ransom money, Giovanna's eyes scanned the little wool coats and seized on a bright red one.

"Can I see that one, please?" she pointed. The color would make it easier to spot Angelina on the street, or to find the little imposter in her daughter's coat.

"Yes, this is the one," she announced to the clerk. "I'll pay for it now, but it's a gift for my cousin's daughter. He'll come get it. His name is Ricco."

"No problem, signora. I'll have it ready for him."

TUESDAY, DECEMBER 7, 1909

All day long Giovanna combed the streets in case the scoundrels simply left Angelina in the neighborhood, and when the children and Rocco returned from work they joined the search.

Much later that night, they had a quiet dinner of broth and bread. There had been no money for meat since Angelina was kidnapped. Her stepchildren were skin and bones.

WEDNESDAY, DECEMBER 8, 1909

"Get the kid," ordered the older brother to his wife. She went into Angelina's cell and pulled her off the straw and out the door.

"Can't you clean her up a little?" asked the older man.

"What do you care?" answered his wife.

"At least wash the blood off her arms and legs."

With a cold cloth, the woman scrubbed Angelina's limbs. "We're getting rid of you today," she said.

Angelina felt relieved. Would they throw her in the trash? In the river by the bridge? It didn't much matter.

"Who's taking her?" asked the woman.

"They are," said Leo, nodding to the brothers, who both now had beards.

Angelina imagined that the droopy-eyed man might hurt her before getting rid of her and wondered if the short men would try to stop him.

"Where's the coat?" asked Leo.

"Here," said the younger brother, tossing him a package. "Look at that color!"

"It's not like the Calabresi. Very flashy," commented the younger woman.

Angelina was happy that she was going to be warm before she died. She hugged the coat around her and played with the black braid at the waist.

"Go," said Leo. "I'll wait for you here."

Angelina turned to wave at the children, who silently waved back.

They walked a long time. Angelina was so weak that she kept trying to sit, but the men with beards would yank her back up. After she fell a few times, the older man picked her up impatiently. Angelina couldn't bear to be so close to his breath, which smelled of wine and cigars.

"I can walk. Put me down," she commanded. She had lost all fear of them. Even the lupo bear didn't provoke her anymore.

"Then stop falling," barked the older man.

At the station, they climbed the stairs and waited on the platform. "They could be taking me to the ocean, not the river," thought Angelina.

Once on the train, she was warm, warm enough to not want to end up in cold water. "I should scream," she thought, "then someone will stop them from taking me to the ocean." But right before yelling, she saw that they were heading over the Brooklyn Bridge to the city, not away from it.

"Where are we going?"

"You're going home," snarled the younger brother.

"He's lying," thought Angelina. "Besides, my parents don't want me." Watching out the window, she recognized the Bowery with the train tracks hugging the sides of the street and darkening the storefronts. They passed the big hotel with the name she could never pronounce. Gazing down at her new coat, she had another thought. One Sunday dinner she had heard the grown-ups talk about people selling children. They were making her look nice because they were going to sell her, not kill her.

At the next stop, the older brother yanked again at her arm, pulling her out of the train. "Walk fast or I'll carry you."

Angelina tried to keep up with them as they pulled her down the Bowery. Ahead of her she saw the black marble columns of the Germania Bank Building across from the brick building that looked like it was holding an ice cream cone. This was her old neighborhood.

"Where are we going?" Angelina asked again, this time more tentatively.

"I told you. You're going home," muttered the younger brother.

"But my parents gave me up," she practically whispered.

They were on Spring Street, a block from the corner of Elizabeth.

"Do you know how to get home from here?" asked the older man.

Angelina nodded but was confused.

"Go, then, go!" commanded the younger brother.

They had let go of her hand. She could run.

"Go!" they shouted at her.

Angelina ran as fast as she could, which wasn't very fast, down Spring Street. She looked behind her, but they were gone. She could go home! But what if her parents didn't let her in? Where would she go? She turned onto Elizabeth Street, because she figured she would at least ask her mother why she gave her away. At the sight of her building in the distance, she ran faster, grabbed the brass handle on the door, ran over the little mosaic tiles and up the slate stairs.

The sound of little feet running up the stairs reached Giovanna. She dropped the baby in the bureau drawer that was his bassinet and lunged toward the door, throwing it open.

"Mamma! Mamma!" Angelina was halfway up the stairs when she

saw her. In seconds Giovanna scooped her up and buried her face in Angelina's neck. "Mamma, you're hurting me!" called Angelina.

"Scusa, scusa, let me see your face!" Giovanna cupped her daughter's face in her hands and sobbed.

Angelina was confused and angry. Hitting her mother, she shouted, "Brutta Mamma! Brutta Mamma! Brutta! Brutta! Why didn't you come and get me? Why did you give me away?"

Angelina's confusion was only magnified when she saw her mother, who was crying, start to laugh. "You talk like a little Sicilian!"

Rocco and the girls burst through the door.

"Angelina! My Angelina!" Rocco took her from Giovanna's arms and kissed her face many times over. The child was completely bewildered. Her father never kissed her. And then he kissed her mother.

Mary and Frances pulled at her shouting, "You're back!"

Angelina struck out at her father and sisters too, her little fists raining down on them. "Why didn't you get me! Brutti! Brutti!" Her cries became louder when they, too, laughed with joy.

"My baby, my baby, don't cry. We are so happy to have you back." Giovanna stroked her face. "If we had known where you were we would have come at once to get you."

"You didn't know where I was?"

"No, bambina."

"But you sent me away with Limonata."

"She was a bad woman." Turning to Frances, Giovanna said, "Go to Zio Lorenzo's house and tell them Angelina is back."

Word had already spread that people had seen a little girl in a red coat running through the streets. Teresa and her children arrived before Frances made it down the stairs.

Angelina had a hard time understanding all the crying and the laughing. There wasn't a moment when she wasn't being kissed and thrown in the air. Arms were everywhere, and her head was alternately pressed into someone's body or cupped in someone's hand. The happier they all were, the angrier Angelina got. "If they like me so much, why didn't they find me?" she thought.

Her mother broke away, and Angelina saw her and Zia Teresa

heating water and pouring it into a big tub by the stove. Frances, who Angelina hadn't even noticed was missing because of all the commotion, returned from the pharmacist, her arms brimming with bottles. At one point in the mayhem, her mother brought her into the bedroom and said, "Angelina, this is your baby brother, Anthony."

"I'm glad you didn't give him away."

Giovanna hugged her tighter.

"Let's get these clothes off," ordered Teresa. Teresa cut the clothes from Angelina's body and handed them and the red coat to her oldest daughter, Concetta. "Burn them, they're infested."

Angelina was dipped in the hot tub. It was the first time in three months her body was immersed in water. The heat actually made her shiver; something inside was thawing.

"My baby, my baby," Giovanna was crying, but there was no laughter as she gently washed her daughter's emaciated body, which was covered in open wounds, scabs, and vermin.

"I'll start on her hair," offered Teresa. Taking a thin-toothed comb, she separated each strand, capturing and killing lice and nits. By then all her cousins were in the apartment as well. Everyone was laughing, and her cousins, especially Domenico, kept trying to ask her questions. But her mother would shush them, "Not now, not now."

Concetta, who had left to burn Angelina's clothes, returned an hour later with food. Soon everyone was eating, including Angelina, who ate in the bath while her mother and Teresa continued to minister to her body. Frances had emptied and filled the tub nearly ten times, and Mary was feeding her sips of hot tea and bites of meatballs.

Hours later, when Angelina was lifted out of the water, her mother wrapped her in a towel and her father poured wine. Someone held a little glass to Angelina's lips as everyone drank.

On the bed, Giovanna removed Angelina's towel and kissed every square inch of her daughter's body, using the towel to wipe the tears that fell on Angelina's clean skin. Uncapping bottles, she dabbed lotion and salves on the cuts, bites, and wounds, muttering prayers the entire time.

"I bought you a new nightgown," said Giovanna, pulling a soft flannel dress over Angelina's head. She picked Angelina up off the bed and knelt with her before her makeshift altar. "I prayed every minute to Saint Anthony to bring you home, Angelina. He answered my prayers."

Giovanna retrieved a brown paper package from under her pillow that was tied with string. "I have something to open with you. I waited for you," she whispered, crying and gently ripping the paper to reveal a photograph with three views. "Look how beautiful you are!" exclaimed Giovanna, crying even harder. "I want you to forget everything from the day after this picture was taken until this moment," she said, placing the photo on her makeshift altar.

Angelina's eyelids fluttered, and her head swayed groggily. Giovanna lay down on the bed with one arm wrapped tightly around her daughter as if she would never let go. Stroking Angelina's hair, Giovanna whispered, "Sleep, child, you're safe. You're home."

PART TEN

HOBOKEN, NEW JERSEY
1918

FORTY-THREE

When they moved to Hoboken, there was no doubt in Giovanna's mind what type of business they would establish. Since that day in Coney Island, she was infatuated with ice cream and ice cream cones. Her passion paid off. They had become masters.

Teresa and Giovanna were in the factory behind their ice cream parlor. Sacks of sugar lined the walls, and in the center of the room sat wood barrels. Inside the barrels, a ten-gallon tin can was surrounded by ice, and the top of the barrel was covered with rock salt.

Over the years, despite their prickly start, Giovanna and Teresa had bonded. Teresa was not someone whom Giovanna would reveal secrets to, but she had come to love her sister-in-law, and they worked well together. Giovanna could read Teresa's moods. Today, making ice cream, she knew there was something on Teresa's mind that she wasn't talking about. Giovanna also knew that Teresa was incapable of holding something in for long, so she waited patiently.

"Teresa, could you bring me another gallon of cream?"

Giovanna filled the silence. "The nights are becoming chilly. Soon we won't need to make so much. Rocco was already talking about switching to selling chestnuts."

When Teresa handed Giovanna the cream, their eyes met, and Giovanna's curiosity got the best of her. "What is it?"

"You know I still see my friends from Elizabeth Street."

"I know. You went this weekend, yes?"

"They told me that Lucrezia is dying."

Giovanna shut her eyes, put down the gallon of cream, and turned from Teresa.

"Giovanna, I didn't know whether to tell you. I know that you don't see her anymore, but I thought you should know."

Giovanna could never explain to Teresa. When she had lied over and over again to Lucrezia during Angelina's kidnapping, she felt that she had violated their relationship and that it could never be the same. It was as if Lucrezia was her lover and Giovanna had cheated on her. She did love Lucrezia, in fact she knew that she still did, but she had forsaken the friendship because she was overwhelmed by fear. When Angelina was returned, she was embarrassed to confess and admit that she hadn't trusted her.

"Why don't you go see her, Giovanna?" suggested Teresa softly.

"I want to go for a walk. Can you finish up?"

"Of course."

Giovanna hugged Teresa and walked into the parlor. Mary was on her hands and knees cleaning the black-and-white checkered floor. Her baby sister, Concetta, was asleep in a cradle braced against one of the wire-backed parlor chairs.

"Mary, that's clean enough!"

"I like it to gleam, Zia."

No one took as much pride in the ice cream parlor as Mary. She had become an artist at making sugar cones. In fact, she did it with such flair that Giovanna had set up her cone-making apparatus in the window, and she never failed to draw a crowd.

"I must go out. I fed Concetta. And please, when Angelina and Anthony get home from school, see that they do their chores."

Giovanna walked a full lap around Hoboken's square mile. She headed up First Street, passing what she called her hometown fish market—the one with a swordfish for a sign. She went north along the waterfront, past the ships, which were being loaded and unloaded by swarms of dockworkers. She shivered at the sight of the big German ship that had just been seized by the Americans at the pier. Her nephew Antonio was already fighting for Italy in the war. She prayed every day for his survival, because she knew that either fate or her will would bring Antonio to America to marry Angelina.

Turning west at the north end where the ships were in dry dock for repair, Giovanna avoided the hustle and bustle of Washington Street by walking south on Willow Avenue. She passed the library with its copper dome and the new high school that Mary had just graduated from. When she walked back east toward the river, this time she kept walking straight onto the ferry.

She was shaking, in part because she was going back to New York City for the first time in five years, and in part because she didn't have a clue what to say to Lucrezia or whether she would even see her. She didn't even know if Lucrezia was in a hospital.

Giovanna had seen the Madonna in the harbor four times. The last time was when they moved to Hoboken. She remembered wondering whether the watery distance created by the river would keep them safe. It was like looking from Scilla across the Strait of Messina at the black smoke of the volcano. On the Hoboken shore, New York became a distant but visible threat.

New York City had never been her choice. And possibly because of that, she didn't trust the place. How could one piece of land support so much weight? How could they keep digging tunnels and not have the streets collapse? How long would it take before one of those trains fell from the overhead tracks? In her search for Angelina, she had traveled all over the city without really seeing it. With her daughter abducted, Giovanna felt every square inch of New York had become inhospitable. Even after Angelina was returned, the metropolis continued to overwhelm her, and she could no longer take comfort in the privacy of its crowded streets because she knew how many eyes were really watching. She had come to, and left, New York City as a foreigner. Hoboken was her home now. She had chosen it.

Pacing the perimeter of the ferry, she tried to sort through her conflicting emotions, starting with guilt but always ending in deep sorrow. She came to the heartbreaking realization that this might be the second time she would lose Lucrezia.

Walking off the boat, Giovanna was struck by how accustomed she had become to life in Hoboken. New York City seemed so crowded and fast—far more than she remembered—possibly because there seemed to be so many more automobiles competing for street space with the trolleys and horses. Anxious to escape the streams of people surging through downtown and exhausted from her walk in Hoboken, Giovanna took the train.

When she got to Lucrezia's block, it felt as if nothing had changed. She could have been arriving after delivering a baby, or coming to visit her friend with a newspaper in hand. The same old woman sat on the stoop next door.

"Did you come to see the signora?" She greeted Giovanna without missing a beat.

"Yes. Is she upstairs?"

"She is."

Giovanna started up the stoop but turned to ask, "Is her husband with her?"

"I saw him leave. But her daughter's up there."

As she opened the outside door, Giovanna became aware that she was visiting empty-handed. She'd been so determined to get there and unsure of whether she would even see Lucrezia that bringing something hadn't crossed her mind. She hesitated, but knew that if she left now, she might never come back. Instead, breathing deeply, she walked up the stairs and knocked on Lucrezia's door.

"Yes?" said Lucrezia's daughter, opening the door slightly.

"Buon giorno. You must be Claudia. I am Giovanna, an old friend of your mother. I was hoping I could see her." Claudia looked exactly like Lucrezia and was just as stately.

"Come in, signora," greeted Claudia, opening the door and looking at Giovanna's work clothes. "Please have a seat."

Catching Claudia's glance, Giovanna mentioned, "Your mother and I used to deliver babies together."

"Oh, yes. I remember her talking about you."

"How is she?"

"Not well. The doctors think it is only a matter of days."

"I'm so sorry, Claudia. Can I see her?"

"She's resting. She gets so little sleep that I would appreciate it if you could return at another time."

Giovanna stood, ready to bolt out the door, embarrassed that she had come. "I'm sorry, I understand . . ."

"Claudia, who are you talking to?" Lucrezia's thin voice drifted from the bedroom.

"An old friend of yours, Mamma." Turning to Giovanna, Claudia said, "She's awake. Would you like to see her?"

Giovanna was waving her hand in an attempt to say, "No, I'll go," but Lucrezia's daughter was leading her by the arm to the doorway of the bedroom.

Lucrezia turned her head, and Giovanna felt like her shoulders fell to her knees. Lucrezia's face and body were skeletal. Her body barely dented the bed.

Lucrezia stared back at Giovanna and smiled. "Sit down next to me."

Giovanna looked to Lucrezia's daughter's face for permission, and when Claudia nodded and left the room, Giovanna did as she was instructed. Awkwardly, and without speaking, she took Lucrezia's hands, which lay on top of the bedcovers, and held them in her own.

"I bet you heard from Teresa," kidded Lucrezia in a voice that sounded like it only fluttered over her vocal cords.

In seconds, Lucrezia had cleared the air. Giovanna laughed hard and remembered why it was so easy to love this woman. "Yes, you're right! She told me this morning."

"I'm glad you came, Giovanna."

Hearing Lucrezia say her name unleashed a torrent of emotion. Cupping and kissing Lucrezia's hands, Giovanna said over and over, tears streaming down her face, "I'm sorry. I'm so sorry, Lucrezia."

"Giovanna." Lucrezia lifted her bony hand to Giovanna's face and caught a tear. "I knew," she said.

Giovanna was not at all surprised but wept harder. "I couldn't tell you."

"I wanted to help."

"I was afraid."

"Were you afraid of me?"

"I was afraid of everyone. I was even afraid of myself."

Giovanna's head collapsed onto Lucrezia's chest, and Lucrezia entwined her fingers in her hair.

"I don't want to lose you again, Lucrezia," moaned Giovanna.

"You never lost me. And with the way you pray, you never will."

Giovanna's laugh became a snort through her tears, and it brought Lucrezia's daughter into the room.

Claudia looked at them, surprised and concerned. "Perhaps you should rest, Mamma?"

"Yes. Lie with me a while, Giovanna?" asked Lucrezia.

Giovanna got up and rearranged the blankets around her friend and then went to the other side of the bed and lay on top of the covers next to her. Lucrezia reached for her hand, and Giovanna held it tighter than she should have.

Giovanna left that evening after Lucrezia had fallen asleep. She returned the next day as she had promised, but Lucrezia had died that morning with her husband and daughter by her side.

"She asked that I give you this," said Lucrezia's daughter, holding out her hand and crying. Giovanna took the small medal of Saint Anthony from Claudia's palm. "It's odd, because my mother wasn't religious. But she said this would be meaningful to you. She also said to tell you that when people love each other, they always find each other in the end."

That night, Giovanna closed the store near nine o'clock but didn't get upstairs until after ten. Not yet ready for bed, she leaned out her first-floor window into the late summer heat.

The store looked so quiet, yet only a few hours before, there'd been a line around the block. Lorenzo was talking about opening his own ice cream business and going to Newark, which was a good thing, because now that Clement was married, there were so many adults in the business that they were stepping on one another's toes. Domenico still helped in the store, but he had started working at the German-named factory on Third and Grand that raised spiders in the basement to supply the crosshairs for submarine periscopes. He had also become a fixture around Hoboken's many social clubs.

Rocco came up behind Giovanna and put his arm around her waist. "I can't sleep either. Let's go downstairs and play cards."

Giovanna smiled. "You set up the table, and I'll be down in a minute."

A moment later, Angelina was in the room. "Mamma, I can't sleep. It's too hot."

"Come here by the window with me."

Angelina was too big for her mother's lap, but she sat on it anyway. Giovanna ran her hands through her daughter's hair.

Below on the sidewalk they could see Rocco setting up the card table and pouring two glasses of wine.

"Mamma, will you rub my back like you did when I was little and had nightmares?"

"In a minute. First I want to give you something."

"What?"

"I know you are responsible, so I am going to ask you something important. I want you to promise me that when I die, you will put this in my coffin." Giovanna reached into the pocket of her dress and handed Angelina the Saint Anthony medal that Lucrezia had left her.

Angelina looked at the medal and then at her mother. "Mamma, you're scaring me. Why are you saying this?"

"Nothing is going to happen to me, Angelina. You won't have to do this for many, many years."

Angelina looked at her mother with tears welling in her eyes. "Promise me you'll never die."

"I promise I'll never leave you. That's the reason I want you to bury me with Saint Anthony." Giovanna put her hand over Angelina's, which now clutched the medal. "When I'm gone, if you need me, or if your children need me, or even their children, you'll always know that I am there. You see, Angelina, people who love one another always find each other somehow."

EPILOGUE

"Nanny, why is Uncle Anthony called Cakey?"

"Because when he was a kid, he liked cake. Aren't you hungry?"

As soon as I graduated college, ignoring my mother's disbelief that I was moving back to the ghetto, I rented an apartment in Hoboken that Uncle Cakey helped me find. Uncle Cakey had also shown me the best places to shop, and now, five years later and a regular, I had visited each and every one to prepare the feast that was in the kitchen.

"I made shrimp scampi." I put another tape in the video camera.

"How did you know how to do that? You don't cook."

"I used a recipe."

"They have recipes for that?"

"Nanny, do you remember when I was about twelve, we were watching this movie and you got really upset. That's the day you told me about the kidnapping."

"Don't put that down. I'll make you stop."

Although Nanny had begun to share memories, this was one topic that remained off-limits. I finally realized she was still afraid. I left the video camera and sat next to her on the couch. "They can't get us, Nanny."

"No, no, I don't tell nobody. I don't even tell my friends. You shouldn't tell. That's the way it is."

"Nanny, I shut off the camera. I just need to know."

"They were so mean and lazy. What they did was wrong. They shouldn't have done that. I was just a little girl."

I watched my grandmother transform before my eyes. The bossy eighty-year-old shrunk into her blouse. Her huge hands didn't flail around excitedly anymore; they clutched at her sides or covered her mouth as she spoke. I could barely breathe as my grandmother talked about the kidnapping in detail for the first time. I would gently ask questions when she slowed down, but I avoided looking at her because I felt like she would snap out of what resembled a trance.

". . . Our neighbor Limonata took me to her brother; he had a butcher store. Maybe it wasn't her brother, I don't know. Then she said she had to go to the dentist, and he took me to the kidnappers."

"How did he get you there?"

"I was a smart little girl. I said to him, 'This isn't the way we came.' We were going over the Brooklyn Bridge . . ."

"If I cried too much they would put this teddy bear at the window to the door and say, 'You be quiet or il lupo will get you.' I thought they were so stupid, because 'lupo' in Italian is 'wolf,' not 'bear' . . ."

An hour later, she had recounted every detail of the ordeal including the color of the blind across the street.

"When I ran up those stairs, they were so happy to see me, everyone was crying, especially my mother. They disinfected me in a tub all night long. And for weeks they brought me toys, a doll, a carriage, a little piano . . ."

"Nanny, did they ever catch the guys who kidnapped you?"

"No! I told you, you couldn't tell nobody. After I got back, the newspapers started to bother us. When I went out with my mother, sometimes a reporter would stand in front of us and say, 'We heard your daughter was kidnapped by the Black Hand.' My mother would yank my hand and we would run away. They would run after us and ask me questions: 'Little girl, did bad men take you?' My mother was so mad, she would yell at them to leave us alone. When we got home she would make me promise to never answer any questions from anyone. Never talk to strangers. Never to tell anyone."

"So that was it? You don't know what happened to the people who kidnapped you?"

"No, not the people who kept me. But my mother found Limonata in Brooklyn."

"And?"

"Eh, what do you think? She nearly killed her. She kicked her and threw her down four flights of stairs."

"Did Big Nanny tell you about that?"

"No, I told you, we never talked about it. My cousin Dominick told me. Dominick, bless his soul, was smart. He was tough too. When they found us again in Hoboken, he scared them away."

"Who found you—what do you mean?"

"Eh, these were bad people. They didn't stop even after I was returned. My brother Clement found a bomb before it went off outside our apartment on Elizabeth Street. So we moved to Hoboken. My parents and uncle opened our ice cream store in Hoboken, Siena's French Ice Cream."

"French!?"

"It sounded fancy. They tried to blackhand us again, but Dominick found the guy. He took the guy by the neck. I think he even cut him. Dominick had Hoboken friends by then. The names probably scared them, because that was the end of it. No more Black Hand. Let's eat. If you made the scampi sit all this time it won't be good."

I dished out the pasta and brought the reheated pan of scampi to the table. When I put the pan on the table, Nanny scowled.

"That don't look nice," reprimanded Nanny, bringing it back to the kitchen.

I let her rummage around my kitchen for a serving bowl. My head was swirling with images of my great-grandmother accosting kidnappers, beating up Limonata, and running from reporters.

Putting the bowl on the table, she tasted the sauce with her finger. "The shrimp likes more garlic than this."

When she finally sat down, I said, "Nanny, I wish I had known Big Nanny better."

"My mother was a beautiful woman. Strong. Smart."

"I remember her a little. I remember her skin was like silk. And she had strong hands like you. But I especially remember her eyes. There was a whole story in those eyes."

Nanny passed me the grated parmiggiano. "Here, take some and we'll say grace."

GLOSSARY OF ITALIAN TERMS

acqua — water

aiutami — help me

ammoratas — girlfriends
    (*Italian-American slang*)

andiamo — we go, let's go

arrivederci — good-bye

aspetta — wait

avanti — come in

bambino — baby

basanogol — basil
    (*Italian-American slang*)

basta — enough

bella — beautiful

bene — well

biscotti — cookies

blu marinos — Navy
    (*Italian-American slang*)

boccalone — big mouth, gullible one

bocce — Italian ball game

bravo — good, congratulations

brigantaggio — thieving

briscola — card game

brutto — ugly

buon giorno — good day

cafone — crude person

Calabresi — people from Calabria

Calabria — southern region of Italy

cannolo — an Italian pastry

capisci? — do you understand?

caro — dear

castello — castle

che cosa fa? — what are you doing?

chiazza — town square

ciao — hello/good-bye

coglioni — balls

come si chiama? — what's your name?

con — with

contadini — peasants

cos'è successo? — what happened?

così bella — how beautiful

cugina — cousin

culo — butt

dago — derogatory term for
    Italian-American

Dio mio — my God

disgraziato — miserable one, wretch

dottore — doctor

due — two

farmacia — pharmacy

festa — party

finalmente — finally

forza — go

fratello — brother

gabbadotz — stubborn
    (*Italian-American slang*)

gedrool — jerk
    (*Italian-American slang*)

glantuomini — the gentry

gombada — friend that's like family
  (*Italian-American slang*)
grande — large
grazie — thank you
guarda — look
inglese — English
l'alta Italia — the north of Italy
La Mano Nera — The Black Hand
l'America — America
levatrice — midwife
loro brutti puzzolenti mafiosi —
  ugly lowlife gangsters
lupo — wolf
ma — but
macchiette — musical theater sketches
maestro — master
mafioso — thug, crook
mala femmina — bad woman
malocchio — evil eye
medza menz — half and half
  (*Italian-American slang*)
Mezzogiorno — the south of Italy
mille grazie — a million thanks
mio fratello — my brother
molto — very
mustasole — a type of hard cookie
Napolitano — person from Naples
niente — nothing
nome — name
nonno — grandfather
non parlo inglese —
  I don't speak English
occhi — eyes
opera buffa — comic opera
padrone — owner/wealthy
paesani — countrymen
pasticcini — pastries

pazzo — crazy
pensione — small hotel
perché — why
per favore — please
pescatori — fishermen
pescespada — swordfish
piacere — please/pleased to meet you
Piemontese — person from the
  Piedmont region in northern Italy
Pokerino — card and board game
pomodoro — tomato
prego — excuse me/you're welcome
principessa — princess
professore — professor
Puglia — region of Italy
puttana — whore
questa — this
Risorgimento — Italian revolution
schifoso — lowlife
Scillese — person from Scilla
scopa — card game
scusa — excuse me
sì — yes
signora — ma'am
signore — mister
sindaco — mayor
smettila — cut it out
sorella — sister
sporcaccioni — pigs, slobs
strega — witch
stronzo — turd, shit
terremoto — earthquake
torta — cake
tre — three
uno — one
va al diavolo — go to the devil
va bene — okay, fine

vaffanculo — go fuck yourself

vai — go

voto — vote

wop — derogatory term for
Italian-American

yia-yia — grandmother (*Greek*)

zia — aunt

zio — uncle

zucchero — sugar

SELECTED BIBLIOGRAPHY

Aleandri, Emelise. *The Italian American Immigrant Theatre of New York City.* Arcadia, 1999.

Anbinder, Tyler. *Five Points.* Plume, 2002.

Ardizzone, Tony. *In the Garden of Papa Santuzzu.* Picador USA, 1999.

Asbury, Herbert. *The Gangs of New York.* Alfred Knopf, Inc., 1927.

Barker, Folger. "What of the Italian Immigrant?" *Arena* vol. 34 (August 1905): 174–76.

Barolini, Helen. *Umbertina.* The Feminist Press, 1999.

Barreca, Regina. *Don't Tell Mama! Italian American Writing.* Penguin Books, 2002.

Binder, Frederick M., and David Reimers. *All the Nations Under Heaven: An Ethnic and Racial History of New York City.* Columbia University Press, 1995.

Bingham, General Theodore A. "The Organized Criminals of New York." *McClure's Magazine,* XXXIV (November 1909): 62–67.

"Black Hand Sway in Italian New York," *Literary Digest* vol. 47 (August 30, 1913): 308–10.

Bodio, Luigi. "The Protection of the Italian Emigrant of America." *Chautauquan* vol. 23 (1896): 42–64.

Brownstone, David M., Irene M. Franck, and Douglas Brownstone. *Island of Hope, Island of Tears.* Barnes and Noble, 1979.

Burns, Ric, and James Sanders, with Lisa Ades. *New York: An Illustrated History.* Alfred Knopf, 1999.

Byron, Joseph. *New York Life at the Turn of the Century in Photographs.* Dover Publications, 1985.

Cannistrano, Philip V. *The Italians of New York: Five Centuries of Struggle and Achievement.* New York Historical Society, 1999.

Cascone, Gina. *Life al Dente: Laughter and Love in an Italian-American Family.* Atria Books, 2003.

Center for Migration Studies. *Images: A Pictorial History of Italian Americans.* Center for Migration Studies of New York, Inc., 1981.

Ciongoli, A. Kenneth, and Jay Parini. *Beyond the Godfather: Italian American Writers on the Real Italian American Experience.* University Press of New England, 1997.

Cohen, David Steven. *America, the Dream of My Life: Selections from the Writer's Project*. New Jersey Ethnic Study, Rutger's University Press, 1990.

Cordasco, Francesco, and Salvatore LaGumina. *Italians in the United States: A Bibliography of Reports, Texts, Critical Studies and Related Materials*. Oriole Editions, 1972.

Corresca, Rocco. "Biography of a Bootblack." *Independent* vol. 54 (Dec. 4, 1902): 2863–67.

Crawford, Francis Marion. *The Rulers of the South: Sicily, Calabria, Malta*. The Macmillan Company, 1900.

D'Agostino, Pasquale. "I Found 5 Million on a Pushcart." *American Magazine* vol. 154 (September 1952): 107–11.

D'Angelo, Pascal. *Son of Italy*. Arno Press, 1975.

Denison, Lindsay. "The Black Hand." *Everybody's Magazine* vol. XIX (September 1908): 291–301.

De Rosa, Tina. *Paper Fish*. Feminist Press, 1980.

DeSalvo, Louise. *Crazy in the Kitchen*. Bloomsbury USA, 2003.

Di Donato, Pietro. *Immigrant Saint: The Life of Mother Cabrini*. McGraw Hill Book Company, Inc., 1960.

———. *Christ in Concrete*. Ballantine Books, 1939.

———. *Three Circles of Light*. Ballantine Books, 1960.

Di Franco, Philip. *The Italian American Experience*. Tom Doherty Associates, 1988.

Douglas, Norman. *Old Calabria*. Jon Manchip White, 1915.

Ermelino, Louise. *Joey Dee Gets Wise*. St. Martin's Press, 1991.

———. *The Sisters Mallone*. Simon & Schuster, 2002.

Fiaschetti, Michael. *You Gotta Be Rough: The Adventures of Detective Fiaschetti of the Italian Squad*. Doubleday, Doran & Company, 1930.

Gabaccia, Donna. *From the Other Side: Women, Gender and Immigration in the United States 1820–1990*. Indiana University Press, 1994.

Gans, Herbert J. *The Urban Villagers: Group and Class in the Life of Italian-Americans*. The Free Press, 1962.

Gambino, Richard. *Blood of My Blood: The Dilemma of the Italian Americans*. Guernica, 1998.

Gotham Comes of Age, New York Through the Lens of the Byron Company, 1892–1942. Museum of the City of New York, 1999.

Hall, Edward Hagaman. *The Hudson-Fulton Celebration 1909, Volumes I and II, Report to the Legislature of the State of New York*. J.B. Lyon Company, 1910.

Hoobler, Dorothy and Thomas. *Italian American Family Album.*, Oxford University Press, 1992.

Howells, W.D. "Our Italian Assimilators." *Harper's Weekly* vol. 53 (April 10, 1909): 28.

"Italian Festivals of New York." *Chautauquan* vol. 34 (1901): 228–29.

Jackson, Kenneth T. *The Encyclopedia of New York*. Yale University Press, 1995.

Kasson, John F. *Amusing the Millions: Coney Island at the Turn of the Century*. Hill & Wang, 1978.

Kimball, C. "An Outline of Amusements Among Italians in New York." *Charities* vol. 5 (August 18, 1900): 1–8.

Laurino, Maria. *Were You Always an Italian?* W. W. Norton & Company, 2000.

Maffi, Mario. *Gateway to the Promised Land: Ethnic Cultures in New York's Lower East Side*. New York University Press, 1995.

Malpezzi, Frances M., and William M. Clements. *Italian American Folklore*. August House, 1992.

Mangano, Antonio. "Associated Life of Italians in New York City." *Charities* vol. 12 (May 7, 1904): 476–82.

Mangione, Jerry, and Ben Morreale. *La Storia: Five Centuries of the Italian American Experience*. HarperPerennial, 1992.

Maquin, Wayne, with Charles Van Doren and Francis A.J. Ianni. *A Documentary History of the Italian Americans*. Praeger Publishers, 1974.

Maurel, Andre. *Little Cities of Italy*. G.P. Putnam's Sons, 1911.

McNamara, Brooks. *Day of Jubilee: The Great Age of Public Celebration in New York, 1788–1909*. Rutgers University Press, 1997.

Miller, J. Martin. *The Complete Story of the Italian Earthquake Horror*. G.W. Bertron, 1909.

Moorhead, Elizabeth. "A School for Italian Laborers." *Outlook* vol. 88 (February 29, 1908): 499–504.

Musmanno, Michael A. *The Story of the Italians in America*. Doubleday & Company, Inc., 1965.

Oppel, Frank. *Tales of Gaslight New York*. Castle Books, 1985.

Pannella, Vincent. *Growing Up Italian in America*. Doubleday & Company, Inc., 1979.

Parrino, Maria. *Italian American Autobiographies*. Italian American Publications, University of Rhode Island, 1993.

Petacco, Arrigo. *Joe Petrosino*. Macmillan Publishing Co., Inc., 1974.

Pitkin, Thomas Monroe. *The Black Hand: A Chapter in Ethnic Crime*. Littlefield, Adams & Co., 1977.

Radin, Edward D. "Detective in a Derby Hat." *New York Times Magazine*, March 12, 1944.

Reid, Sidney. "The Death Sign." *Independent* vol. 70 (April 6, 1911): 711–15.

Riis, Jacob. *How the Other Half Lives*. Charles Scribner's Sons, 1890.

———. "Feast Days in Little Italy." *Century* vol. 58 (August 1899): 491–99.

Sante, Luc. *Lowlife*. Vintage Books, 1991.

Schiavo, Giovanni Ermenegildo. *Italian-American History: Volume I*. The Vigo Press, 1947.

Schoener, Allon. *New York: An Illustrated History of the People*. W.W. Norton & Company, 1998.

———. *Portal to America: The Lower East Side, 1870–1925*. Holt Rinehart and Winston, 1967.

Spalding, Henry D. *A Treasury of Italian Folklore and Humor*. Jonathan David Publishers, 1980.

Speranza, Gino. "Italians in Congested Districts." *Charities* vol. 20 (April 1908): 55–7.

———. "How It Feels to Be a Problem." *Charities* (May 7, 1904): 459–60.

Talese, Gay. *Unto the Sons*. Ivy Books, 1992.

Tamburri, Anthony Julian, Paolo A. Giordano, and Fred L. Gardaphe. *From the Margin: Writings in Italian Americana*. Purdue University Press, 1991.

Tonelli, Bill. *The Italian American Reader: A Collection of Outstanding Fiction, Memoirs, Journalism, Essays and Poetry*. William Morrow, 2003.

Train, Arthur. "Imported Crime and the Story of the Camorra in the United States." *McClure's Magazine* vol. 39 (1912): 82–94.

"Undesirable Citizens." *The Independent* vol. 66 (April 6, 1909): 712–13.

Vecoli, Rudolph J. "Cult and Occult in Italian-American Culture: The Persistence of a Religious Heritage." In *Immigrants and Religion in Urban America*, edited by Randall M. Miller and Thomas D. Marzik. Temple University Press, 1977.

Villari, Luigi. *Italian Life in Town and County*. G.P. Putnam's Sons, 1902.

Von Borosino, Victor. "Homegoing Italians." *Survey* vol. 28 (September 28, 1912): 791–93.

Warner, Arthur. "Amputating the Black Hand." *Survey* vol. 28 (May 1, 1909): 166–67.

Watchorn, Robert. "The Black Hand and the Immigrant." *Outlook*. LXCII (July 31, 1909): 794–97.

Weyl, Walter E. "The Italian Who Lived on Twenty-six Cents a Day." *Outlook* (December 25, 1909): 93–972.

White, Frank. "Black Hand in Control of New York." *Outlook* vol. 104 (August 16, 1913): 857–65.

———. "How the United States Fosters the Black Hand." *Outlook* vol. 93 (October 30, 1909): 495–500.

Wittke, Carl. *We Who Built America: The Saga of the Immigrant*. Prentice-Hall, Inc., 1939.

Woods, Arthur. "The Problem of the Black Hand." *McClure's Magazine* XXXIII (May 1909): 40–7.

Yans-McLaughlin, Virginia, and Marjorie Lightman. *Ellis Island and the Peopling of America*. The New Press, 1997.

Transcript from *Pay or Die*
New York Times
Brooklyn Eagle
Gangrule.com

ACKNOWLEDGMENTS

Elizabeth Street was researched and written over a ten-year period during late nights and weekends. While it was a labor of love, it was also something that I felt I had to do. Some stories need sunlight, and this was one of them.

Our family's story, and in particular my grandmother's kidnapping, came to me in pieces over the years and then in a fuller picture when I finally persuaded my grandmother to tell it to me in detail. However, even then, there were gaps and questions. My research started in the genealogy library of the Church of Latter Day Saints. Countless hours were spent searching through microfilm records to create our family tree. Now, because of the efforts of a hundred thousand volunteers, many of these records are online at www.familysearch.org. I quickly learned that research leads to more research. I first became aware of the 1908 earthquake when I was looking through birth and death records in Scilla's City Hall. It was chilling to see thousands of names all entered under one date. That led me to unearth my family's story of survival and how the earthquake impacted New York's Italian colony. Early on in my research, the Ellis Island passenger ship records became available online. The ship manifests were invaluable, not only for immigration dates but also for a wealth of details that became clues to other information at www.ellisisland.org.

In the New York Public and New York University libraries I read every 1909 newspaper. It was an extraordinary year in New York City's history. My grandmother once said, "My sister Mary was in a big parade when they had me." It was a line that had little meaning until I came across the first article of hundreds about the Hudson-Fulton celebration. Nearly every day the same newspapers also contained articles about the

Black Hand and Lieutenant Giuseppe Petrosino. For information about Lieutenant Petrosino, I am additionally grateful to the officers at New York City's Police Museum and to the officers of the 5th Precinct at 19 Elizabeth Street, where Giuseppe Petrosino worked. It was a pleasure to meet Petrosino's great-grandnephew, Joseph Petrosino, a district attorney, who graciously gave me a copy of an out-of-print book on Lieutenant Petrosino and who became an early supporter of *Elizabeth Street*.

While I read literally hundreds of books, articles, and newspaper stories on the period covered in *Elizabeth Street*, the most valuable information came from my family both here and in Italy. One of the blessings of writing this book was finding my family in Scilla. I am indebted to the Arenas—Cesare, Fortunata, Raffaele, Nunzia, and Christina—and to Rocco Giordano for their warm welcome, delicious meals, and for patiently answering thousands of questions asked in bad Italian. To every family member who participated through storytelling or photos, including my Uncle Joe, I thank you with all my heart and hope that this book will become yours.

When you've spent your life writing memos, presentations, and speeches, you need some pretty serious encouragement to write a novel. My friends, particularly my colleagues at Robin Hood, were the best cheerleaders and the most patient listeners. For rolling up their sleeves at some point, I thank: Sharon Guynup, Joan Rafter, and Donatella Sirtori for their detailed edits; John Fuery for helping make sense of the engineering and construction of the Brooklyn Union gas tanks; and Nancy Green, Azania Andrews, Mark Bezos, Stephanie Adler, Debbie Fife, and Molly Laub for their advice and support.

When the book was completed, I was honored to have the assistance and encouragement of a number of literary agents, starting with Mort Janklow and Rebecca Gradinger, who were early champions of the book. David Kuhn and Billy Kingsland were of enormous help in directing my edit of the first manuscript. I will always be grateful for their time and effort.

Elizabeth Street was available for sale online before being published by AmazonEncore. A number of extremely dear friends helped me promote the book, in particular, the most supportive and generous friend ever—Perri Peltz—and Eric Ruttenberg, Rebecca Prowda, Daniel Lurie, and Jennifer Pitts. The merchants of Little Italy in New York City were quick to embrace *Elizabeth Street*—my gratitude goes out to John Fratta, Mort Berkowitz, Lou DiPalo, and Dr. Joseph Scelsa. Karen Hsu did a brilliant design for the original cover.

At AmazonEncore, it was an absolute pleasure to work with Terry Goodman, Sarah Tomashek, and Jeff Belle. Literally, you would not be reading this version of the book without them. Their belief in *Elizabeth Street* made it possible to bring the story to a wider public, and I will always be grateful. My appreciation also to Melcher Media, my publicist Camille McDuffie, Suzanne Bronski, and Kate Linker.

Thank you to my friend Steve Winter, a *National Geographic* photographer, who took my photo. (I figured if he could capture a charging rhino, he could make a sedentary writer look good.)

While my family was what motivated me to write this book—both to chronicle our family history and to let it go—they were also the source of my inspiration. My mother's love of literature and the arts influenced me from day one and continues to do so today. (She also became the book's biggest fan and never missed an opportunity to talk about it.) My father was, above all, my role model and the person who taught me the meaning of family. I miss him every day. And, as I wrote this book, I was inspired by seeing my sister, Annie, fight her own epic battle for her four-year-old daughter's life and by witnessing my niece Adriana's perseverance.

My grandmother was so proud that my daughter, Siena, had her name. And I am just so proud of my daughter. She's a remarkable young woman, wise beyond her years. (Her suggestions for edits, even though she was a child, were the most insightful.) When I decided to include the ransom notes, Siena ended up having a hand in the book. My grandfather burned the actual Black Hand notes sent to my family many years after the crime. However, in studying other such notes and letters, I was struck by how childlike they were, so I asked Siena, then eleven, to create them. Despite the fact that she thought writing ransom notes for her great-grandmother would necessitate therapy one day, and that she objected to misspelling words, she did a great job.

When you write a book in stolen moments, there is always a victim.

In this case it was my husband, Joseph Della Fave. I unequivocally could not have written this book without him. He made it possible for me to devote long hours to research and writing. And while his practical help was key, his emotional support was far greater. He always, always believed this was something I should do, even when I did not. He was with me in Italy, and was equally enthusiastic about tracking down clues and finding family. He praised each and every chapter, cried at the right moments, and didn't make fun of my bad grammar and spelling. It's his book, too.

Lastly, although my time with my great-grandmother was brief, Giovanna remains my hero. And I am clearly indebted to my grandmother, Angelina Siena Arena, whose experiences and memories fueled this book. Her recollection of events was extraordinary. And while she always maintained "some things you shouldn't tell," I truly believe she would have been proud to see her story in print and agree with Maya Angelou who said, "It is agony to keep a story buried inside you." Angelina Siena Arena died on March 31, 2001, at 96 years old. I was with her on the day she died. I fed her while she once again chastised me about how I wore my hair. Later that night she died in her son's arms. Her last words were, "I want to go home." Nanny, you're home and we love you.

ABOUT THE AUTHOR

Laurie Fabiano has had an exciting and colorful career in the nonprofit world. After graduating college, she moved to her family's hometown of Hoboken, New Jersey, where she established the Hoboken Cultural Council and eventually served as chief aide to the mayor. In 1988, AIDS was at its peak and, motivated by the death of a family member, Fabiano became an AIDS activist. For seven years she coordinated the AIDS Walks and AIDS Dance-a-thons around the country, raising millions of dollars and AIDS awareness. In the past decade, the events she produced as the Robin Hood Foundation's senior vice president raised hundreds of millions of dollars and helped grow the foundation into the largest private poverty-fighting organization in New York City. She is now the president of Fab Tool, a marketing and events company.

Fabiano comes from a creative and close Italian family. *Elizabeth Street,* her first novel, is her family's story. She lives in Hoboken with her husband and daughter.